"Sun Hound." The voice startled him, coming as it did from a deeply shadowed corner of the room, and DiMag rose from the long couch. Kyre turned to face him. "Prince DiMag, I don't know why you summoned me here. Princess Simorh tells me that I am a cipher. I don't see how I can be of any use to you."

DiMag nodded slowly, thoughtfully, crossed to a corner of the room and dragged out a heavy oval object. It was, Kyre realized, a warrior's shield, faced with a layer of bronze. Kyre slowly approached the shield. A strong bony face looked back at him—he wasn't hideous, as he feared. Not a monstrosity, not a freak. DiMag regarded Kyre carefully. "Do you know where Simorh found the spell that created you? She found it in a manuscript which had all but rotted away, and which no one else had studied for centuries." He turned to face Kyre. "That's what you are, Sun Hound. Decayed parchment and faded ink; a jumble of words half in one language and half in one other. Or that's what Simorh believes."

Simorh's sorcery might have driven the anger in Kyre underground, but the fire still smouldered, and he retaliated bitterly, "And you, Prince DiMag? What do *you* believe?"

LOUISE·COOPER

MIRAGE

A TOM DOHERTY ASSOCIATES BOOK

For my mother, Pat—
who told me magical stories
and opened my mind to wonder.
You began it all.

MIRAGE

Copyright © 1987 by Louise Cooper

First Tor printing: June 1988

A TOR book

Published by Tom Doherty Associates
49 West 24 Street
New York, N.Y. 10010

Cover art by Robert Gould

ISBN: 0-812-53397-6

Printed in the United States of America

0 9 8 7 6 5 4 3 2 1

Chapter 1

ARE YOU AWAKE, IN THE DARK AND THE SILENCE?

Do you have eyes to see, and ears to hear? Do you have hands, to reach out and clutch at the emptiness?

Can you feel? Can you know hate, loneliness, love, despair?

ARE YOU ALIVE?

Yes; you are alive. You can sense blood trickling through your veins, count the muffled beats of your heart; and you know that, after what might have been centuries of waiting, sleeping without dreams, without memory or identity, you exist. And although as yet there is nothing for your awakening senses to grasp, something is approaching you. It draws nearer, like a half-recalled nightmare, and it pulls and calls, demanding that the call be heeded.

You don't want to answer. You can't name the instinct that urges you to turn and run in fear, but it's there; it's strong. Yet you have no means to resist or flee the compulsion, and the unknown beckoner is touching you, binding you, dragging you inexorably forward . . .

1

. . . to admit you in blinding agony into a world where you suddenly and violently exist—and in which your first awareness of life is a long-drawn scream of pure terror.

"Wake up!"

The voice was light, crisp, demanding obedience. It spoke so close by his ear that he started; and his muscles contracted sharply with the unaccustomed movement. It took him a few moments to comprehend that the voice was female.

"Wake *up*!" The impatient edge was sharper. "You breathe, you live; I know you can hear me, and you won't gain anything by pretending not to understand. Open your eyes."

He could see no good reason to defy the command. His eyelids flickered open—then shut again instantly as an intolerable brilliance seared his brain. He uttered a sound that was midway between a shout and a groan of protest, and his unseen companion sighed.

"Very well; very well. Wait . . ." A faint hissing. "There. The brazier's extinguished, and if moonlight blinds you you're little use to man or beast and the Hag might as well consign us all to madness. Look at me."

He took no heed: distracted by the sound of his own voice and curious at its unfamiliar timbre, his mind was elsewhere.

"Servant, open your eyes!"

Startled by the cold anger in her tone, he obeyed reflexively. She stood not two paces from where he lay, illuminated by a cold shaft of light. A heavy mass of fair hair framed an angular face which, though still young, was harshly lined. Her eyes, watching him shrewdly and unwaveringly, were the blue-gray of a hostile sea, and she wore a black, shapeless shift, so wafer-thin that he could glimpse the outlines of her breasts beneath the fabric.

The woman stared hard at him and her eyes narrowed coldly. "You're not quite what you should be . . . but no matter. It makes no difference. Now, *listen*. I am Simorh, and the first lesson you will learn is to be obedient to me. Sit up."

There was strength in his arms . . . cautiously he raised his torso, head turning to look uncertainly at his surroundings. He seemed to be in a chamber built from rough and heavy blocks of stone that seeped and ran with water. The chilly glow filtering from above gave little indication of the cave's proportions, but he sensed it was vast; a cheerless, empty place of shadows and echoes. A smell which he identified as brine and rotting weed hung thick in the air, and on the threshold of audibility he heard a regular, rhythmic breathing, as if some monstrous beast lay uneasily sleeping just beyond the dark walls.

He shivered, then looked down at himself. He lay on a barnacle-encrusted rock shelf, and he was naked. His body felt alien. Strong, well-proportioned, but alien. Disturbed, he looked at the woman again and tried to make his throat form words.

"Where is this place?" It was banal, but the question he really wanted to ask eluded him.

"The old temple."

That meant nothing, and he frowned, trying to assimilate the little he knew. She was Simorh; that much she had told him. He knew her name, but . . .

Then the question he had sought crystallized, and with it came a sick fear.

"My name," he said, and the fear colored his voice as it echoed suddenly more strongly in the cave. "What is my name?"

She smiled again, thinly and with a trace of contempt.

"You have no name. You need none, for you're nothing beyond what I've chosen to create."

For a moment understanding eluded him. Then: "You . . . ?" Simorh laughed harshly. "You're slow to grasp the facts, my friend! Let me put it plainly——I have *created* you. You owe your very existence to me, and for that alone you'll learn to be grateful!"

"But I must have a name." He looked at her cold face, and his eyes pleaded.

"Must?" Simorh echoed, unmoved. "Why?"

"Because I exist——I *know* I exist. Please; who am I?"

"You have no identity. I've called you into existence because I need a creature like you. You have a function to perform, and that is your only value. Beyond that, you're worthless."

The fear increased, mingling with hurt, but although he wanted to protest he had no argument to counter her. There were no memories in his mind, no recollection of a past or an identity. It was as though he were newborn; and yet he wasn't a complete stranger to the world. Concepts such as sun, moon, earth, sea, sky, were familiar to him; he conversed with this cold-eyed woman in her own tongue; recognized countless points of reference in his surroundings. He lived, and he was whole. But he was denied the smallest clue as to who, or what, he was.

He put a hand up to his face and felt the contours of bone under skin and flesh. "What color are my eyes?"

Simorh's mouth curled. "Don't be ridiculous! That's of no importance."

"It is to me! I want to know what I look like——please, *I must know myself*!"

"There's nothing to know," she said implacably. "You're just a shade, a creation of sorcery. *My* sorcery. And I could destroy you as easily as I created you." Her smile wasn't pleasant. "So if you value the life you've been granted, you'll do as you're told and ask no more foolish questions. Remember that, and we'll get along well enough."

In a peculiarly detached way it occurred to him that he could have risen from the shelf, taken a single step toward her, and broken her neck with his hands. The thought was fleeting, and quelled by the same impulse which told him not to argue further with her. If what she said was true—and he had no way of knowing—he'd be a fool to put her to the test; for whatever this life might hold, it was surely preferable to oblivion? He bit his lip uncertainly—and, surprised by the small pain, experimentally did it again. Simorh watched him, her expression hovering somewhere between unease and contempt; then abruptly she turned and moved into the embrace of the shadows.

"Here." Her voice, at a distance, was hollow. "Put this about yourself. We've stayed here overlong, and even a creation of sorcery can drown. We must be on our way."

As she spoke she picked up a dark and shapeless object and tossed it to him. It was a cloak, long enough to cover him from shoulders to feet, and he fingered it uncertainly. "Where are we going?"

"Back to Haven. No, don't start your questions again, damn you! Just hurry."

He cast the cloak awkwardly round his shoulders, then, at her impatient urging, swung his feet off the rock shelf and stood up.

Water, shockingly cold, licked at his ankles. He looked down and saw it swirling sluggishly across the floor; dark, brackish, and laced with an unpleasant foaming scum.

"The tide's turned." Simorh was already moving away toward a dark gash in the rock wall which he realized was a doorway. Beyond it steps glimmered in the unhealthy light, leading away upward. "At high tide this chamber floods to the roof; we've little time left." She eyed him bitterly. "I didn't risk destroying myself just to watch the sea take you before you can do your work. Stir yourself—or I'll put you under a compulsion."

The brine smell was stronger . . . not knowing what compulsion the sorceress might be capable of conjuring, and not caring to speculate, he followed her toward the aperture. The surging water splashed around their feet with a thin, furtive sound; then they were through the gap and leaving the slowly flooding cavern behind.

The stairway was narrow, the steps worn and slippery, but Simorh's surefootedness gave him confidence as they climbed toward the source of the light. The flight was quite short: they reached the top and, angling her body against the rock wall, the sorceress beckoned once for him to follow before disappearing into a cramped fissure through which the dim light was filtering. For a moment as the rock's cold blackness pressed in on him he experienced a panic-stricken sense of claustrophobia, as though he were being swallowed and digested by a beast made of living stone. He drew breath, forcing himself to keep his hands by his sides and not push frantically, futilely against the encroaching walls—and then he stumbled out of the fissure in Simorh's wake, and emerged into a nightscape that almost made him bite through his tongue in shock.

He stood amid a litter of rubble and broken masonry, surrounded by the towering, skeletal ruins of what had once been a massive structure. Splintered pillars of stone speared like knives into the green-black sky, long-rotted windows gaped sightlessly, barnacles and weed encrusted the ancient buttresses and twisted them into fantastical shapes. And in the center of the ruin was a humped, featureless slab of rock, threaded with veins of incredible color, that might, untold centuries ago, have been a votive altar.

A cold, sluggish wind soughed through the broken stones, and underlying it he heard a sighing, a whisper that ebbed and flowed in mesmeric rhythm. The sea . . . there was salt on the air, sharp and raw in his nostrils, and he shivered as he was assailed by a disquieting sense of recognition.

"Hurry." Simorh's voice echoed eerily between the shattered walls. "There's little time left."

In the chilly half-light she looked insubstantial but for the now almost brazen sheen of her hair. She beckoned, her movements quick and peculiarly ungraceful, and he began to stumble across the detritus after her—

And stopped, as he was abruptly caught in a cold shaft of light.

The huge, pockmarked satellite that orbited this world had been hidden behind one of the few wall sections still standing, but as he moved it swung into his field of vision; a single, baleful silver-gray eye glaring through the ragged frame of an arched window. He stood transfixed, staring back at it as a sense of dread filled him; then suddenly Simorh was at his side and tugging furiously at his arm.

"Move! Move, damn you! We must *go*!"

The moon's glamour shattered; he shook his head, looked at her, and saw the satellite's sickly color reflected in her eyes. For a reason he couldn't begin to understand her look made him recoil, but he responded to her urging and they scrambled through the rubble, to emerge at last onto a narrow shingle strand, at the edge of which lapped a smooth, shifting, iron-dark sea.

Simorh stopped to catch her breath, then looked over her shoulder at the monstrous moon which, now that they were clear of the ruin, hung alone in the night sky.

"Quickly." She spoke softly. "The strand will be covered soon—we must reach the beach before the sea does."

The shingle bar was a poor barrier against the encroaching tide; already, small, white-edged wavelets were licking at it and soaking the unstable mass of shale and pebbles. Simorh started along the narrow causeway, her robe snatched by the wind and blowing ethereally about her, and—yet again he seemed to have no choice— he followed. The shingle was treacherous, slippery and shifting, but the smooth stones were less painful underfoot than the rubble of the ruin. To their left the sea stretched unbroken to a hostile and distant horizon; after one glance he preferred not to look at it again. To the right, low, crumbling cliffs were half hidden by a thin mist, and the tide seeped between them and the land like a slow-moving river. The mist seemed denser ahead, hiding the unknown goal to which Simorh was leading him, although he thought he had glimpsed a rise in the dessicated cliffland, and the deceptive witchglow of a distant light. Suddenly and sharply the dread came back; the sense that he was moving toward something that he neither understood nor wanted, but was compelled to face. He tried to call out to the sorceress, who was his only point of reference in this eerie world, but the words caught in his throat. The wind soughed, the sea hushed; if he wasn't to drown, he could only follow.

Simorh stopped and turned, her face corpse-white under the baleful moon. "Hurry!" she called. Her voice was all but lost against the vast night. He pulled the cloak more closely about himself, and hastened in her wake.

The shingle bar ended in a gentle slope to the sand of a wide, deserted bay. On the far side the cliffs became high buttresses, and the beach—that part of it still clear of the encroaching tide—stretched away into an unguessable distance. Simorh stopped, waiting for him to catch up, then raised one arm to point inland to the back of the bay. "That way." She set off again without waiting for a response, as though she didn't want to stay on the fine white sand any longer than need dictated. He trailed after her, tired now, and through the shifting mist saw again the fleeting, will-o'-the-wisp glimmer of lights where the sand gave way to rock once more. Then abruptly he realized that they were approaching not a bare rock face, but a crazed jumble of walls and buildings hewn out of the stone and sprawling away behind the bay toward the clifftop. The strange witchglows were nothing supernatural, merely the lights that marked the town's gate; but the realization didn't reassure him.

"Hurry!" Simorh called again. The fog distorted her voice and muffled her figure into little more than a dark smudge. "The Hag is setting."

The moon had slipped down the sky and now hung threateningly over the cliffs, shrouded in mist and surrounded by a sickly corona. Its light gave the scene a cold, steely edge, and he looked away again, disturbed.

Simorh waited for him to reach her, then grasped his arm in a grip that surprised him with its strength. Her nails dug into his bicep and she hissed, "When I give you a command, I expect you to obey me! Don't forget that—don't *dare* forget it!"

He stared down at her, not speaking, and she turned away with an exasperated gesture; but not before he had seen the fear huddling behind the anger in her eyes. They set off again toward the town and the smooth sand gave way to scattered rocks. But these rocks, he noticed, were different; even-edged, as though they had been cut by human hands. They formed, he realized suddenly, the unmistakable outline of a broken wall.

A sick sensation made his stomach churn and he stopped, reaching out to touch the jagged stones. They *had* been hewn, though centuries ago—and wedged between the slabs were traces of slate. He swallowed as a fragment of memory flickered across his mind and was instantly lost.

"The stones." He'd spoken almost before he realized it, and Simorh whipped round as though someone had struck her. "They're not . . . natural."

He couldn't see the sorceress's face clearly enough to read her expression, but her body tensed. "No. They're not natural."

"Then what—"

She interrupted him angrily. "*Damn* you, with your endless questions!"

A spark of rebellion took hold of him and he insisted stubbornly, "I want to know!"

She was silent for a few moments, then abruptly and harshly she said, "Very well; if you must. Nine years ago, the tide flowed twice in one night without ebbing. It receded, eventually, but the sand it brought did not. You are walking on the tomb of more than half of Haven and its inhabitants."

The color drained from his face and he withdrew his hand quickly from the cold stone. Simorh's mouth twisted in a mockery of a smile, and the mist, shifting about her, gave the disturbing illusion of an army of ghostly forms at her back. "Now perhaps you understand why I don't want to linger here."

He nodded, not knowing what he could say. Feeling that the sand was suddenly burning his bare feet with every step, he hastened after her.

Haven—or what remained of Haven—was sheltered behind a high sandstone wall in which was set a wide

arch. Two lamps burned green in the shelter of small
alcoves, and as they passed through the arch he had his
first glimpse of the town.

Haven was a straggling sprawl of low buildings,
narrow, twisted streets, and small squares which seemed
to have grown rather than been carved out of the rock on
which it was founded. Pale stone houses with shuttered
windows stared blindly at him from both sides as he
followed Simorh up the winding lanes. The mist crept
around them like phantom hands, distorting the shadows
and manifesting illusory and half-seen shapes that flickered and vanished before they could be seen with any
clarity. There was no sound save their own soft footsteps,
and no sign of life, human or otherwise. The quiet and
the desolation were intense, and eerie.

As they climbed higher through the town, the sense of
dread that had weighed him down since the moment
when Simorh had dragged him screaming into this world
grew stronger, although still he could find no cause for it.
Questions tumbled one upon another through his mind,
but he dared not ask them.

As they passed through the city he tried to glimpse his
reflection in the windows of the houses but every
window was tightly shuttered as though the householders
had long ago abandoned their dwellings and left them to
the mercies of wind and rain.

Or as though they feared the night . . .

He was gazing uneasily at one of the shuttered houses
when he realized that ahead of them the street ended at a
sheer wall, several times his own height. He stared up,
and was just able to make out the silhouettes of three tall
towers beyond the wall before a deep wing of shadow
seemed to drift across the sky and the images blurred into
darkness.

"The Hag has set. This way, quickly." Simorh turned

aside to where a narrow gate had been set into the wall.
She lifted the latch; the gate opened, and they passed
through.

Steps led up into the mist-shrouded dark, and they
began to climb. It seemed that they were in a garden, but
the thin soil and the unceasing blight of salt-laden air had
mocked the garden-maker's efforts; the flowers and
shrubs were poor and stunted. An occasional larger
bloom showed bloated and pale in the tangle, and dead
or dying vegetation trailed across their path as they
climbed. Then the steps ended, and they stood before a
high, windowed, and dimly lit structure that spread away
into the dark on either side. The three towers he had
glimpsed from the street were clearly visible and he
realized that this place, whatever its nature, must be the
seat of power in the city.

Simorh raised a hand to the arched door that faced
them, and pushed. The door swung silently open,
revealing a wide hallway, floored and faced with stone
shot through with veins of blue, green, amber, and silver.
Tapestries hung on the walls; once they had glowed with
reds and oranges and yellows, but their colors had faded
with age and wear, and now they looked merely shabby.

The sorceress was moving toward a flight of stone
stairs that spiraled up out of sight to the right of the hall.
She was halfway there when footfalls sounded on the
steps, and moments later a man appeared.

He stopped when he saw them, and his expression
changed to astonishment as he looked first at Simorh and
then at the man behind her.

"Princess . . . I—we didn't expect—" He looked at
the stranger again and licked his lips uncertainly. He was
a heavyset man, blond-haired and bearded and perhaps
some fifteen years older than the sorceress. And he was a
warrior; his massive body ran to muscle rather than fat,

and although his clothes—loose shirt and trousers, with a long woolen robe thrown over—suggested indolent and comfortable living, the short but businesslike sword at his hip belied first appearances.

"Vaoran." Simorh stared coldly at the warrior. "You were wrong. *All* of you were wrong. I have succeeded.

"Yes . . ." Vaoran's blue eyes filled with unease and he licked his lips nervously. "It seems, lady, that you are owed an apology by those who doubted you. That I, at least, will offer, and wholeheartedly."

Simorh nodded with tired dignity. "Your apology is accepted. Thank you. Now, if you would be kind enough to inform Prince DiMag that I have returned and—"

The warrior's face closed instantly. "Prince DiMag has retired to his rooms, lady. He left strict instructions that he isn't to be disturbed."

"Don't be ridiculous, Vaoran!" Simorh's mouth narrowed into a tight line.

"With respect, princess, I'm not in a position to question or disobey the prince's order. Believe me, lady, I'm sorry."

Simorh stiffened at Vaoran's words. Curious, her creation watched and waited for her to react. He anticipated an angry outburst, but it didn't come. Instead, her shoulders sagged as though in defeat, though when she tossed her head back there was still a semblance of pride in the gesture.

"Very well. If those are your instructions, I won't argue with you. Perhaps you'd be good enough to have our new guest taken to the Sunrise Tower—and send word to me in the morning, as soon as the prince wakes."

Vaoran bowed. "Of course, lady." He glanced at the stranger again, but briefly and uncertainly. "I'll summon a steward."

"And a word of warning, Vaoran. He asks questions. Don't attempt to answer them—or I, personally, will be responsible for the consequences."

She gave her creation a final look that suggested his presence was more of a curse than a blessing, then before either man could speak she walked quickly away toward the spiral stairs.

Simorh climbed the steps swiftly, keenly aware of defeat and trying to thrust the memory of the last few minutes as far from her mind as she could. The knowledge that DiMag had barred her from his presence, tonight of all nights, was bitter wine. He had known what she was attempting to do, the risks she would run; but still he had avoided her.

At the top of the flight she turned and headed along a corridor toward the furthermost of the palace's three towers, where her private apartments were situated.

Reaching the narrow stairway that led to her tower, she began to climb. Lamps in hanging chains had been lit at intervals on the wall for her return. Someone, at least, had faith in her. She climbed on, not pausing to glance through the tower's narrow windows at the dizzying panorama of the town and coastline beyond, and soon reached the white door with its painted single eye. Almost as soon as her hand touched the latch the door was pulled open from within, and the narrow, elfin face of a young girl peered nervously from the darkness beyond.

"Princess!" Relief and eagerness colored the girl's voice, and as Simorh stepped into the unlit room she dropped to one knee and kissed the hem of the sorceress's thin robe.

Simorh smiled sadly down at her. "Get up, Falla;

there's no need to be so formal. Is Thean in the sanctum?"

"Yes, lady." Falla was hastening to light a lamp, and a warm glow shot through with soft shadows rose slowly into life. "We kept vigil, turn by turn, as you told us." She paused and looked back, her eyes huge and dusky in their frame of pale face and bobbed dark hair. "I'm so thankful you're safe!"

She might not give thanks by the time this is over, Simorh thought, but only nodded and said, "Thank you, Falla. Fetch Thean, and tell her the vigil can end now. I'm very tired . . ."

The girl hastened away through a curtained arch, and returned moments later with Thean at her heels. Simorh's second protégée was taller and fairer than her companion, and her normally vivid blue eyes were dulled, the pupils overdilated, with the effects of the narcotic incense which had sustained both girls throughout their vigil.

"Princess." Like Falla, she knelt and kissed Simorh's hem; unlike the dark girl she was bold enough to ask the question that simmered in both their minds. "Did the work go well?"

Simorh's limbs felt iron-heavy and, partly through reaction and partly because of the night cold striking through her inadequate garment, she was shivering spasmodically. With an effort, she nodded. "It succeeded, Thean. He is here, in the palace."

The girl's eyes widened, and Thean said: "Oh, lady . . . does the prince know?"

The prince doesn't know, and the prince doesn't care, Simorh thought bitterly. She had argued ferociously with DiMag over the advisability of tonight's events, and only the fact that he had no other solution to the threat that

hung over Haven had enabled her finally to gain his
unwilling permission for what she had to do. But DiMag
had disliked having to give way to her—and he would
dislike it all the more when he came face to face with her
creation in the morning.

If he was willing to see her . . .

She must have shown some sign of her distress, for the
girls were suddenly about her like two anxious mother
cats. They ushered her through the smaller of the two
doors that led off the room, up another short flight of
steps, and into her bedchamber.

"Are you sure you've no further need of us, lady?"
Falla's anxious dark eyes scanned her face.

"I'm sure, Falla. Go. You've earned your rest."

She waited until the door closed and the padding
footsteps diminished away down the stairs, then turned
to her wide, curtained bed. The sheets smelled faintly of
salt—everything in this forsaken place smelled of salt,
though she was so inured to it that she hardly ever
noticed—and when she lay down she found she barely
had the strength to pull the blanket over herself. The fire
was burning down to embers; the kettle hissed gently,
and when she snuffed out the single light at her bedside
the crimson-edged shadows loomed and reared over her
like sentinels. She thought of what she had achieved
tonight; thought of the frightened creature she had
conjured into existence out of nothing; thought of
DiMag . . .

Simorh turned over in the bed and pushed a fist hard
against her mouth so that her ever-vigilant apprentices, in
their room above, wouldn't hear her sobbing.

Chapter 2

SIMORH'S CREATION WOKE SCREAMING AN HOUR BEFORE dawn, racked by a nightmare that faded back into shadow only as his eyes snapped open. An involuntary reflex triggered his muscles, and he flung himself from the disordered and sweat-soaked bed, staggering across the circular room until his flailing hands found a door. Fingers clawed the latch, scrabbling and wrenching and drawing blood from under his nails, but the door refused to yield.

At last he stumbled back, not knowing where he was but understanding on an animal level that he was trapped. Still part-drugged with sleep and the remnants of the nightmare, he found himself at a narrow embrasure of a window, and the shock of the cold stone sill against his skin rallied his floundering wits. Remembering, and rubbing at his eyes, he stared out at the vista beyond the walls.

The mist which had stolen up from the sea in the wake

17

of moonset had thickened, casting a milky pall through which the thin predawn light shimmered. Close by, a tower loomed out of the fog, disembodied and drifting, one window gaping like an idiot mouth near its summit; and somewhere far down he thought he could see the ghostly green witch-lights of the town.

He backed away from the window, disturbed as the fragments of memory coalesced in a more complete picture. He was a prisoner in what remained of a coastal city called Haven; that much he knew. And he had been brought here through the spell-casting of a sorceress whose name was Simorh and who appeared to be a princess of whatever dynasty ruled here. But beyond those bare facts, he knew nothing of himself or his origins, or of the world in which he had come to dwell. If the sorceress were to be believed, he had had no existence before last night; she claimed to be his creator, and he had no evidence to gainsay her.

And yet it struck a wrong chord. Nameless he might be, and without memories—but he didn't *feel* like a cipher. Locked away somewhere within him was an identity of his own that Simorh had not created and couldn't tamper with; he was sure of it, and the certainty both angered and frightened him. He *had* to discover the truth—but if the little he'd gleaned of these people so far could be trusted, he'd learn nothing from them.

There were too many ramifications, and too many of them unpleasant, for him to be able to face them now. He was desperately tired and craved sleep still; a sleep free of the evil dreams that had plagued him through the night. If nothing else, he had warmth and shelter; he lived, and, in however bizarre a way, prospered. He'd best serve his own interests, he thought, by biding his time until he could learn more of his circumstances.

He lay down on the bed again and pulled up the coarse but serviceable covering. A faint scent of brine touched his nostrils, as though the weight and warmth of his body had released something sea-born from the pallet into the room; it was a familiar smell, chilly but comforting, and he closed his eyes with a small sense of relief. Sleep came quickly, and this time there were no more dreams.

When he woke again, the false dawn had given way to full day and a dull, colorless light suffused through his room. He sat up, full consciousness returning and with it a memory of the previous awakening that made him determined not to fall prey to the same sense of disorientation and panic. He took several deep breaths, counting each one; then, calmed, climbed out of the bed.

The window was a blank white rectangle; the fog had thickened further as morning broke, and the filtered daylight had a flat quality that made every feature of the circular chamber look faintly unreal and dreamlike. For a few moments he stood on the chill flagstones, not sure of his next move—then he saw that while he slept someone had paid a visit to his room, for folded neatly on a chair near the window were a linen shirt and trousers. He picked the garments up, fingering the coarse fabric; and an observation, unbidden, came to him.

They should surely have provided something better . . .

The thought fled as quickly as it had come, and it left him puzzled. He knew nothing of these people—his captors, for want of a better term. Why, then, should he feel disappointed and faintly insulted by the clothing they had provided for him?

He shrugged. If this was part of the conundrum, it could hardly be significant; the air had a cold, damp edge to it, and he was thankful for something warm to wear, be it peasant's garb or prince's.

The clothes fitted him surprisingly well, though the material of the shirt in particular felt strange, making the muscles of his back twitch with faint irritation. Also on the chair he found a broad leather belt with a clasp fashioned to depict a many-rayed star with a gargoyle face, like a grotesquely stylized solar image; he fastened it at his waist, then, without thinking, turned to look for a mirror in which to study himself.

There was no mirror in the room. He put tentative fingers up to his cheeks, nose, eyebrows. As far as he could judge there was nothing remarkable about his features; no scars, no deformities. He pulled a strand of hair forward over his shoulder to see it: it was a startlingly vivid red, but the unusual color stirred no traces of recognition. Beyond that small detail, though, he knew nothing of his appearance, and although in the wake of all that had happened to him it seemed a pitifully trivial matter, at this moment it was more important to him than anything that he should find out.

He turned toward the window, wondering if the fog-dimmed glass might reflect him—but before he could peer more closely at it and see, someone knocked at the door.

He turned sharply, but the door didn't open; and after a pause the knocking sounded again. The servant, steward, or whoever stood outside clearly had more regard for his privacy than the anonymous dawn visitor, and he allowed himself to relax a little.

"Enter." His own voice was still unfamiliar to him, but the momentary *frisson* vanished as a key grated in the lock and the door finally opened.

The girl who stepped over the threshold was dressed in

a simple linen shift with a woven shawl over it for warmth. Her face was small and heart-shaped, large gray eyes framed by a mass of short, unruly dark curls, and she held a covered tray carefully before her, supporting its weight on her braceleted arms. She couldn't have been above nine or ten years old.

"Good morning," she said with an extraordinary composure for one so young. "You must be Kyre."

Nonplussed, and collecting his wits as best he could, he replied, "You're mistaken, little lady. There's no one of that name here."

She frowned, hesitated, then came forward into the room and decisively set her tray down on the table beside his bed. "I can't be mistaken. The steward told me I'd find you in the Sunrise Tower, and this is the Sunrise Tower." She turned round, scrutinizing him with frank interest. "Aren't you the one who was brought from the old temple last night?"

A peculiar chill seemed to settle in his veins; hardly realizing what he was about, he nodded.

"Then you *are* Kyre." She stepped back a pace or two, studying him critically, then smiled. "You should be proud to have such a name. Do you like it?"

"I . . . don't know." He was struggling to find some recollection of the name, but there was nothing; not the smallest spark of familiarity. "I've never heard it before."

"It means 'Sun-Hound' in the old tongue," the child told him. "Do you speak the old tongue, Kyre?"

Old tongue? He shook his head. "No."

"I do. Or a little, anyway. My tutor says so much of it has been lost that no one will ever speak it properly again, but I'm trying to learn *Ky*—hound, *Re*—sun. Kyre." She seemed to be repeating the name simply

because its inflection pleased her, but the repetition did
nothing to stir his memory. He merely stared back at her
until, meeting his gaze, she laughed self-consciously and
a bright flush came to her pale cheeks.

"My tutor also tells me I babble, like rain in the gutter,
he says. I'm sorry." She smoothed the front of her shift
and then with formal gravity extended a hand. "My
name is Gamora."

"Gamora." Their fingers clasped briefly and he found
himself wanting to smile. He wondered if this child, with
her blend of ingenuousness and attempted sophistication,
would answer his questions.

"Do you live here in this palace, Gamora?"

The child's expression clouded with disappointment.
"Of course I do." Clearly she had expected him to know
more about her than he did. Then she said a little primly,
"I am the *Princess* Gamora. My father is Prince DiMag
of Haven, my mother is the Princess Simorh."

"Your—" He checked, astounded, and for a moment
thought he couldn't have heard her aright. "The sorceress—is your *mother*?"

"Yes, of course. She and my father are cousins—such
a marriage is traditional. You don't know much about our
ways, do you?"

He shook his head, unable to explain the effect her
revelation had had on his mental image of Simorh. He
simply couldn't equate the cold-eyed witch who had
summoned him to this world with the mother of such a
bright and sweet-natured child. And the prince, of whom
Simorh had spoken so bitterly last night, was her
husband . . . the knowledge shed a little unhappy light
on the motivations underlying the sorceress's harshness.

"When my father the prince dies, I shall rule Haven,"
Gamora carried on, matter-of-factly. "Unless I should

gain a brother in the meantime." She looked at him
candidly. "Everyone says that won't happen; so I must be
ruler one day."

He struggled out of the confusion of his own thoughts
and sensed something of the dissatisfaction that lurked,
only partially masked, behind the girl's words. "Don't
you want to rule?" he asked.

Gamora's eyes clouded, and she said: "No."

"Why not?"

"Because by then, there'll be nothing left to rule
over."

The edge of solemn maturity in her simple statement
struck a cold chord in his heart; and reminded him of
something Simorh had told him last night, as they
crossed the sands under the bleak and terrible eye of the
moon. *Half the city swallowed and drowned in a single
night, when the tide flowed twice without ebbing* . . . It
must have happened at almost the same time that Gamora
was born.

Anxious not to alienate the child, yet desperately
needing to learn, he said, "I don't understand what you
say, princess. Why should Haven not continue to
prosper?"

For a moment he thought she might answer him
frankly, but instead her face tightened into a sharp,
uneasy look of distrust. Her dark curls bobbed as she
shook her head emphatically. "Eat your breakfast, Kyre;
or it'll grow cold."

"You haven't answered my question, Gamora."

"I—can't." Pain flickered in her gray eyes, then the
tautness relaxed fractionally and the childish honesty was
back. "I *daren't*. I bribed the steward to let me bring
your tray; if they even knew I was talking to you, they'd
punish me. I heard . . ." She swallowed. "I heard

them say that you must be told nothing; not yet."
Awkwardly, she gestured toward the covered tray on the
table. "You should eat. Please, Kyre. *Please*."

He immediately regretted his attempt to draw more
from her than she was willing to give. Without further
comment he uncovered the tray, and though he was in no
mood to eat he was agreeably surprised by what he
found. A plate of steamed fish, rich and garnished with
some unidentifiable herb; and beside it a cup of dark
liquid that smelled pleasantly spiced. Gamora watched
him gravely as, to please her, he drank the cup's contents
and then sampled the fish. Something about its flavor
was faintly familiar, though he couldn't place it; he ate
more than half of it before he realized that his stomach's
urgings had overcome his mind's reluctance.

He was still eating, with the child sitting attentively
beside him, when without warning the door to the
circular room opened. Gamora looked over her shoulder—then leaped to her feet, her face suddenly dead
white but for two flaming spots of crimson on her
cheeks.

Simorh stood on the threshold. She was dressed in a
dark yellow gown, more formal than her garb of last
night, and her long hair was braided into a tight,
elaborate style. She spared a single careless glance for
Kyre, then stared at her daughter with cold anger.

"I might have known *you'd* find your way here." The
sarcasm in her voice made Gamora's flush deepen; every
muscle in the child's body was locked rigid and she
stared blindly ahead, not meeting the sorceress's eyes.

Simorh stepped into the room and pulled the door wide
open behind her. "Out. Go to your lessons. And tell your
tutor and your nurse that you are not to be allowed out of
your room when the lessons are over."

Gamora unfroze, and her eyes widened. "Oh, Mother, please—"

"*Out!*" Simorh repeated furiously. The child fled. As she ran from the room Kyre saw the glitter of tears in her eyes, and before the sorceress could turn her attention to him, anger got the better of caution and he said harshly, "Are children punished in Haven merely for showing curiosity?"

Simorh swung round to face him. Her lips were set in a sharp, bitter line. "You," she said scathingly. "What do you know of children, or of anything else? And you won't learn the answers to your questions from her. If you don't curb your curiosity, I'll put you under a binding that'll do far worse than simply silence your tongue!"

Some of his confidence evaporated in the face of her threat. She had power, that he knew; he wasn't sure enough of himself to test it. Not yet, at least. He nodded a barely perceptible acknowledgment and she turned her back, lifting her shoulders irritably.

"Make yourself presentable," she ordered peremptorily. "You're to be taken before Prince DiMag, and he doesn't like to be kept waiting."

If mention of her husband's name caused her any discomfort she hid it well. Kyre said, evenly, "I'm as presentable as I can be with no other clothes than these."

Simorh made an impatient sound in her throat. "Very well. Then come with me." She looked back at him. "When you stand before the prince, you will listen without speaking. Don't *dare* to ask a single question or venture a single opinion. No one will want to hear it."

With that she left the room, and he followed. It seemed that he had been housed at the summit of one of the palace towers, for immediately outside the door steps began to spiral down. Simorh skimmed down them at a speed he found hard to match, and he only caught up with her at the foot of the flight. They walked along a passage for a short way, then there were more stairs, until finally these too ended and the stairwell widened out into the tapestry-hung hall through which he had been brought on his arrival last night. Simorh didn't pause, but turned immediately and led Kyre across the hall to a set of double doors which opened to her touch. Through a maze of passages that left him helplessly confused and lost, until at last another set of doors—guarded this time—confronted them where the endless corridors branched away into shadow. Simorh strode toward the guards and was about to issue a peremptory order for the doors to be opened, when hasty footsteps to the right alerted her. She and Kyre turned, to see Vaoran approaching.

"Princess." He halted and bowed. "You weren't thinking of taking the creature to the court hall?"

Simorh's eyes glinted dangerously. "Since when have my activities been of direct concern to you?"

The swordsman's face stiffened. "I beg your pardon, madam. But Prince DiMag is conducting urgent council business."

The sorceress sighed, as though dealing with a recalcitrant and none too intelligent child. "Swordsmaster Vaoran, I received word an hour ago via Prince DiMag's personal steward to bring this creature to my husband in the hall." Her voice sharpened. "Contrary to opinion in some quarters, the prince's memory isn't deficient; so I can only conclude that you have your own unfathomable reasons for wishing to deny me that appointment." She paused. "I hope I'm wrong."

Vaoran's shoulders seemed to lock rigid, and the expression on his face told Kyre that, beneath his arrogant mask, the warrior was afraid of Simorh.

"Lady, I meant no slight; I wasn't aware of the arrangements." With an obvious effort Vaoran forced himself to meet her venomous stare. "But you've obviously not heard the news from the coastal patrols."

"I'm told nothing of what goes on in this benighted place, as well you know!" Simorh retorted savagely. "And I fail to see what relevance the reports of the coastal patrols have to my appointment with the prince!"

"Half an hour ago, madam, they brought in a prisoner."

"A prisoner?" Simorh's fury abated visibly; the storm in her eyes was suddenly edged with an unpleasant blend of apprehension and eagerness. The swordsmaster's gaze flicked dubiously to Kyre, but she made a dismissive gesture. "Never mind him. Tell me."

Vaoran glanced again at the red-haired man. Simorh's dismissal had done nothing to assuage his doubts, but he didn't dissemble any further. "They found it at the high tideline," he said. "It was injured; the patrol commander believes it was caught in a crosscurrent and dashed on the rocks by the north headland. Its own kind had abandoned it, as we'd expect of them, so the patrol brought it to the city."

Simorh nodded. "I see. Where is it now?"

"It was taken for interrogation. We wait only Prince DiMag's order to bring it to the hall."

Simorh looked speculatively at the doors for a few moments, then to Kyre's discomfiture turned an indecipherable gaze on him. She said, quietly, "Conduct us through the bodyguard's door, Vaoran. I'd like to see the creature for myself when it's brought before the prince—and it might provide a salutory lesson for our friend here."

The warrior clearly disliked the order, but could think

of no sound reason to refuse. He made a small, curt bow.
"Yes, lady."

More corridors, more pieces of the jigsaw . . . Kyre
walked behind Simorh and the striding Vaoran, aware
that the poor light illuminating these passages was
diminishing still further, the atmosphere growing danker
and closer. At last they reached a heavy curtain at the end
of a dark, unadorned, and tunnellike walk, and Vaoran
pulled the curtain aside to reveal a low door which
opened on soundless hinges. As it swung back, Kyre
recoiled instinctively. Light flooded from beyond; light,
and voices susurrating like a sullen hostile sea. And with
them, the claustrophobic, uneasy smell of fear.

Simorh went through first, bending and vanishing into
the comparative brilliance. He hesitated and might have
balked, disturbed by an intuitive sense that something
ugly lay ahead, but Vaoran put a powerful hand on his
shoulder and, preferring the unknown to the swordsmaster's touch, he shook the hand aside and followed the
sorceress, to stand blinking in Haven's court hall.

The hall was vast, or seemed so. All the tall, narrow
windows were shrouded by heavy curtains, while lamps
burning at intervals high on the walls cast huge pyramids
of shadow that reached up among stone pillars to meet at
an unguessable height. Tapestries decorated these walls;
like their counterparts in the outer hall they were faded
ghosts of their original glory, all brilliance drained from
them by age and damp decay. The hall's architecture
dwarfed them, and dwarfed the two dozen or so figures
gathered around a raised dais near the curtained door.

"What's this?" A man's voice, angry and with a bitter
edge, cut through the whispering, and Kyre looked to his
left. On the dais stood a carved chair; the chair was
occupied, and Kyre found himself, for the first time, face
to face with the prince of Haven.

The chair was ornate and cumbersome, made of a wood so old that it was all but petrified. The high back was carved with the same sun-symbol that adorned Kyre's belt buckle, and similar amulets had been cut into the elaborate arms. Prince DiMag sat awkwardly in the chair, one knee drawn up and both hands gripping the arms. He was younger than Kyre had expected, lightly built, with long, unkempt hair of the same wheat-gold shade as Simorh's. He was dressed in crimson trousers and a wide-sleeved, narrow-waisted coat heavily embroidered with gold thread; the garments were old, and looked as though they had been slept in. Now the prince turned intelligent but angry hazel eyes on Kyre, staring at him with a mixture of curiosity and resentment. Beyond the throne, the twelve or fifteen men who stood in attendance also peered at the newcomer, their expressions hostile.

"What's this?" DiMag repeated. One hand moved in an involuntary warrior's reflex as he spoke, going to the hilt of a cumbersome sword that hung scabbarded at his side. The gesture, and his tone of voice, raised Kyre's hackles and he felt a furious urge to challenge the prince's dismissive arrogance. Simorh, however, stepped forward, pushing him none too gently aside.

"I have named him Kyre," she said, then added in a sharp undertone, "I told you I would succeed, and I did!"

DiMag frowned. "So I see. Whatever possessed you to bring him here, *now*?"

Simorh's mouth tightened into a hard line. "You sent for me, DiMag, and told me to bring him. If you then sent a second message canceling the first, I didn't receive it!"

The men behind the throne shook their heads at the princess's sharp retort, and one or two hissed through

their teeth with disapproval. DiMag stared at his wife for
a few moments and it was clear from the sudden palpable
rise in tension that no one could anticipate how he would
react. Simorh didn't back down, and abruptly the prince
flexed the fist he had clenched and smiled a lopsided
smile that had little humor in it.

"Well, well. My memory must have failed me for a
moment." He cast a raking, challenging glance that Kyre
couldn't interpret about the company at large. "Perhaps
it's as well; he may find these proceedings instructive."
He raised a hand and beckoned. "Step forward, Kyre.
Let me see you more clearly."

Kyre moved away from Simorh to face DiMag more
directly. He was conscious of a multitude of eyes boring
into his back, making his spine tingle, and he met the
prince's stare with steady, uncowed interest.

"Sun-Hound," DiMag said thoughtfully. His uneven
smile broadened for a brief moment, then vanished.
"The princess obviously has a reason for naming you
after the greatest warrior in our history. Is she justified?"

The prince's words took him aback. "I don't know,"
he said.

One of the men hovering by the throne cut in with
asperity, "Mind your tongue, creature! You'll address the
prince as 'my lord,' not—"

"Spare me your protocol, councillor." DiMag interrupted the man with an irritable wave of one hand.
"There'll be time enough for the niceties later—I'm
more interested in finding out whether our new friend is
as much of a warrior as his namesake." For the second
time he touched the hilt of his heavy sword, and his look
suddenly became closed and almost possessive. "Vaoran—give Kyre your blade."

The burly swordsmaster stepped forward. "My lord,
is this wise? After all, you—" He stopped as DiMag

turned a ferocious glare on him, then hastily amended whatever he had been about to say. "There are more urgent matters to attend to."

"Your view of what is urgent clearly doesn't accord with mine," DiMag retorted. "Give Kyre your blade."

Unhappily Vaoran obeyed, unclipping his scabbarded sword and holding it out hilt-first. Kyre took it with equal reluctance, unable to comprehend the look of intense dislike the warrior gave him as he handed the sword over. His fingers closed round the hilt, and he felt a sudden peculiar sense of familiarity. He had held such a blade before; he understood its weight and balance, and the tactics and skills of using it. And yet instinct told him that his knowledge was flawed. Though the weapon was familiar, it was also *wrong* . . .

Prince DiMag rose to his feet, unsheathing his own blade as he did so. "We'll put your fighting abilities to the test," he said, his odd smile returning. "Let's see if you have the skill to disarm me."

Some of his councillors began to protest, but the prince ignored them and their voices dropped away to disquieted mutterings. DiMag began to descend the steps from the dais. His movements were strangely awkward; he negotiated the steps with difficulty, and Kyre realized that he was handicapped by a paralysis of the left leg that gave him a terrible limp. He took a pace back, appalled. A child could disarm the prince, afflicted as he was; this was a travesty . . .

DiMag reached the floor and stood facing Kyre, who was a head taller. His eyes were dangerous. "Draw your sword, Sun-Hound," he said.

All attention in the great hall was focused on them now, and Kyre felt alarmingly vulnerable. What did this hard-eyed audience expect of him? If he disarmed the prince, as he surely must, would they use it as an excuse to mete out some punishment to him? Or would he fare worse by holding back and humiliating DiMag by allowing him the pretense of winning? He felt as though he had walked into some elaborate trap whose nature he couldn't begin to understand.

DiMag's voice snapped him back to his immediate predicament. "I said, draw your sword. Show us all what you can do!"

The prince's tone goaded him; he tugged the blade free of its scabbard and threw the scabbard aside, hearing it rattle coldly on the stone floor. The sword was a good one, as he might have expected; heavy, but well balanced and maneuverable, and suddenly he no longer cared what this capricious prince or his court might want of him. He'd not asked for a part in their pantomime; if DiMag wished to make a fool of himself, so be it.

He brought the blade up in a curt salute which the prince returned—then he lunged.

DiMag didn't attempt to dodge aside. Instead, he brought his own sword up to block Kyre's, and sparks glittered as metal discordantly struck metal. A shock ran through Kyre's arm to his shoulder; DiMag's reflex had been much faster than he'd anticipated and he rocked back on his heels, quelling his surprise.

"Good," DiMag said, "but half-hearted. You can do better than that."

His tone was careless, but his eyes were still dangerous, the light in them verging on fanatical. Kyre shifted his grip on the sword hilt and advanced again, more slowly this time, watching for any sudden move. He had made the initial mistake of underestimating the prince and he didn't intend to repeat it; DiMag's limitations were obvious and one calculated strike would put an end to this charade.

Kyre chose his moment. He feinted as though thrusting at his opponent's throat, and changed in midstrike to a rapid, sidestepping blow with the flat of the blade which caught DiMag off guard. The prince swore aloud as he realized the tactic—then with a speed that stunned Kyre he pivoted, letting his damaged left leg take his full weight, and his sword came slicing up under Kyre's to intercept the blow. The sheer physical force behind the prince's strike flung Kyre backward; DiMag flicked his wrist as the blades met, and Vaoran's sword was wrenched from Kyre's hand to fly wildly, spinning, across the hall. It crashed on the dais, scattering the councillors behind the throne, and Kyre dropped to his knees, clutching at his shoulder which felt as though it had been dislocated.

DiMag stared down at his opponent. The prince's face was gray with pain, but he forced a smile that, Kyre thought as he returned the gaze, was far more significant than he could imagine.

"Well, you did your best." Laughter, albeit on the edge of anger, lurked somewhere in DiMag's voice. "But it wasn't good enough." He darted a vitriolically triumphant glance at his councillors, then turned back toward the dais. Vaoran stepped forward as though to assist him, but the prince waved him away.

"Thank you, swordsmaster, but as you perhaps now realize I'm not yet a complete cripple." Painfully, clumsily, he made his way to the top of the steps, where the sword Kyre had wielded lay near the throne. No one made any further attempt to help him as he bent, with a ferocious effort, and picked up the blade. Turning, he held it out to Vaoran, who took it in chagrined silence; then he sat down once more and looked at Kyre, who by this time had risen to his feet.

"Come up here," he said, beckoning. "Stand beside me. The court has had its entertainment, even if

Councillor Vaoran and his friends are disappointed by the outcome.'' He smiled thinly. "Now I know I can defeat you, I've no cause to fear you.''

Simorh had turned her head away, her expression unreadable, while Vaoran's face was flushed and the other councillors looked disconcerted. Abandoning any attempt to understand what was afoot, Kyre mounted the dais and stood, as DiMag indicated, beside the throne. The prince studied his face carefully for a few moments, then said: "You don't understand me, do you, Sun-Hound? You haven't begun to comprehend what this is all about.''

Kyre didn't speak, and DiMag shrugged. "You'll learn, soon enough. And you might as well begin your first lesson now." He snapped his fingers toward a nearby retainer. "We've kept our unexpected guest waiting. Tell Paravad to bring it in.''

The order was hastily relayed to the far end of the hall, where liveried guards moved to open the double doors, and one hurried away along the passage beyond. People shuffled and whispered among themselves, and the growing tension made Kyre's skin crawl. Then after perhaps a minute or two came the sound of feet in the corridor, and five men entered, escorting a figure in chains.

Leading the small party was a saturnine man in stained gray clothes. Every gaze in the hall followed him as he walked to the dais, where he stopped and bowed to DiMag before standing aside to allow his companions to approach.

Kyre stared at the being which the four guards half led and half dragged before the throne, and felt a tight, cold knot at the pit of his stomach. He had expected some kind of animal—but this creature was human. Slim, and so young that its sex was hard to determine, the prisoner had a shock of short silver-white hair and its skin, under a thin black shift that barely covered its torso, was faintly tinted a translucent blue-green. Huge dark eyes, disproportionate in a narrow and almost feline face, stared up at DiMag without emotion: either the being didn't comprehend its situation, or it was devoid of fear.

DiMag stared back at the captive, and when Kyre glanced at the prince he was shocked by the insensate hatred that glittered in the hazel eyes. Slowly DiMag ran his tongue over his lips, then he gestured to the saturnine man to approach him. As the gray-clad figure mounted the dais Kyre caught a trace of an unwholesome reek, and recoiled inwardly as he recognized the acrid and unmistakable smell of fear.

"Well, Paravad." DiMag leaned awkwardly toward him. "Have you persuaded it to speak?"

The saturnine man made a small, obsequious bow and shook his head. "No, my lord. It refuses to respond. I've made use of all the customary techniques, but it is unwilling to cooperate."

DiMag twisted a strand of his lank hair between two fingers. "What's your prognosis?"

"To be frank, sir—and in the light of past experience—I can see nothing to be gained by pursuing my efforts any further."

The prince nodded. "I'm inclined to agree. Very well; filth is filth, and should be disposed of before it can corrupt everything it touches." A savage edge, contempt mingled with loathing, had crept into his voice as he spoke. "Was it armed when it was captured?"

"It was, sir; yes."

"Then bring me the weapon it carried."

The silver-haired creature continued to regard the tableau on the dais with the same hollow, indifferent

stare, and Kyre's discomfort increased. Paravad's answers to DiMag's questions, however carefully phrased,
left him in no doubt that the prisoner had been tortured. It
exhibited no physical marks, but something in the
saturnine man's look and in his smooth voice with its
underlying ice told him that Paravad's methods were too
subtle to embrace mere brutality, and that he derived a
good deal of pleasure from his work. Kyre felt a cold
sweat break out on his arms and torso.

Another guard, gorgeous in red and gold and bristling
with self-importance, came striding the length of the hall
to halt and bow with military precision before the dais.
He carried a bizarre weapon which he held out to the
prince, and, peering forward, Kyre saw that it was a
long-shafted spear, the shaft polished to glasslike
smoothness and shot through with opalescent tints of
green and blue. The blade, glinting wickedly in the poor
light, formed a long and ferocious point that branched
halfway along its length into a secondary, shorter blade
angling away into a sweeping hook. It was a superb piece
of craftsmanship, and formidably versatile; it could stab,
slice, scythe, or pin and sever any flesh in its path. *And
with an unpleasant, liquid feeling at the pit of his
stomach, Kyre knew that, if the weapon were placed in
his hands, he could handle it like a master.*

DiMag rose from his chair and took the weapon from
the guard. Briefly, as the spear passed into its field of
vision, a flicker of intelligent interest showed in the
chained captive's eyes; then as the prince's hands closed
on the haft it lapsed back into its former indifference.

Slowly, DiMag paced to the edge of the dais. The
councilors were watching him intently, and the smallest
sound—the rustle of a garment, an incautious intake of
breath—seemed shatteringly loud against the stifling

background of silence. Kyre felt as though his body were under a spell; his limbs were locked and frozen, his lungs had stopped functioning. He could only watch as, with careful precision, and clearly treasuring the moment, DiMag stepped down and approached the prisoner.

It looked up at him as he raised the blade, and for a moment its expression changed, betraying youth and vulnerability and—at last—fear. DiMag's eyes lit with an answering triumphant relish; he renewed his grip on the spear-shaft, paused—and the blade sheared in an arc that slashed the prisoner's head from its shoulders in a single blow. Kyre's stomach lurched violently as he saw blood spatter like thrown water over DiMag's hands and body. The severed head bounced and rolled, and the de-capitated body swayed, arms jerking once in an obscene parody of life, before it collapsed to the floor, darker blood pumping across the marble floor.

DiMag threw the weapon aside and stared dispassion-ately down at the prisoner's remains. Slowly he rubbed his hands together as though washing them, spreading the crimson stains over his own skin. Then he smiled.

"Just a little fear, at the last," he said, as though speaking to himself. "It almost makes the trouble worthwhile."

Kyre felt his leg muscles weakening under him. He couldn't express, couldn't even begin to assimilate, his horror and disgust at the prince's cold-blooded pleasure. Suddenly he collapsed to his knees and, as the surprised councilors turned from the main entertainment to stare at him, he vomited violently onto the floor of the dais.

CHAPTER 3

KYRE WAS HUSTLED BACK TO THE SUNRISE TOWER BY two armed guards. His last glimpse of the court hall showed a party of servants moving in to clear away the remains of the corpse, and that image stayed indelibly with him long after his escort had locked the door of his room on him and gone.

He sat on the bed, staring at the floor before his feet and struggling against the sense of numbing inadequacy that had overtaken him. He had just witnessed the brutal killing of a defenseless captive; and the wanton savagery disgusted him. But he was equally disgusted with himself—he'd made no attempt to intervene, but had merely stood by, passively observing. Perhaps the sorceress was right after all; perhaps he *was* nothing better than a cipher, a shadow-man, and his pretensions to an independent identity were just that: pretensions.

Looking through the smeared window, he saw that the fog which hung over Haven was beginning to disperse.

The dark shapes of towers and walls and roofs showed faint and ghostly through the white pall; the view was eerily depressing, and Kyre turned away with a suppressed shiver.

He loathed this place. He loathed the bleak shore with its moaning tide and shifting strand; loathed the claustrophobic city and its cold-eyed people. Whatever was amiss in Haven, whatever had driven Simorh to call him out of darkness and bring him here, he wanted no part of it.

The bed sagged with a dismal protest as he sat down once more. The room seemed to close in on him, and he put his face in his hands, not wanting to be forced to look at the bare walls. He stretched out on the bed, turning over so that his face was pressed close to the wall. Sleep would solve nothing, but it seemed a better prospect than wakefulness.

With a sigh that the room threw mockingly back, Kyre closed his eyes.

In the shadowy hall, Prince DiMag sat hunched in his chair, watching as the cleaning operation was completed. Four servants had carried away the prisoner's body and severed head in a sacking sling, and the harsh sounds of brooms swabbing the bloodstained flagstones echoed hollowly somewhere among the rafters.

Some of his councillors had left the hall; others conferred gravely at the back of the dais, and the prince noted with some irony that Vaoran was among their number. He deliberately ignored them, aware that he was the subject of their debate, and aware, too, that he could have stopped their whisperings in their tracks with a single look. But DiMag wasn't about to give them the satisfaction of seeing him behave according to their predictions. He shifted his position, drawing up his undamaged leg and resting his heel on the edge of the chair seat.

"DiMag . . . ?"

Simorh was standing a few paces away. Her posture was tautly formal, hands clasped before her; the thought came involuntarily to his mind that she looked beautiful, and it awoke old memories that, to his surprise, hurt. Then he saw the familiar unease in her eyes, and it reminded him sharply that they both no longer felt— _could_ no longer feel—the same toward each other as they had once done.

When he answered her his voice was wearily sharp. "What is it?"

Simorh blanched a little at his tone, but was determined not to be intimidated. "Have you a few moments to spare?"

Her voice gave away the fact that she resented having to all but plead for his attention, and DiMag noticed the strained inflection. He smiled coldly.

"I have a few moments. Especially as my councillors seem intent on conducting the court's business without reference to me." He'd raised his voice deliberately, and was gratified to see, from the corner of his eye, Vaoran's head come up sharply. The swordsmaster glanced at the prince and then at Simorh, and his face flushed before he turned away again.

Simorh moved closer to the throne. "I wanted to speak to you about Kyre."

"Kyre. Ah, yes; the Sun-Hound whose stomach objects to the sight of blood." DiMag smiled lopsidedly. "I admire your choice of name for the creature, Simorh; I didn't realize you had such a sense of the absurd."

She turned abruptly away to hide her anger, and clasped her own forearms. "He has a lot to learn."

"Clearly."

"He *will* learn: I'll see to that." Her voice had a vicious edge. "He's unmolded, untrained—as yet he's no better than an ignorant animal." She swung round to face him again. "But he is what I said he would be. You can't deny that, DiMag—just as you've never been able to deny that we need him."

DiMag didn't answer her. Instead, he levered himself clumsily upright from the chair and moved slowly toward the edge of the dais. Simorh started forward to help him before she could stop herself; he drew back, glaring at her, and her hands fell to her sides.

"We *need* him," DiMag repeated with ferocious contempt. "A single man—and not even a true man, but a *thing* conjured by witchcraft! You may find that enough to satisfy you, but by the Hag, I don't!" Carefully he negotiated the steps to the foot of the dais, and Simorh followed, her cheeks burning with mortification at his all too obvious aspersion.

"You know the facts as well as I do," she hissed, aware that some of the councillors were watching them. "You've read the scripts that Brigrandon translated—you know what Kyre is, and you know, you *must* know, why I took it upon myself to perform that conjuration!" She didn't add that she had run the risk of losing her sanity or even her life to cast the spell that had summoned Kyre to the world; self-pity would cut no ice with DiMag. "You know what my motives were!" She had kept pace with him as he moved toward the door behind the dais, subtly trying to interpose her body in a way that would make him pause, but without success. DiMag looked at her, and his hazel eyes were cynical.

"Yes: you did it for me, or so you'd have me believe. Everyone in this damned place would have me believe that they act entirely in my best interests!" He touched his tongue to his lips, tasting salt. "Haven needs a fighting force now as it has never needed one before. You're quick enough to champion the results of your dark arts against my disapproval—conjure me an army ten times the size of the one we have now, and I'll have good cause to thank you!"

Simorh's expression closed as she realized that nothing she could say would persuade him to unbend. "I can't perform miracles."

"Then you might have saved your energies, because nothing less than a miracle is going to be of any use to us!" DiMag had reached the door, and hacked aside the tapestry that hung across it before pausing to stare at Simorh. His face was white and drawn with fatigue. "I pity that poor creature you dragged from the netherworld. We are nothing to him, he owes us nothing; yet, willing or no, he's destined to be our champion or die in the attempt. No one has taken the trouble to tell him what's required of him. He must simply do what he is told to do, without ever questioning."

"You talk as though he were as human as you or I," Simorh said. "He's not. I gave him life: he has no existence beyond what I've granted him. Questions of his desires or his feelings don't arise."

"I wonder if he would agree with that sentiment?"

She gazed back at him, and for the first time made no attempt to hide the bitterness she felt. "Do you think I care? Only one thing matters, DiMag; only *one* thing! And I'll sacrifice anything for that!"

He paused. Then: "For Haven?"

His words were a challenge; he knew what she

implied, and was daring her to voice it without ambiguity. Simorh's courage failed, and unshed tears glittered in her eyes as she said, "For Haven."

She couldn't speak to him again, but could only watch mutely as he pulled the low door open and walked through. The tapestry curtain fell into place behind him, and a small, cold draft breathed on her face. After a minute or so, when the sound of his uneven footsteps had faded along the corridor, she too went through the door and began to walk back through the maze of passages toward the main palace hall and the upper levels beyond. By the time she reached the hall, DiMag was nowhere in sight. Simorh crossed the marble floor toward the spiral stairs that would lead her to her own tower, and had almost reached them when footsteps behind her made her turn her head.

Vaoran had emerged from the direction of the main council chamber doors and was moving—deliberately, she thought—to intercept her. Too dispirited to evade him, she slowed and allowed him to catch up.

"Princess." The swordsmaster's voice was gentle, and he laid a hand on her arm. She flinched at the contact and saw the shrewd flicker in his eyes as he realized that he had made a tactical mistake. He withdrew his fingers.

"Princess, is anything amiss? I wondered—"

"Nothing's amiss," she replied sharply. "Thank you, Vaoran, but the prince and I were merely discussing a private matter."

"I thought perhaps the prince's action was a little . . . untimely." He nodded in the direction of the Sunrise Tower. "The creature—the warrior—he was obviously unprepared for such vehemence."

"There's been little opportunity to prepare him for

anything he might confront in Haven, Vaoran. Time will
mend that.''

"Of course, lady." The burly man inclined his head.
"And if I can be of service in that regard, I hope you'll
consider me at your disposal."

Oh, yes; Simorh thought: *I know what that means,
Swordsmaster Vaoran! But you'll have no influence over
Kyre while I continue to draw breath!* She hid the sharp
inner flash of fury behind an impassive mask and said
coolly, "I appreciate your concern, but I think it best that
Kyre should remain under my jurisdiction." The look in
her eyes grew hard. "You'll serve me best if you
remember that." And before he could dissemble or
protest, she turned and strode away toward the stairs.

Simorh vanished, and Vaoran, after a few moments,
swung abruptly on his heel and left the hall in the
opposite direction. Believing himself to be unobserved,
he'd made no effort to disguise the sting of his chagrin;
but as his footfalls faded along one of the echoing
corridors, a small figure eased out from the shadows and
across the floor.

Gamora peered along the passage which Vaoran had
taken, and only when she was satisfied that the swordsmaster was out of sight did she hurry on light and silent
feet toward the stairs. There she paused again, flattening
herself against the wall, and peeped cautiously round
into the stairwell, aware that if her mother should by
some mischance return she would earn more than sharp
disapproval for her disobedience. She'd been sternly
instructed to stay with her tutor; but she couldn't
concentrate on lessons with so much afoot, and had
escaped when the aging scholar had left her to work on

her handwriting while he fortified himself with a cup of
wine.

She *had* to see Kyre again. There were so many
questions she wanted to ask him, and she couldn't
contain her impatience. Her first meeting with the
strange newcomer had kindled a sense of hopeful
eagerness that Gamora had never experienced before,
and which she couldn't understand but wanted to grasp
avidly lest it should slip away.

The stairwell was empty and silent. Gamora waited,
counting her heartbeats until she judged that her mother
would have left the main staircase where it branched to
her own tower, then hitched up her skirt and ran up the
steps toward her goal.

At first, Kyre thought that the furtive scratching sounds
at his door must be the remnants of a dream. He had
almost fallen asleep, and the small disturbance had jolted
him back to wakefulness so suddenly that he was
convinced the noise had come from within his own skull.
He sat up, rubbing a clenched fist across his face—then
stopped as he saw the door moving slightly.

A click. The sound was faint but decisive, and his
muscles tensed in response. Then the latch rattled and
lifted, and slowly the door creaked open.

"Kyre?" Gamora's eyes were huge smudges in the
blurred whiteness of her face as she stood framed in the
dim light from beyond. "Kyre, are you awake . . . ?"

"Princess—" He got to his feet in an involuntary
reflex, and the little girl slipped into the room, shutting
the door behind her. "What are you doing here?"

She tiptoed across the floor—pointlessly, as there was
no one in earshot—and smiled ingenuously. "I picked
the lock. My tutor told me a story once, about a prisoner

who escaped from a dungeon, and I remembered how it was done." Proudly she held up a small wire contraption and showed it to him. "I have to wear these in my hair sometimes, but they have much better uses!"

Her fingers were stained with ink; she must have slipped away from her lessons, and Kyre wished that he could have been in a better condition to greet her. In his present mood, he couldn't respond to her childish enthusiasm.

Gamora, however, possessed a sensitivity beyond her tender years, and she knew instantly that all was not well with her new friend. "Kyre, what's amiss?" she asked, her eyes wide and her voice solicitous. "Something troubles you." She touched her tongue to her lips in a gesture unconsciously reminiscent of DiMag. "Did my mother take you to the court hall?"

She must have the eyes and ears of a fox . . . Kyre nodded, and Gamora sighed. "I thought she would. My father would have wanted to see you . . . but there was something else, wasn't there? I heard a prisoner was brought from the shore at dawn."

"You miss nothing, do you, little princess?"

"I can't afford to," Gamora retorted candidly. "Is it true? Is there a prisoner?"

He couldn't judge how much she might have guessed or how much he could tell her without distressing her. It was easy to forget how young she was. After a few moments' hesitation he said: "There was a prisoner."

"Was?" She picked up the hint that Kyre had hoped she might miss. "Ah. Yes, I think I understand. Was it my father who killed it?"

His expression answered her question. Her small face became almost feral, and she said fiercely, *"Good!"*

"You *approve*?"

She stared at him in surprise; then comprehension dawned in her gray eyes and the surprise was replaced by a sad smile. "You still don't understand, do you? Poor Kyre."

Poor Kyre, indeed. Memory of Prince DiMag's expression as he swung the blade to decapitate the creature from the sea knifed into Kyre's inner vision. The thought that a child of Gamora's age could condone such wanton butchery wrenched the ground from under his feet, and he turned away.

Behind him, Gamora said: "Did you speak with my father?"

Kyre drew a deep breath. "No. We—exchanged no more than a few words."

"Then he didn't tell you why we hate the sea-people so much?"

The fierceness in her last few words made him realize that her own hatred was no more than a catechism, a response she had learned from babyhood without questioning and probably without comprehending. It turned his anger to ashes—the fact that she was a child was enough both to explain and to excuse—and it also awoke in him an overwhelming sense of pity for her blighted innocence.

He said, "No, princess. He didn't tell me that."

"I don't think I could explain it to you, not properly." Gamora frowned. "My tutor says that if I attended more closely to my history lessons I'd understand things better. But I don't need to understand, because I *know* that the sea people are our enemies, and that they must be killed." Her face cleared, and she added simply, "It's the way things have always been."

The ways things have always been . . . The words chilled Kyre, and he stared blindly at the window.

"You should talk with my father," Gamora said. "*He* could tell you——"

The ugly image of DiMag in the court hall rose afresh in Kyre's mind, and he interrupted sharply. "Your father? I doubt that he or I would have anything to say to each other!"

"Oh, but you would!" She seemed oblivious to the venom in his voice. "You don't know my father well yet, Kyre, but when you do you'll see how wise and just he is."

"Damn your father! He's——" And Kyre checked himself as he realized that it was wrong, as well as pointless, to direct his disgust at this child, who was surely too young to fully comprehend the motivations of her elders, let alone be held in any way responsible for them. She alone of Haven's inhabitants had shown him kindness; the least he could do was curb his tongue, and reciprocate.

He dropped to a crouch so that their eyes were on a level and took her small hands in his, trying to smile. "Forgive me, little princess," he said quietly. "I didn't mean to speak harshly; but I'm a stranger to Haven and there's so much I don't yet understand." *And perhaps never will*, he appended silently. "If I seem mistrustful, it's only because I don't yet know what my future holds, or even what the sor—what your mother and father want of me."

Gamora looked gravely but cautiously back at him. A shrewd instinct far beyond her tender years told her that Kyre was obliquely asking a vital question, but although she wanted to please him and make him think well of her, she couldn't give him an answer—or none that would be anything but an imaginative guess.

She shook her head at last. "I don't know why you're

here, Kyre. If I did, I'd tell you. Truly I would." She
blinked slowly, then added with a candor that was quite
painful: "My mother hardly ever talks to anyone, and
especially not to *me*."

Having seen something of Simorh's coldness toward
her daughter, Kyre could well believe that, and he felt a
renewed sympathy for the little girl.

"She told me I wasn't to come near you." Gamora
looked over her shoulder at the door and licked her lips
uneasily. "No one's allowed to, not without her permission. I asked why, but she wouldn't tell me." She turned
to look at him again, and her eyes pleaded. "I didn't
want to disobey her, Kyre, but . . ."

He squeezed her fingers, touched by the desperation in
her voice. "But what, little one?"

Gamora's cheeks pinkened. "I . . . hoped we might
be friends."

This simple expression of her feelings gave Kyre a
sudden, sharp insight into the underlying currents of her
life in the palace, and he realized that there was far more
to her efforts to befriend him than childish curiosity or a
desire to be at the heart of any new and mysterious game.
Gamora was lonely. And in recognizing a fellow outcast
she was clutching at a thread of hope.

This time he didn't have to force a smile. "I'd like to
be your friend, Gamora," he said.

Small teeth sank into her lower lip and she gazed at
him uncertainly. "You would? You're not pretending?"

"No. I'm not pretending." And the gods—if there
were gods in this world—knew that he needed a friend
now. Even a friend who was only ten years old.

She tugged her hands from his grasp and performed a
pirouette that took her halfway to the door. "I could
come to see you every day," she told him eagerly. "We

could talk—there are so many things I want to tell you about! May I, Kyre? *May* I?''

Laughter caught in his throat. "I'll be glad of your company, princess. But your mother—"

Gamora shrugged in an eloquently adult way. "If she finds out she'll punish me, but I've been punished before, for all kinds of things." Mischief sparkled in her eyes. "She won't know, Kyre. It'll be our secret. Won't it?"

Kyre allowed the laughter to break free, and felt a tight knot of tension within him unexpectedly loose its hold. "Yes, little one," he said. "It will."

Five days passed, during which Kyre had nothing to do but languish away the hours in the Sunrise Tower while trying not to let his mounting impatience and anger take too great a grip on him. Each morning and evening a steward brought him a tray of food, but his fervent questions as to Simorh's whereabouts or intentions were met with stone-faced silence—and the fact that the steward was accompanied by an armed guard quelled any thoughts Kyre might have had of wresting the information from him by other means.

So he waited, and so the tension grew. He spent most of the daylight hours by the narrow window, at first trying to force it open but, when it proved rusted into place, simply sitting and staring out through the gale-scored glass at what little view was afforded him. Occasional sounds drifted distantly from the city, though they were muffled by the mist, which never truly relinquished its hold. Kyre kept the worst of his thoughts at bay by trying to interpret the sources of those disjointed sounds, but when dusk fell and the outside world was swallowed by darkness, he had no defense against the ugly reveries that crept out of the shadows in his mind to plague him.

Haven. A city rotten with the putrefaction of hatred. A ruler whose sanity was in question, and whose consort's bitterness tainted everything she touched. And a child to whom death and slaughter were a commonplace to be shrugged off with barely a second thought. It made an unpleasant picture; yet it seemed that, willing or not, he was destined to be drawn into it, a new thread in an old and sullied tapestry.

But what manner of thread? Kyre was no nearer to learning the answer to that or a thousand other questions; but of one thing he was certain: whatever Haven and its people might demand of him, whatever the role that Simorh had decided he should play, he wanted no part of it. The sorceress might previously have cowed him with her claim to hold the key to his own life or death; but what was life worth if it held no better prospect than Haven and its corruption? He'd be better dead—or would have been, but for one single spark of light in the darkness.

Gamora had been true to her promise. At least once a day Kyre heard furtive scratching sounds as the lock on his door was tampered with, and the child would slip into the room, flushed and excited with her forbidden triumph, to pass some time with him. In the wake of their earlier encounter he had had some misgivings about the wisdom of encouraging Gamora to befriend him, and to begin with he was cautious, deliberately keeping a distance between them. But Gamora's openness, and her painfully obvious pleasure at having found a new friend, broke down the barriers he tried to build, until he gave in and admitted to himself that he was as grateful for her friendship as she was for his.

Gamora, in her turn, began to blossom. For the first time in her young life she had an indulgent, even willing, audience to whom she could relate her anecdotes, recall her dreams, tell of her brimming ideas. She brought Kyre her lesson slates, showing him the rudiments of the old tongue that she strove to learn; she relayed tales and epithets told to her by her tutor; she gave him small gifts in the form of pebbles and tiny, roseate shells which she had gathered on the beach when she took her morning walks.

But in all the time they spent together, one subject and one alone was never touched upon.

It wasn't that Kyre didn't long to ask the questions that plagued him, questions concerning Haven's rulers and their plans. Nor, he believed, would Gamora have been unable or unwilling to answer them where she could; she was innocently eager to please him, and would have kept no secrets from him. But, perhaps because of that same innocence, Kyre couldn't bring himself to take advantage of her. The truth was that the child's sweet nature had touched him far more deeply than he had anticipated, and he was growing too fond of Haven's little princess to want to embroil her in his own uncertain future.

And that, as he finally and bleakly forced himself to acknowledge, was something that could only bear bitter fruit.

He made the decision that intuition had already told him he must make on the fifth morning of his confinement in the Sunrise Tower. Gamora would come at any time now; though he could do no better than guess at the hour, her visits were beginning to form a pattern of sorts. And when she came, he must steel himself for the unkindness that, in the long run, was the only course he could take. He didn't want to hurt the little girl: yet he knew that, in her eyes, what he was about to do would seem like a cruel betrayal. To encourage her friendship, only to turn his back on her, abandon her . . . the thought caused a wave of self-disgust to roil in the pit of his stomach. But it must be done. There was no future for him in Haven, and to pretend otherwise was to blind himself to reality. There was no future in his fondness and sympathy for Haven's little princess; he knew it, and in time Gamora would know it too, however hard she fought against the inevitable. For now, she might make believe that this happier interlude would last, but in truth that decision lay in Simorh's hands alone. And when she chose to break the hiatus, such trivial considerations as her daughter's happiness would not stand in her way. Better, then, that Gamora should face the truth now— and that Kyre himself should snatch the one chance he might ever have of taking a hand in his own destiny. He could no longer wait passively for the sorceress to mold and manipulate him in some embittered scheme of which he wanted no part. He meant to make a bid for freedom—and Gamora held the only key.

The look on the little girl's face when he forced himself to tell her what he wanted made Kyre hate himself. Her small features became pinched, her eyes introverted, hunted, and she said in a barely audible voice: "Leave Haven . . . ? Why, Kyre? Why?"

"I can't explain it to you properly, little one; not now. All I can tell you is that I have to go."

She bit her lower lip, which was quivering. "Is it . . . that you don't like me?"

"Of course not, Princess." He took her hands, trying to reassure her. "Anything but that!" Yet he couldn't explain the truth—that he feared Simorh and what she meant to do; that he would not knuckle to her will without a fight. Gamora couldn't have understood.

"Please," he said with gentle urgency, "try to believe me when I say that I mean you no slight, Gamora. I don't want to be unkind to you—but I *must* leave the city, at least for a while. And to do that, I need your help."

Her brow creased, twin furrows marking her forehead. "Will you come back?"

Kyre tasted something sour and brittle at the back of his throat. "Of course I will." *Serpent*, said an inner voice.

Hope glimmered in Gamora's eyes. "When?" she asked. "Let it be soon, Kyre—or let me come with you!" Now the light of hope became something more, a new enthusiasm. "Oh, let me! We could have such fun—"

"No, Gamora." He spoke more vehemently than he'd intended, and her face fell again. He squeezed her fingers tightly. "I'd take you with me if I could, truly; but it isn't possible. But I will come back. Soon." Something twisted inside him and he silently cursed the lies that came so easily to his tongue. "I promise."

She didn't quite trust him, but an uncannily adult wisdom told her that she couldn't sway him. Gently tugging her hands from his grasp she turned and walked slowly toward the door.

"This lock is old," she said in a curiously flat voice. "It's very easy to trick it open." She looked back at him, her eyes huge and sad, then took a pin from her hair, holding it out toward him. "You can do it with this, just as I do. They won't know I gave it to you. I promise I won't tell."

She would keep that promise, he knew, far more faithfully than he would hold to his own empty oath. He nodded, unable to speak.

"Then . . . there's a way out of the palace that no one uses any more." Gamora gulped back the threat of tears. "I found it by myself." She squared her small shoulders as though abruptly if reluctantly coming to a decision, and returned to his side. "If I wet my finger and draw you a map on the floor, it'll stay long enough for you to remember it." Licking a finger several times she drew a quick, practiced series of outlines on the flagstones. When she had done, Kyre stared down at the map. It was simple enough.

"You must wait until dark," Gamora told him. "Until the palace sleeps. The fog will hide you."

He glanced toward the window, feeling cold and unreal. "The fog has lifted." His own voice sounded remote.

"It will come back." Gamora smiled obliquely. "It always does." She paused, blinking. "I'll think of you tonight, Kyre. I won't be able to see you in the mist, but I'll watch from my window and I'll imagine you waving to me. Will you wave?"

"I will, Princess." That promise at least he could keep, for what little it might be worth. "And I'll repay your kindness, somehow, one day." On impulse he bent to kiss her forehead. "Thank you."

She hugged him, her cheeks pink, then backed toward the door. "May the Eye protect you, Kyre."

The door closed between them, and he heard the sound of the lock clicking softly back into place.

Waiting was the worst of it. The day seemed endless, and as the hours passed Kyre's thoughts shuttled unhappily between guilt at his deception of Gamora, and fear that some capricious twist of fate might bring a summons from Simorh that would put paid to his plan.

He hadn't considered where he might go once—and if—he escaped from the palace. The city itself held little hope of sanctuary, and he had no idea what lay beyond its boundaries. But that was a problem he would tackle when the time came; for now, his sole concern was to get safely away.

The summons he had feared did not come, and at last the light beyond the window began to dim as the fog closed in once more. Distant sounds faded into an engulfing silence, and Kyre felt as though the blood in his veins had been replaced by a burning, searing river of tension. He rose, paced; then sat down again, afraid that someone below might hear his restless movements and investigate. He thought yet again of Gamora, felt the sharp pangs of conscience and forced himself to banish the memory of her pale little face from his mind. One day, he told himself, he would try to make amends to her. One day . . .

And at last he knew that, whether the palace slept or not, he could wait no longer.

The lock yielded to his probing, just as Gamora had promised. The hinges creaked abominably, but the noise was short-lived and not loud enough to draw attention; cautiously Kyre eased himself through the half-open door and onto the narrow landing.

Around the first spiral of the descending stairs a lamp burned low; it cast a pool of dim, sullen light, and the rancid smell of fish oil assailed his nostrils as he passed. The stairwell beyond was dark; he felt his way down each uneven step, using the rough wall to guide him, and finally reached the foot of the tower. Here were more lamps, but again they were dimmed for the night, their flames nothing more than tiny pinpoints that granted the passage more shadow than light. Kyre waited, neither moving nor breathing, until the stillness and the lamps' soft, uninterrupted hissing reassured him that no one was abroad. Then he moved, a silent shadow among shadows, toward the unused corridors that would lead him to the palace walls.

Thean couldn't sleep, despite the fact that she felt wearied to the marrow. Since the night of her vigil while Simorh was at the ruined temple she had been haunted by formless and disjointed visions that flickered at the corner of her mind whenever she closed her eyes; and often—as now—the images in her head meant that any form of rest eluded her altogether.

Beyond the curtained recess her fellow apprentice Falla slept soundly on her bed; but below Thean could hear the sounds of restless pacing that told her Simorh, too, was wakeful. She'd seen little of the princess these last few days; council business had kept her away from the tower, and on the few occasions when their paths had crossed Simorh had exchanged no more than a terse greeting with her neophytes before retreating to her private apartments. Sensing her mistress's mood, reading the strain in her eyes, Thean needed none of her acute psychic sensitivities to know that something was badly wrong.

The sounds below ceased suddenly, and Thean held her breath, listening. If the sorceress had retired to bed at last, perhaps her own mind would quieten and she could sleep. She rose from her place beside the dying fire, shivering as she moved out of the narrow circle of warmth, and was about to douse the lamp when the door opened.

Simorh stood on the threshold. She wore a linen shift with a shawl thrown over it, and in the gloom her eyes were vast, dark hollows in her face.

"Thean . . . you're abroad late."

Thean curtsied. "Yes, lady. I couldn't sleep."

"No more can I." Simorh paced across the room to the window embrasure, but the night and the thick fog had blanked the glass into a featureless charcoal gray. "There's something afoot; I can feel it." She drew a quick, sharp breath between clenched teeth, almost a hiss; and Thean said: "Perhaps you still suffer from the conjuration, Princess. It took its toll."

"No." The sorceress shook her head emphatically. "It's something else, and I suspect . . ." She paused, bit her lip, then looked at the girl. "Scry for me, Thean. Bring out your glass. I want to get to the root of this, and I won't rest until I do."

Thean didn't know if she would be capable of calling on her talent, but she didn't argue. Crossing to a chest at one side of the room she took out a tiny sphere of green glass wrapped in a black cloth. Simorh watched while she spread the cloth on the floor and placed the sphere upon it; then as Thean crouched over the scrying ball the sorceress moved silently to stand behind her and laid both hands lightly on her shoulders. Thean saw the sphere beginning to cloud and grow milky; from the milkiness an image began to form. What she saw, and what it meant, Thean didn't know; she was merely the medium for Simorh's own power as the sorceress drew from her uncomprehending mind the message in the crystal.

It was over very quickly. Simorh believed she knew the direction in which she should look for the source of her disquiet, and she was right. The sphere, focusing almost immediately on her thoughts and suspicions, gave her a rapid succession of clear images; and she felt her heart miss a beat painfully. *Red-haired man, gray-eyed child, empty room, tide-washed strand . . .*

Thean recoiled with a jolt as her mistress abruptly broke the psychic contact between them. When she gathered her wits, Simorh was already striding toward the outer door.

"Wait here," the sorceress ordered savagely. "And wake Falla. I will need you both." And with that she was gone, the door smacking back against the wall in her wake.

Simorh wasted no time rousing servants who at this hour would be fuddle-headed and little better than useless. Instead, she ran up the stairs of the Sunrise Tower—and at the top, the open door told her all she needed to know.

For a few moments she stood on the threshold, letting her back rest against cold stone and shutting her eyes against a wave of angry despair. All she had tried to do, tried to instill, and it still came down to this wanton disobedience and foolhardiness. Or perhaps Gamora couldn't be blamed; perhaps she herself should have known that a creature of the dark might have the guile of the dark.

Turning, Simorh started back down the stairs again, and at the foot of the flight entered a side corridor that led back past her own tower and on into the depths of the palace. The nurse's room—no light showing there. But beneath the door beyond, a thin bar of comparative brightness gave away the presence of a dimmed lamp.

When she opened the door, Gamora was kneeling by the window. Her hands were cupped between her face and the glass and she was staring, moving her head in an effort to see through the shrouds of fog and darkness. Bitter fury welled in Simorh, and she threw the door shut with a crash.

The child jumped, lost her balance, and sprawled on

the floor. When she looked up, her mother was standing
over her.

"Get up!" Simorh said furiously. Shaking, Gamora
obeyed, backing toward the bed as Simorh advanced on
her. Suddenly the sorceress's hand shot out and she
snatched a handful of her daughter's hair, pulling hard
and forcing her to stop with a cry of pain.

"What have you done?" Simorh hissed. "You disobedient, stupid child—*what have you done*?" With each
syllable she shook Gamora, and, terrified, the girl began
to cry. "You unlocked the door—you let him go! *Didn't*
you?" Another shake. "Answer me!"

"Mother—"

"I said, *answer me*! And don't *dare* tell me a lie!"

Gamora's face crumpled. "He said—he wanted to go
away. Mother, I didn't mean any harm! I only wanted to
be kind to him, because . . ." She caught sight of
Simorh's face and desperately swallowed what she had
been about to say. Miserably, she whispered, "He
promised he wouldn't tell you . . ."

"Oh, by the Hag—" Simorh's rage was doused by a
wave of self-disgust. How could she expect Gamora to
know better? The child was impulsive and quixotic, but
she wasn't truly to blame; she had thought she was doing
a kindness, and couldn't be expected to understand the
consequences.

She released Gamora, and said harshly, "You foolish
child; of course he didn't tell! But you should know by
now that you can't hide secrets from me!"

Gamora climbed onto her bed and curled up, sobbing.
"I didn't mean any harm—"

By all that's sacred, does she think I don't know that?
Simorh thought savagely. She was staring down at the
child, torn between further fury and a regret that made

her want to reach out and bridge the appalling gulf between them, when the door behind her opened. She whirled, and saw Gamora's nurse, her eyes heavy with sleep, standing on the threshold with a lamp in her hand.

"Oh . . ." The woman made a hasty curtsy, clumsily. "I beg your pardon, lady—I didn't realize; I thought I heard the little princess cry out—"

Simorh's voice shook. "Princess Gamora has had a nightmare. You should be more vigilant!"

Gamora's sobs were subsiding, and the nurse looked dubiously from mother to daughter. "A nightmare . . . ?"

"That's what I said." Simorh couldn't build the bridge now; the damage was done. She walked past the nurse, pausing only to say: "Stay with her until dawn. I think she will be glad of your company."

As she hastened away down the passage, her heart was pounding and her mind reeling with the effects of the encounter. She hadn't meant to be cruel to Gamora; her anger had been fueled by fear, not hatred—but how could a child understand that? She didn't realize what she had done, or what Simorh must now do to put matters right. The sorceress shuddered. She didn't relish the task ahead, but it had to be faced; and she would face it.

If it wasn't already too late.

Chapter 4

THOSE WHO SAW CALTHAR MOVING ON THE ENDLESS flights of stairs or traversing the tunnels of the citadel knew what must have brought her from her lair, though none would have dared voice their thoughts in her hearing. And if they had the misfortune to be close by when she passed, they looked only once at her face before hiding themselves in the dark, damp shadows, holding their breath, touching lips that were suddenly cold to the charms about their necks, eyes closed until she was gone.

The tortuous ways through the citadel were unlit and treacherous, but she carried no lamp. Silver hair, a shocking contrast to her darkly green-tinged skin, swung chaotically about her head and shoulders like a mad nimbus, and the robe she wore and which had been worn by a hundred predecessors flapped in crazed tatters too old and too thin to hide the lithe, powerful body beneath.

She found her quarry with unerring instinct, and flung

open the low door without pausing to knock or call out.
As the door slammed back and the icy wind that haunted
the corridors set all the fish-oil lights dancing and
guttering, the old man scrambled up from the pallet bed.
One foot caught in the blanket that covered him, and he
stumbled and fell, pulling the blanket with him to reveal
the naked body of a girl—hardly more than a child—
huddled on the pallet.

Calthar stared at the girl with shriveling indifference,
then pointed, without speaking, to the open door. The
girl snatched up her garments and ran, ducking wide of
the awesome interloper, and her footsteps could be heard
padding rapidly, unevenly away.

The old man stood up, pulling the blanket about
himself and adopting a hunched, suppliant posture, like a
dog not knowing whether to fawn at its master's feet or
turn tail and flee. As Calthar stalked slowly around him
in a wide circle his pale eyes followed her figure with
hungry eagerness: then he looked at her face and the
hunger died stillborn, to be replaced by fear.

"She's gone." Calthar's husky voice was savage, and
her accusation had a deadly edge.

He drew in a sharp breath. "Again?"

"Again, Hodek. Again. Where is Akrivir?"

The old man swallowed. "He's sleeping. The day has
been arduous, and he was—"

She hissed like a snake, silencing him instantly. For a
few moments there was no sound in the chamber other
than her stertorous breathing. Then she said with soft
venom, "I see. So while your worthless son sleeps and
you fornicate with children, who is to watch over
Talliann?"

The old man's fear flowered into panic. "She can't
have left the citadel! I—she was—"

"She was unwatched!" Black rage and searing contempt fired Calthar's voice with loathing, and he cowered
back as though from a physical blow. "You know where
she has gone—and you know what will happen if she
isn't brought safely back!" She advanced, reached out to
touch his face lightly with long fingers, and he smelled
the scent of corruption on her skin. "You have neglected
your duty, Hodek. You know what I'll do if you fail to
make amends for that neglect!"

An ugly, incoherent sound came from the back of
Hodek's throat, and her hand slowly withdrew. Her eyes
glittered like quartz. "Fetch her back. Unless you want
the Hag to reach out and touch your bones tonight, *fetch
her back!*"

Whimpering, the old man scrabbled for his clothes
while she watched him, the harsh staccato of her
breathing making the room claustrophobic. When he
scuttled from the room and shouted for men-at-arms, she
followed him; she stood at his back in the vast cavern
that opened to the sea, and she watched with a gaze that
no one dared meet as the search party left on the sullen
tide. For now, there was no more to be done. But—and
she turned her head slightly to stare at the cringing
Hodek wringing his hands at the sea's edge—if anything
went amiss tonight, there would be payment to exact.
And it would give her a cold, cruel pleasure to exact it.

Though he knew his surprise was illogical, Kyre was
discomfited to encounter a thriving population in the city
below the palace's high walls. He had crept down
through the terraced gardens, past the stunted plants with
their sickly white blooms, to the wicket gate that finally
released him into the outside world. And there, in the
dim, misty streets with their glowing witchlights, figures

moved and faces peered from windows. He heard a door slam, saw a curtain twitch, glimpsed two women, wraithlike in the fog, huddled together and hurrying to be home out of the night. A small square paved with sandstone blocks was littered with the debris of the market day; somewhere a dog howled and a curt voice reprimanded it.

Kyre shivered, moving on. There was an incongruity about the scene that discomfited him; the normality of the sounds, the people, the market refuse, didn't fit with his original, indelible, image of the eerily empty town. It was as though the inhabitants of Haven weren't true people at all, but ghosts from a dead past, and the initial shiver became a cold shudder that scoured the length of his spine.

A shutter slammed nearby; the noise carried on the thick, still air and startled him. He increased his pace, feeling the gradient of the street steepening and aware, too, that he was cold. The fog had a clammy touch against his skin and the clothes he wore hadn't been designed to counter the chill of the open night. And that realization made him wonder, for the first time, where he was going.

Kyre had been so intent on escaping from the palace and its warped inhabitants that it hadn't once occurred to him to consider what he might do once he was free. Instinct had led him down toward the sea, but only because he had come this way once before and knew no other path. Yet the bleak shore had nothing to offer, save for the ruined, skeletal temple on the shingle strand; and no inducement could persuade him to face that terrible place again—unless his only other choice was to return to the palace.

Involuntarily he looked back over his shoulder to

where the town's jumbled streets and rooftops climbed
away into the fog. It hadn't occurred to him that the hunt
might already be up; but there was a good chance he had
been missed by now. He knew he was valuable to Haven
in some way; or at least, valuable to Simorh. He didn't
know how far the sorceress's power extended, but neither
did he care to put them to the test, and once she
discovered him gone she'd waste no time in summoning
the manpower—or something less human—to track him
down.

Kyre began to run, his bare feet thudding on the hard
ground, creating dull echoes. With night deepening, the
last straggling lategoers had left the streets and the lower
reaches of the town were utterly still. The few lights
which burned in windows were going out one by one.
Almost before he realized it he had reached the arch
where the twin green lamps glared like unwinking eyes,
and he slithered to a halt.

Still no sign of pursuit. But the silence was invaded
now by a new sound that set his nerves crawling in the
few moments before he recognized it. Faint, soft,
imbued with a cold malignance, it was the distant,
mournful rhythm of the sea. There was a power in the
sound that drew Kyre against his will; he stepped through
the arch, turning his face toward the huge beach that
opened up before him. The white sand stretched away,
gleaming before it was swallowed by the fog; he smelled
brine and decay carried on a light wind, and his nostrils
flared involuntarily. It was hard to discern any scale or
perspective through the mist: he thought he could
glimpse a deeper darkness, far off, where the tideline
must be, but it was impossible to be sure. Only a dim
patch of light high up and away to his left told him that

the scarred satellite which the townsfolk called the Hag
had risen and was glaring down through the fog at him.

The wind gusted suddenly, making the green witchlights dance, and the shadow of the arch distorted jerkily
and startled him forward. A short, rocky slope, then hard
stone gave way to soft, damp sand under his feet, and he
turned to look back at the town through the arch's frame.

He couldn't go back. Not now; not when he'd come so
far. The beach surely couldn't lead only to the ruined
temple—there must be a way, however difficult, of
climbing the cliffs to one side or the other and escaping
inland. And whatever the hazards of freedom, it was by
far the lesser of two evils.

Kyre turned his back on Haven, tasting the wet wind
and trying not to shiver. Then he set off into the shifting,
banking fog, across the wide emptiness of the beach.

No light burned in Simorh's tower, but this was a work
which demanded darkness. The sorceress knelt on the
floor of her sanctum, aware of the uneasy gazes of Thean
and Falla who flanked her, and her hands shook as they
gripped the two ends of the knotted length of cord she
held. Her fingers felt like lead, numb with the cold that
pervaded the room and unwilling to obey her, but she
fought the chill, feeding on the anger that still burned in
her like a banked-down fire. The rage had been directed
first at Gamora and later at herself; now, though, she
must channel it toward another, and an image of Kyre's
face formed in her mind. She latched onto it like a
hungry dog, and took a deep breath, drawing all the air
she could muster into her lungs as though afraid that
when she tried to breathe again there might be no more.
Her bones ached and she longed to be able to forget this
new trial of strength, turn her back on it and sleep. But

that couldn't be. She had begun this, and she must see it through; to reject her responsibility would be to admit defeat, and for that there could be no consolation.

Feel the anger, she told herself savagely. *Feed on it, take strength and solace from it. You can do this; you must do it. Feel the rage. Even if it leaves you with nothing else, feel the rage . . .*

Simorh's fists clenched tighter on the knotted cord. Then, with slow and implacable deliberation, she began to wind it and wind it in a complex pattern around her hands as her lips mouthed the silent and ferocious words of an incantation.

Kyre had believed he was moving to the south, away from the stark ruin on the strand and toward the higher cliffs which, his confused reasoning argued, might hold some better hope of sanctuary. The sound of the sea was drawing nearer, though he still couldn't tell how far he was from the water, when to his dismay he stumbled suddenly and found his feet ploughing into shingle.

The strand . . . but he'd been walking in the opposite direction; he'd have pledged his life on it! Dismayed, Kyre stopped and peered ahead, praying silently that he was wrong, that he wouldn't see the sight he dreaded.

But it was there, rising out of the fog as though floating on it like a monstrous mirage. The harsh, skeletal framework of the ancient temple, its walls jagged and broken, towering up from the shingle bar. Even as Kyre watched it seemed that the mist was thinning, drawing back from the ruin to leave it clear before him, while directly above the rotting structure the pockmarked moon hung in an otherwise empty sky.

Something that tasted sour and acid mingled with the saliva in Kyre's mouth as he stared, appalled, at the temple. He hadn't meant to come here, he had set his face in the opposite direction; and yet, tricked by the fog and the sea's echoing, he had been unwittingly drawn back to this terrible place as though bound to it by the same sorcery that had brought him to this world.

His lungs heaved as he tried to catch his breath. He wanted to defy whatever glamour it was that had afflicted him and turn back toward the cliffs on the far side of the bay's mouth; but instinct told him that the attempt would be futile. He hadn't misjudged his direction from Haven. Something had invaded his mind, twisting him away from his goal to bring him back to the place of his bizarre birth and, looking up again at the dark sky, he felt certain that the withered moon, or some arcane power linked with it, had been responsible.

His jaw clenched. He was about to turn his back on the bones of the ruin and on the satellite's dead, glaring eye, when he saw something that stopped his breath.

The mist had stolen back from the strand, exposing the giant, quiescent serpent of the shingle bar . . . and out on the bar was something alive. It must have come from the sea, and now, clear of the water, it crawled over the stones, moving slowly and awkwardly as though the element in which it found itself was alien to its nature; a hunched, indistinct shape that shimmered wet and phosphorescent from the sea. Kyre stared at it, repelled and yet fascinated. And then, with painful concentration, it slowly rose until it was standing upright, and it turned to face him.

It was human. Even at this distance there could be no doubt. And one look at the frail, narrow, deathly pale face told him that the interloper was young, and female. Ragged hair the color of jet blew about her head, and eyes which in the darkness were huge, featureless black hollows stared at him across the distance that separated them. The chill moonlight gave a terrible flatness to her white skin so that she looked corpselike, almost two-dimensional, something from a fragmented, disturbed dream. She was clad in a long gown, and as she moved—hampered, he realized, by its waterlogged folds—the gown shimmered, as though its entire surface was covered with a myriad glittering silver pinpoints.

A painful and involuntary muscular spasm racked Kyre as he returned the alien girl's gaze. Yet what he felt was more than a physical hurt. For the first time something he recognized as a memory was lurching to life within him, twisted beyond recognition but stronger than anything he had encountered since being dragged into this world. He *knew* her. She was—he fought for identity, for a name, but it wouldn't come; the memory, if memory it was, was distorted beyond his reach. He could only stand staring at her as though transfixed. *But he knew her*.

She turned her head suddenly, looking out to sea, and the movement broke Kyre's trance. He struggled to find his voice, wanting to call out and reassure her that he meant her no harm, but before he could utter a sound she had regarded him again, once, and was moving slowly backward, step by uneven step, along the shingle bar.

"Wait!" He forced the word out and it sounded flat and dull against the vast night. She didn't respond, only continued to retreat from him with her odd, uneasy gait. The capricious mist was creeping back, and Kyre was suddenly afraid that she would fade into its embrace and be stolen away, leaving him bereft and alone. He had to go after her and, if she could understand him, he had to speak to her.

He took two hesitant steps forward, and the girl

stopped. Though the darkness played tricks and her face
was no more than a pale blur, he thought she smiled with
a peculiar twisting of her lips, as though the movement
were unpracticed. Then she took five rapid paces back,
almost scuttling, increasing the distance between them.

"Wait!" Kyre called again. "Please—wait!"

A sound like thin and fragile laughter answered him,
and the girl turned her back and ran. Her feet made
barely a sound on the shingle, and the glowering
moonlight set the spangles of her gown shivering and
dancing like a shoal of tiny fish as she skimmed away
toward the stark ruin at the end of the bar. Aware only of
the fear that he would lose sight of her, Kyre set off in
pursuit. The shingle was treacherously loose, sliding
under his feet and threatening to throw him off balance,
but even so he was faster than the fleeing girl and knew
he must catch her before she reached the temple. What
he would do then, what he would say, whether she would
be afraid of him, he didn't know. All that mattered was to
catch her.

He was no more than twelve paces behind the
shimmering, hurrying apparition when a ferocious hissing sounded beneath his feet—and without any warning,
five glittering silver columns erupted with the speed of
striking snakes out of the shingle in front of him. Kyre
yelled aloud in shock, trying to twist in mid-stride as
they coiled toward him, and fell, the yell turning to a
scream as one of the silver ropes cracked across his back
like a whip, searing his skin. He rolled instinctively,
digging hands and heels into the shingle to spring up and
back—and five more of the monstrous things reared up
out of the bank behind him, cutting off his retreat. They
swayed menacingly above him, and cold silver sparks
spat and flickered along their lengths, some spinning to

the wet shingle where they hissed like furious cats. The saliva dried in Kyre's mouth as he realized that the hideous things were alive—or at least, directed by some sentient mind that could see him, that was anticipating his next move and only awaiting its chance to strike at him again.

Trapped, and sweating with fear, he turned to where he had last seen the girl from the sea. She had stopped and was staring back at him, and his first conviction that these monstrous supernatural whips had attacked him at her bidding died as he saw that she had her hands to her mouth in shock. Without thinking he reached out, trying to implore her to help him—and the silver coils twisted, cracked, slashing a fresh shower of burning sparks across his face and pitching him to his knees with a harsh cry of pain. He sprawled, and the shingle beneath him began to hiss anew, pebbles heaving and shifting as if some giant, enraged beast were thrashing under the surface. Kyre tried desperately to scramble to his feet but was thrown violently off balance again, rolling aside in a frantic but futile effort to protect himself as more sparks spat down and seared through his clothing to the unprotected skin beneath. The silver snakes reared over him, coiling and writhing as though maddened by the sight of his agony, and amid their triumphant spitting and hissing he heard another cry, a sound of distress and incoherent protest. It wrenched at his mind and, wild-eyed and crazed, he saw through the shimmering ropes the girl's figure, leaning toward him, arms held out in supplication. And behind her, something else—a blur, too indistinct to register fully on his racked brain; but he had a momentary image of dark shapes flowing from the direction of the ruin, moving toward the girl, overtaking her—

She screamed, on a high, full-throated note that

contained anger and terror and protest, and at the same moment the ten silver serpent-whips curled over and came lashing down together on Kyre. The first strike was white-hot fire, and pain exploded through him with such murderous force that the shriek he tried to give voice to was a silent travesty. He had a momentary glimpse of the glittering, sparking coils rising again for a second attack—and as they bore down and struck him, a fresh wave of pain smashed his consciousness into oblivion.

Falla and Thean caught Simorh's arms as she swayed and pitched forward. Lifting her as carefully as the room's cramped confines allowed, they laid her back on cushions, and Thean anxiously rubbed and patted her ice-cold hands to restore the circulation. The sorceress's face was deathly pale and lined from great strain, but after a few moments she forced herself, with a tremendous effort, to open her dull eyes.

"Fetch . . . armed men," she whispered hoarsely. "Tell them . . ." She coughed convulsively, and spittle ran down her chin. "Tell them to bring him back . . ."

"Lady, are you—" Falla began.

"*Fetch them!*" Simorh could hardly speak, but there was venom in her tone. "Obey me!"

"Yes, lady." Falla scrambled to her feet and ran toward the door. As she disappeared, Simorh struggled into a sitting position, refusing Thean's attempts to help her.

"I shall be all right . . . leave me, Thean. Let me sleep." She looked at the discarded cord, and her expression tightened with revulsion. "Just leave me alone."

* * *

Four heavily armed guards, venturing nervously from Haven under Vaoran's direction, found Kyre sprawled unconscious on the shingle strand. His clothes were scorched in places, and there were burn marks on his face and torso. Vaoran stared down dispassionately as his men turned the senseless figure over. He knew the bare details of Kyre's escape and could surmise the methods Simorh had used to apprehend him; though sorcery repelled him he nonetheless felt a distinct satisfaction as he stared at the prisoner.

One of his men, whey-faced in the waning moonlight, glanced uneasily over his shoulder toward the sea, then indicated Kyre. "The tide's getting closer, sir. Should we get him back to the town?"

Preferable to leave him for the fish and crabs to eat, Vaoran thought venomously, then pushed the thought away. He'd do nothing to advance himself in Simorh's eyes if he abandoned her creation to the sea; this setback must be borne a while longer. But he couldn't resist taking a slow pace forward, prodding the unresisting body with his boot and then delivering a carefully judged kick to the small of Kyre's back before the others lifted him. One more bruise to suffer amid the others: a pity the creature would never know its origin . . .

"All right," he said, his voice as harsh as a seal's bark against the whispering sea. "Move him."

They thought Kyre unconscious, but though he was too stunned to make a movement or utter a sound, his senses were returning. Through blurred and half-closed eyes he was dimly able to make out Vaoran's figure, and he had felt the kick that connected with his spine, though he was incapable of reacting to it. As the men tramped back over the sand with his body slung carelessly between them, it occurred to him to wonder why the swordsmaster should have a grudge against him. But his mind was too stunned and cloudy to be coherent. He lapsed back into senselessness as he was borne toward Haven, and knew nothing more until the moment when he was dumped, with no ceremony and jarring force, onto the floor of the palace's entrance hall.

Kyre groaned and tried to roll over, and heard someone laugh unpleasantly. "The Sun-Hound's had his teeth pulled, eh?" It was Vaoran's voice, and his men joined in the laughter. "Well, he'll live. You—inform the Princess that he's here."

Footsteps hastened away, the noise drumming in Kyre's head, and, his pride stung by the swordsmaster's sarcasm, he made a great effort and managed to lift himself onto his elbows. His skin felt as though it had been roasted and sickness churned in his stomach, but he fought down the nausea and the pain and met Vaoran's cold blue stare. The burly man smiled deprecatingly. "Better make yourself presentable, Sun-Hound. It'd be ill-mannered of you to greet your mistress looking like a whipped cur!"

Anger surged in Kyre, but before he could muster it into any physical or verbal form he was interrupted by a sudden flurry of running feet and a woman's voice calling an ineffectual command. The dimmed lamps by the stairway arch dipped and flickered with a rush of air, and a small figure erupted from the stairwell and across the floor.

"Kyre!" Gamora's voice was shrill with distress. "Kyre!"

Vaoran moved to intercept the child, catching her arms and swinging her toward him. "Little princess! You shouldn't be here; where is your nurse?"

"Don't you *dare* touch me!" Gamora struggled so

furiously that he was chagrined into releasing her, and as soon as she was free she darted to Kyre's side. "What have they done to you?" she cried.

Kyre took hold of her hand before she could touch his scorched face. "It's all right, Princess. Don't distress yourself, I'm not harmed!"

"But you *are*—you're burned, your clothes, your face—Kyre, what did they *do*?"

"Gamora!" The voice, laced with exhaustion though it was, carried enough angry authority to bring the child up short. Kyre looked up and saw, in the darker maw of the stairs, Simorh, with a harassed-looking woman of middle years at her back. He had time for the sorceress's haggard features and lank, sweat-damp hair to register on his mind before Gamora had flung herself across the hall and was clutching at Simorh's skirt.

"Mother, they've *hurt* him, and he's my *friend*! Why have they done it? He wasn't running away; he promised me he'd come back!"

"Gamora . . ." This time Simorh spoke more gently, as though she hadn't the strength for a confrontation. "Gamora, you don't understand. Go back to bed. Go with your nurse."

"No!" the child argued. "Not until I know why they've hurt Kyre! I saw them from my window and they were *carrying* him, as if he were something *dead*! Mother—"

Simorh's pallor increased and she shut her eyes. Gamora was sobbing, and Kyre's sympathy for the child, coupled with the guilt he had already incurred over her innocent faith in him, made him fight back the pain he still felt and force himself, unsteadily, to his feet.

"Little princess." His voice stopped Gamora's protests in mid-flow, and she turned, wide-eyed, to look at him.

"I'm not harmed." He spread his arms wide, hoping that his appearance didn't give the complete lie to his words. "See; I'm standing, I'm speaking to you. I can even smile at you." Beyond the child he saw Simorh staring at him, her face frozen into a look of suspicious uncertainty, then his gaze flicked back to Gamora. "I'm not hurt."

Gamora licked her lips. "But—why were they carrying you like that? As though you were something killed on the hunt—"

He met Simorh's eyes again, briefly. "It was a game, little princess."

"A . . . game?"

"Yes."

She wasn't wholly convinced, but he could see that she set great store by his word, and at last she looked up at Simorh again. "Mother . . . ?" It was the last confirmation she needed.

"Yes," Simorh said faintly. "A game." The look she gave Vaoran was venomous, and she might have directed her next remark to him, but a further sound on the stairs drew the attention of everyone in the hall. Uneven footfalls . . . and Prince DiMag appeared, dressed in a light woolen robe.

"So this is the cause of all the noise." His hazel eyes raked them all in turn. "I'd anticipated an invasion at very least—I suppose I should be gratified to find the palace unscathed!"

"Father, I thought they were hurting Kyre!" Gamora broke away from Simorh and ran to him. He stared down at her and absently stroked her dark hair. "Did you?" Then he looked first at his wife and next at the burly swordsmaster, and the look was vitriolic. "Why should you think that?"

Vaoran intervened smoothly before Gamora could speak. "There has been a slight—mishap, sir; and the Princess Simorh was gracious enough to call on my services."

"Was she, now?" DiMag said with a faint smile.

"It was a game," Gamora insisted. "Kyre said so!"

"Then a game it was." The prince smiled reservedly at her. "But the middle of the night isn't the time for games, Gamora. Not if you want to grow to be worthy of your position, and not if you want to allow the rest of us to get a night's sleep!"

The child flushed. "I'm sorry."

DiMag laughed with a gentleness that surprised Kyre. "Then show how sorry you are, little one, by going with your nurse. Back to bed, now." He touched her hair again, and she gazed at him with adoring eyes. "Yes, Father."

The harassed-looking woman, who had not dared to speak in the presence of her betters, took charge of Gamora with obvious relief, and the little girl was shepherded away up the stairs and out of sight, her huge gray eyes looking hungrily back.

No one moved until the two were out of earshot, then DiMag limped down the last two steps and into the hall. His movements were awkward, and Vaoran started forward solicitously.

"Sir, might I assist you?"

DiMag looked at him. "Thank you, no. I'm sure you'll find it edifying to know, Vaoran, that the damp night air does nothing to improve my disability; but I'm still capable of walking unaided." He had by this time reached the center of the small group formed by Vaoran,

Simorh, and Kyre—Vaoran's men had stiffened to
attention the moment he appeared and no one paid them
any heed—and slowly he pivoted on his good leg to
regard the three in turn. Then, so unexpectedly that they
all started, he snapped, "So: who is going to tell me the
truth about tonight's ructions?"

Two vivid spots of color flamed on Simorh's cheeks,
and Vaoran's jaw worked, though he uttered no sound.
Only Kyre's expression didn't change, and DiMag,
seeing his apparent impassiveness, gave him a sharp,
oblique look. "Your skin and your clothes are burned,
Sun-Hound. What did you do—try to immolate yourself?"

Simorh spoke up before Kyre could answer. "The
marks will fade quickly enough," she said.

"Ah. I begin to understand." DiMag looked challeng-
ingly at her. "Why?"

"He fled the palace." She glanced at Kyre. "You
know why he had to be brought back."

"*I* do; yes. But does he?"

The sorceress's expression became defensive and yet
weary, as though she resented having yet again to
propound an old and worn argument. "That isn't
relevant, DiMag."

The prince gazed down at the pattern of the flagged
floor beneath him, and traced a flaw in the marble with
one foot. "I'm sure it isn't; not to you, not to me, and
certainly not to our gallant swordsmaster-councillor here.
But has anyone thought to ask the Sun-Hound what *he*
has to say?" He looked up, and Kyre was astonished to
see a measure of sympathy, albeit detached, in his hazel
eyes. "Decisions are made in which he has no part;
events are set in train in which he is destined to play a
role without being accorded the common courtesy of

knowing what that role will be." He smiled lopsidedly. "Were I in his place, I too might be inclined to rebel."

"Sir, there can be no possible comparison between—" Vaoran began, but the prince interrupted him with heavy irony. "Naturally, Vaoran, there can be no comparison between the ruler of Haven and a mere cipher. But *I* won't deny even to a cipher the privileges I'd grant without second thought to a dog!"

The slight emphasis wasn't lost on Vaoran, but he had no chance to reply, for DiMag had already turned to face his wife once more, ignoring the swordsmaster as though he were of no consequence.

"Salve his burns, make him presentable, and send him to me."

Her lips whitened. *"Now?"*

"Now." DiMag smiled bleakly. "I think the Sun-Hound and I have a good deal to say to each other—and I doubt he's in any better mood for sleep than I am."

And, without waiting for a response from any quarter, the prince turned and limped toward the stairs.

Chapter 5

THE ROOM IN WHICH KYRE FOUND HIMSELF WAS IN CHAOS. DiMag's books and papers littered every available space, and a motley collection of tapestries covered all but a small area of wall. A single lamp, turned low, provided the room's only illumination, and a worn curtain which had once been crimson but was now dulled to the dessicated hue of an old bloodstain half covered the window. Outside, Kyre noticed, the fog had thickened again.

"Sun-Hound." The voice startled him, coming as it did from a deeply shadowed corner of the room, and DiMag rose from the long couch which, it appeared, served him as a bed.

Kyre turned to face him. Uncertain of his own attitude, he made a halfhearted bow which didn't quite convey respect. "Prince DiMag."

DiMag smiled thinly. "We seem to have solved a small mystery," he said. "I'd been asking myself what could have caused the change in my daughter's manner these last few days, and after her little outburst downstairs, I think I now know the answer. You have a worthy champion, Kyre."

Although there was no overt sarcasm in the prince's tone, Kyre felt his hackles rise defensively.

"Is it so wrong for the little princess to choose her own friends?" he demanded.

DiMag looked hard at him. "Certainly not. I for one am glad of it, and I'm not overly interested in the opinions of those who think differently. Friendship is friendship, for all that it might hail from an unexpected quarter." Abruptly then his expression relaxed, and he gestured toward the cluttered furnishings. "But I didn't bring you here to discuss Gamora behind her back. Sit down, Kyre, if you can find the space. Formal interviews are tiresome." He moved to the window, looking out past the partly drawn curtain. "Haven languishes in fog yet again. Sometimes it's hard to remember a time when it was otherwise." He fingered the worn linen, then looked over his shoulder. *"Ha reinn trachan, ni brachnaea pol arcath?"*

Something stirred in an occluded corner of Kyre's mind; the words sounded alien, nonsensical, yet they triggered a flicker of recognition. But it was no more than a flicker, and he shook his head.

"I don't understand."

"Ah; never mind." DiMag shrugged. "The old tongue. My tutor taught it to me when I was a boy, and my daughter's tutor attempts to instill some glimmering of it into her head now. But it's corrupted; mostly lost. I don't doubt my accent makes it all but unintelligible." His hazel eyes were calculating. "I wondered if it might be familiar to you."

It was, but . . . "No," Kyre said.

"No matter. The manuscripts which survive from the time when it was spoken are too faded to make sense anyway." Involuntarily, and regretfully, he glanced at the heaps of papers on a table near his couch, and Kyre asked: "You are a scholar, Prince DiMag?"

"A scholar . . ." DiMag considered this for a few moments as though the idea hadn't occurred to him before, then laughed with irony. "I suppose I have that misfortune these days, as I can certainly no longer call myself a warrior."

"You defeated me easily enough, in the court hall."

"Mm. Perhaps I simply showed you up as inept; I don't know. Certainly you're no true swordsman." Again, that shrewd, calculating look. "Though as to what you are . . . that's another question, isn't it?"

Kyre sighed. The prince was being oblique, fencing with him. Despite the salve his skin hurt and was still sore, his body ached and he was tired; he was in no mood to play puppet to DiMag's or anyone else's whims.

"Prince DiMag," he said, with an edge to his voice, "I don't know why you summoned me here. I don't know what you want of me." He met the prince's gaze and felt a small satisfaction at seeing DiMag surprised by his look. "But I can't answer your question, and I think you're well aware of that. The Princess Simorh tells me that I'm a cipher, and I have no knowledge nor any memories that enable me to disagree with her. I don't see why you should think I can be of any use to you."

There was silence for a minute or so while DiMag moved with his awkward, uneven gait back to the couch. He sank onto it and said tiredly, "Sit down."

Uncertainly, and with some reluctance, Kyre moved some papers from a chair and sat. DiMag nodded, satisfied. "Very well; I'll come to the point if that's what you want. I brought you here to make a bargain with you, Sun-Hound."

"A bargain . . . ?"

"Yes. Does that seem so surprising?" He laughed again. "I assure you, I spend half my life making bargains and coming to compromises, and by comparison with the denizens of my court, you're a rank novice in such negotiations! When—" And he stopped as someone knocked diffidently at the door.

"Come." His change in tone made Kyre lift a surprised eyebrow, and the servant who answered the summons received a glare of undisguised contempt.

"Your food, my lord." The man set a covered tray down on the table and hastily backed toward the door. DiMag lifted the linen cover, then snapped: "Wait!"

The servant froze. DiMag studied the array of dishes on the tray for a few moments, then beckoned the man to his side and pointed at a platter of shredded fish mixed with nuts and herbs.

"That," he said, then indicated another dish which looked like cooked and glazed fruits. "And that. And a piece of the bread."

The servant bowed and, to Kyre's astonishment, took a small sample from each of the plates and tasted it. The prince stared at the wall in stony silence while the man chewed, swallowed, and finally nodded.

"All's well, sir."

"Good." DiMag indicated the door with a wave of one hand. "I'll need nothing more tonight."

The door closed behind the departing servant. DiMag smiled sourly. "There have been six attempts to poison me in the past two years, and I don't doubt there'll be more."

"But who . . ."

"Who? By the Hag, d'you want to sit here until dawn breaks listening to the list of possibilities?" The prince gripped his own leg and heaved it clumsily onto the couch, so that it lay straight before him. "I have my suspicions, but I won't play into their hands by making accusations without proof." His gaze raked Kyre bitterly. "And it's no concern of yours; no reason why it should be. Eat."

He *was* hungry . . . Dubiously Kyre reached out and sampled the fish. It tasted good, and he took more, eating with his fingers.

"Before we were interrupted," DiMag said, "we were discussing a bargain."

Their eyes met briefly, and Kyre replied, "I still don't see that I have anything to offer you."

"You may not; I view it differently. And I'm prepared to help you, Kyre. My wife has thus far refused to answer any of your questions about yourself and why you are here. But I am prepared to answer them—though I'll want something from you in return."

It was the chance for which Kyre had hoped, but he mistrusted it. DiMag's offer seemed openhanded enough, but the prince might be far more devious even than he seemed.

He asked: "What is your price?"

"That, insofar as you cooperate with anyone in this benighted city of ours, you cooperate with me. Not Simorh, not Vaoran: *me*." He smiled thinly. "In effect, I want your loyalty."

It seemed straightforward; yet there had to be a motive behind DiMag's line of reasoning. The little the prince had told him confirmed his suspicions that all was far from well with Haven and its ruler; and he didn't doubt that his eccentric host had private and unfathomable reasons for striking such an apparently reasonable bargain. Kyre had no inclination to pledge fealty to any denizen of Haven, but DiMag alone—if one discounted little Gamora—seemed prepared to treat him as a man rather than a shade, a guest rather than a hapless prisoner. And that was a gesture which Kyre was fast coming to appreciate.

He nodded. "Very well. I agree."

DiMag steepled his fingers before his face and studied Kyre over their lattice. "Do you know, Sun-Hound, I find your attitude quite refreshing," he said at last. "You refuse to be unctuous; you refuse to make the pretense of demeaning yourself in my presence; I detect in you an honesty that's a rare commodity in Haven these days." The lids drooped shrewdly over his hazel eyes. "I'm not saying that I've taken a liking to you: I'm not such a fool as to do that on so short an acquaintance, and by rights I should loathe and despise you, when I consider the purpose for which you were brought here. Perhaps I will come to loathe you, I don't know; it's a risk you'll have to live with." He leaned forward suddenly. "And it *is* a risk. Whatever you might hear to the contrary, I still rule here. But for now, I choose to indulge my whim to treat you as a friend, of sorts." He laughed softly. "When you've lived in Haven a while, you'll come to understand that that's a rare concession!"

It was an extraordinary speech, and Kyre had no answer to it. Seeing that his implied threat had invoked no reaction, DiMag relaxed a little. "We'll waste no more time," he said, taking a piece of grayish, unleavened bread from the tray and biting into it. "To show my good faith, ask me a question. Anything you wish. I'll answer it, if I can."

Kyre hadn't anticipated such a rapid change of tack, and found himself floundering. So much to ask, so many answers he craved—and he heard his own voice saying: "What color are my eyes?"

DiMag stared at him, nonplussed.

"Well," he said evenly, after a pause, "it's an easy enough question to answer, though I can't claim to comprehend why you should have asked it. How is it that you know so little about yourself?"

Kyre flushed. "The sorceress—the Princess Simorh—gave orders that I shouldn't see my own reflection. She was adamant."

"Was she, now? Then perhaps I begin to understand a little more than she intended." DiMag nodded slowly, thoughtfully, and crossed to a corner of the room, where an extraordinary assortment of objects had been stacked, seemingly at random, against the wall. DiMag delved among them and dragged out a heavy, oval object. It was, Kyre realized, a warrior's shield, faced with a layer of bronze. The surface was badly tarnished, suggesting that the shield hadn't been used in many years, but the thinly beaten metal still had enough of a sheen to reflect DiMag's face as he stared at it.

"There." The prince wedged the shield firmly and stepped back. "Not the ideal looking glass, but it suffices. Satisfy your curiosity, Sun-Hound."

Kyre slowly approached the shield. Now that he was at last to see himself he felt a stab of trepidation, and had to fight an impulse to shut his eyes. He reached the shield, stopped, stared . . .

A strong, bony face looked back at him from the shield's dull bronze surface. Wide-set eyes with a slight slant to them, broad cheekbones, generous mouth, determined jaw. Hair that fell heavy and abundant over his shoulders, and very unkempt. His face was scarred where Simorh's silver whips had attacked and burned him; but they would fade. He wasn't hideous, as he had feared. In fact there was a faint echo of DiMag in his features; of others he had seen in Haven, as if, far in the distant past, there had been a link between them.

He turned to look quickly at the prince, who was watching him with lazy interest. DiMag smiled faintly.

"The bronze distorts color, I know. To answer your original question, your eyes are green. That's a very uncommon characteristic in Haven. I imagine the princess meant it to be otherwise, just as I imagine she would have preferred you not to have red hair. Does that strike you as significant?"

Kyre was starting to feel uneasy. "Should it?"

"Ah; now we come to the nub of it. I wonder . . ." He shook his head. "No. That will keep for another time. But it isn't like Simorh to make mistakes. I may dislike her power and the way she uses it, but I can't deny its efficacy—in certain areas." With an effort he stood up, and walked to the window again. He was restless, and his mood lent tension to the atmosphere in the room. "Do you know where she found the spell that created you? Would you *like* to know?" Kyre didn't answer—the thought made him queasy—and DiMag continued with a trace of malice: "She found it in a manuscript which had all but rotted away, and which no one else can have studied for centuries." He turned to face Kyre. "That's what you are, Sun-Hound. Decayed parchment and faded ink; a jumble of words half in one language and half in another. Or that's what Simorh believes."

"And you, Prince DiMag? What do *you* believe?"

DiMag had been walking back to the couch, but he stopped and stared hard at the other man. "I don't know," he said. "I suspect there's more to you than meets the eye, but I don't yet know why I suspect it. If I thought you were privy to that information I might decide to have it tortured out of you, if that's what it took to get it. But you're even more ignorant than I am, and certainly far more ignorant than Simorh. "Perhaps then he saw a dangerous light in Kyre's eyes, for he took an easy but nonetheless calculated pace backward. "A cipher doesn't have a will or a mind of its own, and it doesn't challenge its creator by being something that the creator didn't bargain for. Tell me, Sun-Hound; do you have a religious belief?''

Again the sudden and sly change of subject, as though DiMag's favorite strategy were an oblique and obscure attack. Kyre frowned. ''A religious belief . . . ?''

''Yes. We had gods once, or so history tells us, but we lost them. If they ever existed at all, they probably abandoned us when we started the long descent that has led us to where we are today, and now we can't even recall their names.'' He saw the flicker of surprise in Kyre's expression and added, ''Oh, yes: we thrived, once. If you go inland from the city, you'll find nothing but a few isolated farms and the occasional mining village, and they're poor farms and villages at best. They still tithe a portion of their produce and minerals to us in exchange for our protection—for what that's worth these days—and some still come to Haven to trade.'' He smiled cynically. ''The arrangement does no more than maintain us all at a bare subsistence; but it wasn't always that way. Centuries ago, Haven was a great power. Our influence spread right across the land, and the land prospered. We created, we traded, we had art and music, and poetry and architecture and philosophy. Or at least, that's what the records would have us believe; though for all I know they might be nothing more than the grandiose fantasies of a few drunken dreamers. The only fact that's not in doubt is that now there's only Haven; or what's left of it. And Haven's days are numbered.''

''The sand . . .'' Kyre said, catching the venomous bitterness in the prince's voice. ''The sorceress said that the sea flowed twice in one night without ebbing, and the sand came in with the tide and buried half of the city.''

''She told you that, did she?'' DiMag's eyes glittered. ''And did she also tell you *why* that disaster happened?''

"No."

"No. She wouldn't have wanted you to know that particular truth." DiMag resumed pacing, and Kyre watched his dogged progress with discomfited fascination. "It happened through the agency of sorcery, Sun-Hound. Not Simorh's; but a filthy, evil, corrupted power whose wielders' sole aim is to destroy Haven and all who dwell in it." DiMag stopped suddenly, seeming to realize that he was losing his self-control. He took a deep breath, then exhaled harshly. "I won't deny that Simorh's skills are formidable—but beside those warped and evil demons from the sea, she's as helpless as a child!" He moved to the window. "They draw their power from the Hag, that bloated monstrosity that floats in the sky when the sun has set and rules over the winds and the tides. Every now and then there's a conjunction—we call it the Dead Night—when the Hag rises directly over the sea and throws a spear of light across the bay to Haven's very gate. When that happens, our enemies' power reaches its height, and we can't stand against them.

"The last Dead Night conjunction was nine years ago, when the tide flowed twice without ebbing. The sea demons came in on that tide and we tried to turn them back, but we failed. Our army rode out across the sand and met them as they came out of the sea." He pressed his hands down on the window ledge, knuckles white, as he stared out at the fog. "My wife stood in her tower, from where she could see the battle, and while our baby daughter slept in a cradle in the room below, she used all the power she could comand to keep the city safe, keep our army safe, and it wasn't enough. What she did almost turned the blood to dust in her veins, and it was a year before she could speak again; but it wasn't enough. Maybe it would have been kinder if she had died."

"And you," Kyre said, believing that he knew the answer. "You were wounded?"

"If that's what you want to call it. A spear in the leg is one matter; a spear cursed with sorcery, and wielded by a hand that should have been dead fifty years ago, is another. The wound should have healed, so every physician told me. It didn't. And no spells of Simorh's will ever restore me to fitness."

Creatures from the sea, enemies who drew their power from the baleful moon: the prisoner in the court hall . . . little Gamora's savage hatred to the sea people . . .

Suddenly, his mind cast up the image of the girl on the strand.

DiMag saw the change in his expression, the dismay and confusion that he couldn't hide in time. The prince's eyes narrowed.

"What is it?"

"I . . ." Kyre swallowed. "Demons from the sea, you said. And yet—they look human?"

"You saw the creature in the court hall with your own eyes. They're human enough to die like any of us. Why?"

"On the strand tonight—I saw a girl."

Suddenly DiMag's hands weren't steady. "Where?" he demanded.

"Not far from the ruin."

The room was silent but for the prince's harsh breathing. "What did she look like?"

"Young—I think. Her hair was black, shimmering, almost—" He struggled for the right word but couldn't find it. "A white face, deathly white. Strange, vast eyes. And—"

"*Dark*, you said? Are you sure? Not silver-haired?" DiMag's eyes were ablaze with a feverish light.

"No." Kyre shook his head. "Her hair was black."

"Then it wasn't Calthar . . ."

"Calthar?"

The prince's face was venomous. "Calthar is the source of their power. She's a vampire, a soul-eater. She's the ultimate corruption; the demon-race draws its inspiration from her as a child suckles its mother's milk. But it wasn't her you saw . . ."

"She came from the sea," Kyre said uneasily.

"Oh, yes: I don't doubt that the creature was one of Calthar's emissaries. Which can only mean she's abroad again." DiMag shuddered. "There's another Dead Night coming. Our astronomers have calculated it, and what you saw on the strand only serves to confirm their predictions."

A deathly cold hand seemed to touch the pit of Kyre's stomach as a terrible suspicion entered his mind. He said, not entirely trusting his voice, "And what has that to do with me?"

"Everything," DiMag replied softly. "It's the reason why Simorh summoned you into our world." He stared at Kyre with a mixture of bitter weariness and pity. "When Dead Night comes again, she means you to be Haven's champion."

Kyre's throat was dust-dry, and his voice shook. "She surely can't—"

"She can. That is your task, my friend. Haven is threatened with destruction; a conjunction is approaching, and without a miracle we can't hope to survive the attack that will surely come. Your destiny is to provide that miracle."

Kyre's mind floundered, and his only clear thought was to ask himself whether DiMag, or Simorh, or both, were insane. The idea that he, a single man, should be expected to stand against an army of enemies was sheer, deluded madness. He owed no loyalty to Haven, he had no past to call on: to the best of his own poor knowledge he wasn't even a warrior!

DiMag was still watching him, and said suddenly, "I know what you're thinking, and maybe it *is* a kind of madness. But there's a great deal you don't understand."

"Then tell me," Kyre said tightly.

"No." The prince shook his head. "I'm no true scholar, despite my pretentions; you're demanding your answers of the wrong man." He moved stiffly toward his couch. "You should seek out Gamora's tutor, old Brigrandon, and put your questions to him." Abruptly, he turned toward his couch. "I think, Sun-Hound, that for the time being we have no more to say to each other. I've been honest with you, as I promised, but for now I can tell you no more." Pausing, he looked back at Kyre. "Remember the pledge you made to me in return, and you won't find my word wanting. I'll grant you complete freedom within the palace, and you need answer only to me. But *always* remember your pledge!"

He sank down on the couch, and reached out to pull at a bell rope which hung by the wall. Kyre couldn't speak, couldn't find words to say that made any sense; and, seeing that he wasn't about to argue, DiMag added, "My own guard will show you the way back to the Sunrise Tower." He smiled wryly. "Good night, Kyre. Sleep well—if you can."

Calthar was waiting when they brought the girl back to her room. She stood bathed in the eerie blue glow which suffused through the womblike cavern, watching as the escort party stopped on the threshold. The men would come no farther than the narrow embrasure; the sanctum was barred to them by the twin prohibitions of tradition and their own fear, and Calthar treated them to a glance of withering contempt when she saw how uneasily they shrank back from the girl, afraid to touch her. Then they withdrew, and the girl entered the cavern alone.

After an initial struggle she had suffered her recapture meekly, and as she faced Calthar her huge, dark eyes were empty of emotion. A tranquil and dreamy smile softened the line of her thin lips, and Calthar felt a familiar mixture of rage, resentment, jealousy, and disgust boiling within her like a brew in a caldron. The girl was in one of her lucid phases—otherwise, she could never have had the self-possession to escape in the first place—and was quite capable of speaking if she chose to. But she wouldn't choose; no power could force words out of Talliann unless Talliann willed it.

She paced slowly toward the girl, moving among the stalactites that hung like giant, ossified claws from the cavern ceiling. Her steps were slow and deliberate, and on the cave walls with their cold sheen of abalone a hundred reflections of her lithe form and fluttering, ancient robe performed a distorted dance. Talliann didn't react in any way, and Calthar felt her patience ebbing toward a dangerous level. The girl needed a sharp and bitter lesson to bring her to heel and make her understand the responsibility that lay on her shoulders: but, though the knowledge ate at her like a cancer, Calthar knew that hers could never be the hand to administer that lesson. As Priestess of the Hag and heir to the Mothers who had reigned before her, she was feared by the sea dwellers above all others: save one. And it rankled cruelly that Talliann, this child, this fey simpleton whose sanity had been in doubt from the first day of her existence, should command more respect from her people than Calthar could ever do; a respect made all the stronger by the love and reverence which went hand in hand with it. For that reason alone, Calthar couldn't touch Talliann. She didn't dare.

The priestess stopped pacing, and stared at her charge's impassive back. Still Talliann didn't move, and

Calthar expelled a long, hissing breath that expressed a bare fraction of the frustration she felt.

"Why?" she demanded hoarsely. "Why did you go?"

Talliann raised her head, but that was all. Swift as a snake, Calthar moved across the floor until she was facing the girl. Her face was distorted with anger, but when she looked into Talliann's black eyes something she saw there made her hesitate. The depth of the girl's hollow look was daunting; her gaze seemed to drink in her surroundings, draining the strength from everything she saw. A cold worm of discomfort moved in Calthar and she looked away.

"Child, you try me!" The sorceress's voice was harsh. "Time and again you are told what you must do; time and again you try to thwart me. Will you never learn?"

The girl's vast, dark eyes fastened on her face and Calthar repressed a shudder. "You are precious to us," she added, forcing the words past her tongue and teeth. "More precious than anything, as well you know. We can't risk your safety, Talliann. And if you continue to defy the rules we have made for your own good, then that freedom you have enjoyed must be denied you. Is that what you want?"

Uncertainty flickered in the girl's gaze for a moment, swiftly followed by dread, before her face became an impassive mask once more.

"I thought not." Calthar smiled thinly. "Then if you wish to avoid such a stricture, answer my question."

Small, sharp teeth showed over the girl's lower lip. When she spoke, it was as though words were an unfamiliar medium to her.

"Ask . . ."

Better, Calthar thought. Aloud, she demanded: "What did you find on the shore?"

Talliann's deathly pale brow creased in a frown that, for a moment, made her face ugly. "I saw . . ."

Calthar waited.

"I saw . . ." And suddenly the frown was gone, and the girl's face was radiant. She turned toward the priestess and said, as though struck by a revelation, "He has come back!"

It made no sense, and the all too familiar anger of frustration clutched Calthar. "Who?" she demanded, her voice rising to a furious pitch. "What are you talking about?"

Talliann began to laugh. The sound was like bright water lapping over stones, and it grated on Calthar's ears until she thought she would scream with the pressure of it—and then it stopped as suddenly as it had begun, and Talliann repeated, in the voice of a child, "He has come back."

There was death in Calthar's eyes as she stared at the girl. She didn't understand this new tack, and doubted if Talliann comprehended it either. But the wretched child had encountered someone on the shores of that hated city: someone who seemed to have obsessed her. She had unfathomable but immovable reasons for not wanting to reveal the truth, and Calthar drew only one conclusion from her stubbornness—that the mysterious interloper had some direct connection with Haven.

She spoke, but this time with a terrible gentleness. "My child, my sweeting, you are tired. You must sleep. Sleep until night comes round once more." Moving forward, she took Talliann's arm. "Sleep, Talliann. Rest. Leave it all to me."

Talliann moved meekly under her guiding hand, allowing herself to be steered toward the back of the cavern. A short flight of uneven steps led up to a place where the hanging stalactites formed a forest of twisted, encrusted pillars. Among these lay a single huge shell, its gaping interior lined with the tangled, black and green fronds of sea-bed weed. This was Talliann's resting place, the womb from which, years ago at the Hag's great conjunction, Calthar's sorcery had summoned her: as they approached the shell, Talliann stopped.

"I will see him again." Her tone was flat with utter certainty, and then she tilted her head to one side and gave Calthar an old, sly look. "I *will* see him. For if I don't . . . perhaps there will be no great conjunction. Perhaps it will not come. Perhaps I will see that it does not."

Calthar's breath hissed between her teeth, but her voice didn't give away the fury that Talliann's words had rekindled. "You'll see him, precious one. You will." *Who?* she thought. *Who?*

"Soon . . ." Talliann's voice took on a sleepy, sing-song quality, and Calthar felt relief. The girl's strength was waning fast, her stamina failing as it always did when her emotions were roused; for now, there'd be no confrontation.

"Soon," she echoed. If Talliann comprehended the venom in her voice she showed no sign of it, and Calthar watched as she stepped into the shell and sank down on the bed of weed. Talliann's eyes closed, and the priestess expelled a sharp breath. The girl's sleep would be long and deep; time enough to see what might be seen, and do what might be done. Something was afoot, and it must echo the omens which her Mothers had spoken in her ear since the Hag's last fullness. Their message had grown stronger each night: perhaps now she had the first clue to what they had been trying to tell her.

Within less than a minute, Talliann slept. Calthar watched her for a short while, satisfied by the gentle,

even rhythm of her breathing, then she left the chamber
and traversed the dimly lit passageways that ran like a
maze through the rock. She met no one on her journey,
and at last reached the vast, echoing emptiness of the
cavern which led out to the open sea. Here she stood for
a while on a rock spur, staring down at the black water
that slapped with a sluggish yet inexorable rhythm
against the stone beneath her feet.

Time and inevitability . . . the sea ate eternally at
the rock, wearing it away with inhuman patience,
content to let aeons pass in the knowledge that it would
eventually triumph. Calthar felt no such contentment.
Her soul was warped with thoughts of chaos and
destruction and she scorned the sea's stoicism. Damn
time, and damn patience. The Hag's night was at hand.

She drew breath, and with sinuous grace slipped into
the sea. The water's buoyancy lifted her and she drew its
strength into her bones, becoming one with the swell,
moving smoothly out on the undertow as a wave drew
back toward the cave mouth and the vast, empty night
beyond. Her robe flowed around her like decaying weed,
tangling about limbs that shone beneath the water with a
silver-green phosphorescence. She drew breath again,
feeling brine flow through her mouth and nostrils and
into her lungs as she dived deep, deeper into blackness,
water replacing air as the medium of life, breathing and
drinking, eyes wide and filled with an aching, lusting
hate as Calthar, sorceress, priestess, Mother born of
Mothers, swam with the ease and grace of a sea serpent
toward the open water.

Chapter 6

THE VERBAL KNIFE WHICH DiMag HAD INSERTED INTO what was left of his composure was no match for the sheer exhaustion that overtook Kyre when he reached his room in the Sunrise Tower. He slept too deeply for dreams to plague him, and when he woke the fog had cleared and a weak sun hung above the horizon, throwing a spear of light through his window.

Recollections of the bizarre interview with Haven's prince came back as Kyre opened his eyes, and his first reaction was a surge of furious anger. At last he had discovered what Haven wanted of him, and the revelation was a goad that fired and fueled the rage in him. A champion—or, more accurately, a pawn, a fool to stand up in the face of a deadly enemy and fight a battle which he had no hope of winning. How they expected him to fight, what they expected him to do, he couldn't begin to imagine: the entire concept seemed utterly mad. But it was the purpose for which Simorh had called him to this world.

And as for DiMag . . . his view of him was now
utterly ambiguous. Though he still couldn't say that he
liked the prince, he had learned enough last night to
understand and sympathize with his ingrained bitterness.
Yet despite his openness, and his avowed belief that Kyre
had an identity which owed nothing to sorcery, DiMag
had made it clear that he was as ready as Simorh to use
him without scruple. His escape attempt had proved,
painfully and beyond doubt, that Simorh could control
him, and if he proved unwilling to cooperate with her
plans, he had no illusions that DiMag would prevent her
from using her powers to force him into compliance.
Man he might be, with a soul and mind of his own: but to
DiMag and Simorh he was no better than a slave chained
to their will.

Or was he? The fury was under control now, banked
down like a smoldering fire, and Kyre knew that he had
two choices. He could allow his confusion, his fear of
Simorh's sorcery, to gain the upper hand, in which case
he was a coward and deserved nothing better than the
metaphorical collar and chain with which the people of
Haven meant to hold him. Or he could stand up to them,
resist their efforts to intimidate him, and show them that
he would neither cower nor submit.

DiMag had perhaps sensed the rebellion simmering
within Kyre when he offered his bargain last night. Kyre
was still prepared to stand by their agreement, but
whether DiMag would keep *his* word was another matter.
The prince was mercurial at best, and Kyre didn't care to
place too much trust in his pledge. But DiMag had
promised him freedom within the palace bounds, and
that at least was something he could put to the test. At the
same time, he might serve his own purposes further by
seeking out Gamora's tutor and putting to him some of

the questions which DiMag had been unable or unwilling to answer.

He climbed out of bed, crossed the room, and tried the door. It was unlocked, and he smiled faintly. Well and good; but how far would his new freedom extend? Everything depended on DiMag's preparedness to abide by his word. Testing that preparedness would prove an interesting experiment.

He opened the door wide and looked out. There was no one to be seen, nothing but the dimly lit and empty staircase. Kyre listened for a moment to be sure, then, hearing no sound, left his room and began to descend the long, winding stairway into the heart of the palace. No one attempted to impede Kyre as he made his way through the palace's corridors. He encountered a steward, who stonily ignored him, two female servants who whispered behind their hands, and a pale-haired, uneasy-eyed page who pressed close to the wall and slid by, avoiding the tall man's gaze. Reaching the deserted main hall he paused for a few moments to look again at the tapestries which hung on the walls. What little remained of their faded richness was washed out by the cool daylight filtering from outside; surrounded by cold stone and with no lamplight to soften their edges they looked ghostly and wan. The main doors stood ajar and a shaft of sunlight cut a narrow swathe across the floor, bringing with it a scent of fresh, salty air that lured him. He crossed the marble floor, pulled one of the great doors wider open, and stepped outside.

The morning was chilly, and though the chill struck sharply through his clothes and made him shiver, its freshness helped to dispel the sense of cloying uncleanness that had been growing during his imprisonment. He stood on a terrace that ran the length of the

palace wall and curved away round the side of the
building, edged by a low and intricately carved balustrade. Overhead the sky was a pale, washed blue,
patchworked with clouds that scudded before a strong
wind, and below him the palace garden sprawled, sere
foliage and struggling, bloated flowers given a touch of
life by the sunlight. In the distance Kyre could hear the
hushing moan of the sea, and instinct—he had nothing
else to go on—told him that this was, for Haven, a
perfect autumn day.

He stood still for a few minutes, breathing in the
mingled scents of brine and damp soil and warm stone;
then as the sun's strength began to counter the bite of the
wind he turned and walked slowly along the terrace
toward the palace's seaward side.

The perimeter wall was too high to allow him any
sight of the town, but the lack of any noise from beyond
the wall was something he found a little disturbing. With
the fog gone and the day fine there must be bustle and
activity in the streets of Haven; but no sound of it
reached the palace. The quiet was profound, and eerie.

But the quiet wasn't to last. Kyre had almost reached
the corner of the palace where the terrace swept round in
a graceful, flying arc, when a door rattled somewhere
nearby and light footsteps scurried on stone. A shadow
skittered across his path, and Gamora appeared round the
curve of the terrace, running.

"Kyre!" She just managed to stop before cannoning
into him. She was pink-cheeked and breathless, her dark
curls bobbing, unbrushed, around her face, and the sight
of her gave Kyre's spirits an unexpected lift.

"Princess!" Reflexively he caught her in his arms,
almost lifting her off her feet. "What's the great rush?"

"I saw you from the window," Gamora told him,

tripping over her words in her eagerness. "And I told my tutor you must come with us, that I *insisted*—Kyre, I was right, wasn't I?"

"Right?" The chaotic mixture of subjects made him want to laugh but he squashed the impulse, not wanting to offend her dignity. "About what?"

"About you coming back. You *said* you would and I *knew* you would, because you promised. And I was *right*!"

Kyre's conscience stabbed him as he realized that she was blissfully ignorant of the truth. But he couldn't disillusion her. And he couldn't deny the simple fact that he was glad to see her again.

He said: "Of course you were right, Princess."

She searched his face, and her eyes suddenly narrowed suspiciously. "But you really suffered no hurt? *Really*?"

He smiled. "None. May the Eye close on me if I tell a lie!" And instantly he was nonplussed by the phrase he had used. Where had it come from? He'd never heard it before; and yet it had come easily and naturally to his tongue, a careless oath . . .

It seemed, however, to satisfy Gamora, for she said, "Good! Then you won't be too tired to accompany us."

This time he did laugh. "I'll accompany you gladly, Princess—if I know where it is you're going."

"We are going, I suspect, wherever the little princess's whims lead us!"

The new voice, with its underlying hint of weary humor, startled them both, and Kyre looked up. The man who had followed Gamora's flying progress at a more leisurely pace was probably as tall as Kyre himself, though the stoop he affected took the edge from the impression. He was getting on in years, lean, and dressed in a motley of subdued colors that indicated

either lack of taste or complete indifference to his own
appearance. In youth his hair had clearly been peppery-
fair, but now it had turned gray and was swept back from
his face in two unruly wings. Broken veins under the
coarse skin to either side of his nose suggested that
drinking was something more than a pastime. But his
smile, as his gray eyes met Kyre's, was frank and
friendly, if a trifle sardonic.

"The Sun-Hound, if I may presume to make an
educated guess?" he said. "Good morning. I'm most
intrigued to make your acquaintance."

"Tutor Brigrandon?"

"Ah." Brigrandon's look became self-deprecating.
"For my sins, yes. And there was I, hoping to keep you
guessing for a while. Clearly I'm not the only one whom
the little princess takes into her confidence!"

"Prince DiMag spoke of you last night."

"Did he?" Kyre realized suddenly that, despite the
manner he affected, Brigrandon could easily match
DiMag for shrewdness.

Gamora danced on the spot, catching her tutor's sleeve
and tugging it. "Master Brigrandon, you *promised*! And
if we don't hurry, the tide will turn!"

Brigrandon looked down at the little girl and said
severely, "When you reach my time of life, Gamora,
you'll understand that hurry is not a polite word!"

She was unimpressed. "But you promised! And you
said that Kyre could come with us!"

"Very well; very well." The tutor sighed and looked
at Kyre again. "I throw myself on your mercy, Sun-
Hound. The little princess insists that you accompany us
on our recreational walk, and if you don't agree to her
demands I'll never hear the end of it. My future is in your
hands."

The request suited Kyre's purpose admirably, as it would give him the opportunity to question the tutor without making his motive or his eagerness obvious. Besides, he was beginning to like Brigrandon. He smiled again.

"My conscience wouldn't let me live with the consequences of a refusal," he said. "I'm at your disposal."

There *was* activity in the town, but it had the same muted, faded, and secretive quality that seemed to typify everything about Haven. Kyre was surprised when Brigrandon led him and Gamora to the same wicket gate through which he had entered the palace on his arrival, and disconcerted to find three more solemn-faced children, two girls and a boy, waiting there to join their party. The girls curtsied to Gamora and the boy bowed, but no one made any attempt to introduce Kyre, and he had to suffer the discomfort for their mute and poorly disguised curiosity as the gate was opened and they left the palace grounds.

It seemed odd for the heir to the throne of Haven to be walking through the streets without any form of ceremony or security. Kyre might have expected crowds to line the way for a glimpse of their princess, but to the people they passed Gamora might as well have been any fisherman's child. One or two women making their way toward the market square paused and smiled with sad fondness at the little girl, and Brigrandon nodded to a few of the folk they passed, but aside from such small courtesies they were ignored. Even the presence of the red-haired stranger—and Kyre reasoned that rumors, at least, of Simorh's sorcerous creation must have reached the streets by now—did little to rouse the townspeople's interest.

And so they walked down through the town until they came to the city wall. Kyre hadn't expected Brigrandon to lead them this way, but he said nothing, only quelled a small shiver of memory as the small party went under the arch and out onto the vast sands of the bay.

The tide had withdrawn to a brilliant line on the horizon, reflecting the sky in a hard, sapphire blue. Its restless murmuring was a deep and constant vibration which Kyre sensed in his bones rather than heard; breakers gave a glittering white edge to the sapphire and added to the feeling of distant menace which he couldn't dislodge. To either side the coastline stretched away, the cliffs deceptively colorful in sunlight: he made himself look at the tall, impassive rock faces to the right of the bay, not wanting to gaze in the opposite direction where the gauntly malignant silhouette of the ruined temple marred the scene.

The four children, freed from the constraints of the palace and the town, broke away immediately from Brigrandon's supervision and ran across the white sand toward a cluster of fallen rocks that held sheltered, secret pools. Their exuberance made Kyre think of young animals newly released from cages; but as he and the tutor followed at a more leisurely pace he couldn't banish the thought of what lay beneath the sands. The disturbance must have shown in his face, for Brigrandon, having studied him obliquely for a minute or two as they walked, suddenly said: "Princess Gamora was less than a year old when it happened, Kyre. The others weren't even born. No reasonable man can expect them, at their age, to respect something that played no direct part in their lives." Brigrandon's long, flat-knuckled fingers fidgeted at his side, tapping a deep pocket in his faded coat as though he debated whether or not to delve into it.

In the pocket something bulged, and at last the tutor sighed.

"One shouldn't mourn forever. It's unhealthy, and life continues with complete indifference to our sorrows. But now and again it's hard to put the old memories away."

Kyre looked down at the sand beneath his feet. For a moment he felt as though, with only a small effort, he could have seen through it to the carnage preserved in gruesome tableau beneath, and the thought struck him to the core. "You lost someone in that tragedy?" he heard himself ask softly.

Brigrandon's eyes were bright and hard as he stared at the children, who by now were indistinguishable figures in the distance. "Both my sons fought with our army on that night, and my daughter's husband with them," he said, putting a detachment into his tone that didn't deceive Kyre for an instant. "My duties kept me at the palace, but my wife went to my daughter's house to keep vigil with her. The house was only one of many engulfed by the sand, and the young men were only three of hundreds killed in the battle." He shrugged, blinked, then thrust his restless hand into his pocket and drew out a small leather flask, reinforced with silver filigree. The cork came free with a faint sucking sound, and Brigrandon held the flask up toward the sea in a mocking and faintly defiant gesture. "Here's to them all. May the Eye always watch for their enemies." He drank deeply, then held the flask out to Kyre without a further word.

He didn't want the drink; he felt queasy and his stomach rebelled at the thought. But to refuse would be to insult the memories that tormented the old tutor. He took the flask. "The Eye preserve them all," he said, and drank.

Brigrandon put the flask away again and they walked

on in silence for a while. Gamora and the other children had reached the rocks and were climbing among them, oblivious to the somber mood of the two men. At last Brigrandon spoke.

"So you, too, curse or bless by the Eye." He glanced at Kyre. "I'm surprised you've developed the habit so quickly. Or was it simply a courtesy?"

Kyre stopped walking, aware that they had both been waiting for this moment when the first barriers would be breached.

"I don't know," he said. "All I can say is that it's not the first time I've called on it—despite the fact that I don't even know what it is I'm calling on."

"Ah." Brigrandon turned to stare at the distant sea. "Now the picture begins to make some sense." He paused, then, with the manner of one who had considered a number of options and come to a decision, added, "Let's walk a while. The children won't miss my attention, and I'd like to talk to you. I imagine we might have quite a lot to say to each other." He nodded toward the shingle bar. "The old temple seems as good a place as any to make our goal."

Before he could stop himself Kyre said, "I'd prefer—" then bit his tongue.

"You'd prefer to avoid the place?" Brigrandon regarded him shrewdly. "Yes; a lot of people feel that way. But in your case, I think it might be wiser to fight those feelings." Without expanding on that cryptic statement he set off toward the shingle bank, and Kyre had little choice but to follow. As they walked, he forced himself at last to look up at the grim skeleton of the temple. Under the bright sun it looked less baleful than when the cold moonlight had etched it, but nonetheless he couldn't stop his mind's eye from superimposing the memory of

night and darkness and the horrors they had brought over
the comparatively peaceful scene.

*That, and the image of a white-faced, hollow-eyed girl
in a bizarrely spangled gown . . .*

Brigrandon's voice broke into his uneasy thoughts.
"Do you know anything of the temple's origins?"

"No. Nothing."

Shingle crunched under their feet as the sand gave way
to the bar. Now that he'd faced the ruin, Kyre found he
couldn't stop staring at it. "If you want the full story,
you'd have to learn the old language of Haven,"
Brigrandon said. "And that's an impossibility now; it's
so many centuries since it was spoken that our knowledge of it is unreliable at best. We keep the remaining
fragments alive out of some misplaced sense of tradition,
but for any practical purposes it's little short of useless. If
you saw the numbers of rotting manuscripts preserved
for posterity, which now we can't even translate with any
accuracy—" He broke off and smiled. "I'm sorry; I'm in
danger of being diverted onto my favorite topic. We
scholars are uncomfortably aware of the shortcomings in
our historical knowledge, and it rankles. To return to the
point: the temple fell into disuse far back in our history,
but—as far as we know—its original name was the
Shrine of the Eye."

Kyre looked sidelong at the older man. Unprompted,
Brigrandon was moving into the territory he wanted to
explore. "A shrine?" he said. "I thought that shrines
were the homes of gods. And according to Prince
DiMag, Haven has no gods."

"That's true enough; or at least we've lost the gods we
might once have had. But we still have the sun that
shines in the sky, and though we see little enough of it, it
still rises each day and grants us continuing life. In

Haven, the sun is known as the Eye of Day; hence the naming of the temple."

"Sun worship?" Kyre forced himself to look at the ruin again.

"I don't believe our ancestors ever personified the sun as a god," Brigrandon said. "Their view of the powers that influence this world was a little more parochial. But certainly the Eye has always been revered. And in times gone by it had a human champion, whose sworn duty was to defend all that the sun's image stood for. One might well think of him as the Hound of the Sun."

His tone was so mildly careless that it took Kyre a few moments to realize the significance of what he had said. When it struck him, he stopped walking, feeling a cold, ghostly hand clutch at his vitals.

He said, quietly yet dangerously: "What?"

"Ah." Brigrandon, too, halted, and rubbed at his chin. He seemed a little disconcerted. "So they *haven't* told you about the original Kyre? The one after whom you were named, and in whose image you were made?"

Kyre was stunned by the question. He managed to maintain a calm expression, but his eyes burned hotly. "They have not."

"Ah," Brigrandon said again. "That is rather as I suspected." He reached toward the pocket where his flask was concealed, then changed his mind and let his hand fall to his side. "I'm well aware of the Princess Simorh's injunction that you should be kept in ignorance; and I'm aware, too, of the interest that Prince DiMag is taking in you, although"—and he smiled wryly—"the prince's reasoning is sometimes a little cryptic. But I imagine DiMag anticipated that you'd eventually find your way to me with your questions."

Despite the angry uncertainty that Brigrandon's revelation had reawoken in him, Kyre smiled thinly. "He did."

"Then he'll expect me to answer those questions. The prince knows me well enough to realize that, whatever my shortcomings, I won't be a party to deception or evasion. So he wants you to know the facts; that much we can deduce, though I wouldn't care to take a wager on his reasons." He sighed and shook his head. "It's as likely as not that his sole motive is to spite Simorh. A sad state of affairs . . . But, however convoluted the reasons, the circumstances have at least placed you in DiMag's favor. That's more of an advantage than you might think."

He echoed the prince's comment of the previous night, and again there was an implication that Kyre didn't comprehend. "Why should I not think it an advantage?" he asked.

"Oh, there are some who might not view it in that light. Think on it: a crippled ruler who has become a virtual recluse, no prospect of a son to succeed him, a decimated army which he can no longer lead . . ." Brigrandon paused. "In such circumstances there's no shortage of ambitious men who might be tempted to view Prince DiMag as a lost cause."

I want your loyalty, DiMag had said last night. Kyre was beginning to understand.

He turned and looked back across the bay to the straggling sprawl of Haven against the cliff face. In sunlight the old city was quite beautiful, the stone mellow and specked with tiny, glittering diamonds of brilliance where the light caught particles of quartz embedded in the rock. The three towers of the palace rode high and proud over the scene, their windows glittering. Yes; a beautiful city. Beautiful, and riddled with intrigue, corruption, decay . . .

Brigrandon said quietly: "I'm willing to answer your questions, Kyre; or at least I'm willing to try. But I don't know whether you'll like what you hear."

Kyre smiled bleakly. "I want to know the truth, Master Brigrandon."

Shrill voices impinged on them from somewhere in the distance, and the old scholar looked toward the sea. "This isn't the time or the place for further talk," he said. "Here come the children—we must return to the city, and I've lessons to give them this afternoon. We'll meet again later, my friend. Come to my rooms this evening, eat with me, drink with me. Then we'll see what can be done."

They turned their backs on the ruined temple and walked back to the sand, intercepting Gamora and the other children as they came racing from the direction of a rocky outcrop. Gamora's skirt was wet and she carried her soaked shoes in one hand; in the other she held a shell she had found and which she was anxious to display to Kyre.

"Look, Kyre!" The little girl's face radiated delight as she held her treasure out to him. "Look how thin the sea has worn it—and the colors are so beautiful!"

The shell was as large as Gamora's hand, and almost translucent. Its inner surface was lined with mother-of-pearl and, catching the light, it shone like a coruscating rainbow. Kyre smiled. "It's lovely, Princess."

"I shall keep it in my room, and look at it every day," Gamora declared.

The other children hung back while she chattered happily, though Kyre was aware of their curious eyes surreptitiously watching him. At last the small party

started back toward the city gateway. They had almost
reached the sandstone arch when a group of some half-
dozen men, armed and wearing crimson sashes over the
shoulders of their heavy leather jerkins, came marching
in quick formation out of the city. Their leader saluted
Gamora, who was too engrossed with her shell to notice,
then the patrol tramped away across the sand toward the
tideline.

Kyre hung back from the arch, watching the men.
"Do they patrol the beach every day?" he asked.

"Each time the tide turns," Brigrandon told him.

It was yet another ritual, another hollow tradition.
Though sometimes, Kyre thought, the patrols found
more than just the sea's flotsam. He recalled the sea
creature which had died at DiMag's hand in the great hall
of the palace, and suppressed a shudder.

"Cold?" Brigrandon asked.

"No." Kyre shook his head. "Just—thinking."

With the children trailing behind them, they walked
under the arch into the claustrophobic city.

Hodek's palpable fear of her was a goad to Calthar's
temper, fueling the loathing she felt for the man and for
the spineless sycophants he gathered around himself to
bolster his flagging confidence. She had deliberately
summoned them to her outer chamber rather than to one
of the main halls of the citadel as precedent dictated; she
wanted them to feel the power that cocooned this place,
and she wanted them cowed by it. She would show them
that, whatever the grandiose titles with which Hodek and
his minions dignified themselves, the Mothers ruled
here, and she alone spoke with their voice.

She sat cross-legged on a dais that had been carved
from a single giant slab of obsidian. This chamber was

small and cramped, unfurnished save for the dais and a few fish-oil lamps set on high ledges and placed so that their light cast grotesque and unnerving shadows. Calthar knew the value of outward impressions, and took satisfaction from the unease in the faces of the council as they shuffled into the chamber and arranged themselves as best they could in its confines. She waited until they had settled, then said, without preamble, "You have all had my message, and I assume you understand both its urgency and its significance." They heard the rage underlying her tone, and exchanged glances. "I have summoned you in order to inform you of how I intend to deal with the matter."

Hodek cleared his throat, the sound hollow and dead. "Before we move to that, Calthar, I—ah, we all—feel that certain aspects might need further clarification."

At Hodek's side, a young man whose hair was a bizarre pattern of silver streaked with black, and who bore an ugly birthmark on his right cheek, nodded. His blue eyes watched the sorceress levelly as he said, "It's my opinion that we should speak to Talliann, and hear for ourselves what she has to say—"

Calthar glared at him, and the young man instantly subsided. Akrivir, son of Hodek and second only to his father as an object of Calthar's contempt. It was rare to find them speaking on the same side, for Akrivir loathed his sire, and, though he'd never been able to uncover the full truth, held him responsible for his long-dead mother's untimely end. His hatred for his father was matched only by his hatred for Calthar; though where he despised the one, he feared the other. He was no threat to the sorceress: indeed, she found in him a further source of amusement, and had deliberately elevated him at an early age to her council so that she might enjoy the bitter quarrels which invariably developed between him and Hodek.

As Akrivir withered beneath her savage stare, Calthar knew full well what had prompted his desire to speak to Talliann. Akrivir had hopeless dreams of becoming Talliann's lover or even consort, just as Hodek wanted Calthar and had once dreamed that he could tame her. The boy, in Calthar's view, was as big a fool as his father: Talliann was not for him, and he could no more hope to court the fey girl than to possess the Hag herself.

"Clarification." Calthar repeated Hodek's word with soft venom, her tone making it into an obscenity. "Speaking to Talliann." The words hung in the stale air until their very last resonance had died away. Her eyes were huge and deadly, reflecting splinters of light from the veins of pyrites and quartz that shot through the rock walls. Her tongue flickered out over her lower lip, then with a violence that made every man in the chamber start with shock she barked out, "You are *fools*!"

She rose, uncoiling, and the lamps flickered, giving off streamers of oily smoke as her sudden movement disturbed the still air. Calthar stepped down from the dais and faced the councillors, who shrank back at her approach. She was a head taller than any of them, and stared down at their pale faces with undisguised scorn.

"My message needs no clarification," she said savagely. "I haven't called you here to listen to inept bleating about the finer details of what has happened— nor," she added with a searing look at Akrivir, "to listen to the blandishments of a lovesick sea worm!" Ignoring the suppressed fury that showed in his eyes at the taunt, she whirled, her ragged robe dancing about her body. "The simple facts are these: our enemies have a new champion whom they intend to use against us on the night of the Great Conjunction. Talliann—who was allowed to leave the citadel through the laxness of those who should have known better—encountered this precious new pet of theirs, and she has taken it into her head to want him brought here to the citadel."

Calthar began to pace. "Talliann, as we know, has always been given to unpredictable whims and fancies, and in the past her thoughts have been easy enough to steer in more profitable directions. This time, however, she is immovable. I have cajoled her; I have reasoned with her; I have threatened her." She glanced toward the back of the chamber, where a low, heavy door, bolted, marred the rock, and from the corner of her eye saw Hodek blanch. "But my efforts have availed nothing. Talliann is adamant—and if her desire is not granted, she will refuse to play the part required of her during the Great Conjunction, when we launch the final assault on our enemies."

Someone swore softly, others set up a troubled muttering. Calthar turned to face them again. "I see you appreciate the nature of our problem. Without Talliann, the opportunity afforded us by the Great Conjunction is worthless. Yet if we don't accede to her in this, we will have nothing from her."

Akrivir spoke up sharply. "It won't be an easy conundrum to solve. We can hardly send warriors into their stronghold simply to—"

Calthar silenced him with a look. With soft venom, she retorted, "When your advice is required, you will be informed of the fact. Until then, hold your prattling tongue!

"The solution to our conundrum is something that I and I alone can contrive. I need no help from the council—all I need is, by tradition, to inform you of what I intend to do, and to have your sanction. I assume that sanction won't be withheld."

It was a threat rather than a question. Akrivir, who alone might have voiced another objection, thought better of the idea, and Hodek nodded eagerly.

"Tell us, Calthar. Whatever you want, we'll do your bidding!"

Calthar's sanctum was dark. She needed no illumination; she knew every inch of her domain, and knew that no uninvited foot would ever dare trammel her privacy. Crouching now on a narrow ledge that overlooked a small and bottomless pool, she was utterly still, as she had been for hours past, waiting and watching with the awesome patience of a hungry predator. And at last her vigil was rewarded.

Such a pitifully simple device in her hands, yet it was more than enough. The land-dwellers' command of sorcery was beneath her contempt; they'd know nothing of the alien presence in their midst until matters had moved far beyond their influence. And the mind of a child, so innocent and malleable, was a dark delight to manipulate.

Inwardly, Calthar felt a desire to laugh. But no sound escaped her throat except for the steady, rhythmic breathing which had continued hour after long hour. She gazed into the pool, seeing beyond its featureless black surface to something that moved in another place and another dimension. Now and then her lips formed an invocation to the Mothers whose guiding inspiration lived within and around her, but the invocation was silent and she made not the smallest sound. She watched. And she smiled.

Chapter 7

THEAN WAS ON AN ERRAND, AND, LACKING HER MORAL support, Falla hadn't the courage to stand up to the first of the two visitors who called on Simorh that morning.

Swordsmaster Vaoran had heard the news that the princess was unwell and unable to leave her tower, and it offered him the opportunity for which he'd been waiting and hoping to speak to her alone. Falla's insistence that her mistress was not strong enough to receive callers met with polite but icy disinterest, and it took the burly warrior less than a minute to browbeat her into leading him to her private room.

Simorh had attempted to rise at her usual hour, and had collapsed. The power she had wielded against Kyre last night, following so closely on the heels of the ritual with which she had conjured him into the world, had drained and exhausted her and the damage would take some time to heal. At last, with the help of Falla and Thean, she had left her bed, but she was too enervated to do anything other than lie on a couch by the window. At the sound of Vaoran's heavy tread she looked up, and the swordsmaster was shocked by her appearance. Her fair hair was lank and lifeless, hanging in brittle tendrils around a face made haggard by strain and exhaustion. Her skin had become parchment-yellow and deep shadows smudged her eye sockets, while her hands, folded on the embroidered wool blanket which the girls had wrapped about her for warmth, kept shaking in unpredictable, palsied fits. Youth and vitality had deserted her, and she looked desperately sick. Yet her sickness didn't prevent a spark of anger from flickering in her eyes when she saw her visitor.

Anxious to forestall that anger before she could give vent to it, Vaoran approached the couch and made a knee to her. It was an archaic gesture, long fallen into disuse, yet it had the desired effect, as Simorh couldn't ignore such a compliment without giving unjustifiable offense.

"Swordsmaster." With an effort she pulled herself more upright on the couch. Falla ran forward to help, but Simorh waved the girl away. She was beginning to understand how DiMag must feel . . .

"Princess, I came as soon as I heard the news of your illness," Vaoran said solicitously as he rose to his feet once more.

Simorh looked up at him. *Shrewd eyes, as blue as the sky, calculating . . . yet there was something else in them which he couldn't quite mask and she couldn't quite recognize.* She returned a wintry smile.

"Thank you for your concern, Vaoran, but I assure you it's misplaced. I'm not ill; I'm merely exhausted. I'll be fully recovered in a day or so."

He smiled. "So I heard, lady, but I confess I couldn't banish my doubts. I wouldn't have dreamed of intruding

on you, but my anxiety was such that I had to set my
mind at rest."

"As you see, I'm in no danger."

"Indeed, and I'm very thankful. I feel a keen
responsibility for what happens."

"You?" She looked at him, surprised. "Why should
you be in any way to blame?"

He made a small, self-deprecating gesture. "As both
councillor and military commander, the fact that the
creature—the Sun-Hound—" he uttered the name as
though it were distasteful to him—"was allowed to
escape from the palace *must* be my responsibility. You
had personally given orders that he should be confined
and watched, and those orders were not complied with.
If I find the man who allowed—"

Simorh interrupted him with a sigh. "Neither you nor
your soldiers nor any palace servant was at fault, Vaoran.
The culprit was my daughter."

"Princess Gamora?" The swordsmaster was taken
aback.

"Gamora is quixotic and impressionable," Simorh
said tiredly. "And easily dazzled by anything unfamiliar
or mysterious. No doubt she found it exciting to
champion a new friend."

Vaoran frowned and moved toward the window. After
a few moments' silence he said: "I see. I'd wondered . . ." He hesitated, then shook his head. There
was a long pause, during which the sound of Falla
moving about at the far side of the room set Vaoran's
nerves on edge. Then Simorh said sharply, "*What* had
you wondered, Vaoran?"

He turned to face her again, his movements ponderous
and deliberate. "It's of no moment, madam; not now."
His blue eyes focused on hers. "I'd simply wondered if

Prince DiMag had countermanded your order and hadn't informed me of the fact."

In the ensuing stillness he could hear her breathing. The sound was sharp, quick, unhealthy; fury underlay it, though she hadn't the physical strength to give it form.

"Haven asks a great deal of you, Princess Simorh. You have made great sacrifices for this city, and I wouldn't want to see such sacrifice come to nothing."

Simorh stared down at her hands, willing them to stop shaking and twitching. Her fingers gripped the blanket, though the grip was weak. "And what," she asked evenly, "has this to do with Kyre's escape?"

Vaoran hesitated, then: "I am simply concerned lest the control you have of him should be undermined. The Sun-Hound is your creation and your slave; but there could be factions within the palace which might wish it otherwise. I . . ." He hesitated, then smiled at her, a little sadly. "I simply wish you to know that, if I can be of help to you in resisting such factions, I'm at your service."

There was silence for some time. Simorh was aware that Vaoran watched her carefully, alert for any reaction. He was a hard man to read: she thought she had the measure of him, but she could never be certain, and his apparent solicitousness made her doubly wary. At last, her voice utterly neutral, she said: "Thank you, Vaoran. I appreciate your kindness—and your honesty."

"Believe me, lady, I have only the best interests of Haven at heart."

"I know. And I shall think on what you've said." She looked up again and gave him a smile that he hadn't expected. "Thank you."

It was a signal to leave, and Vaoran had the wisdom to acknowledge it. He had achieved what he wanted; the

seeds were sown and as yet he could expect no more.
Time and changing circumstances would dictate what
occurred from now on. He only hoped that he had
succeeded in winning at least a small measure of
Simorh's trust and appreciation.

Simorh watched the curtain fall behind the swordsmaster, then listened to the sound of his heavy footfalls
as Falla led him down the stairs to the anteroom. She
thought she heard a murmur of voices from below,
though they were too faint to be recognizable: then more
footsteps sounded on the stairs and her eyes widened as
the curtain was pushed aside again and DiMag stood
facing her.

"DiMag—" She started up, as he came into the room,
his eyes intent on her, and took a chair a short distance
from the couch. "Well." He continued to look at her,
and she couldn't interpret the look. "I'm sorry to find
you in such straits."

"I'll be fit enough in a few days." She smiled
uncertainly, wondering whether she had imagined the
flicker of sympathy and concern in his eyes and hoping
that she hadn't.

"You shouldn't have done what you did. It wasn't
necessary—Kyre could have been brought back by other
means, without the need for you to endanger yourself."
He paused. "Do you still mean to go ahead, even after
the risks you've already run?"

"Yes."

"Knowing that what you plan might kill you?"

"Does that matter?" she fired back. "It seems to me
that I must take that chance, or sit and wait passively for
Haven to be destroyed! Death might lie at the end of
either road; but my way at least leaves no room for
shame."

DiMag drew breath in a sharp, angry hiss. "You failed nine years ago." The pitch of his voice dropped. "We both failed."

"Yes. But I succeeded this time. I brought Kyre to us."

He turned to face her. "Did you?"

"I don't know what you mean."

"You summoned a creature to this world, I'll not deny that. But what manner of creature? For I'll tell you this— he's no cipher, and you didn't create him."

Simorh stared at him, but didn't speak.

"One." DiMag counted the fingers on one hand as he spoke. "He doesn't look as he was meant to. Oh, don't think I'm not familiar with the ritual you used; I may not be a sorcerer, but I can read those rotting manuscripts and I'm acquainted with the old tongue! What was it: 'his hair and eyes shall be like to the earth that gives us life, brown as the bark and the sweet nut that grows on the tree.' And here is your Sun-Hound, red-haired and green-eyed; not what you bargained for at all. Two: he has a will of his own—again, not what was intended. Three: the fighting skills, which should be the pivot of his motivation, seem to be nonexistent; or at least, if he *can* fight, it's with no weapon familiar to us. Oh yes, Simorh; you summoned him. But *what is he*?"

Inwardly, Simorh was fighting down the small voice that told her—as it had tried to tell her since the night of the ritual—that DiMag was right. She couldn't allow that thought to gain a hold on her, for if she did, her hopes would crumble to nothing. She *must* believe in herself.

"Whatever Kyre is," she said, "it doesn't matter. I'll use him, DiMag, as I always meant to. And don't think you'll stop me. You won't."

The prince turned away, back to the window once

more, and she couldn't see his face. "Very well. We
understand each other, and I'll waste no more of your
time or mine." He swung round and his hazel eyes were
hot with suppressed anger. "You'd best build up your
strength for your creature, Simorh. I've no doubt that
you'll need it!"

For a moment they stared at each other, and the
barriers between them were a suffocating, palpable
presence. Then DiMag bowed formally and curtly, and,
without a further word exchanged, turned on his heel and
limped from the room. As the outer door closed—
quietly, and not with the slam she expected—Simorh
realized that she was biting her tongue so hard that she
could taste blood. She leaned back, closing her eyes and
forcing her jaw to relax, and wished that she had it in her
to cry.

Descending the tower stairs was a slow and difficult
process, but DiMag welcomed the distraction of the
effort, for it took the worst edge from the turmoil in his
mind.

He had gone to Simorh's rooms with the intention of
trying to bridge the chasm between them, at least enough
to make her understand his own doubts and fears.
Meeting Vaoran on the threshold of her chambers had
surprised him considerably and the glint of triumph in the
burly man's eyes had set his hackles up.

In times past DiMag had never doubted his wife's
loyalty, but now so much had changed that even that
foundation had cracked. The love they had once shared
was gone, wiped out in a single night of events that had
left him a cripple and almost destroyed her mind; for nine
years they had been espoused in nothing but name while
the gulf between them grew ever wider. And what use

was a maimed man, a warrior who could no longer fight,
a prince who could no longer properly rule, to a woman
like Simorh? DiMag had faced that question long ago,
and had made the decision to turn away from his consort
rather than live with the hypocrisy of maintaining a false
image. He had nothing to offer her; she wanted nothing
from him. And so perhaps it was natural that she should
have begun to look elsewhere.

But Vaoran, of all men? It made his own position
begin to look very precarious. Vaoran was shrewd,
intelligent, and ambitious, and being at the beck and call
of a crippled master wasn't to his liking. And Simorh
. . . whatever her loyalties in the past, she, too, looked
to the future. If Vaoran could convince her that her
consort no longer served Haven's interests, her old
allegiances might well be changed.

DiMag reached the foot of the stairs, where a wide
corridor led away toward his private rooms, and paused
to regain his breath, angered by the lameness that had
made the descent so arduous. If only he could be *sure*.
Half-founded suspicion was worse than certainty, for it
let the imagination run riot. He needed to delve, to
discover whether there was truth in the doubts that had
been sown in his mind—yet who could he trust to help
him? That, perhaps, was the greatest irony of all.

Slowly he moved along the corridor toward his
chambers. As he approached, the guards who stood on
permanent duty moved forward to open the door for their
master. DiMag didn't acknowledge their presence, but
walked past them into his sanctuary and, with a brief
exertion of angry energy, slammed the door at his back.

Swordsmaster Vaoran rarely entertained guests in his
modest apartment on the fringe of the palace's barracks.

His habits tended to be ascetic; he drank only in moderation and, as far as any of his men could tell, was uninterested in the women who would have made themselves readily available to a man of such high standing. But on returning to his rooms after his visit to Simorh, he found, as he had anticipated, a visitor awaiting him.

The caller rose as Vaoran entered. He was a plump man of advancing middle years, dressed in the red tunic and gold sash of a royal councillor, and he nodded with grave courtesy as the swordsmaster closed the door.

"Good morning, Councillor Vaoran. I fear I was a little early for our appointment: I trust you'll forgive my invasion of your privacy?"

"Not at all, Councillor Grai. I'm later than I'd planned: my apologies." He indicated for Grai to sit down again and crossed to a carved cupboard that dominated the sparsely furnished room. "Some refreshment?"

"Ah—thank you. Wine would be welcome." The plump man's gaze followed Vaoran as he poured drinks for them both, and he accepted the cup that was put into his hands.

"Thank you. Did you succeed in seeing the Princess Simorh?"

"I did, yes." Vaoran took a chair opposite his guest. "Though I'll admit the interview fell short of my expectations." He smiled, a private smile. "Or at least, my hopes."

Grai pursed his lips. "Her attitude, then, hasn't changed?"

"Not to any degree."

"I see." Grai sighed. "It makes me sad to see her so inflexible. I would have thought that by now she might

be coming round to the view that there can be little hope
for the prince's future. Lame as he is, embittered as he
is—Haven needs a much stronger man.''

Vaoran fingered his cup. "You know I agree with you,
Grai. But without the princess's support, our position is
still too tenuous for us to risk making our views more
public. They're shared by a good proportion of the
people—but the people also share our sympathy for the
princess's predicament, and any move that could be
construed as a threat to her would be a grave mistake.''

"That's true, so far as it goes. But the princess has no
political standing, not by comparison to—''

Vaoran interrupted him, an edge to his voice. "Political standing doesn't enter into it; she has power of
another sort, as we both know. But even that's not
relevant, Grai. It's vital—vital to *me*—that the Princess
Simorh should come to see the situation from our point
of view, and that she should not be coerced in any way.''

"Ah." Understanding showed in Grai's eyes: he had
forgotten Vaoran's personal considerations. "Of course.
But if she persists in her loyalty to the prince, who is,
after all, her husband—''

"In name only." Vaoran smiled again, a little bleakly.
"And that can't be an easy burden for her to bear. She
knows that under DiMag's rule Haven has little to hope
for, and she has the future of little Gamora to consider.''
He looked up, met Grai's eyes with a hot, hungry gaze.
"Simorh is loyal to the man she married, but she is more
loyal still to Haven and her child. A time will come when
she must decide between them. And when it does come,
I shall be on hand to help her in any way that I can.''

There was a long pause, then Grai nodded. "Time,''
he said reflectively. "More time.''

"Yes. Just a little more. For Haven's sake.''

* * *

"If anyone had told me I'd be taking on a new pupil at my time of life, I'd have called him a liar or a fool or both." Brigrandon smiled dryly and raised his mug in Kyre's general direction. "Bad luck to your enemies!"

Kyre returned ·'.e smile with an element of reserve and took a mouthful of ale. They were sitting in the clutter of the old scholar's private study, the table between them strewn with the remains of a substantial meal, and beyond the tall, narrow window darkness had finally fallen, bringing back the creeping fog.

Brigrandon had been drinking steadily for two hours or more—ever since Kyre's arrival, in fact—but though his speech was a little slurred and his movements beginning to lack coordination, the brain behind the physical mask was still active enough. As both set their mugs down again, Brigrandon slapped the heap of parchments that lay beside his empty plate.

"Well, my friend, there you are. The entire history of Haven, myth, legend, and fact, painstakingly sifted and translated and written into comprehensible form by my humble self!" He paused, then patted the pile more gently and let his hand rest on it. "The pinnacle of my life's achievement; a pretty story for the edification of little children." Ironic bitterness crept into his voice, showed in his faded eyes for a moment as he looked up; then the dry smile was back. "Don't worry; I don't expect you to read it. It's simply my credential; proof to you that I can answer your questions."

Kyre returned the smile. "I don't need proof, Master Brigrandon. And I'm grateful to you."

"Ach!" Brigrandon waved a hand dismissively, almost swatting the near-empty flagon that stood perilously close to his elbow. But despite his studied carelessness,

Kyre could see the old man was touched. "You haven't had your answers yet," Brigrandon added. "Wait and see if you still feel like thanking me by morning." A long pause, then: "Well, my good friend who thirsts after knowledge—I'm at your disposal. Where would you like to begin?"

On the brink, at last, of the revelation he craved Kyre felt a sudden reluctance, and found himself dissembling. "Are you sure I don't inconvenience you, Brigrandon? The hour's late."

The scholar shook his head. "These days I tend to spend my nights drinking rather than sleeping, so I might as well talk while I drink." He reached for the flask and poured himself a generous measure of ale, spilling a fair quantity over the table. "Yes; I know what you're thinking, and you're right: drunkenness and I are old acquaintances. But it doesn't impair my mind, more's the pity; so it needn't give you an excuse to put off the moment. If you back away from the questions now you'll only crave the answers another time, and that kind of torment isn't pleasant to endure. So." He took a long swallow from his cup. "Ask."

Kyre was tempted to follow Brigrandon's example. More drink would bolster his courage, and he needed courage to counteract the formless fear that lurked inside him. But he also needed a clear head, and that was the most vital thing of all. So he resisted the temptation, only fingering the stem of his own cup as he forced himself to formulate the one question that was at the nub of everything.

He said: "Prince DiMag tells me that Haven needs a champion, and he and the Princess Simorh intend that I should fulfill that role." As he spoke, the old anger was rekindled and it helped him to elucidate. "You tell me

that there was another Kyre, another Sun-Hound, long
ago, and that I've been made in his image and given his
name. I can only conjecture that I'm meant to do what he
might have done, were he alive now.''

Brigrandon pursed his lips. "A few inaccuracies, but
that is, in essence, true.''

"Then I want to know this. Who was the first Kyre?
What did he do? And why does Haven want me to
emulate him?''

There was silence for some while. The fish-oil lamp
that illuminated the room sputtered fitfully to itself, and
in the far distance Kyre thought, or perhaps only fancied,
that he could hear the uneasy moan of the sea. Then at
length Brigrandon spoke.

"Three questions, and I think they require only one
answer." He leaned forward and refilled his cup again,
this time with greater deliberation. "I'll have to admit
that our records are incomplete. The old language hasn't
been spoken for so many generations that it's all but lost,
and the fragmented version we *have* retained is probably
inaccurate. But, in essence, Kyre—the *original* Kyre—
ruled Haven many centuries ago. He was a warrior as
well as a prince, and under his rule the city's army was a
powerful force—a very far cry from the pitiful remnants
you see today. The sea demons must have feared Kyre
and his soldiers; and—''

"The sea dwellers?" Kyre interrupted him abruptly.
"You're saying that even then they were at war with
Haven?''

Brigrandon smiled sadly. "My friend, that is the oldest
of conflicts. We have only shards of knowledge from that
time, but everything points to an enmity as ancient as the
Hag herself. And it was the sea dwellers who, finally,
were Kyre's undoing. Have you heard of what is known
as Dead Night?''

"Yes. Prince DiMag spoke of it."

"Well, such a conjunction took place during Kyre's reign, and the sea demons planned to use the power it gave them in a single massive assault against Haven. There was a sorceress who lived among them then; we don't know her name, but she was a vampire, a devourer of souls—"

Vampire and soul-eater . . . Kyre recalled DiMag's description of the sorceress Calthar, who he said ruled in the sea dwellers' realm now. Surely, they couldn't be one and the same?

"She drew her power from the Hag, and she used that power to bring about Kyre's downfall during the Dead Night battle," Brigrandon went on. "They met face to face out on the strand, and though he was the finest warrior Haven has ever known, he couldn't prevail against the demon-inspired sorcery she used. She slew him."

Brigrandon paused for more ale, drinking slowly and then wiping his mouth with the back of his hand. "It's said that when Kyre died, at the very moment when the soul-eater's spear struck him down, the world stopped in its track and a great and terrible cry of protest echoed up from the very bowels of the earth." He smiled with dry self-deprecation. "Of course, that's an embellishment—I don't doubt that there were ancient historians as guilty of poetic license as I confess I've been at times. But no matter: whatever protest the world might have made, the Sun-Hound died."

Kyre's mouth was dry and there was a bitter taste on his tongue: he drank more ale. "And?" he prompted.

"And . . . ?" Brigrandon repeated.

"There must be more."

"Oh yes; there's more. The Sun-Hound had a consort.

Her name is lost, and we know nothing of her, save for one fact." The old scholar fingered his cup. "She was a witch, a sorceress. Not of the order of the monstrous creature who trapped and slew Kyre; but she had power. She didn't fight at Kyre's side, but she stood in the very same tower that the Princess Simorh occupies now, and tried to use her magic to save him. When she realized she had failed, she killed herself rather than live on without him. But before she died, she wove a spell, a talisman to protect Haven from the demons from the sea. And the spell formed part of her dying prophecy." He looked up and his eyes met Kyre's uneasily.

Kyre said: "Tell me, Brigrandon, what was her prophecy?"

The old man shrugged. "Do I need to tell you? She decreed that, should Haven ever be threatened with final annihilation by its enemies, one could be summoned to the world who was made in the image of her lost lord. And she left behind a rite by which that one—that cipher—could be imbued with the spirit of the first Sun-Hound, so that he might face the vampire-witch from the sea and defeat her."

For a long while there was silence. Brigrandon was staring into his cup, his face tight and uneasy. Kyre stared blankly ahead; in his mind's eye was a picture of DiMag in his gloomy sanctuary, then, superimposing that, the image of Simorh's taut and bitter face.

He said at last: "They want me to fulfill the prophecy and be a second Sun-Hound. They want me to face that same creature, that—that soul-eater—who killed the original Kyre—"

"Not the same creature," Brigrandon said. "She's long gone from this world. But her descendants live on."

"The same creature, or another—what's the difference? They want to pit me against her, in the hope that *I* can succeed where the greatest warrior in your history *failed*!'' He drew in a violent breath. ''They are *insane*!''

The scholar looked away, lifted his cup and drained it. ''You wanted the facts from me, my friend. Now you have them. I warned you that you might not like what you heard.''

Kyre took a cold grip on his rising fury. He had no justification for venting his anger on Brigrandon: the old man had done no more than answer the questions put to him. ''This prophecy,'' he said. ''It's in one of these manuscripts of yours?''

''As far as we can translate it, yes. It exists. Don't doubt that.''

Another long silence, while Kyre's eyes lost their focus again. At last he spoke. ''Go to bed, Brigrandon. I owe you a debt, but I can't repay it. I need time to be alone, to think.'' He frowned, seeming to drag himself back from another, unimaginable plane of thought and existence. ''I'd like to stay here, if you'll allow it: at least until the sun rises.''

''Of course.'' Brigrandon rose, lurched, and a sheaf of papers fell to the floor with a heavy thump. The lamp in the center of the table rocked alarmingly, throwing grotesque shadows across the wall, and the scholar began to move slowly toward a curtained recess, steadying himself by clutching at the furniture. He was drunk, and Kyre envied him.

Brigrandon reached the curtain and hacked it aside at the second attempt, revealing a narrow, unadorned bed in the recess beyond. He hesitated, swaying a little on his feet, then shook his head sadly. ''Stay as long as you will, if my snores don't disturb you. And if you need a sympathetic ear when tomorrow comes, I shall be here.'' His fingers tightened on the curtain fabric and he stepped into the recess. "I have one last thing to say to you, and it's something you may heed or ignore as you choose. The first Kyre was prince and ruler of Haven, and he was beloved of a sorceress. He was also free from those disabilities that cripple the man who rules Haven now. Bear that in mind, my friend, in all your dealings with Prince DiMag. Good night."

Kyre waited until the small sounds of Brigrandon readying himself for sleep had ceased, then reached out to the lamp and turned the wick up so that shadows shrank back from the table. The smell of fish-oil pervaded the room but he barely noticed: a peculiar and terrible sense of peace was settling on him. He knew: at last, he *knew*. And there was something awakening in him, a new courage and a new certainty that he would not accept the fate that Haven had planned for him. Whatever its perpetrators might name him, he was not Kyre. And that was a lesson they would soon begin to learn . . .

The tide had risen to the full, drawn back to the ebb, and now was rolling in again, following the slow, muffling march of the fog. It crept over the shingle bar, over the bay's smooth sand and the streets and houses petrified beneath, and as it quietly, rhythmically ate the land away, the Hag rose and rolled with it, first a gray, bloated specter on the horizon, then a shining eye that gazed down on the sea and shot the wavetops with silver. Crosscurrents and undertows moved among the stark black rocks and beat in the mindless rhythm of centuries against the crumbling cliff faces; out at the end of the submerged shingle bar the ruined temple rose from the swell, impassive, an old skeleton etched against green-gray dark.

Haven slept, while two green witchlights under a
sandstone arch burned defiantly against the night. One
lamp glowed in a window of the palace, casting its dim
radiance over the struggling white blooms in their
wasteland of a garden. A prince tore unknowingly at the
woven blanket which covered him, lost in the grip of an
all too familiar nightmare. In her tower Simorh also
dreamed, and tried to interpret her dreams even as she
slept. And the Princess Gamora, smiling with the illicit
pleasure of knowing that her nurse slumbered soundly in
the next room and would never, ever guess that her
young charge lay wakeful, played in the dark with the
shell she'd found on the beach, watching its shimmering
surface catch and reflect the refractions of moonlight that
shone through the fog, through the chink at her curtained
window. It seemed to speak to her, whispering stories of
strange and beautiful places, conjuring vivid pictures in
her mind, and she longed to answer the shell's call and
see the dream worlds it promised her, to slip away and
tell no one of her secret, not even Kyre. It would be such
an adventure.

And Calthar, a motionless and infinitely patient predator in the pitch-black of her sanctum, gazed into the
fathomless dark pool that told more than was natural, and
smiled as her lips formed silent, secret words. While not
far away in the labyrinth which Calthar ruled, Talliann
turned in an unnatural sleep, unconsciously fighting the
strictures that shrouded her mind, and whispered a name
that her waking mind didn't know. A name from long
ago, another age, another history. Something that had
been dead when the history she knew began.

Chapter 8

DAWN CAME, THE SUN SHOWING AS A DIM, PALE GHOST amid the fog that shrouded the city and muffled all sound and all movement. Kyre had fallen asleep at Brigrandon's table, and only stirred when the first diffused rays touched his face. In the recess the old scholar slept on: and as the strengthening daylight slowly dwarfed and dimmed the lamp at his side Kyre rose, stiffly and with an effort. A glance toward the curtain that separated Brigrandon's bedchamber, a moment's hesitation, then he strode to the door. His quarrel wasn't with Brigrandon. He was determined to face those who were responsible for his situation: when he did, his fury would know no bounds.

The early morning air was bitingly cold, with a clammy, bone-penetrating dampness permeating it, and by the time he had entered the main wing of the palace via the terraced walk—the only route he as yet knew—the damp

was clinging to his face and arms, and mingling with the
chill sweat of his anger. The hall was cold and desolate,
with no lights burning and no servants in sight: he
hesitated only a moment before striding toward the
stairs. At this hour DiMag was likely to be in his
chambers, and that was well and good. He wanted the
prince alone, without the encumbrance of his court.

As he climbed the stairs, taking them two at a time,
Kyre's hands were beginning to shake. He clenched and
unclenched his fists in an effort to stop the spasms, but
they continued to assail him, spreading through his arms
until he felt like a coiled spring ready to explode from
confinement at the smallest provocation.

The landing: still no one in sight. But as he turned the
corner he saw the one obstacle he had forgotten—the
constant guard set at DiMag's door. Two men, anonymous in their uniforms, staring fixedly at the opposite
wall, unmoving.

Kyre slowed. The sentries paid him no attention.
Then, at some unknown signal, one of them turned about
and opened the door beside him. Kyre heard a murmur of
voices; DiMag's, quick and sharp, another which he
knew but couldn't place; and then the bulky figure of
Swordsmaster Vaoran emerged, ducking his head to clear
the low lintel. The door slammed at his back and he
turned toward the stairs—then stopped.

"You—" He didn't dignify Kyre with a name, and
contempt underlay the irritation in his voice. "What are
you doing here?"

Kyre's fists clenched again, involuntarily this time, as
the anger latched quickly onto his dislike of the warrior.
"My business is no concern of yours."

Vaoran's eyes narrowed, and as the other man made to
brush past him he reached out and gripped Kyre's arm.

"You're not planning on seeing the prince, are you, my friend?"

His words were an open challenge. Kyre froze, and stared at him, glad to find that he was the taller by a few inches. Skilled swordsman Vaoran might be, but suddenly such considerations were irrelevant. Beyond them, he saw, the guards were surreptitiously but avidly watching.

"And if I am?" he retorted softly.

Vaoran smiled. "Prince DiMag has no time for you, creature. He isn't interested in you. I'll give you one warning, for the sake of your own continuing good health—"

He got no further before Kyre's fury erupted. He could no longer control it; his clenched right fist came up and slammed with all the force he could put behind it into Vaoran's face, while at the same moment he swung his left arm and followed with a bone-cracking blow that knocked him off his feet. The swordsmaster hit the floor like a boulder; even as he rolled over, and the two sentries started forward to help him or restrain his attacker or both, Kyre swung round. The guards couldn't coordinate themselves in time to prevent him from thrusting between them, and before they could stop him he had flung open the door to DiMag's rooms.

The prince froze, startled, as Kyre burst in. He had been in the act of putting on the crimson coat he wore during court business, and looked faintly ridiculous with one arm half in a sleeve. When he saw the look in his unexpected visitor's eyes, the muscles of his face tensed visibly.

"I want to talk to you," Kyre said savagely, *"Now."*

"My lord—" One of the sentries appeared at Kyre's back, sword drawn. "We couldn't stop him, he was—"

"Get out!" DiMag interrupted the man with such

ferocity that he jumped back, and Kyre helped him on his way by pushing the door shut, hard, at his back.

DiMag let his coat drop to the floor and limped slowly across to the bed. He fingered the tasseled rope that hung beside it and said levelly, "If I should pull this, my servants would be instantly summoned. Though whether they'd reach me before you had committed murder is a matter for conjecture." He turned to face Kyre again. "What do you want?"

Striking Vaoran had blunted the edge of Kyre's anger, but enough remained to fuel the fires inside him. He took a step forward, noted with some satisfaction how DiMag matched him with a pace back, and said, "Last night I talked with Brigrandon. He told me the legend of the first Kyre."

"Ah," said DiMag.

"And I learned the nature of the legacy which he and his consort left to this benighted city."

"Ah." DiMag had the good grace to look away.

"Haven wants a hero," Kyre said viciously. "That's what you told me, isn't it? A hero, to save its corrupt and decaying bones from final ruin!" He clenched his teeth, trying to get his breathing under control, then swung round. "You are a *liar*!"

He couldn't, in the grip of his anger, find the detachment to read the expression in DiMag's hazel eyes, but an observer might have seen the flicker of regret and sympathy that touched them briefly. Then the prince said evenly: "I didn't lie to you, Kyre. Perhaps I distorted the facts a little, or put my own interpretation on them. But I didn't lie."

"You're a master of rhetoric, my lord prince!" Kyre cried. "You knew the truth. You knew what the word *hero* meant in your terms! Not a fighter, not a savior—

just a human sacrifice to be cloaked in the trappings of a myth and sent to face impossible odds, to satisfy the doubtful premise of a prophecy which no one understands, and which probably doesn't even exist!"

Silence fell sharply in the wake of his accusation, and the two stared at each other until, abruptly, DiMag broke the deadlock by glancing aside.

"You're growing eloquent. Somehow, I hadn't expected that of you. No—" He raised a hand as Kyre seemed about to erupt again. "Don't take offense. I'm simply saying that it adds more weight to my conviction that there's more to you than any of us knows." A brittle smile. "Though you might accuse me of putting my own interpretation on that, as well as on everything else."

"Damn your interpretations!" Kyre retorted. "I've heard enough of your dissembling—I want the truth from you, and I won't be satisfied until I have it!"

"No. I don't suppose you will. Very well—I should at this moment be in the hall, but it seems court business must wait a while." He moved toward his couch. "Sit down, Sun-Hound, and stop being so stiff. Now: the truth."

"All of it."

"As you wish." DiMag lowered himself carefully onto the couch. Kyre made no move to sit but paced to the window; after a few moments DiMag steepled his fingers and stared at them. "You have, it seems, correctly anticipated the Princess Simorh's plans for you. And I won't deny that they're my plans too, though not from choice; but I'll come to that later. Yes, there is a prophecy, and yes, it is fragmented and we can't be sure that our interpretation of it is accurate. We lost any true understanding of our old language at about the time we lost our gods, whoever or whatever they were. But the prophecy exists, my friend. You are living proof of that, for the spell that summoned you to our world is an integral part of it. And the prophecy says that, when Haven is faced with final ruin, our enemies' sway can be broken only if one created in the Sun-Hound's image faces and defeats the sorceress from the sea."

"But I'm *not* the Sun-Hound!"

"Created in his image," DiMag repeated with emphasis. "Maybe my wife failed in fine physical detail, but in all other respects she fulfilled what was required. No; you're not the true Kyre. But you will *become* Kyre, and you'll face Calthar. It's the only hope Haven has." He stared at the wall. "And bitterly, bitterly regret that it has to be so."

The angry words that Kyre had been about to utter died on his tongue. He hadn't expected such an admission from DiMag, yet the prince's tone and his expression told him beyond doubt that he meant what he had said. And it set all his preconceptions suddenly adrift.

"Why?" he said.

The prince looked at him. "Why do I regret it?"

"Yes. It makes no sense."

"Oh, but it does," DiMag insisted. "I don't revel in the idea of human sacrifice. I faced Calthar once: it was her hand that gave me the wound that won't heal, and the fact that I'm still alive and not consigned to whatever torment she inflicts on her victims is her joke on me. I wouldn't willingly wish such a fate on any living creature: I'm not that much of a monster, whatever you might believe." His face hardened. "But neither am I such a fool as to plead high principles when we are threatened by a power which we can't combat by honorable means. If we must fight sorcery with sorcery, I'm not about to spurn a valuable weapon—especially when it's the only weapon we have left."

He got up and walked slowly to join Kyre at the window. "I didn't think Brigrandon would tell you so much, so early or in such a way. I'd hoped to introduce you to the idea a little more—shall we say—gently. And I don't mind confessing I'd nursed fond hopes that, given time, you would come to sympathize with our plight and could be persuaded to take on the Sun-Hound's mantle of your own free will. That was a mistake." He smiled bleakly, then turned to look directly at Kyre, his gaze steady and very frank. "I realize now that, had there ever been a chance of such an unlikely hope being fulfilled, we destroyed it by keeping the full truth from you."

Kyre stared back at him. "There could never have *been* such a chance. Haven means nothing to me; I have no loyalties here. How could you possibly think I would comply willingly?"

"Oh, I know; I couldn't reasonably expect it of any mortal man. A cipher, maybe; but not a mortal man. But you're not entirely devoid of pity or affection. You might have been persuaded to agree for the sake of the child who must one day rule in my place."

"Gamora . . . ?"

"Yes." DiMag gazed out into the mist. "She's touched you; even I can see that. And I'm not surprised; there's something in my daughter that the rest of us have lost. Innocence, gentleness, goodness, call it what you will; I haven't the right words. But I know you've grown fond of her, and I'd begun to hope that—"

"No." Kyre interrupted harshly. "You'll not appeal to me that way; not by using Gamora. You've told me what you want of me, but I'm not willing to make such a sacrifice. Not for Gamora, not for you, not for *anyone!* You have no right to demand it of me!"

"Right?" DiMag tensed, his eyes angry. "I have

every right—and indeed a *duty*—to use any means at my
disposal in the fight to save my city and the people who
dwell in it! Dead Night is almost on us, and we can't
stand against it as we are! What makes you think I owe
you any more than you owe me?"

Kyre's jaw clenched. "I won't do it, DiMag. And if
you think I will, may you be damned for it!"

"Your will doesn't enter into it!" DiMag snapped. "If
we have to force you, we'll force you. And you've
already experienced what Simorh can do. I doubt if
you'll stand for long against the torment she can inflict
on you, to secure your cooperation." He turned, limped
across the room like a caged animal. "Do you think I
want to do this? If you were the cipher that Simorh meant
to conjure with her sorcery, the question wouldn't arise.
The fact that you're not complicates matters, but in the
end it can make no difference!" He stopped, turned to
face Kyre, his face strained. "If there was another way,
I'd take it. My conscience doesn't rest easy with the
thought of sending a man who has done me no wrong to
almost certain death. But if there's a chance—*any*
chance—that you might be my sole means of defeating a
deadly enemy and giving my daughter a future, then I'll
gladly live with my conscience!"

Kyre said, his voice shaking: "I could kill you, Prince
DiMag. That, too, would solve your dilemma."

"You could try," DiMag sneered. "But I doubt if
you'd succeed; even lame as I am, I'm a far better
swordsman than you'll ever be. And besides, it would do
you no good. Destroy me, and you'd still have Simorh to
contend with. Can you cut down her silver whips with a
blade?"

Kyre sucked in his breath, remembering the experience and not wishing to relive it.

"Kill me, and you'll not have a friend in this world,"
DiMag added. "Leave Haven, and Simorh will bring
you back. Jump from the Sunrise Tower or drown
yourself in the sea, and death is the best you can hope
for." He looked up. "This way, at least you have a
chance. So why not take it?"

Kyre felt fury rising in him again, and it was made all
the stronger by the knowledge that DiMag was right.
Abruptly he turned away, and his voice was harsh as he
said, "We have nothing more to say to each other."

"Apparently not. But think on what I've said, Kyre. It
might bear further contemplation."

There was silence for a few moments, acute and
claustrophobic. Then Kyre strode to the door, and as
DiMag stared moodily out over the fogbound city he left
the room without a further word.

"Kyre! Kyre, wait for me!"

He stopped at the sound of the eager young voice, and
felt every muscle in his body tense as the renewed anger
threatened to get control of him. Gamora's feet pattered
in the corridor and then she was beside him, catching
hold of his hand and smiling happily up at him. She had
come from the direction of the Sunrise Tower, and he
surmised that she had been searching for him.

"Kyre, come and see what I found in the garden this
morning! There is a flower that—"

Kyre interrupted her. "Shouldn't you be at your
lessons?"

She was taken aback by his tone, but it only dimmed
her enthusiasm for a moment. "Master Brigrandon was
drunk last night and he's still sleeping it off, so he can't
teach me! Oh, Kyre, you *must* come—"

"Must?" The word was like salt in a raw wound and

he turned such a look on the little girl that she took a step
back, her gray eyes wide with hurt. DiMag had tried to
use Gamora as a weapon, play on Kyre's fondness for her
in order to blackmail him. It was a despicable act, a
coward's act, and the anger it engendered in him was
almost beyond Kyre's ability to control.

With an effort he calmed his thoughts, reminding
himself that Gamora couldn't be expected to comprehend
his mood and certainly didn't deserve to bear the brunt of
his ire. Then with a greater effort he forced his face
muscles to relax, shaking his head as though to clear it.
"I'm sorry, Princess. I'm a little . . . distracted."

"Then let me cheer you! We could walk on the beach,
or I could show you some more of the old passages
through the palace!"

She was pitifully eager to please him, but he couldn't
bear the thought of her company. It would be a goad, a
constant reminder of DiMag's attempted ploy. And
whatever debt his conscience owed the little girl, no
power in the world would ever make him do what the
prince wanted of him. Not even for Gamora's sake.

"I'm sorry," he said again, more sharply. "I'm a busy,
Gamora—I have things to do."

"Can't they wait?" Gamora pleaded.

Kyre felt as though he were trapped between fire and
ice, and he wanted only to escape from the pressure she
was putting on him. His eyes hardened, and he disen-
tangled his fingers from hers with an abrupt movement.
"No. They can't wait."

Tears filled Gamora's eyes, but she made no further
attempt to appease him, only watched with uncomprehending misery as he walked away from her toward
the stairs.

*   *   *

Kyre only stopped when he reached the terrace that ran
along the palace's seaward side. The fog had if anything
grown even thicker, so that it was barely possible to see
three paces ahead; but the silence in which it cloaked the
world, and the emptiness of the terrace, offered desperately needed solitude.

He sat on the balustrade, staring into the fog's blank
wall and trying to ignore the rank, vegetable smell of the
decaying garden below him. He hadn't meant to hurt
Gamora, but her innocent face and bright chatter were
more than he could bear now; he needed to be utterly
alone, while the rage in him burned itself out.

He'd gone to challenge DiMag, had found his worst
fears confirmed, and at the last had had nothing with
which to fight back. The prince was right: no matter
which way Kyre turned, all roads led to the same
inevitable end. If he believed for a moment that he could
call on reason and justice to sway DiMag, he was as
wrong as it was possible to be; and he had no power to
prevent Haven's rulers from using him in any way they
chose.

What was it DiMag had said? *If there was another
way, I'd take it*. Surely, Kyre argued with himself, *surely*
this ancient, obscure, and barely understood prophecy
wasn't Haven's only hope? So much of the city's history
had been lost, or twisted in translation from a dead
language: Brigrandon, whose knowledge couldn't be
faulted whatever his weaknesses, had freely admitted as
much. And if the prophecy was wrong, or misunder-
stood, then somewhere in the moldering records there
must be another answer. Haven's rulers wanted him to
fight an enemy he had no chance of defeating, and on
that futile thread hung all their hopes. So great was their
desperation that they were willing to sacrifice him in a

cause that could avail them nothing. But Kyre was
determined that he shouldn't be forced to die for Haven
without fighting that destiny to his last breath. And he
believed—perhaps foolishly, but it was all he had to cling
to—that if an alternative could be found, DiMag would
be true to his word.

But how and where to search? He raised his head,
drawing the clammy air deep into his lungs, and faced
the realization that he didn't know where in all of Haven
to begin. And yet a thought was invading the darker
recesses of his mind; something that had no logic yet
which refused to let him alone. Instinct; intuition. He had
no reason to trust it, but it had sown the seeds of a
conviction that the answer lay not in the walls of Haven,
but in the conundrum of his own lost identity.

It didn't make any sense. Kyre shook his head and rose
from the balustrade. His hair and clothes were damp
from the cloying fog, and he was cold; but the cold went
deeper than mere physical chill. He didn't know how or
when Simorh meant to perform whatever moldering
ceremony it was which would theoretically place the
Sun-Hound's mantle on his shoulders; but he believed
that she would delay no longer than she had to, and then
nothing he did or said could save him. He might have
less time than he realized.

He needed to think. Gamora wouldn't be likely to seek
him out again today—when he could, he promised
himself, he'd make amends to her for his unkindness—
and so the Sunrise Tower seemed as good a sanctuary as
any other, and more palatable than this eerily forsaken
place. What his efforts could avail him, Kyre didn't
know. But he must at least try.

He turned, and walked slowly back into the palace.

* * *

DiMag was tired. These days he didn't seem to have the stamina he had once possessed, and the earlier clash with Kyre had taken more of a toll than he'd anticipated, so when it became clear that the court business would drag on well into the evening he felt depression settling on him like an unpleasantly heavy cloak. He hadn't eaten all day and his stomach felt hollow, yet the idea of food made him queasy. All he wanted was to sleep without dreaming.

Earlier in the day, a vigilant servant had discovered the presence of a virulently poisonous herb known colloquially as Forktongue in the palace kitchens. It was obvious that the deadly leaves had been intended for DiMag's own table, and, once alerted, the court had gone through the ritual of setting an investigation in train. For the sake of protocol the prince's advisers had felt obliged to formally express their shock that anyone in the palace could have planned such a crime, and be seen to pursue the conspirators diligently. They had failed to trace the culprit, but DiMag had no illusions: he knew that his councillors would have been better pleased had the matter never come to public notice. Had the herb been discovered and removed without fuss or recrimination, the entire incident could have been set aside and conveniently ignored. And there were some who might have preferred that the discovery had never been made at all.

He pulled himself upright in his chair. The councillors were debating the nature of repairs needed to a ceiling in the palace's west wing, and DiMag forced himself to crush a black desire to stand up, damn them all for bleating sheep if they had nothing better to occupy their minds, and walk out. His head hurt, his leg ached more fiercely than it had done for some time—but if he was to continue to rule Haven unchallenged, he must be *seen* to rule Haven, however trivial the business at hand.

Two of the councillors were beginning to argue. Their rising voices shook the prince out of his stupor, and he was about to call them to order when a new disturbance, beyond the door at his back, made him pause. Women shouting, or sobbing; he couldn't tell which . . . His advisers also heard it, and fell silent, frowning in surprise.

"My lord—?" one began.

DiMag made a quick negative gesture, then signaled to one of the guards at his back. "See what's afoot."

The man moved to obey, but before he could reach the curtained door it burst open and Simorh flew into the room.

"What is it?" Alarm colored DiMag's voice as he looked at his wife. She was in her night clothes, barefoot, and her face was white, haggard, and blotched with tears. "What are you doing here? You should be abed—"

In a great, sobbing breath, Simorh cried, "DiMag, Gamora has gone!"

"Gone . . . ?" He didn't comprehend; his mind was too fuddled with tiredness to think clearly. "What do you mean?"

"She's not in the palace! She's run away, and I—I can't touch her! I scried, I used all the power I could muster, and she wasn't there, I couldn't touch her mind. She's *gone*, DiMag—there's no trace of her anywhere in Haven!"

Chapter 9

"SHE THOUGHT GAMORA WAS WITH ME." SIMORH DARTED a look of bitter venom at the nurse, who stood wringing her hands in mute anguish. "It was only when it began to grow late that she thought to *look*, to *see*—"

DiMag's grip tightened on her shoulders as her voice rose toward a hysterical pitch, and she subsided against him, though she was still shivering violently. Even through his own fear and distress a part of his mind was disturbed by the strangeness of the familiar yet all but forgotten sensation of holding her. His wife, known but long estranged, yet instinctively turning to him in a time of great need . . . it stirred a complex tangle of emotions which he couldn't begin to interpret.

He said, thrusting the thoughts away and praying inwardly that he sounded more certain than he felt, "We'll find her. She can't have been gone long, or go far."

"But *why* did she go?" Simorh cried. "She had no *reason*!"

DiMag knew what she was thinking, and he shared her unspoken terror. There were people in the palace whose interests might be well served by Gamora's disappearance. As a hostage she would provide the one certain means of ensuring his own acquiescence to whatever her captors wanted of him. Abdication, his life in exchange for hers—there was nothing he wouldn't agree to for his daughter's sake, and the fact was well known.

But he dared not dwell on such a possibility, or allow Simorh to dwell on it either. The search had already begun, directed by Vaoran, who, whatever DiMag's differences with him, could be relied on in a crisis. If Gamora was still in the palace she would soon be found; if not . . .

He'd already heard the bare bones of the story, such as they were. Gamora's nurse had missed her shortly after darkness fell; finding that Brigrandon hadn't seen the little girl all day, she sent a servant to see if Gamora had visited Kyre, and when this, too, produced no sign of the child the nurse assumed that Gamora must be with her mother. She didn't like to disturb the princess—who frightened her more than she cared to admit—and so it was only when Gamora's bedtime had long passed that she began to worry. She had plucked up enough courage to approach Simorh at last, and it was then that the truth began to dawn.

Simorh couldn't begin to explain the sense of dread that crept through her when she realized that Gamora was nowhere to be found. There was no logic in the feeling; chances were that the child had gone off on some secret errand of her own devising and would return soon enough to face a scolding. Yet the sensation persisted, and when Gamora's favorite haunts were searched without result, Simorh knew with an unassailable instinct that something was desperately wrong.

Thean and Falla had pleaded with her not to overtax herself, but she wouldn't hear them. Using her scrying glass, she had fought back her weakness in a frantic attempt to touch her daughter's mind, and had found nothing. She knew her own skills well enough to reach two possible conclusions. Either Gamora had gone somewhere far beyond Haven, where her mother's magic couldn't reach, or she was dead. And so, hurling the glass aside in a frenzy of grief and terror, the sorceress had fled from her tower and run to the court hall where DiMag and the council were in session.

DiMag told himself over and over again that Simorh must be wrong when she claimed that Gamora wasn't in the palace or even in the city. She was ill, her abilities at a low ebb; it must be that she was simply too weak to touch the child. Over and again he tried to convince her, too, though he couldn't tell if he had succeeded. And in the meantime, they could do nothing but wait.

He looked up suddenly as the doors at the far end of the hall banged open, and saw Kyre coming toward him. A sharp spear of suspicion flared in DiMag as he recalled the acrimony with which they had parted; but as the other man approached and the prince saw his expression better, the suspicion abated.

Kyre stopped in front of the dais, looking quickly from DiMag to Simorh and back to DiMag. "She isn't found?"

"No. But she can't have gone far."

"What can I do?"

"As much as any man can do." DiMag smiled with no humor. "Though of course, you have no obligation."

Kyre colored. "In this, I have." He was thinking of the unhappy encounter with Gamora that morning, of the misery on the little girl's face as he walked away from

her. Could she have been so upset by his treatment that
she had run away? It was unlikely in the extreme, but it
couldn't be ruled out. Gamora was impulsive, her
emotions easily moved: if the hurt had gone deep, who
could predict how she might react?

He said: "Where are you searching?"

"At the moment, in the palace." DiMag frowned.
"Though if you have any thought, any clue that might
lead elsewhere, for the sake of all that's holy don't hold it
back!"

Simorh's head came up sharply. "Why should he know
anything?" she demanded venomously. "What does *he*
have to do with it?"

"Hush." DiMag touched her hair, trying, though
awkwardly, to soothe her. "Gamora looks on Kyre as her
friend. She might have said something to him that will
help us." And as she bowed her head again he looked
over her shoulder at Kyre. "Did she? Did Gamora say
anything to you?"

Kyre shook his head helplessly. There was nothing—
except, ridiculously, the image of Gamora on the beach,
holding up a shell she had found and turning it so that the
sunlight glinted on its rainbow surface.

"No," he said. "Nothing."

Simorh looked up again. In her thin, strained face her
eyes were dark and featureless hollows that reminded
Kyre shockingly of the deathly pale girl on the strand.
"Find her," she said, and her voice was as empty as her
eyes. "I don't care what you have to do; what any of us
has to do. Just *find* her!"

Gamora's talent for avoiding people she didn't want to
see was as finely developed as her talent for finding those
she did; and, still smarting from the sting of Kyre's

inexplicable rebuff, she had made her way back to the gardens that morning by a tortuous route that avoided the gazes of all but a few unimportant servants. There she hid herself among a tangle of limp and fading bushes, careless of the damp underfoot and of the leaves' unpleasantly slimy caress, and while the short day wore on she idled her time away, scooping the thin soil aimlessly into little heeps, shredding foliage with her fingers, sometimes singing tuneless dirges to herself in an effort to pass the hours without thinking about her own disappointments. But that was impossible. Her father was busy, her mother ill—they wouldn't tell her what the illness was, but Gamora knew well enough— and her tutor would give her no lessons today. Her nurse did nothing but fuss and scold, and now her friend, her only real friend, had been unkind to her and she didn't know why. Several times the sense of injustice brought tears to Gamora's eyes, but she bit them back stoically, reminding herself aloud that she was a princess and future ruler of Haven, and future rulers didn't cry.

She cradled her shell, which she'd taken to carrying everywhere with her. When she was older, it would be different. When she was older, people wouldn't simply smile and ruffle her hair when she gave an order; they would obey, the way they obeyed her father. She didn't want to rule, but if she must then she would make the most of it. And when she was older, she would marry Kyre. *Then* he wouldn't speak sharply or turn away from her, because if he was unhappy she would know how to cheer him.

She looked up, and realized that the light was fading. The fog hadn't lifted all day, and now as the invisible sun dipped toward the sea it seemed to be closing in, like the dark, formless cloak that sometimes haunted her in bad

dreams, rising up from the floor around her bed to slowly
engulf and suffocate her. Gamora shivered. She could
hear moisture seeping in the ground beneath her and it
sounded like the fog breathing, *in—out, in—out*, a
waiting, predatory animal. She scrambled to her feet,
shuddering as the tendrils of the undergrowth seemed to
snatch at her ankles, and ran for the comparative safety
of the overgrown path. She kept running until the terrace
wall loomed out of the darkening mist ahead, and only
stopped for breath when she reached the safety of the
steps.

Gamora didn't want to go back into the palace. The
gathering dark unnerved her, but at this moment it
seemed a better prospect than the scolding she was sure
to receive from her nurse if she returned to her room. She
felt alone, unloved, unwanted. Very well then; she'd go
away. And if her disappearance gave them all a fright, so
much the better; it might shake them into paying more
attention to her in the future.

She turned the shell over and over, marveling at the
way the rising moonlight reflected every color imagin-
able in the mother-of-pearl. Then she held it to her ear, to
see if she could hear the sea. But instead of the sea the
shell seemed to be whispering her own name.

Gamora . . . Gamora . . .

Gamora smiled, hesitantly at first then with growing
eagerness as she realized her imagination wasn't playing
tricks on her.

*Gamora . . . Come and see, Gamora. Come and
see.*

Images crowded into the little girl's mind, of night and
the sea and the world transformed by the pale shimmer of
moonlight into something magical and wonderful. Such
places! Such beautiful, unknown lands . . .

Come and see, Gamora. Come to me, and I will show
you wonders beyond imagining. Come to me, and all
these wonders will be yours . . .

The shell seemed to take fire with an inner light of its
own; sparkling like pearl and diamond and emerald and
sapphire all at once.

Come and see. It isn't so very far. Come and see . . .

She wanted to see with her own eyes, instead of
merely in her imagination, the beautiful things that the
shell-voice had promised her. And they were out there,
in the night, only waiting for her to come.

She left the grounds by a back way, rarely used, that
took her around the palace's outer wall and down into
Haven. The fog muffled her footsteps and distorted
shapes and shadows in the empty streets; it created an
eerie illusion of being deep under water, and more than
once Gamora started, heart pounding painfully, at imagined horrors looming out of the dark. Under other
circumstances she might have turned tail and bolted for
home, but the shell in her hands gave her confidence, and
in her mind she seemed still to hear it whispering
encouragement to her.

She reached the archway at last, and stopped between
the alcoves with their dimly glowing lamps. Ahead lay
the bay, vast and empty, no longer the familiar play-
ground of bright days but something unknown and
fraught with danger. Yet even as Gamora's courage
faltered, the shell seemed to speak to her again,
whispering her name, calling her, urging her to be brave
enough to leave the town's dull lights behind and move
on into the dark. She stepped through the arch, felt the
hardness of paving under her feet change to the yielding,
shifting texture of sand. Grains trickled into her shoes;
she kicked them off, and started barefoot across the huge
expanse of the beach.

Fog enfolded her in soft shrouds. Somewhere high
above, she knew, the Hag sailed the sky and gazed down
at her, but the old moon's scarred face was lost in the
dense whiteness. Even the sea was no more than a
distant, muted susurrating without form or direction; but
though she could see no more than a few inches before
her, Gamora padded swiftly and unerringly across the
sand. Now that the shell had assuaged her fears she felt
exhilarated; the challenge of being alone in the night
thrilled her, and she believed fervently that the promised
something to which the shell was leading her would be
worth any risk and any peril.

The sound of the sea grew louder, closer. A capricious
gust of wind pounced from the west and ruffled the fog,
momentarily pushing its veils aside so that Gamora had a
brief glimpse of sullen, dark waves, crowned with
yellowish scum, a bare twenty yards away. The tide was
very low and must be about to turn: she ignored the
sudden *frisson* of unease that assailed her, and hurried
on.

Moments later, the sand turned to shingle beneath her
bare feet. Gamora stopped, realizing that she must have
reached the long bar that stretched out into the bay's
southwesterly arm and knowing that there was nothing
now between her and the ancient, ruined temple.

Surely, the shell didn't mean for her to go *there*? She
couldn't—fear of the place was inbred in her, as in all the
people of Haven, and even her insatiable curiosity had
never been enough to overcome it. But as she hesitated,
not knowing whether to wait, turn aside, or flee back to
the town, a voice, lilting and gentle and so sweet that it
made her ache inside, called out to her.

"Gamora . . ."

It wasn't the shell this time. The voice was different—

and it had come from a way off, somewhere out on the shingle bar. The little girl bit her lip . . .

"*Gamora . . .*"

She wanted, so desperately wanted, to answer. The sweetness of the voice hinted at love and kindness and beauty, assuaging her loneliness and reaching to the depths of her soul. Yet she dared not answer. The shingle strand was too grim a barrier.

"*Gamora—come to me, Gamora. Don't be afraid . . .*"

The breeze rose again, from the north this time, shredding the mist so that it rolled aside—and Gamora saw an unearthly figure waiting for her on the bar.

Vast eyes, as black as the night-shrouded sea, gazed at the child from a deathly white face about which the wind flung tatters of raven hair. Dressed in a dark, sleeveless robe, the woman looked so fragile that her bones might have been spun from strands of glass, her flesh insubstantial as sea foam. A faint, silver nimbus surrounded her, tiny motes sparkling and dancing, as though she had come down from the moon and brought a trapped piece of its light with her; and love, longing, and an inexplicable pity welled up in Gamora as, transfixed, she returned the unwavering gaze.

The woman inclined her head with a slow and almost childlike movement, as though to regard Gamora from another angle. Then she smiled—Gamora saw only a darkness where her mouth must be—and, raising one long, frail arm, beckoned with a fluid motion.

Gamora felt her feet starting forward involuntarily. For an instant she tried to fight the impulse, but the momentary doubt was eclipsed by a renewed surge of emotion. This was what the voice in the shell wanted; this strange, fey creature, whoever she might be, was the

one who would lead her to promised wonders. And she
trusted the voice. It was her friend.

As the little girl broke into a run, the woman laughed,
bright, shimmering laughter that the fog couldn't quell
and that made Gamora want to laugh with her. Then she
turned, her robe rippling suddenly with dark hints of blue
and green amid the black, and skipped away along the
shingle bar. Dropping her precious shell—somehow it no
longer seemed important to her—Gamora picked up her
skirt and broke into a stumbling run, her voice cutting
through the murky night like the cry of a small, lost bird.

"Wait! Oh, wait for me!"

The figure ahead of her stopped, jerkily like a
marionette, and spun back to face Gamora. Her laughter
pealed out again and she held out both her arms, feet
dancing restlessly in the shingle, unable to stay still.

"I'm coming!" Gamora cried. "Wait for me!"

Their progress along the shingle bank was a bizarre
game of catch-if-you-can. Just as Gamora thought she
would reach the strange woman and touch her she
skipped away again, dancing across the slippery stones,
so light that the little girl believed she might at any
moment take to the air and fly away into the fog.

She couldn't tell how long the weird game went on;
time was meaningless, and only her elusive quarry
mattered. But suddenly there were walls looming out of
the fog; huge, crumbling ramparts gashed by the decayed
eyes of what had once been windows; shattered columns
towering among them, great, fallen stones impeding the
way. Gamora stumbled to a halt, catching her breath on
an involuntary, indrawn gasp of shock as she realized that
the shingle bar had ended and she stood among the ruins
of the shunned temple.

Not fifteen paces away the strange, shimmering

woman had also stopped, and waited between two
monstrous piles of broken masonry, gazing back at
Gamora. This time, Gamora knew, her elusive friend
would not run away; there was nowhere left to run.

"Gamora." The woman smiled, and the dark hollows
of her eyes were suddenly lit with an inner fire that drew
an answering smile in the child. Gamora didn't hesitate,
but ran across the uneven ground, arms held out in
greeting. Their hands linked, and the little girl felt
fingers that were slender, frail, yet strong and warm curl
round her own. A sensation that she had rarely felt in her
short life flooded through her; the knowledge that she
was wanted and welcomed, that she, and no one else,
mattered.

The woman laughed again. Now that they were at
close quarters, Gamora was surprised to see how young
the stranger was. There was something otherworldly in
her look: her face was small, sharp, and narrow, her lips
thin if gracefully curved, her eyes, like her hair, utterly
black. Without the seashell's enchantment to cloud her
mind Gamora would have feared her, but the spell had
too great a hold on her, and she felt nothing but the
adoring eagerness that had led her to this moment.

"Pretty. So pretty." The woman's voice was melliflu-
ous and dreamy, and Gamora's captivation deepened.
Hesitantly, not sure if she dared speak lest she broke
some unwritten rule, the little girl said: *"You* are pretty.
What's your name? Tell me, please!"

"I am Talliann." The dancing silver motes in the
nimbus around her spun faster, shimmering.

Gamora's fingers tightened on the thin hands she held.
"Will you be my friend, Talliann? I want so much to talk
to you, and the shell said there were things you'd show
me."

Talliann inclined her head as though considering the
child's plea, and her eyes took on a faraway look. "There
are so many things I can show you," she said at last, still
dreamily. "So many . . . and so much I want to know
of the place where you come from."

"I can tell you!" Gamora cried eagerly. "We *can* be
friends—please say we can!"

"Yes." Talliann raised her head slowly. She seemed to
be gazing at something high on the ruined wall, though
when Gamora followed her direction there was nothing
to be seen but the ancient stones and the grotesque
silhouettes of carved figures, gargoyles mutilated by age
and the elements. Perhaps, she thought, Talliann was
trying to see through the fog to the moon—and then the
breath caught violently and painfully in her throat as one
of the broken gargoyles moved.

Fear broke through the enchantment, and Gamora
made an ugly, inarticulate sound, stumbling back, eyes
wide and staring in horrified disbelief. She tried to let go
of Talliann's hands, but Talliann's grip abruptly tightened
and she couldn't free herself. High overhead, distorted
by the fog, an indistinct shape was detaching itself from
the crumbling wall, moving unevenly yet with an
appalling, reptilian grace, like something fast and lithe
awakening after a long sleep. And as it moved, climbing
down toward a window embrasure, Talliann watched its
progress with empty eyes.

"No!" Gamora found her voice at last, and pulled
with all her strength to free herself from Talliann's grasp.
"No, let me go! Stop it, Talliann, *please!*"

The grip on her fingers tightened still further, belying
Talliann's gossamer-frail appearance, and despite the
panic exploding within her Gamora couldn't help but
look again at the wall and the thing that moved on it. It

had reached the embrasure now and crouched there, a
nightmare making ready to pounce. A cascade of tangled
hair flowed over its hunched shoulders, and though its
features weren't discernible, the glitter of its eyes was
visible under the wild mane of hair. Then a voice, husky,
triumphantly malignant, floated down through the fog to
where Talliann and Gamora stood rigid.

"Good, Talliann. Very, very good."

Gamora screamed and twisted violently in an effort to
free herself, but Talliann's grip slid to her wrists. She
jerked once, hard, and Gamora was pulled off balance,
staggering across the rough ground and colliding with
her. With her arms securely pinned, the child could do
nothing but watch in frozen trepidation as the creature on
the wall—human, animal, demon, she didn't know and
was too terrified to guess—contorted its limbs to a
seemingly impossible angle and, like a monstrous spider,
began to descend, climbing lithely among the smashed
stonework. As it neared the ground deep shadow
swallowed it, but still Gamora could hear its movements
above the harsh sound of her own gasping breath. Then it
was down—she heard the slither of feet on shingle, and a
rustling sound—and something detached itself from the
shadow-pool at the wall's base. It crawled, flowed,
across the broken ground, then its shape changed and it
rose upright, solidifying and resolving into human shape.
Its crown of tangled hair shivered like an animal's mane,
and around the long, powerful limbs the tattered shreds
of ancient garments fluttered and coiled. Gamora tried to
shrink back as it advanced, but Talliann blocked her path;
the child felt hot tears sting her cheeks as terror and an
awful sense of betrayal fought for precedence in her
reeling mind. The figure drew closer, then a hand, the
fingers bony and tipped with long, ragged nails, shot out

and took hold of her jaw in a pincer grip. Gamora shut
her eyes tightly, but couldn't open her mouth to scream or
plead or be sick, though she wanted to do all three at
once. A powerful smell of brine assaulted her nostrils,
mingled with the reek of decaying seaweed, and she
uttered a small, helpless, wordless sound.

"Look at me, Gamora." Close to, the husky voice had
an undercurrent of terrible cruelty. "Open your eyes, and
look at me."

Gamora tried to fight the compulsion to obey, but it
was impossible; her eyelids were forcing themselves
apart against her will. The fog and the walls of the ruin
swam before her, then her vision focused and she looked
into Calthar's face.

The green eyes, chillingly, unhumanly, and calculat-
ingly malevolent, sapped the last shreds of Gamora's
will. The child's limbs stiffened and she could only stand
rigid and helpless as the sorceress tilted her head at a
painful angle to see her the better, her fingers making
small, stroking motions across Gamora's chin in an
obscene parody of affection. Then she smiled, and in the
darkness the effect was savage.

"Good . . ." she said again. "We have what we
came for." She glanced at Talliann, the old resentful
malice stirring behind her eyes. "Release her, Talliann.
Your part is done."

Talliann's grasp relaxed a little but she didn't let go.
When she spoke she was incoherent, as though Calthar's
presence had disturbed her composure and clouded her
thoughts. "I don't want . . ." she said. "I don't
want . . . you to harm my friend."

"Why should I harm her?" Contempt gave a rasping
edge to Calthar's voice. "She's valuable to me—and you
know full well why; just as you know that this whole

affair is at your behest!" She gave Gamora a venomous little shake. "Don't try to argue with me now. Let go of the child!"

Slowly the defiance faded from Talliann's eyes, leaving her face expressionless, and her hands fell away limply to her sides. She stepped aside with a shuffling, crablike motion, and Calthar turned her head to stare up into the fog. The tide had turned and the first sliding incursion was inching its way across the shingle bank; somewhere below her feet the sorceress could hear water moving into the temple's underground chambers. Dawn was still far off, but the Hag would set soon; she sensed the old moon's lights waning, and with it her own power. The return journey should be delayed no longer.

She turned once more to Gamora. The child still stood frozen, all movement arrested. Only her eyes held any animation, and the stark terror in them irritated Calthar intensely. Still gripping Gamora's chin, she raised her left hand and drew a symbol in the air before the little girl's face. Gamora's eyes closed instantly, and as she slumped, Calthar caught her and swept her up in her arms. Then she looked at Talliann.

"Go," she commanded.

Talliann frowned faintly. Her lips parted and she half raised one arm before letting it drop again. "I . . . don't want . . ."

Calthar's mouth hardened into a vicious line. "Go," she said again, softly, in a tone Talliann knew well.

All intelligence left the fey girl's eyes. She bowed her head, black hair whipping across her face as a capricious gust of wind caught it. Then she turned and began to move with her odd, shambling gait to where the sea waited.

Chapter 10

THEY GATHERED AT FIRST LIGHT IN THE WALLED COURT-
yard behind the palace; some two hundred hard-eyed
soldiers together with courtiers, councillors, and as many
palace servants as could be spared from essential duties.
A soft, dreary rain had just begun to fall. darkening
stonework, soaking clothing, and dripping from hair and
cloak hems.

DiMag waited until the entire company was assembled, then emerged onto the palace steps to address
them. The prince looked haggard and ill; from his
vantage point just inside the doorway Kyre saw him
falter twice as he stepped outside, and feared for his
ability to get through the necessary formalities. But
nothing would induce DiMag to stop now, however
exhausted he might be. A night's intensive and organized
searching had proved that Gamora was not in the palace
precincts, and DiMag sensed in his bones that, whatever
had befallen her, time was of the essence if she was to be
found.

The assembly fell silent as he appeared. His gaze swept over the sea of upturned, uneasy faces for a few moments, then he cleared his throat.

"My friends of Haven." The prince's voice mirrored his bleak weariness. "As you all know by now, my daughter, the Princess Gamora, is missing. She disappeared last night and despite extensive searches we can find no trace of her. We have established beyond doubt that she is not in the palace, and therefore the search must be intensified and extended to the city and all surrounding areas." He hesitated. "I don't need to tell you that her well-being is of paramount importance to me and to my wife. Nothing else matters beside her safe return, and I ask you, *urge* you, to stint nothing in the search for her. She must be found, whatever the cost." Another pause, and DiMag seemed to be struggling to get himself under control. "If she is found—*when* she is found, and brought safely back—then whoever finds her will earn the highest measure of reward that I can bestow.

"I can say no more to you at this stage. You have all been assigned to search parties; your leaders should now report to Swordsmaster Vaoran, who has designated areas of the city and its surrounds for each party to comb. And if any one of you can provide a clue to my daughter's possible whereabouts—any recollection, any hearsay, *anything* at all—then I urge you to bring the information to me in the court hall immediately.

"That is all. Search diligently and thoroughly—and thank you."

DiMag turned and walked back into the palace. At his back a murmur of voices was rising, and the search-party leaders were already pushing their way through the crowd and climbing the steps to find Vaoran. The prince moved away into an antechamber, accompanied by several of his more senior advisers, and Kyre hesitated, unsure of what he should do. Across the room, on the far side of the window, men were congregating around the burly figure of the swordsmaster, and for a moment, as Vaoran glanced up, Kyre caught his eye. The look he received mingled open hostility with contempt and an unpleasant edge of triumph: Kyre felt his hackles rise, and looked quickly away. But he could still sense the cold blue eyes staring at him, and after a few moments he turned his back with a deliberate movement and walked quickly away into the side chamber.

DiMag saw Kyre enter the room, and left the knot of anxiously conferring councillors to intercept him. Kyre took in the appalling strain on the prince's face and made a quick, formal bow. "How can I be of use?"

With the shadow of their last encounter still hanging over them, DiMag hadn't expected him to maintain such an openhanded response. For a moment his mask slipped and a flurry of emotions showed on his face; then he had himself under control again.

"I want you to go with Vaoran." He gripped Kyre's upper arm and steered him out of the councillors' earshot. "I know it's not an assignment you'll relish, but I have good reason." He looked up shrewdly at the taller man. "Take his orders, Kyre, and do what he tells you. But if the orders he gives seem to detract in any way from the urgency of finding Gamora, I want you to report to me immediately. Do I make myself clear?"

"You're not suggesting that Vaoran—"

"No, I'm not. I don't believe for a moment that Vaoran would harm my daughter. But no more do I believe that he'd be above using her, if he could, to secure my cooperation in his own schemes." DiMag paused, and studied Kyre's face suspiciously. "I'm

gambling on my instincts by being this frank with you,
Sun-Hound, and despite our differences I think those
instincts are sound. But if you fail me, or if you betray
my trust, you'll suffer for it."

Kyre's eyes narrowed. "I won't see Princess Gamora
hurt. Or used—against anyone."

The prince nodded. "That's what I thought, and it's
why I'm taking the risk of relying on you. Go, now.
Report to Vaoran and tell him I've assigned you to his
search party."

Kyre turned to leave, then stopped and looked back.
"How is the Princess Simorh?"

DiMag shrugged. "Much as anyone might expect. She
suffered a bad relapse, but she's well tended in her
tower." His eyes were suddenly haunted, belying the
estrangement between himself and his wife. "As things
are, we can't hope for anything better."

Kyre could make no reply to that. He headed toward
the door, and the prince turned back to his councillors.

Horse riding was a new experience for Kyre, yet one
which seemed elusively familiar. As Vaoran's party filed
out of the courtyard gate and into the twisting city
streets, he sat easily on his mount's high, narrow back,
controlling it with relaxed and practiced movements of
his fingers on the reins. The swordsmaster made no
secret of the fact that he resented Kyre's presence in his
party, and, bar an initial curt order to mount up and move
out, pointedly ignored him.

They rode through Haven, not toward the sandstone
arch but up, along streets that grew narrower and steeper
until finally they emerged from the city onto the clifftop.
The open emptiness of the high ground was a shock after
the close and claustrophobic atmosphere that permeated

Haven; gray moorland stretched away into the wet haze, broken only by the occasional patch of windburned gorse and untrammeled by any path. In the distance Kyre glimpsed what appeared to be a cluster of low buildings, and beyond them an indefinite spread of crop-bearing fields; but the drizzle made it impossible to discern any real detail. The prospect did not look appealing.

At Vaoran's order the riders turned right along a hard-packed track that followed the cliff's ragged edge; the swordsmaster waited until the party was strung out along the path before jerking his horse to a halt and looking back.

"We'll ride beyond the bay, until the track ends. I want the first five in line to watch inland, the rest to look down to the beach. Use your eyes as you've never used them before; and if any man sees anything untoward—*anything!*—report it to me immediately!"

His voice carried harshly on the still, damp air and the edge of emotion was unmistakable. Despite his dislike of the man, Kyre couldn't fault Vaoran's zeal. He spurred his horse as the party moved on again, and kept his gaze fixed firmly on the huge crescent of the bay below. The tide was half out and ebbing, and the shingle bar lay like a shining snake in the shallows, gleaming under the dull sky, the ruined temple reduced, from this height, to the dimensions of a child's toy. Grief constricted Kyre's throat as he thought of Gamora and what might have befallen her. She was the one innocent undeserving of any harm, and the memory of how he had rejected and dismissed her so cavalierly at their last encounter added guilty remorse to the sorrow. If Haven had had gods, he thought, he would have prayed fervently to them at this moment that she might be found safe and unhurt.

It took two hours to traverse the winding path along

the clifftop, and when the track at last petered out into dead patches of shale and thin grass, no clue had been found to Gamora's whereabouts. The weather was worsening; the cloud cover had thickened and crept lower, seeming to meet the land in places, and the early drizzle had developed into steady rain that drove stingingly in from the sea and soaked the men and their mounts through. The tide was by this time at its lowest, and Vaoran pointed toward a steep but negotiable gully that cut a scar in the cliff and led down to the sand.

"We'll make our way down to the bay, spread out and comb the beach while the tide's at the ebb," he shouted back.

He turned his horse toward the decline and one by one the men followed. Kyre, at the tail end of the file, experienced a brief but nauseating moment of vertigo as his mount began to slither down the gulley and the cliff fell away to either side; with an effort he collected his wits and concentrated on the saddle pommel as the riders made their cautious way toward the beach.

Reaching the sand, they spread out in a wide arc that stretched from the cliff face out to the tideline. Kyre positioned himself in the lee of the cliff—it offered no shelter from the driving rain, but he felt happier with the greatest possible distance between himself and the restless sea—and slowly the line of riders began to move forward, eyes focused on the ground around them, alert for any clue. Kyre hung back a little behind the main formation, anxious to take in every detail of the rocks and pools that littered the foot of the cliff, and morbidly aware that at any moment he might glimpse a tangle of dark hair or a small, white limb protruding from the weed and boulders. Ahead of the party, perhaps a quarter of a mile away though obscured by the mist and rain, the ancient temple stood between them and Haven, and he couldn't banish a purely intuitive yet powerful gut feeling that Gamora's disappearance was somehow connected with the ruin. Though he couldn't see it, it drew him, its presence a constant and disconcerting goad.

Someone shouted suddenly, the sound peculiarly flat in the heavy atmosphere, and a horseman broke from the line to canter toward Vaoran. Kyre reined in, watching though he could hear nothing of the conversation between the two men. He saw Vaoran shake his head and clap the rider's shoulder as though in commiseration, then the swordsmaster raised his arm and signaled everyone to move on.

The temple drew nearer, its jagged pillars looming out of the gray day as though they hung in midair with no foundation to support them. Kyre's horse shied nervously at the apparition and he had difficulty calming its stamping and sidestepping. At last he reined it to a halt, meaning to settle the animal before riding on; and as he leaned forward to stroke the horse's neck in an attempt to reassure it he glimpsed a flicker of movement by the cliff face.

Involuntarily, Kyre jerked so hard on the reins that his horse snorted sharply and almost sat on its haunches. The cliff here was pocked with caves, some no more than narrow slits in the rock wall, others gaping like dark, idiot mouths; and it was in the shadows of one of the wider caves that he had seen the movement.

"Who's there?" Kyre moved his horse a cautious pace or two nearer the cliff, peering forward and mentally cursing the water that dripped from his hair into his eyes. "Come out—show yourself!"

A slithering sound answered him, as though someone or something was climbing carefully across the piles of

rank seaweed that littered the place. Then he saw a pair
of eyes, shining luminously in the gloom, and the outline
of a pale arm that rose and, jerkily, beckoned.

He looked quickly over his shoulder. The rest of the
search party were still making their slow way onward
and no one seemed to have noticed the fact that he was
now some way behind them. Kyre thought of Vaoran's
order, then recalled DiMag's last words to him, and
stilled the shout that had been on the tip of his tongue. He
neither needed nor wanted anyone to back him up, least
of all Vaoran . . .

His horse grew nervous as he edged it toward the cave,
fighting the bit and kicking up flurries of sand until he
was forced to dismount and lead it. The hand still
beckoned, though he could no longer see the shimmer of
the eyes; whoever lurked in the cave had drawn back into
the darkness as he approached.

He called out softly, "I'll come no further. Who are
you, and what do you want?"

Again there was a slithering sound: then a figure
emerged slowly from the cave's black interior into the
twilight just beyond the entrance. Small, thin, skin pale
with an odd blue-green tinge that he'd seen before, and
white hair that whipped around its shoulders as a wet
gust of wind caught it. It was dressed only in a loincloth
and its body was so scrawny as to be all but sexless. In
one hand it held a spearlike weapon, identical to the one
with which Prince DiMag had killed his prisoner; its grip
on the spear seemed negligently careless but Kyre wasn't
inclined to take any chances. He held up one hand, palm
outward, in what he hoped would be interpreted as a
pacific gesture.

"Can you speak?" he asked. "Do you understand
me?"

The sea dweller smiled, showing small but ferally sharp teeth. Then it said, in a voice that was bizarrely modulated and sounded as though water rather than air flowed through its lungs, "Sun-Hound?"

Kyre's throat constricted. *How could it know?* He swallowed and replied with an effort, "Yes. I'm the one called Kyre."

It nodded. "You're searching for the little princess."

"Gamora . . . do you know where she is?" His pulse was starting to pound.

The creature laughed, and revealed its free hand, which hitherto it had kept hidden behind its back. Something glinted like a captive rainbow in its grasp; then it brought its arm up in a sharp motion and threw the object directly at Kyre.

He stumbled back, and caught the thing by reflex rather than judgment as it arced toward him. It was a shell, the inner surface brilliantly pearlescent and reflecting every color of the spectrum. Gamora's precious shell, which she had found on the beach while they walked with Brigrandon . . .

The pounding in his blood swelled to a suffocating pitch and he looked up, wild-eyed. *"Where is she?"*

"With us. Safe. I can take you."

Kyre felt sick as he realized what the sea creature was telling him. Gamora was in the hands of her people's deadliest enemies. How they had snared her he couldn't begin to guess, but the shell was proof enough. They had taken her.

He tried to get a grip on the fury and panic that threatened to overwhelm him. If Gamora was a prisoner, why was this creature so eager to take him to her? Gamora was a far more valuable hostage than he could ever be; her captors could surely want nothing from him?

The creature impinged on his chaotic thoughts. "I can take you," it said again. "But you only. No other."

"Why?" Kyre demanded hoarsely. "Why me?"

It shrugged. "I didn't question the order." Another feral smile. "If you want her to live, you must come."

It was an ultimatum that he couldn't argue with, and he dared not doubt for a moment that if he didn't comply Gamora would be harmed. Yet if he did, he might be walking to his own execution . . .

"Well?" The sea creature cocked its head in a faintly mocking challenge.

I'll repay your kindness, somehow, one day. His own words to Gamora echoed in Kyre's memory. Had they been as empty as the other promises he'd made to her? He cast another look back toward the sea. The horsemen were well ahead now, his absence still unnoticed. A debt that was overdue . . .

And, said a voice within him, *a chance—perhaps just a chance—to explore a few more unanswered questions. What have you to lose, Kyre? What have you to lose?*

He focused on the figure of the sea dweller; thought again of Gamora. "Very well," he said tersely.

The creature's smile became a wide grin. "Come, then," it told him. "This way—quickly."

It emerged from the cave mouth and started away at a run in the opposite direction to Vaoran's receding party. Taken aback, Kyre loosed his horse's reins and set off in pursuit. The sea dweller moved with a peculiar, loping gait that looked ungainly but nonetheless covered ground fast; keeping up with it on the wet, soft sand was hard work. They were still in the lee of the cliff, and at first Kyre didn't hear the hoofbeats approaching from behind, as the rush of his pulse pounding in his ears masked all other sound. Only when a voice bellowed at his back did he realize with a sudden shock that his absence had been discovered.

"*You!* What in the name of the Eye d'you think you're doing?"

The sea creature stopped in a tangle of limbs, hissing with alarm. It cast a rapid glance back, then snatched Kyre's arm, pulled hard, and snarled, *"Run!"*

Jerked almost off his feet as his companion dragged him away from the cliff and in a direct line toward the sea, Kyre had no chance to think what he was doing and time only for the briefest glimpse of the horsemen bearing down on them. Someone must have looked back and seen him with the sea dweller; now the soldiers were pounding head-on toward them, Vaoran in the lead and yelling at them to stop. He looked desperately at the sea, and knew they couldn't reach it before they were run down.

"Run!" the creature screamed again, furious or frightened, Kyre couldn't tell which. He tried to force his legs to move faster, but his calf muscles ached savagely and he could make no better speed.

The leading horses changed direction, stringing out in a curve that would cut the fugitives off before they reached the tideline. The animals were far faster than any runner, and suddenly the dark form of Vaoran's horse swept between them and the sea. Kyre and the creature instinctively swerved, only to reel back as another horse veered in from the left. The two animals converged, forcing them into a narrow bottleneck, and as other mounted men came to reinforce their leader, Kyre and his companion stumbled to a halt, hemmed in and trapped.

Vaoran stared down at Kyre, and though the swords-master's heavy figure was little better than a silhouette against the sky Kyre could sense the undisguised loathing radiating from him.

"So what have we here?" Vaoran said with soft malignance. "A turncoat and a traitor, a sandworm who consorts and plots with sandworms . . ."

The sea dweller bared its teeth and snarled. Vaoran's horse shied violently, alarmed by the aggressive movement and not liking the smell of brine from the creature; Vaoran jerked the reins viciously to discipline it, and his blue eyes focused on the white-haired being. His chest heaved as though with some livid emotion he was determined to contain, then he gestured to one of his men.

"Kill that," he said with flat disinterest. "We'll give the prince's pet a more protracted lesson; but kill that now and leave its entrails for the gulls."

Kyre wanted to shout a protest, remembering Gamora, but the sea creature was faster than he was. Before anyone else could move, it brought its spear up in a bizarre movement from the wrist, and the weapon cut a whirling, lethal arc through the rain, slashing across the unprotected chest of Vaoran's horse. The animal shrieked and reared, tipping the swordsmaster out of the saddle; other horses milled in panic, their riders frantically trying to keep them from trampling their fallen leader, and in the confusion the sea creature thrust the bloody spear, shaft-first, into Kyre's hands.

"Follow me!" it hissed, its huge eyes glittering with a fanatical light. "Or the child will be dead before nightfall!" And it was gone, darting like quicksilver through the melee and running toward the sea.

Kyre cursed, a voluble oath that he hadn't realized he knew, and tried to shoulder his way through the stamping animals in the creature's wake. Vaoran, hoarse with shock and rage, shouted, *"Stop him!"* and a horse slewed into his path, the rider snatching his sword from its scabbard and lunging toward him. Kyre felt fear and fury and desperation well up like a tidal wave; and with them came an instinct that surged out of his lost memory. The spear in his hands suddenly seemed to be alive; he flicked his wrists, holding the shaft double-handed, and the ferocious blade sheared like a striking steel cobra to meet the sword as it came down. The metals clashed with a searing, discordant note that set Kyre's teeth jarring, and sparks hissed in the rain. The swordsman swore, trying to untangle his blade: Kyre held it trapped on the divided point of the spear until the moment was perfect—then with another swift, expert twist he brought the spear blade back and, in the same movement, hamstrung his assailant where he sat.

The man's screams were an ugly counterpoint to the renewed whinnying of the horses as the smell of blood panicked them afresh, and even Vaoran's roaring frustration couldn't cut through the din. Still gripping the spear, Kyre shoulder-charged the wounded man's horse; the animal jumped aside, stiff-legged with terror, and he was through the knot of men and free. He started to run, following the faint footprints of the sea creature; inspired by desperation he gave no thought of what might lie ahead of him, and halted only when his feet splashed into the shallows of the turning tide.

Behind him there was shouting: he looked back and saw someone stumbling across the sand toward him. Vaoran . . .

"Come back!" The swordsmaster was mad-eyed, his rage beyond control, and at the sight of him the shock of what he'd done struck Kyre like a physical blow. He had wielded the sea dweller's spear as though born to it—

he'd hamstrung a man, perhaps killed him—he'd had to do it, for Gamora's sake: *but where had that deadly skill come from?*

He looked frantically over his shoulder at the sea. Vaoran meant to kill him, and he couldn't trust himself to defeat such an expert warrior.

He backed away into the sea until the water was swirling round his thighs. There'd be no chance for explanations; the swordsmaster wouldn't listen, and perhaps in his place Kyre might have felt the same. The sea was his only chance.

He took another step backward and felt the beach begin to shelve steeply under his feet. He didn't even know if he could swim, but it was too late to consider that now; he must learn, or drown.

Vaoran was closer; he couldn't afford any more time. Taking a deep breath, Kyre shouted, "They've got Gamora! I *have* to go, or they'll kill her! Tell DiMag—they've got Gamora!!"

Whether Vaoran either heard or understood, he didn't know; he turned and, with a silent mental plea to any benevolent power that might be listening, flung himself into the path of a breaking wave.

Green water smashed over his head and bore him down; it was stunningly cold and he almost gasped in a lungful of the sea before his head broke surface and he found himself beyond the wave and carried on a strong crosscurrent. Instinct took over and he kicked out, feeling his legs and the sea's buoyancy propel him clear of the current and into deeper water. Salt stung his eyes, nose, and mouth before he learned to breathe between the swells of the breakers. He thrashed his arms, trying to match their stroke to the thrust of his body—and suddenly coordination came; it was easy, and he was swimming strongly.

As though he'd been born to it . . .

He forced the chilling thought away, knowing he must concentrate on pure physical survival. He'd swim until he was clear of the bay, then come ashore at a place where Vaoran's men couldn't reach him: it was impossible to think beyond that point until he was safe—

Kyre yelled aloud and swallowed sea water as something gripped his ankle. He lost his stroke and twisted, flailing; then whatever held him pulled violently and he went under in a swirl of bubbles and foam. Down—he kicked but couldn't free himself—and then through the murky, turbulent darkness he saw luminescent eyes and a hand that grasped his foot, while another hand beckoned with a slow, smooth motion. Beckoned him down . . . He turned his head frantically from side to side, trying to tell the sea creature that he must breathe air, not water, but it only showed its teeth in its feral smile and beckoned again, nodding so that its pale hair flowed like waterborne weed.

It must know he couldn't survive more than a minute or two under water—it meant to drown him! Kyre kicked again, with all his strength. He'd lost most of the air in his lungs with the shock of being pulled down; there was a mad drumming in his ears and his head and chest felt as though they were about to burst apart. He had seconds, at most, before muscular reflex would force him to open his mouth in a fruitless and desperate compulsion to breathe.

The creature nodded, more emphatically, as though reading his thoughts and urging him to begin the terrible process of drowning. The gloomy undersea world seemed to be turning crimson; the sea was like blood, his captor an appalling scarlet apparition, and the drums in his ears were beating harder, deeper, louder—and suddenly he could bear it no longer. A spasm racked his

throat and diaphragm, his mouth opened and he gasped
for air.

A fountain of bubbles gushed by his face and blinded
him, and he felt the stinging, searing attack of salt. He
shut his eyes, limbs flailing helplessly . . . and the
drumming in his head faded, the pressure in his chest
receding as his lungs expanded in relief. Expanded
. . . contracted . . . expanded again . . . *he was
breathing*! Shocked and bewildered, Kyre opened his
eyes to see the sea dweller, one hand still gripping his
foot, grinning at him in the murk. It nodded and made an
open-palmed gesture as if to say: you see? Kyre stared
back at it, aware that they were both drifting on the
heavy undertow—he could see neither the sea bed, nor
any glimmer of light from the surface—but suddenly not
caring. He was breathing, as easily as he breathed on
land, but what flowed through his lungs was *water* . . .

Realizing that he at last comprehended what had
happened to him, the sea creature released its hold. It
turned, moving with lazy grace, and backfinned with its
hands to keep its position against the current. Then it
pointed ahead, into swirling darkness.

Stunned, wondering, Kyre turned his body about until
he was angled forward halfway between the vertical and
the horizontal. The caress of the sea, buoying him and
giving strength and flexibility to his limbs, was relaxing
and invigorating. He felt as though his stamina could be
endless here in this gentle, watery world.

Tentatively he nodded to the creature ahead of him to
show that he was ready. Then, as it moved slowly away,
he flexed his muscles and propelled himself forward,
following it into the deeps.

Chapter 11

DiMag said evenly, without looking up from the notes he was making, "I see."

Vaoran stared down at him. Two spots of color were flaming on the swordsmaster's cheeks, and he couldn't keep the anger he felt out of his voice as he asked sharply, "My lord, what do you intend to do about it?"

"*Do?*" The prince turned round in his chair so fast that Vaoran took an involuntary pace back. They were alone in DiMag's private apartments. DiMag's eyes were venomous with dislike and disappointment, and his mouth set in a tight, ugly line. "What, my good swordsmaster, would you *suggest* that I do?"

"The creature is a traitor! He has betrayed Haven! My lord, I've believed all along that he shouldn't be trusted; though I don't wish to sound sanctimonious, I—"

"Then don't!" DiMag snapped viciously. He got up, the chair scraping noisily back. "According to your own report, the last you saw of Kyre was when he plunged

181

into the sea to escape your wrath. Which, as I doubt if he can swim, probably means that he is dead. In which case, you've had all the satisfaction you're going to get—unless you want me to have the sea fished until his corpse is found, so that you can take pleasure in dismembering it?"

Vaoran didn't answer, but DiMag could hear suppressed fury in his stertorous breathing. The prince smiled sourly. His swordsmaster and councilor might well harbor deep-rooted resentments, but he wouldn't dare act on them. Not yet, at any rate. Then the smile faded.

"Vaoran, you have done me a great disservice," he said, turning his back and walking away toward the window. "Thanks to your prejudice and stupidity, the sorcerous work which my wife"—he stressed the word, subtly but noticeably—"performed at great risk to herself has been destroyed and brought to nothing."

Vaoran's face purpled. "The creature betrayed you, Prince DiMag!"

"Did he?" DiMag looked back at him, eyes narrowed. "How can you be so certain?"

"By the Hag, he murdered one of my men! One of my best soldiers—he bled to death on the sand before my eyes!"

"Maybe Kyre killed him to save his own life? Maybe you didn't give him the chance to explain himself?"

Vaoran stared at him. "What in corruption was there to explain? The creature was *consorting* with those demons, in league with them! I'm not about to start doubting the evidence of my own eyes!"

"No, of course not. And so you were ready to kill him without a further word being said."

Vaoran sucked in a harsh breath. "Yes. I was. Because

my faith lies in Haven, not in the unproven mouthings of
a creature dragged into the world out of hell!"

DiMag turned slowly to face him, and wished fervently that he had a sword in his hand. He said, softly, "Get
out of my sight."

Vaoran held his gaze for a few moments. Then, with a
disgusted exclamation, he turned and left the room,
slamming the door behind him.

Grai was waiting where the corridor turned at the
junction with the main stairs, out of sight and earshot of
the sentries at DiMag's door. He stepped out of the
shadows as Vaoran approached and, judging the swordsmaster's mood, prudently said nothing while they de-
scended the flight together. Only when they reached the
entrance hall did Grai at last speak.

"Well? Did it go as you anticipated?"

"Worse." Vaoran glanced sidelong at the plump
councillor. "My evidence wasn't enough for him; he
began *defending* that monstrosity as though it were his
blood brother!"

"Um." Grai sucked at a strand of his beard, a habit
which irritated Vaoran, and his eyes focused on the
middle distance for a few moments as he contemplated.
"Well," he said at length. "Then it seems our prince is
as unreasonable as ever."

"Indeed. In fact I might go so far as to suggest that
he's on the verge of losing his reason. Not a happy omen
for the future of our city."

Grai nodded sagely. "Certainly it isn't. Though
whether the time is yet right to suggest such a thing more
publicly . . . ?" He let the question hang unfinished,
and Vaoran hunched his shoulders.

"Not yet, Councillor Grai. We need, I think, just a

little more time." He smiled grimly. "If the condemned man is given a long enough rope, then he'll sometimes save the hangman a tiresome task."

The councillor uttered a short, wheezing laugh. "Succinctly put. I take your meaning, and I agree with you. We've learned patience; we can endure it a little while longer. Now, I shall leave you to refresh and victual yourself after your arduous morning." He patted Vaoran's arm in an absentminded gesture and started to move away, then stopped and looked back. "Oh; one small matter. The last words the creature shouted to you, about Princess Gamora. Did you mention that to the prince?"

"No. I thought it might be more—tactful—not to reveal it as yet."

"Tactful." Grai smiled. "Tactful. Yes. What the prince doesn't know can't trouble him. Wise of you, Vaoran." He smiled, and walked away.

"DiMag!"

Simorh's scream brought Thean and Falla running from the room below. They found the sorceress collapsed on the floor among a tangle of blankets, hands flailing and sweat gleaming on her skin as she struggled out of the grip of a dream.

"Lady! Lady, it's all right, you're safe in your tower!" Thean, who was the stronger of the two girls, pinioned Simorh's arms and fought to calm her while Falla unraveled the blankets that cocooned the sorceress. Simorh moaned and burst into tears, and between them her apprentices lifted her back onto the couch from which she'd fallen.

"Falla, fetch the physician!" Thean said urgently.

"No!" Simorh's body jerked and she swatted weakly

at the ministering hands. "Not the physician—send for
the prince, send for DiMag. I must speak to him!"

"Madam, you're in no condition—"

"*Ohhh!*" Bitter exasperation was in Simorh's groan
and she wiped at her face with the sleeve of her robe.
"Don't argue with me! I *must* see DiMag." She gripped
Thean's wrist, her nails digging so painfully into the flesh
that the girl winced. *"Do as I say!"*

The girls exchanged an uneasy glance, then Falla
straightened and ran toward the door.

DiMag was still seething from his interview with Vaoran
when a servant brought Falla's message from Simorh.
For a moment it was on the tip of the prince's tongue to
dismiss the man with a curse, but an odd instinct
forestalled him. His senses were unnaturally and painfully acute today, and something in the tone of the message
alerted him. He found Falla waiting nervously in the
corridor, and smiled to reassure her.

"Well, Falla. What's amiss with your mistress?"

The dark girl shook her head. "I don't know, my lord.
She woke from a bad dream and she was very dis-
tressed—she begged to see you."

"Very well. Lead the way."

They made as good speed as DiMag was able, and
within minutes were climbing the stairs to Simorh's
tower.

"DiMag!" As they entered her bedchamber the
sorceress tried to rise, pushing the anxious Thean aside.
The prince read the urgency and strain in her face, and
glanced at the two girls. "Leave us."

He waited until the door closed behind them, then
knelt beside the couch. "What is it? Have you had a
vision?"

Under other circumstances Simorh might have been gratified by his eager concern, but she was too distraught to notice. She caught hold of his wrist and the words spilled chaotically from her tongue. "I saw Gamora. In a dream—DiMag, I saw her!"

DiMag felt his chest constrict. He knew his wife well enough to set great store by the dream-images that sometimes came to her, and to trust her interpretation of them. His fingers clamped over hers and he demanded urgently, "Where? Is she alive?"

Simorh nodded. "She's alive, and unharmed, but . . . the place where she is; it's . . ." She shook her head helplessly. "I don't *know*, DiMag; I can't see it clearly. It's as though she were in another world, another dimension." Tears sprang to her eyes. "I don't know that place, and I can't touch it."

Dread settled like a monstrous weight in DiMag's gut. "Simorh, what you saw—" He could hardly bring himself to utter the suggestion, but forced the words out. "It wasn't a place of death . . . ?"

"No!" She was vehement. "She is alive; I *know* she is. Besides—Kyre was with her."

"Kyre?" His face lost its color and her eyes widened.

"Yes, Kyre. Why is that significant?"

DiMag released her hand and stood up. He couldn't bring himself to meet her frantic gaze as he said, "Vaoran came to me half an hour ago, with news—"

"Of Gamora?" Simorh's voice was shrill.

"No. Listen to me. Kyre was with Vaoran's search party; I sent him. He encountered a . . ."—he hesitated, swallowed— "one of the sea creatures, and Vaoran tells me that he and the creature were attempting to slip away when they were apprehended."

Her face was suddenly very still. "What happened?"

DiMag shrugged. "Much depends on what you choose to believe. According to Vaoran, there was a fight, one of the soldiers was killed, the creature escaped to the sea— and Kyre went with it. He was last seen in deep water, swimming."

Simorh didn't speak for some while. From stillness her expression had taken on a pinched, tight look, her eyes haunted and introverted. At last, she said: "Do you believe that report, DiMag?"

The prince sighed. "I don't know what to believe. All I do know is that Kyre hasn't returned." He looked up. "And yet you Saw you—"

"With Gamora. Yes."

He bit his lip. "Does that mean they are dead?"

"No." Less vehemence this time, but her conviction was unshaken. "They both live; I know it, and I feel— sense—that they're together. But wherever they are, DiMag, we can't reach them, and the search parties won't find them."

DiMag sucked in a long breath. "I don't know what to do, what to think. If you're right, then—" He shook his head violently. "There are so many possibilities. Why did Kyre go? How did he find Gamora?"

"I'll find out," Simorh said savagely.

He looked at her. "You're not strong enough."

"I don't care. I don't care what I have to do. I'll find out what's happened." Her eyes were feverishly bright. "There's no other choice."

DiMag paced the room slowly. Tiredness made his limp more pronounced than usual, and Simorh had to look away, disturbed by the awkwardness of his gait. "Is our Sun-Hound a traitor?" he said at length, speaking more to himself than to the sorceress. "Vaoran believes it. I don't." He turned, faced her again. "You brought him here; you should know the truth."

She cast her eyes down. "When I get him back in the palace, I'll find out," she said viciously.

"If you get him back."

"When."

"As you please."

Simorh gripped her upper arm. "It *has* to be *when*; don't you understand that? Kyre is our only link with Gamora!" She stared at DiMag's taut, bitter face for a few moments, then abruptly turned over on the couch, away from him. "Go away, DiMag. Send out our search parties and leave me alone; I can't talk to you." Her shoulders heaved and she drew in a gulping breath. "I know what you're thinking. Kyre has brought this on us, and I brought Kyre to Haven. Very well: it's all my fault, and I confess it. But I'll change that. If I die trying, believe me, I'll *change* it!"

She was crying, and DiMag couldn't touch her, couldn't even approach her. The division between them was too wide. He turned away and limped toward the door, only pausing when his hand was on the latch.

"I don't believe Kyre took Gamora from us. There's far more to this than we understand, and I'm not such a fool as to take Vaoran's glib tales at face value." He looked down at his own feet and added softly, "You don't know me very well, do you, Simorh?"

Simorh jammed a clenched fist into her mouth in an effort to stem the shuddering, silent sobs that racked her and seemed to jar from the top of her spine through to her heels. She didn't hear the gentle sound of the door closing as DiMag left the room.

* * *

Time had become a meaningless concept. They might
have been traveling for an hour or a day or a year,
moving ever onward through the dim, swirling world of
the deep, a world of greens and blues and grays, ever
changing, ever revealing some new wonder as they
swam on. Here was a formation of crystalline rock,
shaped into fantastical sculptures; a castle from a
childhood dream. Here was a vast bank of weed moving
above their heads with slow, inexorable grace as though
directed by some alien intelligence. Here were shoals of
fish with brilliant eyes, which darted aside like a shower
of glass slivers at their approach, passing by a fingerbreadth away yet always eluding capture.

Kyre felt as though a new and unplumbed range of
senses which he hadn't known could exist had been
suddenly and stunningly awakened. The freedom he felt
at moving with such ease and speed through the water
was like a heady drug; there was a new dimension of
power in him and he wanted to laugh and scream and
weep all at once with the sheer exuberance of it. The
fight on the beach was forgotten, Gamora was forgotten,
Haven was forgotten; he knew only this deep and
beautiful new world and he wanted to experience it with
every part of his being.

But the sea creature that guided him knew the urgency
of its mission, and though it was content to indulge his
eager exploration, it nonetheless continued to lead him
toward their goal. To Kyre, the creature was a flickering
will-o'-the-wisp that he followed without pausing to
consider the wisdom of what he did; he was too caught
up in the miracle that had overtaken him to think beyond
the moment. But at last something new impinged on his
mind. The smooth tide on which they swam was
changing: crosscurrents buffeted them, stirring up sand

from the sea bed and churning the water into murk. And then above his head there were traces of shimmering, shivering light, and a distant booming sound that seemed to echo in his bones.

His companion jackknifed gracefully to cut across his path as, suddenly confused and unsure of himself, he twisted about in the water. It took hold of his wrist and gestured toward the surface before turning upward and kicking out strongly. Kyre's limbs moved reflexively to match the creature: there was an exhilarating sense of speed, of energy—and then their heads broke out into salt-laden air.

The sea dweller snorted a stream of water from its nostrils, then took several shallow, rapid breaths, drawing oxygen into its lungs. Kyre, unprepared for the transition, found himself choking and spluttering in a medium that was suddenly alien to him; only when the creature gripped his jaw in one hand and punched the palm of the other against his chest did he cough water from his lungs and feel his throat begin to work again. The change was agony, a stinging clash of wet salt and cold air, and he continued to cough convulsively, offering no resistance as his guide towed him toward what his streaming eyes could only dimly make out to be a high ledge. A wave helped them on their way; Kyre's body scraped painfully against rock, and then hands were taking hold of him, dragging him from the water, pulling upward. He fought them, not wanting to leave the sea, but his efforts were feeble and, like a stranded fish, he was dumped on the harsh, barnacle-crusted surface of the ledge.

Three men were waiting for them on the ledge. Two were getting on in years; the third was a good deal younger, a bizarrely distinctive figure with his silver-streaked black hair and the ugly birthmark on his face. He watched Kyre with intent interest as the guide climbed lightly up the side of the ledge and stood before the reception party.

"I have done as I was instructed," it said, and bowed quickly to the assembled company. "This is the one she wanted."

Hodek stared down at Kyre, who was only now beginning to try, painfully and not yet with any success, to sit upright. He ignored the waiting guide, and it was Akrivir who finally answered.

"You've done well," he said, a little bleakly. "You'll be rewarded." He nodded a dismissal, and the guide headed toward a dark recess in the cavern wall. As he passed, Akrivir intercepted him; they exchanged a few words in low tones, then the guide disappeared.

Hodek's companion stroked his own chin thoughtfully. "It seems a pity that we have to maintain this charade. My vote would be to kill this creature now."

Akrivir smiled cynically, and Hodek scowled at his colleague." Take a blade if it pleases you, and run the creature through," he countered sourly. "You'll be the one who answers to Calthar, not me!"

The other man shrugged and turned away, and Kyre, whose fuddled mind had been alerted by the exchange, managed at last to raise his head.

"Who are you?" His voice was roughened by the salt and cracked on the last word. He rubbed at his eyes, trying to clear them—and as he focused on the group before him, he remembered at last why he had been brought here.

Hodek glowered down at him. "You are the one they call the Sun-Hound?"

Tension began to replace the weakness in Kyre's

limbs. "Gamora . . ." he said, then the strength returned to his voice. "Where is Gamora?"

Hodek sighed with theatrically exaggerated patience. "I asked you a civil enough question. Be so good as to reply in the same manner!"

Kyre felt himself starting to shiver. *A cave, above sea level—the stronghold of Haven's enemies . . .*

"Yes," he heard himself say. "I am the one called Kyre . . ." He shook his head, trying to clear the last vestiges of confusion and shock, then repeated, "Where is Gamora?"

"The child is well," Hodek told him.

"I want to see her!"

Hodek cleared his throat with genteel deliberation. "I think," he said, "that we might do well to establish one or two minor details before we progress any further. The child, as I said, is well—for the time being. While you cooperate with us, and do as we ask rather than wasting our time with tiresome questions, she will remain well. If, however, you decide to be contentious, her health may take an unexpected turn for the worse. Now." He smiled unctuously. "Shall we begin again?"

Kyre forced himself to nod.

"Good." Hodek clasped his hands together and Kyre heard the knuckles crack loudly. "Akrivir will escort you to your destination. Ask no questions, say nothing; simply follow." He stepped aside, nodded to Akrivir, who, without speaking, jerked his thumb toward the mouth of a black tunnel at the back of the cavern.

Suspicious, but not willing to argue in the face of the explicit threat to Gamora, Kyre went with him. As they reached the tunnel he looked back and saw Hodek watching him. His demeanor was far from reassuring, and Kyre turned his head quickly away.

As Akrivir and his charge vanished from sight, Hodek
let out a long, hissing breath. Like his fellow councilor,
he'd wanted no part of this ridiculous charade, but
Calthar had insisted on it, down to the finest detail and,
as usual, without deigning to make her reasons known.
The familiar mixture of desire, fear, and loathing
churned in his blood as he thought of the priestess, and it
awoke his old fantasy that one day he would defeat
Calthar at her own game. A delusion perhaps, but a fond
one: nothing would have given Hodek greater pleasure
than to reverse their established roles and see her
crawling at his feet.

His colleague was still staring at the tunnel mouth, and
his voice broke in on Hodek's pleasant reverie.

"I still don't begin to comprehend why Talliann should
want such a creature brought here," he said. "What
could she possibly want with him?"

"How should I know what moves Talliann?" Hodek
retorted. "The girl's even madder than Calthar." He
smiled, not pleasantly. "Perhaps she's at last beginning
to awaken to the joys of the flesh?" And he cackled.

"Let her have her diversions while they last," he said.
"Once she's done what's required of her, there'll be no
more need of troublesome children or recalcitrant Sun-
Hounds, and Calthar will know exactly how to deal with
them both." He patted his companion's arm. "You'll
see, my friend. You'll see."

Chapter 12

KYRE WAS HOPELESSLY DISORIENTED. HIS ESCORT HAD LED him for what seemed like mile upon mile through the unlit tunnel; he could see nothing, and only the sound of Akrivir's footsteps a few paces ahead kept him on course. In the pitch darkness the sounds echoed disconcertingly, and he had lost all sense of perspective, so that it seemed the blackness before his straining eyes was a solid wall that he must at any moment run hard into. But the impact he feared didn't come; and at last a glimmer of light showed ahead.

They emerged from the darkness so suddenly that his pulse missed a sharp and painful beat. One moment there was nothing but the featureless tunnel, with only a faint, nacreous patch of illumination drawing indistinctly closer; then with no warning the passage turned at an acute angle, and opened onto a shocking vista.

Kyre swore aloud and flailed wildly for support as vertigo hit him like a solid wall. Akrivir caught hold of him, steadying him and smiling grimly at his shock, and he could only stare and start at the impossible scene.

They stood on a ledge that jutted out from the soaring wall of a titanic cavern. Before them and to either side sheer rock fell away into an echoing chasm, swallowed by a blackness so intense that Kyre had the terrible feeling he could have reached out and down and taken physical hold of the dark. Across the abyss's sickening gulf the opposite wall of the cavern rose towering toward an invisible roof, and to Kyre's stunned eyes it seemed that the far cliff before him was alive with a scene out of an unimaginable hell. Staircases scarred it, like great swathes cut from the rock by a huge and petulant hand, while distorted, spindled towers and mad buttresses reared out of the wall at grotesque angles, each one pricked by windows that shimmered and flickered with deathly pale light. And it seemed—though his battered and straining senses could never be sure—that tiny figures moved against the monstrous backdrop, dimly phosphorescent as they were caught by the lights like moths in a flame, throwing the whole scene into crazed and terrifying perspective. And somewhere, so far below that he didn't dare think on it, he heard the confined and angry moan of the sea.

Akrivir took his arm, pointing with his free hand, and spoke for the first time. "That way," he said curtly.

Reluctantly Kyre looked in the direction he indicated. To the right of the ledge a flight of narrow stairs swept down in a sharp curve, hugging the cave wall. They ended—or seemed to—just before utter blackness devoured them; and Kyre's stomach lurched as he saw, meeting the stairs, the slender span of a rock bridge that arched away across the chasm. From here it looked as fragile and insubstantial as a single thread from a spider's web, and all his senses recoiled at the thought of what his escort expected of him. But Akrivir wasn't about to take any argument, and shock had drained Kyre of the strength to resist. Like a man dreaming he stepped onto the first stair, the second, beginning the dizzying descent toward the bridge. Akrivir went before him: he forced himself to concentrate on the odd piebald of his hair immediately ahead to keep thoughts of what might lie below the stairs' sharp outer edge at bay, and, mesmerized and numb, arrived at last at the point where the slender bridge speared away into emptiness.

He was hardly aware of the crossing. What hidden mental reserves he called on to enable him to walk out over the abyss he didn't know; but somehow his feet moved, one before the other, and by slow and halting degrees he saw the far cliff with its insane architecture draw nearer, nearer; until, sick with fright and tension, he stumbled from the bridge's quivering span and into the heartland of the sea dwellers' citadel. His legs threatened to give way beneath him in sheer reaction, and Akrivir watched him patiently. When he was finally able to straighten up, he thought he detected a glimmer of amused sympathy in the other man's blue eyes.

"The crossing takes a little getting used to," Akrivir said.

"Yes . . ." Kyre fought back an impulse to laugh, aware that it might turn into hysteria, and, encouraged by the fact that his escort was at least willing to speak, ventured a question. "Where are you taking me?"

Akrivir shook his head, smiling faintly again. "Don't ask me: I won't give you any answers." He hesitated, then added more quietly: "Not yet, at any rate. Come on."

Taking Kyre's arm again, he drew him away from the

edge of the bridge and into a tunnel which could have
been twin to the one by which they had reached the cave.
But this black corridor was short: within less than a
minute they had entered a wide passage lit by chain-hung
lamps, with side lanes leading off at intervals. And in
this maze there were sounds of voices, footsteps,
people—*people?* Kyre asked himself dazedly—talking,
laughing, shouting, the sounds of voices echoing like a
faint, random chorus from all directions. Akrivir led
Kyre through caverns that might have been a deliberate
parody of the marketplaces of Haven, roads and squares,
streets and alleys—this whole cliff was a single, vast
warren, a city within rock within the sea; a living
microcosm of a world. And as they threaded their way
deeper into the citadel the distant voices became more
substantial, and Kyre began to see more and more of the
sea folk who inhabited this crazed place. They emerged
from their dwellings or paused at their work to watch the
two men pass, and the impressions they left on his
spinning mind were as varied as he might have found
among any gathering in Haven. Here was a man, sly-
eyed and suspicious; here an ancient, toothless couple
who pointed at him and mumbled to each other and
shook their heads; here a naked child, silver-haired and
so beautiful that it might have been the very personifica-
tion of innocence, snatched away by its mother before it
could stray too close to the interloper. And he *was* an
interloper, Kyre realized. This was a world apart from
Haven; a world populated by beings to whom he was a
freak and an oddity. His skin was the wrong color, his
hair was the wrong color, his face and limbs were
misshapen, his eyes and mouth in the wrong proportion . . . if humanity was judged by the norm, then in
this citadel he was unhuman.

And yet he could breathe water as they did; and he could wield the double-bladed spear as their warriors learned to do . . .

Bewildered though he was, the sights and sounds and salt smells of the citadel fascinated him as surely as though he were under a spell, so that when Akrivir halted with no warning he collided with him.

Akrivir, who had lapsed once more into taciturn silence, pointed to a side tunnel that led away from the main thoroughfare. Kyre's eyes were drawn to the tunnel, and it was a few moments before his vision adjusted to the brilliance that lit its carved and curving walls. The whole passage must have been carved through a vein of pure quartz: it shone and sparkled with a rainbow of colors brought to brilliant life by the myriad lamps depending from the ceiling, and in the vivid light he could see carvings—beautiful carvings, of fish and shells and strange forms he couldn't name—decorating the entrance. They turned into the tunnel, and as they traversed it Kyre could only stare in admiration at the sheer beauty of the place. Whoever had cut this passage from the living rock had been a master of his craft.

The passage was short, and ended at a door which, incredibly, seemed to be made from a single gigantic shell, fluted bands of coral and green creating a perfect symmetry. It swung easily, gracefully back at a touch, and Kyre stepped through into a lofty-ceilinged hall.

For one bizarre moment he thought he must be back in the raftered court hall of Prince DiMag's palace. The chamber was huge, lined with tall, arched windows and dominated by a raised dais on which was a great, carved chair. Between the windows hung tapestries woven in shades of blue, green, and gray, shot through in places by threads of vivid crimson that drew the eye. Below the

dais stood a long table and several chairs, all empty. Kyre
stared, trying to assimilate the shock of such a familiar
scene. And then he realized that the windows weren't
true windows at all, but shapes cut from pure white
quartz, opaque, giving on to nothing. And the tapestries
weren't woven from flax or linen or wool, but from the
sea's harvest; weed and coral strands and the skins of
unnameable, water-dwelling things. The table and chairs
were made from pieces of shell, exquisitely crafted and
dovetailed in organic curves. And the great chair was not
wood, but a single piece of jade hewn from the ocean
bed.

Akrivir indicated the table. As they drew nearer Kyre
could see that a place had been set before one of the
chairs as though anticipating a solitary diner in the
bizarre hall; around it were dishes brimming with what
must have been food but looked, to Kyre, alien and
strange. They reached the table and Akrivir drew out the
chair. "You might as well sit," he said. "And eat. You'll
be waiting a while."

Still dazed, Kyre obeyed; he picked up an ornately
carved silver knife but made no attempt to do anything
other than finger it abstractedly. Seeing that he wasn't
about to serve himself Akrivir sighed, and, at random,
heaped delicacies from the dishes onto the plate before
him. Kyre paid no heed; he was too stunned by the
bizarre anomalies of the treatment he was receiving at the
hands of those who, in theory, were his mortal enemies.
All he could do was stare around the fantastic hall, his
eyes drinking in the shimmer of quartz, the cool glow of
marble, the elusive glitter of small fountains—*fountains?*
Yes: they weren't an illusion; he could see them along the
walls, cascading down into small pools near the floor and
reminding him that this was a world where water reigned
unchallenged.

He was forced out of his fascinated trance by Akrivir's voice. "Eat," he said again. "Nothing's poisoned." To prove the point he picked up a handful of food and carelessly devoured it. Kyre came back to earth and, not knowing or caring what he chose or whether it might poison him or not, stabbed at something which looked like a small, spined fruit, and tasted it. The fruit gave as he bit, and an exquisitely fragile and elusive flavor filled his mouth, tingling on his tongue. He looked up, startled, and Akrivir suppressed a laugh before pouring a pale gold liquid from a ewer into the cup at his right elbow. "Try that," he said. "You'll find they go well together."

Again, a delicacy to the drink; whether it was strong or innocuous he didn't know, but the taste left him longing for more.

It was only when he heard footsteps that he realized his escort had turned away from the table and was leaving. Akrivir made no farewells, said not a word, but merely headed for the door; and Kyre rose quickly, thinking to call out to him. But before he could speak Akrivir stopped, looked back, and shook his head, forestalling anything Kyre might have said. For a moment only there was something akin to sympathy in his eyes: then they hardened again and he strode away, leaving Kyre alone in the hall.

For some moments he stayed motionless, half on his feet in an awkward, ungainly posture, simply staring at the shell door while awareness of his solitude slowly dawned on him. It was a discomfiting sensation to be left alone in such vast and impassive surroundings, and slowly he subsided back onto the chair. His hosts—if that was an appropriate term for them—wanted him to remain here, and they wanted him to eat. Very well: he would play along with their wishes. It seemed he had little to lose; however royally he might be treated he was effectively a prisoner, a hostage for Gamora. He would wait, and let them reveal in their own good time what they wanted of him.

Kyre looked down at the food on his plate. Trying, with poor success, to quell the sick pounding of his heart he began, cautiously but deliberately, like a man who knows the meal before him might be his last, to eat.

Gamora gazed up wide-eyed at the woman beside her and said, her voice awed, "I didn't think he'd come . . ."

Calthar met her stare and was amused by the admiring innocence she saw in the little girl's face. Aloud, she said, "You must learn to trust me, child, and understand that what I say, I mean."

Gamora blinked and peered again through the quartz window that overlooked the hall and its solitary occupant. The window was a device of Calthar's, showing an opaque face to the hall yet allowing any watcher to view the great chamber, albeit distortedly, from the far side, and the fact that something so simple was heralded as a work of genius by the citadel's council irritated the sorceress almost to distraction. Gamora pressed the palms of her hands against the quartz as though willing it to melt and allow her through. She seemed to be thinking hard: then suddenly she turned to Calthar again. "*Why* did he come?"

"For you, sweeting." And that was no less than the truth. At first Calthar had doubted that Haven's new pet could be moved to fulfill Talliann's desire through the lure of this child. Though she'd given no hint of it to Hodek and his acolytes, she had had severe misgivings about the viability of her scheme to bring the creature to the citadel, and the ease with which it had been accomplished had surprised her.

But then, she'd reckoned without the qualities of Gamora herself . . .

Calthar had no maternal instincts, and scorned the idea. But in this child who stood at her side, this little princess of Haven and designated future leader of her sworn enemies, Calthar had seen something of the qualities that motivated other, less pragmatic souls, so often to their own downfall. Gamora's initial defiance, when she had woken to find herself in the citadel, had roused grudging respect in the sorceress; the child had more courage than Hodek and all his crew together. She hadn't cried, she hadn't screamed, she hadn't groveled; she had simply demanded, with an imperious indignation that belied her years, to be released. Calthar had been very amused by her determination. And later, when she realized that she was a hostage and there would be no release, she had accepted the fact of her imprisonment with mature dignity. A child worthy of her station, Calthar thought. A pity that she had been born to the scum of Haven; in other circumstances she would have been ideal material for the sorceress's own schemes.

But there was nothing to be gained by wishing. Gamora had other uses; and second only to her value as a lure for Kyre was her ability to add to Calthar's knowledge of affairs in Haven, and now the pattern was beginning to make some sense.

Calthar was amused by the Haven rules' fond delusion that they could turn the tide of events by invoking such a worthless prophecy. She knew enough about the true Sun-Hound's story to scorn the idea that any cipher created in his image could hope to live up to such a

legend, and considered that, if her enemies were prepared to put faith in such a vain hope, they were greater
fools even than she'd thought them. In truth, their new
champion was more valuable to the citadel than he could
ever hope to be to his creators—and now, with Gamora's
innocent revelations to guide her, her plans were beginning to resolve exactly as she had wanted.

Gamora's voice broke in on her thoughts. "My mother
couldn't command Kyre," the little girl said somberly.
"She wanted to, but—" And she broke off as she
realized that Calthar was listening intently. Calthar saw
doubt in the child's eyes and said gently, "But what, little
one?"

"Nothing." Gamora hunched her shoulders and
turned away, and Calthar felt an odd sense of satisfaction.

She let her hand come to rest lightly on Gamora's
shoulder. "No one controls your Sun-Hound, my sweeting. He came because of you." She dropped to a crouch
so that their faces were on a level. "Haven't I told you
how much he cares for you? Don't you believe me
now?"

"I . . ." Gamora bit her lip. "I *think* so . . ."

"Look." The priestess rose, drawing Gamora with her
as she moved closer to the quartz window. "He eats: he
drinks. I promised you he would be treated as an honored
guest, and so it is." She smiled thinly. "Don't people
keep the promises they make to you in Haven?"

Gamora's face closed and she hung her head mutely,
unwilling to answer. Well enough; her silence was
confirmation in itself, and helped to weaken any hostility
she might have left.

Calthar gestured toward the window, drawing
Gamora's hungry gaze. "Well now. Don't you want to go
and greet your Sun-Hound?"

Gamora looked up at her dubiously, and Calthar gave a soft laugh. "I told you that I keep my promises. Come; we'll go together. You shall greet him first, and then I'll join you and meet him for myself. You've told me so much about him that I'm very eager to make his acquaintance." She held out her hand and, after an uncertain pause, Gamora slipped her fingers into the sorceress's palm. Calthar smiled, and led her toward the door.

"Kyre!"

The familiar voice was so unexpected that Kyre started violently where he sat, knocking his cup over and spilling a small flood of wine across the table. Staring to the far end of the hall he saw a small, dark-haired figure racing toward him, arms outstretched, and in astonishment he rose and hastened to meet her.

"Kyre!" Gamora's headlong rush ended in a chaotic collision, and as he lifted her into the air she flung her arms round his neck, kissing him soundly on both cheeks. "Oh, Kyre, you *came* for me! You're really *here*!

"Princess!" He hugged her tightly, far more moved than he could have anticipated by her welcome. Then, remembering their circumstances, he set her down, held her at arms' length and looked carefully at her. "Are you well, Gamora? Have you been hurt in any way?"

"No, Kyre, of course I'm not hurt!" She was laughing at his absurdity. "This place is beautiful, *wonderful*— and the lady has been so kind to me!"

"Lady?" There was something in her look, something he couldn't quite pinpoint, and it made him uneasy. "What lady?"

"She gave me this." Gamora put a hand to her hair,

where a circlet of exquisitely fashioned pieces of mother-of-pearl sat atop the chaos of dark curls. "And this—" She pointed to a similar necklace around her throat. "And a bracelet and a ring, too, and a new dress . . ." She stepped away from him and pirouetted, childishly coquettish. "She says I'm a princess, and a princess should have a crown, and jewels, and beautiful clothes . . . Kyre, do you think I look pretty?"

"Of course you do . . ." He fought back the doubts, knowing that she needed his reassurance. "You're every inch a princess, Gamora. But—"

The child interrupted him, words spilling eagerly from her lips. "And she said you'd come here, if I wanted you to. She promised—and you did; so she was right!"

She, again and again . . . Kyre said: "Who is *she*, little one? Who is this lady?"

At last Gamora stopped skipping and twirling. "Her name is Calthar," she said. "She rules here, and everyone's afraid of her. I was afraid of her at first, but I don't think I am any more; or not very, anyway. She's so kind, Kyre, and she's shown me so many lovely things." The flow of words paused, and the child gazed wide-eyed around the hall. "I haven't been in here before. It's *lovely*."

That look in her eyes again . . . there was something underlying the bubbling high spirits, and Kyre's growing misgivings grew. Before she could continue, he caught her under the arms and lifted her onto the empty chair next to his own, searching her face for the elusive clue. She smiled happily at him, and he forced himself to smile back.

"Gamora, you must forgive me—I've only been here a little while, and I don't really understand all you've told me. Princess, how did you come here? And *why*? All Haven is searching for you!"

Gamora's gaze slid away from his and she made a moue with her lips. "I ran away," she said flatly. One hand hovered over the dishes on the table; she selected a morsel and ate it. "This is nice."

Kyre persisted. "Why did you run away?"

She shrugged, still not looking at him. "Nobody took any notice of me. Father was busy, Mother was ill. Master Brigrandon was drunk again. And you didn't have any time for me." At last she met his eyes, though obliquely, and her gaze was reproachful. "And the shell told me that I could see some wonderful things, so I went." Another shrug. "Why shouldn't I?"

Though he had no memories of childhood, Kyre began to understand what had moved the little girl; the loneliness and desolation she must have felt. And he was largely to blame for it. Gently, he asked, "But how did you get here, Gamora? Who brought you?"

Gamora paused with her hand, clutching another morsel of food, midway to her mouth. "The other lady," she said, and now she sounded dubious. "The one with the black hair." Then she looked up and met his gaze candidly. "She's very strange, Kyre. I went out to the strand by the old temple, and I saw her there. She ran away and I tried to catch up with her, but when I did, she . . . she was strange. She's very beautiful, but I think she must be ill. Calthar told me she's sometimes ill, and I mustn't mind her. But I think she brought me, though I can't really remember much about it."

The picture Gamora painted was bizarre and disjointed; but one image caught in Kyre's mind. *The lady with the black hair*—he recalled the unearthly looking girl he had seen on the shingle bar; the black-haired one who had run from him. A vampire, DiMag had called her . . .

"Gamora." He took hold of the little girl's hands, knowing that he had to cut through her innocent enthusiasm, even if it meant shattering her happiness. "Gamora, don't you understand where you are? These people are Haven's enemies!"

Her face clouded with uncertainty. "That's what everyone's always said. But—"

"It's the truth! Your father and mother are half out of their minds with fear for your safety—how d'you think they'd feel if they knew you were in their enemies' stronghold?"

"Oh, Kyre . . ." Gamora's eyes were suddenly tragic. "You don't *understand*. Calthar says—"

He interrupted sternly." Calthar says. Why should you trust Calthar?"

"Because she's *kind* to me! She made promises, and she kept them. You've got to meet her, Kyre, then you'll see!"

And suddenly he knew what was wrong. Gamora's voice, her inflections, her gestures, were all as he knew them. But beneath the sparkle in her eyes was a blankness, an emptiness, as though all she had ever known or believed or experienced had been leached from her mind.

Gamora was bewitched . . .

"I've told Calthar all about you," the child went on eagerly. "She's waiting to meet you—" She screwed her head round at an impossible angle, looking toward the far end of the hall, then cried delightedly, "Here she is!"

Kyre looked up, and saw that a full figure had silently entered the hall and was moving toward them. By some means which he couldn't guess at, Calthar had judged her moment perfectly. The precision of her entrance made something deep within him turn as cold as ice.

Gamora turned back to him, her face lit with triumph. "Now you'll see, Kyre—now you'll see!"

Kyre rose as Calthar approached. The movement was unconscious; an involuntary combining of courtesy with the realization that he didn't want to be at a disadvantage when face to face with her. Impressions assailed him: her height—she was as tall as he was; the faintly phosphorescent sheen of her skin; the nimbus of shimmering silver hair; her easy but reptilian grace; the gaunt yet voluptuous body beneath the tatters of the ancient robe. And her eyes. They were molten fire in a face that was, by a crazed paradox, repulsively beautiful; they drew Kyre as surely as if she'd put him under a spell with one flick of her fingers. Then the hpynotic moment broke as Calthar stopped two paces from Kyre and extended her hand.

"Sun-Hound. Welcome to our citadel."

Her voice was a throaty contralto, and unexpectedly warm. Kyre joined his fingers with hers—and as they made contact, he felt something in her touch that sent a shivering cascade of sharp needles through all the nerves in his spine. She had real power, there could be no doubt of it; the way she regarded him made him feel that her eyes saw far deeper than the planes and contours of his face.

Gamora had scrambled down from her chair, and now skipped to the sorceress's side. "Isn't he handsome, Calthar? Isn't he just the way I told you?" She looked quickly from one to the other, then added with satisfied finality, "I'm going to marry him when I grow up."

Over the little girl's head Calthar caught Kyre's eye, and there was amusement in her wry smile. "I'm sure he'll make you a worthy consort, sweeting," she said, and her use of the affectionate term chilled Kyre's blood.

Calthar pulled out a chair and sat down with sinuous

grace. She continued to study Kyre for a few moments more, then said: "Gamora has told me a great deal about you, Sun-Hound. It seems that you have at least one loyal and true friend in Haven."

Kyre glanced sidelong at the child, wondering just how much she had told this woman. "I know," he said.

"And in fact," Calthar continued, "it was for her sake and her sake alone that you were willing to come to the citadel. Am I right?"

"Yes." He had nothing to gain from hiding the truth.

She smiled. "Then by showing your loyalty to the little princess, you've unwittingly done me a great service, Kyre." Turning, she reached out to stroke Gamora's hair. "Sweeting, I want to talk to your Sun-Hound, and it's talk that would bore you. In your room there's a present waiting for you; a new plaything. Why don't you go along and see what it is, and I'll bring Kyre back to you later."

Conflicting desires made Gamora hesitate. She wanted to stay, but . . . "A present?" she asked uncertainly. "For me?"

"Waiting for you in your room. Go and see."

"Yes . . ." Curiosity overcame all other considerations. "Yes, I will." Gamora smiled shyly at Kyre, then left the table and ran toward the door. Halfway across the hall she remembered her dignity and slowed to a careful walk, pausing once to look back over her shoulder and wave. Just for a moment he saw again that utter blankness in her look: then the shell door closed behind her and he was alone with Calthar.

And far away, in Haven, a sixth sense brought to his mind the sound of Simorh screaming . . .

Chapter 13

CALTHAR SMILED, STRETCHING OUT HER LONG LEGS AS SHE reclined in the chair next to Kyre. "As I said a few moments ago, you've done me a great service, Sun-Hound."

Kyre watched her, fascinated by her easy grace yet too wary to unbend. "My service was to Gamora," he replied shortly.

She shrugged a concession. "From your point of view, yes; I won't argue with that. But there's someone else here to whom your presence is equally important. And what matters to her, matters to me." She sat up abruptly. To all intents and purposes, Kyre, I alone rule in the citadel. But everything I do, everything I decree, every move I make, is for the sole sake of Talliann."

Black hair and a deadly white face; the shingle strand and the cold stare of the Hag; a girl he knew, and yet did not recognize . . . The image passed fleetingly through his mind and the shock of it must have shown on his face, for Calthar laughed softly.

"Yes: it was Talliann you saw on the bar near the
ruined temple."

She saw immediately that the gamble she had taken
was paying off. She knew the power Talliann possessed,
however innocently or erratically it might be wielded;
her one doubt had been as to whether the girl's influence
could snare Haven's champion as easily as it had snared
her own people. Now, the doubt was assuaged.

She coiled about into a new posture on the chair,
enjoying his inability to stop staring at her. "Talliann
wants to see you again, Kyre, and my first desire is to
please her. That's why you come to us as a guest—"

"Guest?" The blatant contradiction snapped Kyre out
of his trance, and the spell of Calthar's fascination broke
a he interrupted her angrily. "I hardly think so! Your
emissary made it clear that Gamora's safety depends on
my compliance—and that message was uncivilly stressed
by another of your minions when I was hauled out of the
sea. Is that your idea of how a benevolent host should
behave?"

"What other device would have persuaded you here of
your own free will? Kyre, the little princess is in no
danger: she never has been. I used her to lure you here,
but believe me, that is the full extent of my crime!"

She was lying. The emptiness behind Gamora's bright
eyes had told him the real truth. And yet, despite what he
knew, Kyre's interest was aroused beyond his ability to
stem it. Betraying nothing of his inner turmoil in his
voice, he asked, "Why should I be important to
Talliann?"

Calthar made a display of hesitating before she
replied: "Because I believe you may be able to help
her."

"Lady," he said carefully, "I came here from Haven,

the city of your enemies. I'm no friend to you, nor to your Talliann. I owe you nothing; I have nothing that you can possibly want. Why should I be able—even if I were willing—to help either of you?"

It was the reaction Calthar had expected: she hid her amusement and leaned toward him. He didn't back away—that pleased her—but when she laid a long-nailed hand on his arm she felt the skin beneath her fingers flinch involuntarily.

"Are we your enemies?" she asked, quite gently. "Since your arrival here you've met with no violence, no unkindness, no threat: nothing that suggests hatred." She saw reluctant confirmation in his face, and continued, "You may be from Haven, Kyre, but you're not of Haven; that much I know from Gamora. You owe loyalty only to those who have proved themselves your friends. And by bringing you to our citadel, I'm backing my belief that you're wise enough to acknowledge that."

He couldn't deny that her argument was valid. He'd heard only Haven's side of the conflict between the two cities; he knew nothing of the rights and wrongs surrounding the grievances that had begun the unending war. Haven had done him few favors so far: and then there was Talliann. He savored the name. It was familiar, strangely familiar. *Talliann* . . .

Calthar saw the seeds of uncertainty in his mind and felt the inner pleasure of vindication. She said, softly and with a hint of apparent reluctance: "I'm also gambling on my instinct that you were—shall we say, not entirely unaffected by your first meeting with Talliann, and that her well-being might be of some interest to you."

Her eyes, in the hall's peculiar light, seemed to have caught fire, and Kyre felt something contract and constrict within him. Calthar had struck to the heart of

his greatest weakness. That first encounter, brief though
it had been, haunted him: he could still recall every detail
of the shock of recognition, of realizing that he knew her.
Somehow, Talliann held a key to his lost identity—and
now he had the chance to see her again. Despite his fears
for Gamora, despite the danger they might both be in, he
couldn't turn his back on that chance.

His pulse had quickened and there was a suffocating
sensation in his throat. He said: "You say I might help
her. But why should she need my help?"

Calthar sighed, and looked down at her own bare feet.
"Because, Kyre, Talliann is afflicted."

"Afflicted . . . ?"

"It's not a word I like using, but I can think of nothing
better," Calthar continued. "She is . . . childlike.
Given to moods and whims that no one else can fathom;
moved to joy or grief or fury by random emotions that
even I can't begin to divine." She pursed her mouth
painfully. "At times she's lucid enough, but more often
than not her mind is like a whirlpool that she can't
control. For her own safety she has to be constantly
attended and watched lest she unwittingly do some
mischief to herself. She has no worldliness, and not the
smallest sense of personal danger."

"Are you saying she's mad?"

The sorceress shook her head emphatically. "No.
Flawed, perhaps; but not mad." She looked up again and
met his eyes with apparent candor. "Talliann is like a
daughter to me. Her well-being and her happiness matter
more to all of us than any other consideration." *And that*,
she thought with private amusement, *is no less than the
truth!* "I admit to you, Kyre, that I don't understand her
reasons for wanting you here. But you have had a very
profound effect on her; when she speaks of you she

speaks more coherently than at any other time; and that gives me hope." Her voice took on an angry edge as she added, "Do you really think I would allow Haven's prized champion free run of my citadel without a vital reason?"

That challenge forced a new twist on Kyre's perspectives. He couldn't trust her, *dared* not trust her; yet what she said had a seductive kind of logic. And the fascination, the chilling lure that Talliann held for him weakened his resolve still further.

His face, as he struggled to reconcile conflicting thoughts, was an open book to Calthar. She moved closer to him, until they were mere inches apart.

"I won't try to influence you against your will, Kyre," she said softly. "You can leave the citadel now and go back to Haven, if that's what you want: no one here will prevent you. But what have you to lose by one meeting with Talliann?"

She knew she was taking a risk; if he was contrary enough to call her bluff, then her plans would need rapid alteration. But her judgment was almost sure, and it proved so again. Kyre had no grounds for arguing with her. And he *wanted* to see the girl.

"Very well. If it'll please Talliann, I'll agree to it." He managed a faint, wry smile. "As you say, what have I to lose?"

To Kyre's inexpressible relief, the way to Talliann's sanctum didn't involve a second crossing of the dizzying bridge over the abyss. It was a short and simple route, the only anomaly being the utter absence of any other soul to see them go by. No curious faces gazing from doorways, no passersby pausing to point and whisper to each other, no ingenuously gaping children drawn

quickly out of his reach by anxious parents. Word of a
stranger's presence in the citadel must be widely abroad
by now, but no one came near them.

They climbed stairs, Calthar moving with such an easy
agility that he was hard-pressed to keep up with her, and
finally the stairs ended before yet another shell door. As
it swung open, Kyre felt as though his stomach had
inverted itself within him. The sickness of doubt, of
fear—but most of all, of a ravening anticipation. Cool,
blue light poured out from beyond the door, and shapes
moved within it like phantoms, coming toward them. He
saw the shimmer of wide green eyes, the outlines of
young bodies, filmy shifts, pale, flowing hair: then the
four girls who guarded Talliann's sanctum moved aside
like a tide ebbing, bowing before Calthar. Kyre couldn't
be sure whether or not he had imagined the flicker of
stark terror in their eyes before they lowered their gazes
and fled.

The cavern beyond the door was like something from a
bizarre dream. Around the curving walls, abalone reflected an incredible montage of images, distorting color
and perspective. Stalactites speared down from the roof
and were multiplied a hundredfold by the mirrored
surfaces. Disoriented, Kyre let Calthar take hold of his
hand and lead him deeper into the incredible maze: then,
at the back of the cavern, something moved independent-
ly of the reflections.

She stood halfway up a short flight of uneven steps
where the floor rose steeply at the back of the cavern.
Black hair, hollow eyes, a faint sound like a child's first,
shivering breath—

She saw them, and came down the steps so fast that
she almost lost her footing and fell. Her body was young
and lithe, and modest in a gray shift that fell to her

ankles. For the first time Kyre was able to look long and clearly at her, and he felt something within him constrict as the shock of recognition renewed itself. The small, fragile face, the unclipped black hair falling like ragged silk about her shoulders, the wide, deep eyes, dark as her hair was . . . She wasn't truly beautiful—Simorh unencumbered by bitterness and illness would have been far lovelier—yet she was more familiar to Kyre than anyone or anything he had encountered since he had been brought to this world.

But Talliann ignored him. Instead, she stopped five paces from Calthar, her slight frame shaking with anger. *"Where have you been?"* Talliann's voice was shrill and she wrung her hands together as though violently washing them. "You *told* me, you *promised* me; you—" And she stopped as, with a silent gesture, Calthar indicated the man at her side.

Talliann swung round, and focused on Kyre for the first time. Her eyes were like twin lunar eclipses, vast black pupils surrounded by a glittering silver corona. For a terrible moment Kyre felt as though they were sucking out his soul: then the girl's lips parted to reveal sharp, even teeth as her breath caught in her throat.

"You've come back . . ." She whispered the words as if they were some dreadful, secret talisman, and as she continued to stare at him she began to shiver feverishly. Then she put a hand to her mouth, biting at her knuckles; and Kyre was shocked to see bright blood trickle down her wrist—

"Talliann!" Calthar spoke sharply, as if reprimanding a disobedient child, then when Talliann paid no heed the sorceress swore volubly. One long-nailed hand snaked out and pulled Talliann's arm forcibly away from her mouth. "Stop that!" She glanced quickly at Kyre, and her voice changed. "See your guest, sweeting. He came, as you wanted him to."

Talliann's mouth puckered. She looked uneasily from Calthar to Kyre, back to Calthar again, and whispered: "Thank you . . ."

There was an uncomfortable silence. Then Calthar said: "Well?"

Talliann looked at her blankly.

"You wanted to see him, child. He's here. "Impatience tinged Calthar's voice. "Don't you have anything else to say?"

Talliann's eyes took their fill of Kyre again, until he had to look away from her hollow stare. She wiped her bloodied hand thoughtlessly on her shift. "No," she said flatly.

Calthar sighed as the girl turned her head away. "I feared something like this might happen," she said softly. "Best leave her."

"No—" The protest was involuntary, and had little to do with the sorceress's admonition. In a single moment Talliann had taken Kyre's soul and then rejected him, and the sense of loss was almost beyond bearing.

"Yes, Kyre." Calthar drew him back, toward the door. "You can do nothing for her at this moment. Leave her, and in a while she'll recover." She glanced at the girl, who hadn't moved a muscle but stood rigid, the picture of mute stubbornness. "She knew of your arrival, but the shock of seeing you . . ." She shrugged, leaving the sentence unfinished.

He could only acquiesce. Calthar led him toward the door, and as they reached it he hesitated, looking back. Talliann had turned her head, and was staring over her shoulder at him. Her blank expression had vanished, replaced by a fearful and painfully intelligent urgency, and she mouthed something that Calthar couldn't see. Kyre frowned, not comprehending, and might have spoken; but she shook her head frantically, a plea for secrecy and silence, and hastily turned away.

Calthar hadn't noticed the swift exchange. As she stood back to usher Kyre through the door, she glanced briefly over her shoulder. Talliann was standing with her back to them, head bowed, immobile. Calthar smiled faintly, and left the chamber.

As always when Calthar stalked the citadel's corridors, no one impeded her progress. Young and old alike studiously avoided crossing her path, withdrawing into doorways or side streets, moving back to the edges of the wider public areas as she passed by. Voices were lowered to whispers at her approach and faces were averted: no one wanted to catch her eye for fear of also attracting her volatile and unpredictable temper.

But for once they needn't have worried, for Calthar was lost in thought. She had seen Kyre escorted from Talliann's chambers to the unused stateroom that she had ordered prepared for him; the room had housed a retired but still respected military adviser until old age had recently sent him to his final rest, and the former dwelling of a high-ranker was ideal for an apparently honored guest.

Calthar intended to maintain that particular charade for the time being, despite the grumblings of Hodek and some of the other senior councillors. Haven's new pet had aroused her curiosity, for Gamora's picture of him had been far from accurate. Whatever else he might be, Kyre was not a sorcerously created shell. Had he been so, Calthar would have recognized the signs immediately; but this man had a will, a personality, a self-

motivation that no cipher could ever possess. That led
her to draw two possible conclusions: that the information Gamora had given her was wrong—which she
wasn't inclined to believe—or that Kyre wasn't what his
professed creaters had expected.

So, then, if this new Sun-Hound wasn't a cipher of the
original, what was he? A number of possibilities had
occurred to Calthar, but none of them satisfied her. She
wanted—*needed*—to learn more. And she suspected that
Talliann might hold the clue.

Calthar hadn't been deceived by the girl's behavior at
the fiasco of a meeting; but Talliann's motive in behaving
as she had done was another matter. Her fascination with
Haven's pet bordered on obsession—Calthar had never
known her to react in such a way to anything before, and
the possible implications intrigued her. Since the moment of her arrival in the citadel Talliann had been
flawed, and even the power of the Mothers hadn't been
able to unravel the mystery of her strangeness. Hers was
the one soul in the citadel that Calthar couldn't read
easily, and yet within Talliann resided a power on which
the sorceress had come to depend. As a medium, the girl
was unsurpassed; but though Calthar could influence
her—by terror if by no other means—and channel power
through her to her own ends, she needed Talliann's
cooperation if such sorcery was to achieve its full
potential. Usually her cooperation was simple enough to
secure, but occasionally something in Talliann rebelled,
and she would make some demand, something irrational,
incomprehensible, which must be fulfilled before she
would be compliant again. That particular trait lay at the
root of Calthar's contradictory feelings toward the girl:
on the one hand Talliann was a prize, a jewel, to be
cherished and protected; on the other, the sorceress

violently resented her, envying the fundamental hold that she exercised, however unwittingly, over all around her. Without Talliann to impede her, Calthar could fulfill her own ambitions to rule unchallenged. Yet those same ambitions relied on Talliann's innate powers. There were other means, other methods, but they were more perilous; and to destroy Talliann, as in dark moments Calthar yearned to do, would be to destroy one of the roots of her own strength.

But now Haven's new champion had come into the picture and had touched something deep within Talliann: so much so that the girl's well-being and sanity seemed to depend on his presence in the citadel. That was what intrigued Calthar most of all. There was no logic, even by Talliann's bizarre standards, in her sudden preoccupation, and the sorceress could only surmise that she had sensed something within Kyre that had so far eluded her own judgment. Trying to wring that information from Talliann would be a fruitless exercise, as what she didn't know she couldn't tell; she'd do better, Calthar thought, to make Kyre her target. His wouldn't be an easy mind to manipulate, but in Talliann and Gamora she had in her possession two invaluable weapons. With care, and a modicum of manipulation at the right moment, she might create for herself an advantage that would ensure her enemies' final downfall. And she had waited a long, long time for that.

Talliann had been waiting, tense with impatience, when Akrivir cautiously opened the door of her sanctum. He had hardly been able to believe the nature of the message that had reached him via one of her servant girls, suspecting that either Calthar or his father might be playing some joke at his expense. But Calthar didn't indulge in petty games, and even Hodek was unlikely to trouble himself with such a small spite. No: Akrivir believed that the summons must be genuine—and one look at Talliann's pale face as he entered the cavern had confirmed it.

But when he heard what it was she wanted of him, the stirrings of faint hope which had moved within him died. Her plea was simple. And he didn't want to do it.

She stood before him now, close enough for him to have reached out and taken hold of her hands, though he made no attempt to do so. He was staring at the floor, not wanting to see what was in his eyes, and he felt as though invisible fingers had taken hold of the muscles in his chest and were squeezing them. To do what Talliann asked of him would be to admit finally to what he had always subconsciously known: that she was not, and could never be, for him.

She was waiting for an answer, and bleakly Akrivir realized that he couldn't refuse her. Whatever the outcome, whatever blow it might deal to his own dreams, he cared enough for Talliann to help her in any way he could.

She said, her voice desperate, "I *have* to see him, Akriver. I *must* speak with him alone, without Calthar knowing." She turned away. "You're the only one I can trust." A pause. "I'm sorry."

So she understood. He hadn't realized it, and the knowledge was both a comfort and a bitter irony. He couldn't let her down: she was prepared to put her trust in him, knowing the risk she ran, and if he could do no more, he could at least justify her faith in him.

He stepped forward and, knowing that she'd forgive his presumption, laid his hands lightly on her shoulders. "I'll bring him, Talliann," he said gently. "And I'll make sure that no one knows of it."

She swung round to face him again, her dark eyes wide with gratitude—and, he thought, with sympathy. "I don't know what to say. Thank you, Akrivir." Her hands came to rest on his arms. "You're a true friend."

He smiled wryly. "I hope I always will be."

The quarters that had been assigned to him were, Kyre was forced to admit, rooms fit for an honored guest. No comfort had been spared; he had a huge bed liberally draped with woven covers, a table and chair made of what looked like coral and inlaid with abalone, floor coverings that were warm to his bare feet, tapestries on the walls, even a small fount of sweet water playing into a pearl-lined pool, though how the sea dwellers could obtain fresh water in this vast undersea fortress he couldn't imagine. He wanted for nothing . . . save the answers to some very disturbing questions.

The last look Talliann had given him, and her failed attempt to convey a message, flickered knifelike in his brain. On the strand, when he had first set eyes on her, a thread of his uncharted memory had been twisted violently to the surface, and this second confrontation had painfully and unnervingly confirmed it. Now he knew that Talliann in her turn had recognized him, but she had been anxious not to reveal that fact to Calthar. That didn't fit with the image of Talliann's protector, friend, and mentor that Calthar claimed for herself; but it *did* fit, all too well, with Kyre's instinctive mistrust of the sorceress and her motives.

He wanted to see Talliann again—it was more than a desire; it was an aching need inside him. But he was also aware of the value of caution: and one barrier was the presence of Gamora.

Kyre glanced sidelong at the little girl, who sat beside

him happily devouring the remains of a tray of food. It
seemed that she had only to ask for something and it was
done: her wish to see Kyre's quarters and then share the
meal prepared for him had been granted instantly, and
when she had expressed dissatisfaction with his clothes,
which, though dried out, were stained and stiffened with
seawater, new garments had been brought for him
immediately, made from a cool, thin silver-blue fabric,
and Gamora had triumphantly placed one of the narrow
twisted-shell circlets favored by many of the male
seafolk on his head, declaring that now he looked as fine
as she did. It was an exaggeration: for Calthar had spared
nothing in fulfilling her promise to make Gamora every
inch a princess. She wore a sea-green and silver gown in
the elaborate style of citadel noblewomen, and a filigree
of silver threads had been twisted cunningly through her
hair so that her bobbing curls glittered when she moved.
Even her own father and mother in Haven would never
have dreamed of granting her such luxuries; they would
have been no more than an unfulfilled dream in the
child's mind.

But Kyre knew Gamora well enough to realize that the
lure of such trappings, however desirable they might be,
could never undo the conditioning that had taught her to
hate the sea dwellers with as much passion as anyone
else in Haven. Her own father, whom she loved, had
been crippled by them; though she was a baby in her
cradle at the time, she had been brought up with the story
of the Dead Night battle that had buried half of the city,
and its inhabitants with it, beneath the sand of the bay.
Kyre himself had been shocked by the eager light in her
eyes when she heard of DiMag's slaying of the captured
sea warrior. No: it would take far more than a green and
silver gown and the shimmer of abalone to make Gamora
forget her own heritage.

Yet now, in Gamora's eyes, Calthar could do no wrong: and that gave Kyre a chilling insight into the strength of the bewitchment the sorceress had cast over the little girl.

He could imagine how easy a target a child like Gamora must have been for Calthar's spellbinding. For a while, as he talked with the sorceress in the great hall, he too had come close to succumbing to the allure of this strangely beautiful place and its fey-looking inhabitants, and he could understand the effect it must have had on the mind of a lonely, imaginative child. Haven by comparison was an ironically named travesty, at least on the surface; he had seen nothing of beauty within those crumbling walls, or in the minds of its people. Simorh, vicious and embittered; DiMag with his warped and unpredictable moods; Vaoran, ambitious, untrustworthy; even old Brigrandon, who preferred the relief of a drunken stupor to the demands of cold reality . . . the contrast with what he had seen in the sea citadel was acute—

And invidious. A man dying of thirst in a desert might sell his soul for the chance to find an oasis. But all too often, the oasis proved to be nothing more than a mirage.

"Don't you think so, Kyre? Don't you?"

Gamora's voice at his elbow broke the web of his concentration. He looked down to find that she had finished the last of the food and was watching him eagerly.

His train of thought fled. "I'm sorry, Princess. What did you say?"

She pouted. "People *never* listen to me. Except for Calthar: she does. I *said*, don't you think the great hall here is so much nicer than at home?"

He forced himself to smile at her. "It's very beautiful, yes."

"All those fountains, and the windows that aren't really windows at all but quartz. And the tapestries aren't faded the way all of ours are." She swallowed a last morsel that she'd been chewing and rolled her eyes appreciatively at the taste. "When I grow up, I'll have fountains like those."

Kyre couldn't bring himself to meet her gaze and see again the emptiness behind the look in her eyes. This hiatus had to be broken—but he was no sorceror; he could do nothing against Calthar's skills. There must be another way . . .

He was about to make some inconsequential reply to Gamora's last remark when a sound alerted him, and he turned quickly to see the door swinging open. Expecting a servant, he froze when, instead, he saw Akrivir on the threshold.

"Sun-Hound." Akrivir nodded to him, and forced a quick smile for Gamora, who was watching him with interest. His eyes, as he looked at the little girl, were wary.

"Come in." Kyre rose, wondering what could have brought the young warrior to his room. "Join us."

"Thank you, but I—haven't the time." Akrivir darted another look toward Gamora, and suddenly Kyre realized what he was trying, silently, to convey. He took a step forward. "You wanted to speak to me?"

"Yes. I won't detain you for more than a few moments."

Gamora had already begun to lose interest in the exchange, and Kyre walked to the door. Akrivir caught his arm, drawing him outside, and pulled the door to behind them so that they were hidden from the child's view. He glanced swiftly in both directions, then said without preamble: "I bring a message from Talliann. She

wants to see you, and it's vital that Calthar shouldn't
know of it."

Kyre's pulse quickened. "When?"

"As soon as possible." Akrivir hesitated, and Kyre
saw an odd mixture of resentment and fellow feeling in
his blue eyes. "I'll take you to her myself: but there's a
problem." He nodded back toward the room. "The
child."

"She isn't—" Kyre began, but Akrivir cut him short,
gripping his sleeve.

"You know as well as I do what Calthar's done to
her!" Undisguised hatred flared in his voice momentarily
before he got himself under control again. "She can't be
trusted. The Hag alone knows it isn't her fault, but if she
knows anything she may betray you." He bit his lower
lip. "I'll do anything to help Talliann, but I don't want to
die doing it!"

Kyre realized abruptly what lay behind Akrivir's blend
of friendship and hostility toward him, and suddenly he
felt shamed. Akrivir must be a true friend indeed if he
was prepared to sacrifice his own hopes for Talliann's
sake—and it meant that he was the one inhabitant of this
citadel whom Kyre could trust without reservation.

He eased the door open a crack and looked into the
room. Gamora's small head was drooping over the table;
as he watched, she yawned widely, seemingly hardly
aware of what she did, and slumped further forward.

"She's falling asleep," he said quietly, then looked at
the other man again. "If I put her to bed, she won't wake
for some hours. I can come with you now."

Akrivir didn't meet his gaze for a few moments, and
when he did his eyes were intense. "Very well. But on
one condition."

"Name it."

"I want your promise that you'll do nothing that could harm or endanger Talliann in any way." He paused. "For I tell you now, Sun-Hound; if you hurt her, I'll kill you." He smiled, jerkily and without humor. "That's my promise."

Kyre said: "I'd never harm Talliann, Akrivir. And I think you know it, or you wouldn't be here now."

Akrivir continued to stare at him for a while. Then he nodded, acknowledging the tacit understanding between them.

"I should hate you, Kyre," he said. "But if you can help Talliann, there'll be no enmity between us." And with that he turned away. "I'll wait for you at the end of the passage."

Kyre returned to his room feeling tense with excitement. Gamora was by now asleep; the sound sleep of a happily exhausted child; and she didn't stir as he lifted her from her chair and carried her to his own bed. Laying her down, he covered her with a blanket and stood for a moment gazing down at her with sad affection. Then—he couldn't name the emotion that moved him, but had to make the gesture, however small—he bent down and kissed her forehead.

"Sleep well, little princess." His voice was a whisper. "I'll open your eyes, and restore all that's been lost to you. I swear it."

Akrivir led Kyre on a complex and clearly little-used route to Talliann's sanctum, and in the distance he could hear the murmuring sounds of the citadel's great warren about its business. Since his arrival here he had lost all sense of time; without the strictures of night and day to contain it, it seemed that the sea dwellers' stronghold never rested, and it could have been noon or deep night in the world outside for all the difference it made.

At first they hastened along in silence. Akrivir was constantly alert for any sign of movement ahead or behind, and Kyre felt it prudent to say nothing. But there was one unanswered question which wouldn't let him alone, and at last he had to ask it.

"Akrivir—why are you doing this?"

The young man looked back over his shoulder, surprised, and slowed his pace. "For Talliann," he said shortly. "Because she wants it—and because I think you may be able to help her where I've failed."

Kyre stopped, suddenly suspicious: he'd heard almost those exact words before. "That's what Calthar told me," he said. "And she—"

Akrivir interrupted him with a laugh, a short, sharp bark that conveyed cynical disgust. "Oh yes: I'm sure she did!" He stepped closer to Kyre, gripping his upper arm. "If you take anything that Calthar says at face value, then you're running your head into a noose!"

Pure loathing burned in his eyes, and Kyre said, "Do you hate her so much?"

"*Hate* her?" Akrivir echoed. He hunched his shoulders, staring at Kyre and apparently weighing the risks of revealing what he wanted to say. "If I could kill her, Kyre, if I could eradicate her filthy corruption from this citadel, I wouldn't hesitate for one instant!" He turned, started to walk on but more slowly. "She isn't the only cancer that I want to cut from our city; but she's the most malignant." Furious emotion made his voice shake. "I wouldn't care about what she's done to me; I can live with that if I must. But Talliann . . ."

"What about Talliann?"

"Don't be a fool!" Akrivir said ferociously. "You've seen it for yourself! Talliann's a prisoner—Calthar keeps her that way because it suits her machinations, and any

tales she spins you about Talliann being like a daughter to
her are lies. Calthar uses her, just as she's using your
little princess, and trying to use you. She's far more
dangerous then you know, Sun-Hound. And there's not a
living soul in this citadel who dares speak against her."

Slowly, the pieces of the jigsaw were beginning to fit
together . . . More quietly, Kyre asked, "And what of
you, Akrivir? What has she done to you?"

He made a dismissive gesture. "It's an old tale now,
and it doesn't bear repeating. Besides, it's no longer
relevant: it's Talliann who matters." Abruptly he stopped
walking and turned to Kyre again. His blue eyes were
blazing, and Kyre saw fear, hope, and bitter, impotent
anger in his look.

Akrivir said: "Get her away from the citadel, Kyre.
Get her away from Calthar's influence, before she's
destroyed by it. It's her only hope. It's the only hope for
us all!" And he swung round and strode on.

Kyre hastened after him, but the words that came to
his tongue died unspoken. He realized that to make such
a plea had cost Akrivir dearly: but the young warrior's
outburst had confirmed his own suspicions beyond all
doubt. Talliann, Gamora, himself—all victims of Calthar's scheming.

But why? he asked himself. *What did the sorceress
mean to gain from them?*

They were climbing a flight of stairs, and he realized
that Talliann's door lay directly ahead of them. He *had* to
know more—

"Akrivir." He caught his companion's arm, halting
him, and spoke in an urgent whisper. "What does
Calthar plan to do?"

Akrivir looked back. "Ask Talliann about the Great
Conjunction," he said flatly. "And if you can, believe

me when I tell you that I'd kill Calthar to stop it if I could." He took the last few steps two at a time, and laid his hand on the shell door. "Go to her, Kyre. Talk to her. Help her." Their eyes met briefly, then Akrivir looked away. "I'll be waiting."

Cool, blue light washed over Kyre as he stepped through Talliann's door. The mirrorlike walls of the cavern played tricks on his eyes; as he moved, strange reflections skipped among the stalactites and he tensed, anticipating a challenge. None came . . . and then he realized that one of the reflections wasn't a reflection at all.

She moved quickly toward him, eyes widening with eager recognition—then stopped, like a frightened animal surprised far from the safety of its nest. Her voice was fearful.

"Akrivir brought you?"

"Yes." Kyre gazed at her as unfamiliar emotions moved within him.

She nodded. "Did anyone see you? Are you sure you weren't followed?"

"As sure as I can be." He closed the door behind him, feeling his pulse quicken anew.

For a moment Talliann seemed to be struggling to find words, then abruptly she said: "He was the only one I could trust, and I was so afraid of Calthar finding out . . . Kyre, I have to talk to you."

He took her hands, wanting to reassure her: she was wary of him, and acutely aware of the risk she was taking in trusting him. He wished he could find a way to tell her that he shared her fears.

"We may have very little time," she said. "Calthar never sleeps: she may come here at any time." She glanced again toward the door. "Often I can sense when she's near, but not always."

"There's so much I want to ask you," Kyre told her. "Since I saw you on the strand by the ruined temple, I've—"

"I know. I felt it too." Her hungry gaze searched his face. "I know you, Kyre. I don't know who you are, but I know you. And my dreams—"

"Dreams?" Something clutched at his nerve ends.

She nodded. "I've had those dreams for as long as I can remember. They're like . . ."—she hesitated— "like an omen, a portent. Something I must tell you, and something I must do." She looked at him again, her gaze painfully candid. "I forgot so much, Kyre, and my mind is often confused—but I always remember those dreams. *Always.*"

Her fingers clenched in his grasp. He said nothing, sensing that there was more she wanted to impart and that she needed to take her own time. But his stomach was churning with excitement.

"I've often slipped away from the citadel, and gone to the bay where the ruin is," she said at last, the words coming more hurriedly now. "I've seen the town lights glowing through the fog, and I've wanted so much to go there, but I couldn't. *Dared* not. Yet I knew that was where I'd find you, Kyre. And I so much needed to tell you . . ." She shook her head, bereft of further explanation, and he prompted gently, "Tell me what?"

"What the dreams have warned me I must tell you. About Calthar. About what she means to do, what she *will* do, unless . . ." She stopped again, drew a painful, gasping breath, then calmed herself with an effort.

"You must leave here, Kyre," she said urgently. "You must return to Haven, and warn them, and help them." She bit her lip. "In five nights from now, the Great Conjunction will occur. Do you know what that means?"

She echoed what Akrivir had said, what he had told Kyre to ask her: and he remembered the Dead Night of which DiMag had spoken with such bitter loathing. "It's the night when the moon throws a path of light direct to Haven's portal. There'll be a battle—"

"No," Talliann said quickly. "Not *a* battle. *The* battle: the final confrontation. That's what Calthar means it to be. She says Haven is so weakened, so racked with internal conflict, that it can't hope to stand against the power of the Hag." Her teeth clenched, as though the next words were painful to her. "Calthar will send that power against Haven on the night of the Conjunction. And I shall be the medium through which she wields it."

"You?" Kyre was stunned.

"Yes." Talliann's gaze was hollow. "Don't you understand? Calthar has told you that I'm—afflicted, she calls it. But this thing, this force, that sometimes possesses me—it isn't madness. It's the Hag. And it's Calthar's doing. I'm her puppet; I've been her puppet since I came to the citadel. She binds me by the power of the Hag, and she used me to bring that power to manifestation. I'm the key to her strength."

Kyre stared at her as Akrivir's cryptic words suddenly and shockingly made sense. A prisoner, an unwilling victim of Calthar's machinations—now he understood Akrivir's bitterness, and the young warrior's urgent plea for him to get Talliann out of the citadel. He put his arms around the girl, wanting to comfort her and soothe the distress that her words had aroused. She pressed herself closely against him, her body rigid with tension, fighting against tears.

"I don't want it to happen," she said desperately. Her voice was muffled by emotion, and he felt her fists clench against his chest. "I want to stop it, but I can't; my will

isn't strong enough. But you . . ." She shuddered, then
looked up at him. "You can stand against Calthar. That's
what the dreams have been telling me. You must go back
to Haven, and you must help them!"

Again he remembered what Akrivir had said, and in
that moment he knew that no power in the world would
persuade him to flee the citadel without her. He started to
speak, but before he could express what was in his mind
Talliann said: "There's one more thing I must do. The
dreams told me of it, and I've been waiting all this time
until you came to me . . ." Freeing herself from his
grasp, she stepped back and fumbled with something at
her throat; he glimpsed an elusive shimmer of silver
under her groping fingers, then heard the small, thin
sound of tiny metal links snapping. The girl expelled a
long breath, as though she had been relieved of an
onerous burden, and held out to him the pendant that she
had taken from around her neck.

"Take it," she said, and there was a tremor in her
voice. "It's yours by right—the dreams told me so."

He stared down at the necklace in her palm. Threaded
on the broken silver chain was a piece of ice-blue quartz
shaped like a droplet of water. A glimmer of recognition
flicked through his mind, startling him: he looked closer,
and saw, embedded in the crystal structure, the unmistakable image of a shimmering, open eye. The Eye of Day,
by which the people of Haven swore . . . the symbol
of the Sun-Hound!

He looked at Talliann, his eyes wide and his voice
unsteady with disquiet. "How did you come by this?"

"Calthar gave it to me. When I first came to the
citadel."

The disquiet blossomed into a terrible foreboding.
"When you first came . . . ?" Kyre's throat was

suddenly very dry. "But I thought you were born in this place."

She laughed, the sound shocking him with its mixture of bitterness and irony. "No. Didn't Calthar tell you that much? I wasn't *born*, Kyre. I was *summoned. She summoned me.* I know nothing of myself before the moment when I opened my eyes to find myself lying in a great shell, with her looking down at me." She clenched her teeth and shivered. "I don't know how long I've been here, or where I was before, or even who I really am . . . if I have an identity at all I know nothing . . . save for my dreams. Kyre, does that mean I'm mad?"

She could have been telling him his own story . . . and something moved deep within him, lost memory stirring again. "No," Kyre said emphatically. "You're not mad, Talliann. *"Far, far from it . . . yet the recollection wouldn't come; he couldn't unlock the door—*

She fingered the pendant again. "I've always worn this, for as long as I can remember. Yet whatever Calthar says, I know it isn't truly mine. It's yours, Kyre. *Yours.* And you must take it. That's what my dreams have been trying to tell me."

She was shivering with confusion and distress, and as her grip became unsure the pendant began to slide through the lattice of her fingers. Reflexively Kyre caught at the chain, supporting the quartz in his palm—

The shock of the contact made him shout aloud and drop the pendant. It fell to the floor, and they both stared at it. Then Talliann put a clenched fist to her mouth and whispered: *"Please . . ."*

He didn't want to pick it up. For an instant, as the quartz touched him, he'd had a revelation that had struck

him like lightning from an empty sky. Now it was gone,
spinning away back into the locked rooms of his mind.
But though he'd lost it, the memory of its presence still
reverberated in his head: he knew that if he should touch
the quartz again, the revelation would return.

And that thought terrified him.

Then a voice inside him said: *Coward! This is what
you've been looking for, yearning for, since the moment
when you woke in the ruined temple and knew you
weren't Simorh's cipher! You have the chance you've
craved to learn the truth at last—are you going to balk
now?*

Talliann was watching him. Her eyes glittered unnaturally brightly, and he felt the depth of her longing,
her hope. He couldn't betray her trust.

Kyre stooped, his hand hovering over the pendant. For
a moment, terror overcame him like sick, toppling
vertigo: he fought it back, knowing that he had to do this,
that there was no other way for him.

His hand closed over the quartz.

And in his head, the world exploded.

Chapter 14

TALLIANN!

Her name was a litany in Kyre's mind, and it brought with it the centuries-old pain of love and loss, of agony, of longing. Long days under the sun of Haven; cold nights when the heady perfume of the palace gardens drifted up like strong wine to their open window. Haven had been whole then, her streets and squares sprawling cheerfully out over the bay, her markets thronged, her harbor alive with industry as the fishing fleet which was her living, beating heart scudded in on the friendly tide. By day she was a peaceful golden refuge basking under the sun's eye: by night she was veiled and mysterious, glittering with a myriad tiny pinpoints of light while the old man gazed quietly down from her dark throne . . .

The past jarred suddenly with the present. The old man . . . the *benevolent* moon, not a maleficent object of loathing and fear, but a friend, a guide, a light in darkness. They had ruled, he and Talliann, under the beneficence of sun and moon together—until the greed and treachery of an enemy within the gates had shattered their idyll.

He remembered a name then, and with it a memory that woke bitter hatred. *Malhareq* . . . There had been fear, pain, and at last the long, black road through agony to death. Then centuries of nothingness, before an ancient ritual, in the hands of a desperate sorceress who meant only to conjure a creature in his image, had called him back from the void.

He *was* Kyre. No cipher, no surrogate: he was the Sun-Hound who had ruled Haven so long ago. The quartz pendant which he now clutched tightly in his hands had been his own talisman and a thing of great power; lost on the night his betrayor took his life on the sands of the bay, it had waited through the centuries for him to reclaim it, waited for the moment when the key locked within its crystal facets would at last turn the lock of his memory and release him from limbo.

Haven had forgotten so much! The realization went through him like a sword blade and he wanted to weep for his city, and for all that its inhabitants had lost. He knew, now, what he had known in those far-off days: that there should be no conflict between the worshippers of the sun and the worshippers of the moon; that they had been one, that the circle had been complete. Land and sea in equal measure had formed their domain; until the avarice of one woman, one sorceress, had betrayed them all.

Slowly, Kyre raised his head and looked up. He couldn't remember falling, but he was on his knees on the floor of Talliann's sanctum. She stood like a statue before him, her black eyes huge with awe, uncertainty, and fear, and he felt as if his heart were shattering as he

realized that, though she knew him in her dreams,
though she sensed and clung to the link between them,
she recalled nothing.

*Talliann, my beloved, don't you remember how we
were betrayed? Don't you remember Malhareq, whose
soul ached for power, the priestess who called down the
moon and turned her benevolence to evil? Remember her
face, Talliann. Don't you see her in the woman who uses
the Hag's power against you now, the woman who has
ensnared Gamora, the woman who means to destroy
those who were once our people? Don't you see that
long-dead sorceress come back to life in Calthar?*

"Talliann . . ." He spoke her name aloud, rising
unsteadily to his feet. As he approached her, the look in
her eyes changed and hope began to replace the confusion. In her damaged subconscious mind she knew that
he had undergone a revelation; she saw the change in
him—but she couldn't share it. Remembrance of her own
true self, of their past life together, was still beyond her.

Calthar must have used the pendant, the Sun-Hound's
talisman, to conjure Talliann here to the citadel. How the
talisman had fallen into her hands Kyre couldn't begin to
guess, but he believed that the sorceress must be unaware
of its origins. Her motive in summoning Talliann to the
world had been a mirror image of that which had driven
Simorh to summon him; and, like Simorh, Calthar didn't
yet know the true identity of her creation. If she were to
discover it—as she surely must before long—Talliann
would be in mortal danger.

He believed, too, that he now knew the nature of the
driving force behind Calthar's desire to destroy Haven.
So much had been lost with the dying of the old language
that Haven's history as DiMag and his scholars interpreted it had become grossly distorted. They had made a

legend of his life and the manner of his dying, and the
legend was false. They spoke of an age-old war, of the
vampire-priestess from the sea who had lured the Sun-
Hound to his death. But when he had lived and ruled in
Haven, there had been no war. There had been no sea
citadel. And the enemy who brought about his downfall
had been within his own gates.

He remembered Malhareq's face as though she were
standing before him: he had seen the echo of her warped
soul in the eyes of the sorceress who now ruled over the
citadel. And if Calthar should triumph, and Haven fell,
she would betray the people from the sea as surely as her
long-dead paradigm had once betrayed Kyre.

He had to return to Haven. His mind was moving like
a riptide, propelled by the shock of his reawakened
memory. There was still so much confusion, so much he
had to unravel: but his first and most urgent need was to
get Talliann and Gamora away from the citadel and
Calthar's malignant influence. DiMag and Simorh must
be told the truth, and warned of the imminence of Dead
Night. And Talliann . . .

He looked at her again, and the emptiness in her eyes
nearly shattered his heart. She must be healed, her
memory unlocked as his had been—and he had only one
hope. Once, Talliann had worn a talisman that was twin
to his own. The two stones had been symbols of Haven's
pride and prosperity. Singularly or in conjunction they
had great power; as this quartz he now held in his hand
had restored his lost self, so its twin would surely restore
Talliann.

If it could be found . . .

"Talliann." He took hold of her hands, saw her
surprise at his sudden urgency. "This pendant—it was
given to you by Calthar?"

"Yes."

"Has she another? Think, Talliann, please—is there another stone like this one?"

Her brow creased in unhappy confusion, and she shook her head. "No, I—I've never seen such a thing." The silver chain was tangled in their linked fingers; she stroked the quartz uncertainly. "She sets great store by this stone: she told me that I must wear it always. But she has no other."

Kyre shut his eyes in relief. *Then the talisman's twin was somewhere in Haven* . . .

He remembered Akrivir's warning and opened his eyes again. "Talliann," he said, "do you trust me?"

"Trust . . ." She searched his face, her look clouded, but only for a moment before she replied, "Yes. I trust you, Kyre."

"Then leave the citadel with me. There's not time to lose—we must go back to Haven, you, me, and Gamora. I can't explain it to you now; there isn't time." *And you wouldn't understand, my love; not yet* . . . "But in Haven you can be free of Calthar's influence. And we can stop what she means to do. I know we can!"

Talliann's eyes filled with terror. "No," she said. "I can't flee; I daren't try! If she finds us together and realizes what we're doing, she'll—she'll—" A shudder shook her body and Kyre asked urgently, "She'll what? What is it?"

She shook her head violently and made an inarticulate, ugly sound. "She'll take us to the Mothers."

"The Mothers?" Something unpleasant lurched in the pit of Kyre's stomach. The name signified nothing to him, and yet it triggered a warning.

"Don't ask me what that means," Talliann pleaded. "I can't explain . . . there are things in her inner sanc-

tum that shouldn't exist; things she can summon out
of . . ." She shuddered again. "I can't talk about it.
Kyre, I'm frightened!"

"Talliann, she won't know we've gone until it's too
late, Akrivir will help us, and once you're safe in Haven
she'll have no hold over you!" He squeezed her hands
more tightly. "You said that you trust me—trust me in
this!"

The quartz that lay between their palms seemed to
pulse suddenly hot under his skin. Talliann gave a little
cry of surprise, as though she had felt it too—and when
she looked at him again, there was a glimmer of dawning
understanding in her face.

She said, slowly, as if awed by the realization of her
own feelings, "I *want* to come with you. I'm afraid, but I
want to . . ."

"Then come. There's nothing to fear!"

She couldn't entirely shake off her doubt, but his
urgency and her desire were giving her confidence.
"Yes." She looked up at him with shaky determination.
"I'll come."

He wanted to kiss her; but the gesture would have been
incongruous. She wouldn't yet have understood his
reasons, and he couldn't afford the time to try to explain.
The urgency of their predicament was too pressing.

He said, "Akrivir is waiting outside. I think we can
trust him to help us."

She nodded. "He . . . loves me." A sad little smile
twisted her mouth. "More, I think, than he has ever
dared to show. He's been a true friend to me, and he
won't fail me now." She touched his arm lightly. "Call
him, Kyre."

Akrivir had maintained a discreet distance between
himself and the door, but at Kyre's soft call he came

quickly into the sanctum. As the two men looked at each other, Akrivir's narrowed: he sensed the change in Kyre even if he couldn't guess at its nature; and mingling with the wariness in his look was a new understanding—and a new respect.

Briefly, Kyre told him what they meant to do.

"Yes." Akrivir looked at Talliann for a few moments, his eyes pained. "It's for the best. She'll be safe with you; safe from Calthar." He frowned, as though touched by something he'd have preferred not to recall, then his expression cleared and he added briskly, "The sea cave is your only means of escape, but there are many ways to reach it. This place is riddled with old, forgotten passages. I'll guide you as far as the bridge, and Talliann knows the way from there."

"We must take Gamora with us," Kyre said.

Akrivir frowned. "She won't go willingly; not while she's still under Calthar's bewitchment."

"I know. But she'll still be sleeping—if we can get her away from the citadel before she wakes, she won't fight us." Then an alarming thought occurred to him—how to transport Gamora through the sea? He'd learned that he could breathe water as easily as air, and now he understood why; but the little princess was another matter.

"Talliann," he said urgently, "how was Gamora brought to the citadel?"

"In a shell." She realized what he was thinking. "There are several—like great clams, in which someone can lie and be drawn through the sea without water getting in." She hesitated. "Calthar has often used them, to—to bring victims from the land . . ."

Akrivir's expression said clearly that he understood her meaning, and Kyre pushed away thoughts of the fates those victims might have suffered. "Can we take her back to Haven in the same way?" he asked.

Talliann nodded emphatically. "I know how to seal the shells. And I know where they are kept."

"Then we must waste no more time." He looked at Akrivir. "Is it safe to leave now?"

"I'll check."

"Akrivir—" The young man looked back, and Kyre added, "What of you? If Calthar discovers that you've aided us, she'll kill you."

Akrivir smiled humorlessly. "She won't find out. I've learned ways of averting any suspicions Calthar might harbor about me." Hot determination showed in his eyes. "Just concern yourself with taking good care of Talliann." And he turned toward the door.

Abducting Gamora was unnervingly easy. Akrivir led Kyre and Talliann back through a maze of dark tunnels, and waited in the shadows while they slipped through the shell door to fetch the little girl.

The cavern was dimly lit; on the wide bed Gamora slept soundly. She didn't stir when Kyre wrapped her in a light blanket; and when he lifted her into his arms she simply sighed and put one thumb in her mouth before sinking back into her dreams.

Talliann peered at the sleeping child. *"If she wakes . . ."* she began in a whisper.

"Pray she doesn't." He tried to smile reassurance at her, but knew it was unconvincing: the real danger still lay ahead of them.

Outside, Akrivir pointed at an unlit side tunnel. He was clearly nervous, but tried not to convey it. "This is the safest way. Take care how you step; the floor isn't even."

They moved as quickly as the darkness and Kyre's burden allowed. Akrivir's knowledge of the tortuous warren was sure; he led them through so many twists and turns that Kyre was soon utterly disoriented, but at last, after an unguessable time, a patch of light glimmered hazily ahead.

"The bridge is directly ahead," Akrivir whispered. "I won't come any further; I'll serve you better by diverting anyone who might come this way in the next few minutes." He looked at them, and even in the gloom Kyre could see the strain in his face. "This is the most dangerous part of your journey. If anyone should see you as you cross, they could alert Calthar." He touched Talliann's shoulder gently, tentatively. "Take care."

Talliann laid one hand over his. "I'll never forget what you've done, Akrivir. Good fortune go with you!"

The young warrior turned away so that neither of them could see his expression. Gruffly, he addressed Kyre.

"I don't pretend to know what will come of this, Sun-Hound, but if we've thwarted Calthar's plans I, for one, will rejoice." He looked up, blinking rapidly. "Five nights from now, we'll know the truth of it. When that time comes I may have to face you as an enemy—believe me when I say I hope it doesn't come to that."

Kyre acknowledged his words with a grave nod. "I, too," he said. "Goodbye, Akrivir. Thanks are inadequate, but you have them."

Akrivir's smile was fleeting. He squeezed Talliann's fingers once, quickly, and was gone.

Talliann waited until his footfalls had faded into silence, then said softly, "Well . . . now we must face the worst of it."

Kyre drew a deep breath in an effort to control the sick feeling conjured by the knowledge of what lay ahead.

They approached the tunnel mouth and Talliann moved slowly, cautiously out onto the ledge beyond. He saw her poised against the dim phosphorescence filtering through the titanic chasm, then she looked over her shoulder, put a finger to her lips, and beckoned for him to hurry.

He stepped out onto a ledge that was no more than a narrow buttress hanging over emptiness. All round him the vast dimensions of the cave reared into the dark, and far, far down in the abysmal depths below the sea boomed its muted, threatening song. There before him was the bridge, arching from the cliff wall and soaring out into the gloom. In stark contrast to the mad jumble of towers and minarets and stairways that clung to the face above him, the cavern's far wall seemed all but blank; only one solitary light, glowing like a lost firefly, marked the point where the bridge finally joined with the distant cliff.

Talliann glanced up fearfully at the insane vista toppling out of the gloom at their backs, scanning for signs of anyone moving on the network of staircases, but Kyre couldn't bring himself to risk looking at that vertiginous horror. At last, as satisfied as she could be that all was clear, Talliann beckoned once more to him and stepped out onto the bridge.

He knew the span was wider than it looked. He knew he had crossed it once without mishap, and could do so again even with Gamora in his arms. But no logic or reason could banish the black terror that closed in on him as he set foot on the spearing arch of rock. The hollow immensity of the surrounding dark clutched at his bowels, attacked his sense of perspective until he sensed himself only as a crawling speck in an infinity of indifferent nothingness, a tiny spider teetering across a single, frail gossamer strand. He struggled to drag his

awareness out of the abyss's grip and focus on the figure
of Talliann moving steadily and surely through the gloom
ahead; but it was hard, so hard. The bridge beneath his
feet seemed to quiver fractionally, sending horrifying
messages through every nerve to his brain: if he spoke, if
he so much as dared to breathe, he knew that the echoes
of the sound would fall away and away, on and on until
they were swallowed in the vast distance, and that would
take a very long time . . .

Kyre was beginning to lose hold of his desperate
conviction that the nightmare of the crossing would ever
end when he saw that the light that marked the limit of
the bridge, and which had seemed so minute and so far
away when he began, was only a few paces ahead of
him. He heard the slap of Talliann's bare feet as she
gained the safety of the ledge, then he was following her,
casting off the yawning emptiness, and the bridge was
behind him.

They exchanged a look that expressed their relief at
the end of the ordeal far better than any words could have
done, then Talliann peered cautiously at the bundled
figure in Kyre's arms.

"She still sleeps," he murmured, and privately
thanked fate for it. If Gamora had woken while they were
on the bridge, she might easily have panicked and sent
them all to their deaths.

Talliann nodded, and they moved on. Two flights of
narrow stairs slanted up the cliff wall from the ledge; but
instead of climbing upward as Kyre anticipated, Talliann
instead took the lesser flight that led down into the deeper
dark. Some twelve steps—which, though nothing in
comparison to the bridge crossing, were nerve-racking
enough—and then a side tunnel opened in the cave wall.
They hurried through blackness: then more light ap-

peared ahead, and moments later they emerged into the sea cave.

Cool air wafted against their faces; Kyre drew breath and tasted salt on his tongue. The cavern was deserted, and lit only by a soft phosphorescence from the water that lapped just a few handspans below the rock shelf. Kyre could hardly believe the good luck that had followed them thus far: superstitiously he thrust the thought away, forcing himself not to look back over his shoulder, and set Gamora gently down as Talliann hurried to a recess at the far side of the cave.

"Here . . ." She tugged at something invisible in the shadows, breathless. "The shells . . ."

He went to help her. In the alcove lay what looked like two giant clams; but the double shells had long since lost their original occupants and were worn smooth, their surfaces shining softly in the reflected light. Kyre himself could have huddled within the capacious space they offered; for Gamora, they would make as comfortable a refuge as he could hope to find.

Between them they dragged one of the shells out onto the rock shelf, and Talliann ran her hands along the ridge where the two facets met. There was a faint sound, as of air escaping, and the shell's two halves sprang apart.

"Quickly," Talliann said. In the strange light her face was devoid of all color. "Fetch the little princess!"

Kyre turned to where he had left Gamora—and his heart lurched. Gamora was sitting up, her eyes wide and astonished, tousled curls falling over her face. Her gaze flicked around the cave, taking in her surroundings, and she said in a small voice, "Kyre . . . ? Kyre, where are we? What are you doing?"

Talliann made a small, frightened sound in her throat and covered her mouth with one hand. Kyre hastened to

Gamora's side, crouching beside her and taking her small
fingers in his.

"Don't worry, Princess." He hoped he'd succeeded in
keeping the trepidation he felt out of his voice. "There's
nothing amiss; you're quite safe."

"Safe . . ." She repeated the word mistrustfully.
"But—"

He had to tell her the truth: if he lied, she'd know it
instantly. Glancing quickly at Talliann, he said, "Gamora, we're going back to Haven."

For a moment the little girl simply stared at him. Then
her brows knitted together and her mouth turned down in
an ugly line.

"No!" she said.

"Gamora—"

"No!" A peculiar light sparked to life in Gamora's
eyes. "I don't want to!"

"Princess, listen to me, please!" Without realizing
what he was doing he took her by the shoulders and
shook her. "It isn't safe to stay here! If Calthar—"

"Calthar's kind to me!" Gamora shouted defiantly.
"She's my friend, I like her! I won't go home! This is my
home now!"

He couldn't argue with her. There was no time; and
Calthar's bewitchment stood as an impassable barrier to
any attempt at reason. Frantically, he looked back over
his shoulder at Talliann.

"Prepare the shell," he exhorted her; and to Gamora:
"Princess, we're leaving. And you're coming with us!"

As he spoke, he snatched her up from the rock floor. A
terrible, adult look came into her eyes, a look of
shrewdness, guile—and Kyre had no time to wonder
why she didn't struggle before Gamora opened her
mouth and screamed like a thing possessed.

"Calthar! CALTHAR!!"

"Gamora!!" Kyre's yell expressed shock and fury in equal measure; he swung the child off her feet, spinning round and starting toward where Talliann crouched by the open shell. Gamora was still screaming, he couldn't silence her—and then Talliann's eyes started with horror as she focused on a point behind his back.

They erupted from one of the entrance tunnels, a running phalanx of armed men, their spear points glittering cruelly in the reflected light from the sea. He couldn't count them; there might have been ten, twelve, fifteen—but they moved with trained precision, fanning out to circle the three frozen figures on the ledge and leaving only a narrow, impossible escape corridor between them and the water.

From the corner of his eye Kyre saw Talliann's lips form words, as though praying for salvation; though no sound escaped her. The circle of warriors closed in; fine-honed blades bristled inches from his body . . . then one man, clearly their leader stepped out from the group of spearmen and stood, feet braced, his own spear held at an arrogantly negligent angle. He smiled.

"Put the child down."

Slowly, heart pounding, Kyre set Gamora back on her feet. The little girl darted out of his reach then looked back at him, triumphantly defiant.

"Good." The warrior took another pace forward, gratified when Kyre backed away from the menacing point of his spear. "We'll see, shall we, what the land cur is made of?" He feinted with the blade; its tip skimmed past Kyre's collarbone and missed cutting him by a hairbreadth.

"*No!*" Talliann shouted furiously.

The man licked his lips. "*Yes*, lady," he said. His tone hung midway between reverence and patronage as he attempted to shore up his authority in her eyes. "You have been the unhappy victim of a conspiracy, and until your eyes can be opened to the truth, I must command your obedience. I ask you to stand aside!''

"How *dare* you!'' Talliann fired back. Her voice rose shrilly, echoing against the sea's boom in the cave. Her black eyes glittered and she shrieked, "Leave Kyre alone! *Leave* him, do you hear? *Obey me!*''

Terror spiked her voice, and Kyre realized that her desperate effort to command the sea warrior wouldn't work. She was losing control of herself, too inexperienced to demand obedience: but she gave him the chance he needed.

The warrior leader turned his head toward Talliann. His eyes focused on her—and Kyre sprang at him.

His tormentor yelled with surprise as two hands locked on his spear shaft. Instinctively he pivoted, trying to jerk the weapon free, and Kyre twisted his body and kicked out. His heel slammed against ribs, and the warrior's shout choked off into a rattling hiss of pain. He went down, taking four of his soldiers with him in a flailing tangle of limbs, and Kyre shouted to Talliann, "Get Gamora away! Don't wait—get her away!''

He had no time to see if she obeyed him, for the sea warriors surged at him and he was suddenly in the midst of a chaos of clashing blades. He heard Gamora scream and it sounded like a scream of protest, he saw his opponent getting to his feet, face distorted with rage: and then he was fighting for his life.

He should have known that the odds were too great, the outcome of the fight a foregone conclusion. Someone in the warriors' ranks had thought fast, and any seaward escape was blocked before he could hope to use it. He was surrounded, and though by the time it was over two sea warriors were dead and another three wounded, he couldn't hope to prevail against so many. He'd sustained more cuts than he could count, though none enough to disable him, but at last a spear point whirling at his face made him duck, he lost his footing and, trying to defend himself from the stabbing blade, went down. Something connected with sickening force against his temple, stunning him; he sprawled face down on the rock, his own spear pinned under his body, and two warriors pinioned his arms and knelt on his spine and legs before he could try to rise.

He heard someone sobbing wildly, though the sound seemed to come from a very great distance and was confused with the surging noise of the sea. He felt as if the sea was inside his skull, roaring in his ears: one cheek was pressed painfully against the cold, damp rock floor and his blurred vision only extended as far as ankle height. All he could see was a pair of feet, and the wicked glint of a spearhead as it hovered inches from his face. A toe prodded painfully into Kyre's kidney. He forced himself not to react, and watched the spear intently. It tensed, poised—Kyre hoped against all hope that he could judge the moment of the impending strike and roll clear—and then a new voice, appallingly familiar, cut through the babble and commanded immediate quiet.

"Cease that!"

The spear tip grated against the rock as the warrior stumbled back, and a wave of cold nausea went through Kyre as he heard Gamora's childish voice cry out "Calthar!" in tearful relief.

He sensed the tight circle of warriors around him falling back; in the ensuing silence the sound of Calthar's feet padding across the rock, and the rustle of her robe, was nerve-racking. As she stood over him his nostrils caught a breath of something unclean.

"Get up, Sun-Hound," she said. He held his breath,

didn't move. She sighed. "I know you're conscious, and you hear me. *Rise*."

He raised his head, painfully. Calthar stood two paces away gazing down at him, and Gamora hovered at her side. The little girl was also staring at Kyre, but her eyes were empty and her smile meaningless. A short way away Talliann stood beside the open shell. She was gazing down at the rock beneath her feet, and though he couldn't see her expression Kyre could sense the aura of rigidly fearful defeat that emanated from her.

Calthar said nothing for a few moments, but her gaze bored through Kyre as though her eyes could strip away skin and flesh and bone and see through to his innermost thoughts. Then she raised one hand and snapped her fingers at the warriors gathered at her back.

"Leave."

Her tone demanded instant obedience: they started to shuffle away. Kyre watched them go, and the sickness returned to his stomach. Calthar saw the burgeoning light of fear in his eyes, and smiled. Then she held out a hand. "Talliann. Child, come here."

"N-no . . ." Talliann shook her head: her body jerked as though an invisible hand had violently shaken her, and her fists clenched at her sides.

"Don't argue with me, Talliann." Calthar's voice was soft, cajoling, lethal. "Come here."

Impelled by a force she was incapable of controlling Talliann shuffled across the rock floor, reminding Kyre of the ungainly, shambling creature he had seen on the shingle bar; the creature she became under the Hag's influence. But her face didn't reflect her compliance. Every muscle was tightened almost beyond endurance, and tears of bitter impotence shone on her cheeks. She stopped some six paces from Calthar, then sank to her knees as if unable to bear the weight of her own body any longer.

Calthar nodded, satisfied, and looked again at Kyre. While he watched Talliann he had been aware of the spear still lying beneath him, and one hand had moved, tentatively, to close over the haft . . .

"No, Sun-Hound," Calthar said.

His hand stopped moving. She was smiling at him again, and there was murder in her smile. Then she raised one hand and made a small, careless gesture, as though brushing away a small, buzzing insect. Kyre found himself sprawling aside, his elbow smacking painfully against the rock as he lost his balance: before he could haul himself up again Calthar reached out with one foot and carelessly kicked the spear out of his reach. Then she took a single pace toward him.

Talliann made a thin sound, halfway between a gasp and a sob, and the sorceress's hot stare fastened on her. She looked back, not flinching, but her expression was bleak with despair.

"Wh-what are you . . . going to . . . do?"

"Child." Again that terrible gentleness, that appalling parody of affection. "You have disappointed me. You have both disappointed me. And now you must pay my price. You know that price, Talliann."

"No!"

"Yes." She looked at Kyre again, and abruptly the last remnants of the mask she had worn slipped from her, revealing the true nature of the soul behind Calthar's face. Kyre stared back, transfixed, and in that moment he relived his first encounter, so many centuries ago, with the embodiment of evil who had led him to destruction.

Calthar said: *"Sun-Hound, you will meet my Mothers!"* And in that moment Kyre understood what was to come, and the horror of it nearly split his mind.

* * *

It was as though a vast, rotting throat had opened and breathed the stench of the grave into the sea cavern. Kyre heard Talliann's high-pitched whimper of fright, saw her clap a hand over her mouth as though to stop herself from vomiting. He couldn't help her; he couldn't move as the appalling fetor swept over him, assaulting his nostrils and his lungs. Bile erupted in his mouth and he choked it back, his eyes widening as he stared, unable to rip his gaze away, at Calthar—or rather, at the thing that Calthar was becoming.

Part of his mind tried to hold on to reason, tried to tell him that the light in the cave wasn't being eaten by a darkness so black that it defied sanity. But the rock walls were fading, the sea's roar dimming away, and Calthar, sorceress, priestess, Mother born of Mothers, was metamorphosing. A cold, deathly, nacreous light flowed from within her, the awful phosphorescence of something long dead. Her wild corona of hair grew rank, a crown of moldering seaweed; the tatters of her robe were a spider's-web scum clothing her shimmering body; the flesh of her face melted until her skull was a gaunt and sunken sculpture of skin stretched taut over the jagged contours of naked bone. She smiled and she was lipless, teeth locked in a hideous rictus. She threw back her head, and her indrawn breath was a death rattle.

And Kyre understood the true nature of the Mothers.

They had ruled the sea citadel since Malhareq, their first matrix, had fled Haven with her followers after his death. They were its founders, its motivators, its controllers, each Mother born and shaped and trained to follow her predecessor and take the reins of power. And though no sorcery could keep the eventual death of their bodies at bay, they clung to this world with a terrible tenacity, unwilling to relinquish their hold on the forces that kept alive that first principle of hatred for the land dwellers, who had been their kin until the betrayal that had sent the Sun-Hound to his death. They could not rule Haven as Malhareq had planned to do; so instead they sought to destroy what they could not have.

Though centuries passed and each Mother's body died, still their minds, their wills, their power, lived on and returned to the citadel through their rotting corpses: and Calthar was every one of them, and every one of them was Calthar. She made her lair among their bones; she drew her strength from the dust of their mortal remains; she took her inspiration from their corruption. And each and every one inhabited her body and her soul. As her mask fell away she became her own immediate predecessor; a corpse, worm-eaten, its hair crumbling, its flesh shriveling toward disintegration; then that disguise slipped, too, and Calthar was a living skeleton whose only adornments were tatters of shriveled and blackened skin. And further back, and further back, through brown and brittle bone, through crumbling marrow, through an apparition in which motes of rotting dust made mockery of the human form . . . until eyes that Kyre knew too well—the eyes of Malhareq, first Mother of all, who had hated him and coveted what he was and what he had— glared like twin suns from the empty memory of a skull.

Then, shearing like a blade through the mesmerizing horror of what Kyre was witnessing, came the shrill sound of a child's scream.

Gamora! The name was a talisman, snatching him back from the monstrous corridors of memory into the reality of the cave. Kyre's mind jerked into focus, and the scene before him resolved into a ghastly tableau that slammed into his brain. Talliann on her knees, arms flung

across her face to protect herself from the horror that
Calthar had become. The sorceress, changed beyond
recognition as the primeval force of the Mothers surged
through her and stripped away the trappings of life: bone
and skin and mold and decay flickering about her in a
gruesome aura, her arms outflung as she welcomed and
relished the monstrous intrusion of the dead—

And Gamora.

The bewitchment was broken. In her fury, Calthar had
forgotten her precarious hold on the child, and the spell
that had held Gamora in her thrall had shattered. The
little girl was hunched on the rock floor, arms clapped
over her head, shrieking in panic as the full horror of
what Calthar had become smashed into her mind. And
her screams, the pity and fury they awoke, broke the
thrall in Kyre's own brain. *This monstrosity had bested
him once—she'd not best him again!*

He flung himself across the ledge, hands groping
blindly for the spear that Calthar had kicked aside, and as
his fingers closed round the shaft he felt a surge of
energy, of the old power he had once commanded. He
brought the spear up, feet finding purchase as his
muscles propelled him upright, and, not allowing himself a moment for thought, he lunged at the hideous,
shimmering thing before him.

The spear plunged in just below the apparition's heart,
and a high, wailing screech threatened to split his
eardrums. The searing eyes erupted, changing into a
decayed skull that opened the hinge of its jaw and hissed
a foul wind of putrefaction into his face: he twisted the
blade, his screams blending with Gamora's, and the skull
grew skin, yelling insensately. Then flesh appeared,
tendrils of hair writhing and snatching at him, and
suddenly the monstrosity was Calthar and nothing but

Calthar, and the nacreous glow was devoured by the
natural light of the cavern, and at his back the sea was
booming while the sorceress doubled over, bright blood
flowing from the gash the spear had opened between her
ribs. Hatred blazed amid the shock in her eyes and she
staggered as though drunk, then fell to her knees, hands
scrabbling on the rock, a choking, rattling sound emerging from her throat as she coughed more blood—

"*Run!*" Kyre's own voice roared in his ears and he
was dimly aware of Talliann's shocked face swimming
before him. He started toward her, stumbled over
something that lay in his path, and Gamora's huddled
form registered in his stunned brain. He swept her up and
bundled her unceremoniously into the open cavity of the
shell. Talliann rushed forward, and the shell's two halves
slammed together. Almost before Kyre knew what was
happening the shell was sliding toward the edge of the
rock ledge. It hit the water with a resounding splash, and
Talliann was poised to follow it, arms outspread,
momentarily frozen like a statue on the edge of the sea—

The creature behind him snarled. It was a desperate,
defeated sound, but there was still a horrible, malevolent
strength to it. Kyre cast a glance back over his shoulder
and saw her crouched on the shelf, hunching over her
wound which flowed scarlet. Only her eyes were alive,
and they burned, burned—

He heard the break in the sea's rhythm as Talliann
dived. With a tremendous effort he tore his mesmerized
gaze away from the sorceress, and his muscles propelled
him in a powerful arc as he launched himself into the
welcoming ocean.

Chapter 15

A BREAKING WAVE CARRIED KYRE IN TO SHORE AND DREW
back to leave him sprawled on the shingle bar. In his
hand he clutched a spear. A violent fit of coughing
racked him as his lungs struggled to cope with the change
from breathing water to breathing air. He raised his head
and looked around him.

"Talliann!" His voice was hoarse, and the cry brought
on another bout of coughing. Painfully he tried to
struggle to his feet. *"Talliann!"*

There was a movement further along the shingle bar.
Kyre forced himself to stand on legs that felt too weak to
support him properly; then saw her. She was on all fours
further along the bank, water streaming from her black
hair as she wrestled with the great closed shell, which
had beached close to her, trying to drag it clear of the
sea's pull. He stumbled across the loose shingle to lend
his strength to hers, and between them they hauled the
shell out of the undertow, securing it above the waterline.

They straightened to catch their breath, and Talliann went into Kyre's arms and clung to him, feeling small and desperately vulnerable in his embrace. It was some while before they released their hold on each other, and when at last they moved apart neither of them could speak.

Talliann dropped to her knees again, and slid her fingers between the shell's two halves. It sprang open, revealing Gamora's huddled figure inside.

"Princess." Kyre spoke gently, reaching out to ruffle the little girl's dark curls." We're home, Princess."

She didn't stir. Her eyes were shut and she seemed to be asleep. He shook her shoulder, but still there was no response.

"Gamora?" She should have come out of her faint by now . . . Kyre gathered her into his arms, lifting her from the shell's confines. She was a limp, dead weight in his arms, her head dropping back at a disconcerting angle, and he looked uneasily at Talliann.

"I can't rouse her . . ."

Talliann crouched at his side. She reached out as though to touch Gamora—then withdrew her hand quickly and uttered a sharp, fearful cry.

Kyre's stomach turned over within him. "What is it?"

"Calthar!" There was stark horror in Talliann's voice, and she looked up involuntarily toward the sky. Nothing was visible through the night fog, save for the dim, jagged silhouette of the ruined temple at their backs; but Kyre could feel the presence of the bloated moon beyond the fog's gray shrouds.

Talliann whispered: "She's under an enchantment, Kyre. Can't you see?" Her eyes were huge with fear. "Calthar isn't dead. She's regained her strength, and she's cast a bewitchment. She couldn't reach you or me; but the little girl . . ."

A desperate desire for her to be wrong made Kyre protest. "Calthar couldn't have recovered, not in this time!"

"She could. You've seen for yourself the sources from which she draws her strength." Talliann shuddered. "Kyre, we daren't stay here. We must get Gamora to Haven, quickly, before she strikes again!"

As she spoke, Kyre felt an awful premonition seize hold of him. Involuntarily he looked seaward, and his blood ran cold. Adding its own terrible confirmation to Talliann's urgency, the fog was ripping apart, slowly, softly, like a fine fabric tearing, letting through a shaft of cold light that spilled down from the sky and turned the entire scene into a savage etching of black and silver. Talliann was a specter drained of all color, and Gamora's small body looked like a corpse in his arms under the Hag's deadly glare.

"Hurry!" Talliann pleaded, her voice near to breaking. Kyre needed no further urging: he gathered Gamora more closely and securely to his chest, Talliann snatched up the spear he had discarded, and they set off across the unstable shingle toward the dim gray miasma of the bay's crescent. Reaching the sand they quickened their pace, and Kyre was thankful at last to see the witchlights of Haven's portal ahead, glowing through the fog like remote, feral eyes. He couldn't judge the hour but guessed that it must be deep night; there'd be no one abroad in the town now, and little chance of their being challenged before they reached the palace.

They arrived at the arch and Talliann faltered, terrified of what lay behind them yet balking at the thought of what might await her within the hostile walls of the

town. Despite his burden Kyre managed to reach out and
touch her arm reassuringly: she drew a deep, grateful
breath and then nodded, indicating that she was ready to
continue. As they entered the portal, Kyre resisted an
urge to look over his shoulder lest he should see the
Hag's pockmarked face staring balefully down at them:
then they had passed by the twin green lamps, and Haven
enfolded them.

Fog lay in pale, still pools in the winding streets,
deadening even the small sounds of their bare feet on the
stone paving. Shuttered houses stared with blank, empty
eyes; not even a scavenging animal slunk through the
shadows. Kyre could feel Talliann's fear of the town as a
palpable aura, but he himself was looking at it with
newly awakened senses. So familiar, yet so decayed; its
old glories and beauty long gone . . . as they padded
through a twisting maze of alleys, avoiding the squares
and public places, old memories came back more and
more strongly until he could almost have superimposed a
ghost-image of Haven as he had once known it over
Haven as it was now. The sensation was disquieting,
disturbing; as it assailed him the quartz pendant burned
hot agaist his skin, as though some sentient force within
it shared and echoed all that he felt.

And then at last the high perimeter wall of the palace
showed ahead, the wicket gate a darker blur in the pale
sandstone. In the wall's shadow Kyre gently set Gamora
down—but as his hand came to rest on the wicket gate's
latch Talliann said softly: "Kyre . . . I'm afraid to go
in there."

In the darkness her face was a white oval, her eyes
black hollows. He took her hands. "It's all right. I'm
with you—nothing can hurt you, Talliann. *Nothing.*"

"But they—" She stopped, swallowed. "Will they

accept me? I've come from the citadel; that means to them, I'm . . . evil. And if Calthar—"

"Calthar can't touch you." He squeezed her fingers hard, and the urgent determination he felt lent an edge to his voice. "And no one here will harm you. You're safe here; we're both safe. Trust me, Talliann."

She lowered her head, her expression hidden from him. Then with a quick, impulsive gesture she lifted his hands to her face and kissed them. "Yes," she said. "Yes: I trust you." She met his gaze again and added, her voice stronger, "You know I do."

She watched as Kyre lifted the latch of the wicket gate and slowly, cautiously, eased it open an inch or two. Nothing moved in the dark beyond, and no voice challenged him. He pushed the gate wider . . . still no sound and no movement. Kyre gathered up Gamora's inert body again, and, with Talliann close behind him, slipped through the portal into the dank, silent grounds.

He heard Talliann's soft gasp as she stared at the strange vista of the gardens. Mist drifted in thin, milky coils among the rank shrubbery, giving the low-lying bushes a bizarre semblance of independent life; the bloated white flowers that haunted the garden were beginning to rot now, releasing the sweet-sick odor of decay into the damp air. The girl stayed close, touching his arm as though needing the reassurance of physical contact and shrinking back from the dead blooms as they made their way along overgrown paths toward the terrace.

Only the ornate stone balustrade was visible above the pooling fog; the terrace seemed to float on it like a ghostly ship on a curdled sea. But there was a light shining dimly from a window near the top of the steps, and Kyre realized that it came from Brigrandon's rooms.

The old scholar was still awake: he above all other would be able and ready to help them reach DiMag.

He turned to Talliann, and indicated the soft blur of light.

"Those are the quarters of Brigrandon, Gamora's tutor," he whispered. "He's a good and trustworthy friend—we'll find sanctuary with him."

Her answering look told him that she still couldn't assuage her fears, but she said nothing, only nodded and followed him up the terrace steps. As they stood before Brigrandon's door she started to shiver, then when Kyre rapped a quick, furtive staccato on the wood she shrank back into the shadows. For a few moments it seemed the knock hadn't been heard, and Kyre was about to rap again when the door abruptly jerked on its hinges and opened a crack, spilling a finger of warm yellow light out onto the terrace. The figure in the doorway was a silhouette, but Kyre recognized the set of the scholar's shoulders, and the unruly wings of his hair.

"Master Brigrandon." His voice was a whisper.

"Who's that?" The door opened a fraction wider, but Brigrandon was cautious. Kyre wetted dry lips.

"It's Kyre, Brigrandon."

There was a pause, then, slowly, the door opened wider. They stared at each other for what seemed a very long time; then Brigrandon said softly, "Well, now. I'd always believed that sobriety was a certain cure for hallucination. It seems I was wrong."

The dry, familiar tone—and the old man's calm resignation—gave Kyre a sense of acute and desperately needed relief. "I'm no phantom, Master Brigrandon," he said. "And I urgently need your help."

Brigrandon stepped back, pulling the door fully open. "Come in, quickly," he said. "Where by all that's sacred

have you—'' And his voice choked off, his eyes staring
in their sockets as the lamplight from the room beyond
him spilled across the huddled figure in Kyre's arms.

"May the Eye preserve us!" The incredulous oath
came on a harshly indrawn breath. ''You've brought her
back!'' He looked as though he were about to cry.

"Brigrandon, I have to see DiMag and Simorh!" Kyre
stepped over the threshold, shouldering the old man
aside, for Brigrandon seemed transfixed by the sight of
the child. "Gamora is bewitched—she's in a trance, and
I can't rouse her. And there's more, far more.'' He
looked over his shoulder and called softly: "Talliann . . .''

She emerged from the darkness and stood under the
lintel, every muscle tensed like a wild animal poised to
flee at the smallest sign of danger. Brigrandon stared
at her, not comprehending, and Kyre added quickly,
"There's no time for full explanations, Brigrandon.
We've come from the sea dwellers' citadel, and we've
news—it's desperately urgent!"

"Bewitched . . .'' Brigrandon repeated in a bemused
tone: and then abruptly he shook his head as though to
clear it. "Kyre, forgive me. Your appearance was such a
shock, I—I hadn't dreamed anything like this might
happen. It caught me unawares.'' He straightened his
back, and the old, shrewd intelligence was back in his
eyes as he crossed the room to a couch by a banked but
still warmly glowing fire. "Set the little princess down
here. And your friend . . .'' He looked up at Talliann,
who hadn't moved. "Come in, child; come in and get
warm. You're soaked, both of you.'' He watched as Kyre
laid Gamora down on the couch, then gave him a
searching look. "Bewitched, you say?"

Kyre thanked providence for Brigrandon's pragmatism: no histronics, no rebuttals; even his questions were brief and to the point. "It's the work of a sorceress called Calthar," he said.

"What?" Brigrandon's eyes narrowed.

"You know of her?"

"Enough. And if this is her doing, then I can only pray that the Princess Simorh has the power to counter it." He glanced again at Gamora's motionless form. "We must get word to her immediately. And the prince—have you tried to get into the palace?"

Kyre felt Talliann press close against him. She'd come further into the room at Brigrandon's bidding, but she was still nervous. "No," he said.

Brigrandon's mouth tightened to a hard, thin line. "That's just as well. As things are now, I'd give little for your chances of reaching him unscathed. Orders have been issued to kill you on sight."

Kyre was appalled. He had anticipated hostility from DiMag, but nothing so extreme. "But surely the prince doesn't—" he started to say.

"They're not Prince DiMag's orders," Brigrandon interrupted grimly. "They're Swordsmaster Vaoran's. And he has enough men willing to obey his authority over their prince's, and put a blade in your back before you have a chance to tell your story."

So matters had moved on . . . DiMag had hinted at the precariousness of his position on more than one occasion, but Kyre hadn't imagined it could come to this so quickly. It made his own mission all the more urgent.

Brigrandon said, compounding his unease, "There are few enough servants who can be trusted in these days, my friend, let alone soldiers. I'm not even sure that I can rely on my own men any more." He hesitated, considering, then added, "I'll take you to the prince myself." He met Kyre's eyes, and his look was painfully candid. "It's the only safe way."

Talliann was beginning to shiver violently as the warmth of the room clashed with the deep cold in her bones. She was unsteady on her feet, her eyes heavy, and Kyre said, "Talliann is exhausted, Brigrandon. She needs to rest."

"Then she shall stay here." There was sympathy in the old man's expression as he looked at the girl. "It might be for the best anyway. But we must take the little princess with us. If you carry her, that will force Vaoran's followers to think before they make any attempt on your life." He sighed. "It doesn't please me to have to say such a thing, but it's the bald truth."

Kyre didn't argue. He knew Brigrandon well enough to realize that the old scholar was given neither to fabrication nor exaggeration. If anything, he would have understated the situation.

He nodded. "I'll do whatever you think best."

"Then he must go." Again Brigrandon looked at Talliann, and his smile was kindly. "Dry yourself, my child, and warm yourself. You'll find blankets in that alcove there: take as many as you need. We'll lock the door behind us, so you'll be quite safe until we return."

She turned uncertainly to Kyre, and he stroked her wet hair back from her face. "Brigrandon's right. You can trust him." He kissed her forehead lightly, felt her relax a little. "Sleep, Talliann. There's nothing more to fear."

They left two minutes later, Brigrandon leading the way with a lantern, while Kyre, carrying Gamora in his arms, followed. Again Kyre felt the bizarre clash of past and present as they entered the palace's outer hall: the faded tapestries, the dulled marble, the chill air of neglect all clashed with his newly awakened memories of past prosperity and glory. The hall was virtually unlit; only Brigrandon's lamp kept the depths of shadow at bay as they moved toward the arch and the stairs beyond. No footstep broke the quiet, no voice challenged them as they climbed, and within minutes they had reached the corridor that led to DiMag's rooms.

"The prince will probably be awake," Brigrandon said in a low voice as they paced silently along the passage. "He hardly sleeps these days; since the little princess disappeared, he . . ." And abruptly he stopped speaking as they both heard the sound of footsteps ahead of them.

There were five men in the party that came round a corner of the passage, and Vaoran led them. Kyre had time to recognize the faces of two senior councillors and a high-ranking army officer before the burly swordsmaster's eyes focused on him. Vaoran stared for a moment in sheer disbelief: then his stocked voice hissed, *"You!"*

"No, swordsmaster!" Brigrandon stepped in front of Kyre as Vaoran pulled his blade out of its scabbard. "Kyre is here to see the prince!"

Vaoran looked contemptuously at the old man. "Get out of my way, scholar," he said softly. "You know the order I've given regarding this creature." Behind him, quietly, the army officer also drew his own sword. Brigrandon, however, wasn't to be intimidated.

"I take my orders from Prince DiMag," he replied crisply. "And Kyre and I have business with him— urgent business. I'll thank you, Vaoran, not to impede us!"

He started to move forward, then stopped as he found himself face to face with the tip of Vaoran's sword.

"Stand aside," Vaoran said.

"Vaoran, don't be such a fool! Don't you understand?" Brigrandon flung out one arm and pointed to the bundle in Kyre's arms. "Kyre has brought the Princess Gamora back to us!"

There was a stunned silence. Then, so quickly that the old man had no time to react, Vaoran struck Brigrandon with the flat of his sword, knocking him out of his path. Brigrandon reeled back, striking his head against a lamp bracket on the wall. He lost his balance and fell, and Kyre and Vaoran were left facing each other.

Vaoran glared for a moment at Kyre, the challenge of disbelief in his eyes. Then he stepped forward and snatched back a corner of the blanket that covered Kyre's burden.

One of the men at his back swore softly as he saw Gamora's still, pale face, and the muscles in Kyre's jaw tightened convulsively. Had it not been for the precious burden in his arms, he would gladly have killed Vaoran. He had encountered men like this before; ambitious men, who sought to take power from their rightful ruler and invest it in their own hands. He had been their victim once, when Malhareq had aroused their greed; now, it seemed, it was DiMag's turn. And looking into Vaoran's eyes, he saw the confident satisfaction of a man who had almost achieved his goal.

Vaoran's face suffused with angry color, and he brought up the point of his sword so that it hovered inches from Kyre's face.

"Set the child down," he said, enunciating each word with careful, deadly precision.

"I'm taking her to DiMag."

Vaoran stepped closer, the sword point now no more than a fingerbreadth from Kyre's mouth. "I'll count to five, creature, and then—"

"Vaoran, stop this!" Brigrandon, though still groggy from the blow to his head, stumbled forward. Seeing what was afoot, the army officer moved to intercept him; they grappled, anger leading strength to Brigrandon's struggles, and Vaoran shouted, "Get that old fool out of the way! Quiet him, if you have to run him through!"

"*Swordsmaster Vaoran!*" The new voice cut savagely through the clamor. Startled and chagrined, the officer sprang away from Brigrandon, and Vaoran froze. The other councillors shuffled aside, making way for DiMag, who had emerged from his rooms at the sounds of the disturbance.

The prince had lost weight, his fair hair was ragged and unkempt, his face gray and pallid. Only his hazel eyes burned with feverish energy. He was fully dressed—if he slept at all, he slept in his clothes—and one hand gripped the hilt of his heavy, unsheathed sword. He ignored Brigrandon and the councillors, and gazed with undisguised hatred at Vaoran.

"Put down your blade."

"My lord, this cur—" Vaoran began explosively.

"I said, put it down." DiMag's face was stony. "Or I'll cut off the hand that holds it."

His tone left no one in any doubt that he both could and would carry out the threat unless his order was obeyed. Vaoran hesitated a bare moment, eyes reflecting his fury at being humiliated before his companions. Then, slowly, he lowered the sword until its tip touched the floor.

Now DiMag stared at Kyre. His eyes registered doubt, suspicion, and above all a terrible weariness. He opened his mouth to speak, but before he could say a word Brigrandon stepped forward and touched his sword arm lightly.

"My lord prince." The old scholar's voice was gentle. "Kyre has brought the Princess Gamora back to us."

"Gamora . . . ?" Every trace of color vanished from DiMag's skin, as for the first time he focused on the wrapped figure in Kyre's arms. He put the back of his hand to his mouth, and for an instant Kyre saw terror in his look—terror that he might wake at any moment to find he had been dreaming. He said: "It's true, Prince DiMag."

"My lord—" Vaoran started to bluster angrily, and the prince rounded on him.

"Silence!" He limped forward, and peered into the folds of the blanket. He stared at his daughter's face for a very long time, then closed his eyes and swayed. Brigrandon hastened to steady him as he seemed in danger of falling, and after a moment DiMag pulled himself together. He patted the old scholar's arm in a gesture of thanks, then said, "Brigrandon, find a servant. Send for the Princess Simorh and tell her to come at once to my chambers."

"I'll go myself, sir—"

"No. No; save your legs, my friend. Send a servant. I'll want you in my rooms . . . and Gamora's nurse; she must be roused—"

"My lord," Brigrandon said, "there's something more you should know." He glanced helplessly at Kyre, and Kyre decided that there was nothing to gain from hedging.

He said quietly, "Prince DiMag, Gamora has been bewitched. We can't rouse her."

"Bewitched?" DiMag frowned, then his eyes hardened with a glimmer of understanding. "Yes," he said. "Yes . . . I suppose I should have anticipated something of that nature. It was what Simorh dreamed."

"And who has bewitched her?" Vaoran demanded. His confidence was returning, and his expression was dangerous. Kyre was about to make a furious retort when DiMag held up a hand, forestalling him.

"Swordsmaster Vaoran," the prince said icily. "I have heard enough from you for one night. I want none of your accusations, your spites, your vendettas." His eyes met the taller man's, and Vaoran blanched. "Get back to your quarters."

"Prince DiMag, this is an outrage! This creature comes crawling back to Haven after betraying us all, and you—"

"He has brought back my daughter!" DiMag snarled. "And that's more than you and your entire army could do!"

Vaoran recovered himself, and sneered. "Oh, yes; he has brought the little princess back! But at what price?"

For a moment DiMag glared at him. Then he said, with incredible venom, "I told you go. I expect to be obeyed."

"My lord, I demand—"

"You're in no position to demand anything!" The prince's hand tightened on his sword hilt and Vaoran, disconcerted, backed away an involuntary step.

"Go, all of you," DiMag said more softly. "My daughter has been returned to me, and for the moment that is all I care about. You may convene the council in the morning, and they'll have a full report from my own lips then. Until that time, I will kill any man who dares to disturb me." He raked the small group one last time with a withering stare, then looked at Kyre.

"Bring her to my chambers," he said quietly.

As he followed the prince along the corridor, Kyre could almost physically feel the heat of Vaoran's hatred.

DiMag still clung to enough authority to best the swordsmaster in a direct confrontation, but the situation was obviously deteriorating fast. Vaoran had influential friends among both the council and the army; it might only be a matter of days before he felt sure enough of himself to make his bid to oust the prince from rulership. And DiMag knew it—Kyre had seen the unease in his eyes, the awareness that his future was balanced on a knife edge. When the council convened in the morning, and heard the full story of what had happened in the sea citadel, it would divide them even further.

The guards at DiMag's door saluted and stepped aside to allow them through. They entered the familiar room—doubly so now to Kyre, for he recalled that it had once been his own—and Gamora was laid gently on the prince's couch. DiMag sat beside her, taking her hand and chafing gently at it as he gazed at her. Kyre stood by, not wanting to disturb him, and neither spoke until Brigrandon returned from his errand. Then, as the door closed behind the old man, DiMag looked up.

"I don't know what to say to you, Sun-Hound," he said quietly. "You've brought my daughter back, and that's a service I can never repay. But this . . ." He indicated the child's immobile form. "I don't know what to do. I don't know what to think."

"She's alive, Prince DiMag," Brigrandon broke in. "That at least we can all be thankful for. And if the Princess Simorh can—"

"*If,*" DiMag stressed harshly, then looked at Kyre again. "Who did this, Kyre? Who was responsible?"

"It was the sea sorceress: Calthar," Kyre said.

DiMag's expression became a dead mask, as though all reaction, all emotion, had been instantaneously shut off. "Calthar." He repeated the name, but Kyre could tell that to do so cost him dearly. "So she still rules?"

Kyre nodded.

"And she has enchanted my daugher . . ." He rose, limped across the room to a small table on which stood a flask and several cups. As he poured wine for himself his hand was unsteady.

"She should have been dead these fifty years," he continued, and now his voice was dangerous. "Her worm-eaten corpse should have rotted away while my grandfather was still young, not lived on to—to—" He shook his head, unable to express what he felt.

"I know," Kyre said, and something in his voice made the prince pause. Their eyes met, and DiMag saw a haunted echo of the horror that the other man had witnessed in the citadel.

"Prince DiMag, there's more behind Calthar's evil than even you realize," Kyre went on. "What she has done to Gamora is only the beginning. What she plans to do—*will* do, if we're unable to prevent it—is far worse."

DiMag studied his face for a moment. Then: "Tell me," he said. "The sooner I—"And he broke off as the door flew open.

Simorh stood on the threshold. She was clad only in a night shift, and her eyes were wide and frightened. Her wild stare focused on each man in turn, then she said in a small, confused voice, "DiMag . . . ?"

The prince pointed wordless to the couch. Simorh turned, saw Gamora: and burst into tears.

Kyre and Brigrandon looked away in discomfort as the sorceress dropped to her knees at her daughter's side, head bowed over the child's body, racked with sobs which were all the more pitiful for being silent and desperately controlled. This was a side to Simorh that Kyre had never thought to see, and he was moved by her distress. He exchanged a glance with Brigrandon, but neither spoke; and DiMag simply stood gazing toward the window, seeming to see into a private world. Then Simorh looked up. Her face was blotched with tears and her voice shook as she cried, *"Who did this to my child?"*

She didn't need to be told of the enchantment; like Talliann she could sense it. Kyre would have answered her, but DiMag forestalled him and said, with quiet bluntness, "Calthar."

"What?" Her eyes narrowed, and she got unsteadily to her feet.

"Kyre brought Gamora back," DiMag said. "And he says he has news that—"

"Damn his news!" Simorh's voice was razor-edged. "That whore's spawn has enchanted my daughter—I'm not about to waste time listening to tales!" She swung round. "I want Gamora taken to my tower, *now*! If anything can be done, I'll—"

"Lady, wait," Kyre said sharply.

She stopped and stared at him, astounded and infuriated by his temerity. "How *dare* you—"

"I dare because I must!" Kyre cut across her fury. "Calthar has done far worse than bewitch Gamora. If you don't listen to me now, all your efforts to rouse her will be worth nothing—for in five nights' time Calthar plans to destroy every soul in Haven!"

Simorh stared at him, and DiMag said softly, *"Dead Night . . . ?"*

"Dead Night. They call it the Great Conjunction. And it will take place five nights from now."

"Fourteen," Simorh said sharply. They both turned to look at her. "Not five nights. Fourteen. Our astronomers have calculated it." But her voice didn't carry conviction.

"Your astronomers are wrong," Kyre told her. "The sea dwellers know to the moment when the conjunction will occur, and this time Calthar means to annihilate Haven."

"How can you know that?" DiMag demanded.

"Because I was in the sea dwellers' citadel, with Gamora."

Simorh was about to retort angrily, but DiMag's hand on her arm stayed her. "You followed her there?" he said.

"Yes."

Simorh turned angrily at her husband. "DiMag, you surely don't believe him? If it's true—if he has been among the sea demons—then how did he reach their stronghold? And how was he able to get Gamora away?" Her angry gaze raked Kyre. "He claims to have rescued her, but for all we know he could be in league with our enemies! How do we know that his story isn't part of a trap?"

For a moment there was a painful silence. Then Kyre said: "Princess Simorh, I don't expect you to trust the man you summoned out of limbo. But would you be ready to take the word of the one after whom you named me? Would you trust the true Sun-Hound?"

Brigrandon was the first of them all to grasp the implication. The old man sat suddenly down on a chair, and DiMag looked at him in surprise. "Brigrandon? What is it?"

The scholar was staring at Kyre, and after a moment he replied, "I think, my lord, that something has happened which none of us had bargained for. Am I right, Kyre?"

"Yes. You're right, my friend." And Kyre held out his arm to display the quartz pendant tied about his wrist on its silver chain. "How it came to be in the citadel I don't know. But when Talliann placed it in my hand, it turned the key in my mind—and I remembered what I truly am."

DiMag said querulously, "Talliann?" but Brigrandon ignored him. He was staring at the pendant with an almost childlike awe and, looking quickly into Kyre's face for permission, reached out to touch it with a reverent fingertip.

"This is the one," he whispered at last. "Just as our oldest records describe it. The amulet of the true Sun-Hound . . ."

"What?" Simorh's eyes widened and she came forward. Shock registered on her face and she said in a low voice, "No . . . it isn't possible!"

DiMag came to stand beside her. His arm slipped round her shoulders as he, too, looked at the pendant, though Kyre doubted if he was even aware of the gesture. Then he looked up, and understanding began to dawn in his eyes.

Kyre smiled wryly at him. "Prince DiMag, at one of our earliest encounters you asked a question of me that I couldn't answer. You said: *"Ha reinn trachan, ni brachnaea pol arcath?"* He saw the prince's face pale at his flawless accent, and repeated the question in DiMag's own language. "Can a prince return, if his land is lost?" I can answer you now, by saying, *Kena halst reinn crechen ha brachnaea voed creich.*"

DiMag whispered a translation. " 'Only with the death of the last prince can a land truly die' . . ." His voice was barely recognizable, and Kyre smiled.

"Even in my time the old tongue was used only by sorcerers and scribes," he said. "It's little wonder that it's all but vanished now."

"DiMag!" Simorh turned to him in sudden panic. "DiMag, this can't be true! I know what I did, I know what manner of creature I brought to this world! What you're thinking, what you're saying—*it isn't possible!*"

"Madam," Brigrandon put in gently, "you believed that you had created a man in Kyre's image, but you were wrong." She looked wildly at him, and though she fought to refute it, realization was in her eyes. Brigrandon smiled at her with infinite pity and infinite respect. "Your powers reached further than any of us ever dreamed, Princess. You have call our Sun-Hound back from the dead!"

Servants had carried Calthar back to her chambers, but they didn't dare enter her inner sanctum. And so, inch by maddened inch, she had crawled through the door that held such terror for others, and into the heavy darkness beyond. Blood trailed across the floor in her wake; her face was twisted with pain but also with a black, ravening fury. One would pass: the other would endure.

She should have known what he was! Clutching her rib cage with one shuddering hand, feeling her own life force spilling between her splayed fingers, Calthar knew hatred of an order she had never before experienced. No ordinary mortal could spill her blood: many had tried during her long life, but the power of the Mothers made her impervious to any weapon wielded by her enemies. Yet this creature, this false champion of Haven, had succeeded where all others had failed, and that could mean only one thing—he was no false champion. Centuries after Malhareq, first and greatest Mother of all, had sent him to his death, the Sun-Hound had returned.

And she had let him slip through her fingers, taking Talliann with him . . .

There were steps in the gloom, leading down. Calthar
clamped her teeth together and dragged herself over the
rim of the pit. Halfway down she was forced to pause to
allow the air that eluded her to return to her lungs. Her
breath rattled in her throat and rib cage and she tasted
blood in her mouth: she spat, coughed, spat again, and
crawled onward. And at last her groping hands felt
something soft that yielded beneath her fingers, and she
knew she had reached sanctuary.

She lay panting like an exhausted animal, spittle and
blood mingling on her chin as she marshaled her
thoughts. There must be a reckoning. Sun-Hound or no,
Kyre would pay for what he had stolen; and the price
would be Haven's destruction. The Mothers were angry
and demanded recompense; she, as their avatar, would
be the instrument of their revenge.

Calthar wanted Talliann back: but if need be, she could
and would do without her. Though she had created the
girl for a purpose, Talliann's flaw had always made her at
best an uncertain channel for the power Calthar drew on.
The price was worth paying—but if her recapture proved
impossible there was another vehicle for her power, a
darker vehicle; one that had lain dormant and waiting
throughout the years of her rule. It could be summoned
only once, and could not be banished again save by
destruction; but Calthar no longer cared for the risks. The
Mothers' hour had come. From the grave, from rotting
dust, they would rise again in triumph: and Haven and all
who dwelt within its walls would die.

Calthar's breath hissed in her throat, an insane blend of
pain and pleasure and anticipation. She huddled further
down among the debris that carpeted the floor of the pit,
closed her eyes, and her mind reached out. Heal me, she

said silently. *Heal me, and I shall bring about a vengeance to fulfill our deepest dreams!*

Later, she couldn't have said how long she lay in that place before the first tingling of returning strength began to course through her veins. When the sensation came, she smiled, and her limbs moved, sluggishly at first but then with great confidence, through the bones and dust among which she sprawled. She felt the wound Kyre had inflicted healing, fading to nothing more than a ragged white scar. She felt the blood she had lost regenerating within her, flowing fresh and alive in her arteries. And she felt the strength, the life force, seeping from the mortal remains of her predecessors in the pit, the crumbling, powdering corpses from which she drew both knowledge and an awesome rejuvenating power. She breathed deeply and drew the force into her, letting it spread through her to make her whole again. And when she was whole, she closed her eyes and spread her limbs wide, listening to the vengeful thoughts of the Mothers among whom she lay; until the inchoate sounds and words in her head coalesced into a single clear prospect, and she knew what she would do.

Calthar rose to her feet. Dust and cobwebs clung to her hair and to the tatters of her robe. For a few moments she stood motionless, reveling in the sensations of union with and regeneration by her long-dead predecessors. Then she moved toward the steps that would lead her out of the pit, and her wide mouth twisted in a terrible, purposeful smile.

Chapter 16

Simorh watched the departure of the servants who had brought Gamora to her tower, then said: "There must be no disturbance. Nothing."

"I've posted guards to stand watch at the outer door, and also at the foot of the stairs." DiMag smiled painfully. "There are still a few I can trust."

She nodded. "Very well. Then we'll begin."

Kyre felt Talliann's fingers entwining nervously with his, but his thoughts were too chaotic to allow him to do more than squeeze her hand in an attempt at reassurance. Since the shock of his revelation, much had happened—and much had changed. He had feared that DiMag and Simorh would find it impossible to accept the truth, but he had underestimated them both: they believed, and the pendant had added more than enough fuel to the fires of their belief. They had listened in silence while he told his full story: his encounter with the sea dwellers' messenger and the ensuing fight on the beach; Calthar's serpentine

scheming; his secret meeting with Talliann and the
revelations the pendant had brought; and finally, the
horror of confronting the Mothers and their escape from
the citadel. And he had told them the truth about the sea
people and their war with Haven: that the history to
which they had adhered for so long was flawed. The old
tongue, corrupted by centuries of change and neglect,
had led them into the false belief that the conflict was
unending and unresolvable; an eternal battle between two
separate races who could never hope to find accord. Kyre
knew better: for when he had lived and ruled in Haven,
the two races had been one. And he believed that, were it
not for the legacy which that first power-hungry sorceress
had handed down through the Mothers to Calthar, they
could be one again.

The truth, Kyre had told them gently, was in their
manuscripts. But even in his time the old language had
fallen into decay; since then the decline had progressed
so far that truth had become occluded and the legends
distorted by generations of misunderstanding. He
couldn't expect DiMag and Simorh to abandon the
teachings of generations past and accept what he told
them without question. But he could offer them one thing
which was, perhaps, more valuable than anything else—
the presence of the first Kyre, the real Sun-Hound with
his knowledge and his memories of their lost past,
among them once again.

He wished he had had the chance to speak with DiMag
alone, for he knew that, now his identity had been
revealed, the prince feared him. DiMag's attitude was an
uneasy blend of deference and defiance, and Kyre
wanted to reassure him that he had no wish to rule in
Haven as he had once done. The city was DiMag's by
right; Kyre was no usurper. He had returned, but his

place was at DiMag's side, not on his throne. Yet DiMag, beset by opposition, painfully aware of his own instability, had doubts. So far he had quashed them, but nonetheless Kyre wanted to give him the reassurance he craved.

And then there was Talliann . . .

Brigrandon had brought her to the prince's chambers at Kyre's request, and DiMag's first encounter with the girl who, for nearly ten years, had been the embodiment of all that was evil and corrupt had been hard. Talliann had no knowledge of her true self—but, unexpectedly, it had been Simorh who had had the insight to see past the myth to the underlying reality. And it was Simorh who had told Kyre of the second amulet—Talliann's amulet—which, so legend had it, had been lost when the Sun-Hound's consort committed suicide after her lover's death. The story she related had hurt Kyre like a sword thrust; yet it gave him a glimmer of hope. Talliann had died in Haven, and the clue to her talisman's whereabouts lay somewhere in their most ancient manuscripts. With both its twin and its rightful wearer gone, they believed, beyond recall, no one had ever troubled to search for it. But now Brigrandon, who in his capacity as royal tutor was also curator of Haven's historical records, was about to begin that search. Kyre could only hope and pray that the scholar would succeed in time.

Talliann herself had so far had little to say. She was still dazed with weariness, and most of what was revealed had been beyond her ability to comprehend. Kyre had hoped that with their return to Haven some of her forgotten past might come back to mind, but he had been disappointed: nothing seemed familiar to her. She was still very wary: she sensed DiMag's hostility and feared him because of it, and even with Brigrandon, who

had shown her nothing but kindness, she was cautious.
But to Kyre's great surprise, the one person whom
Talliann seemed prepared to trust was Simorh, and,
perhaps a little unwillingly on both sides, a rapport was
developing between them. The sorceress's sixth sense
had forced her to overcome her prejudices: she saw and
recognized the nature of the power latent in Talliann, and
knew that if she was prepared to acknowledge the true
Sun-Hound she had no choice but to acknowledge his
consort.

A sudden darkening of the room broke his chain of
thought and he looked up, blinking, to see that Simorh
had extinguished the lamps. The only light now came
from a small brazier placed near the head of the pallet
where Gamora lay, and by its uneasy glow everything in
the deeply shadowed sanctum looked grotesque and
distorted.

Simorh had changed her shift for the same thin black
robe she had worn on the night she conjured Kyre to the
ruined temple. Her hair, loosed, shone faintly in the
dimness, and her eyes were bright pinpoints as she
silently gestured to them all to take their allotted places.

They took up their stations: Simorh before the brazier
at Gamora's head, DiMag by the child's feet, Kyre and
Talliann on opposite sides of the pallet. The only sound
in the room was the slow, regular hush of Simorh's
breathing as she focused her concentration on the spell
and began to slip into a trance. Then, slowly, she closed
her eyes and held out both arms, fists clenched. The
brazier's light reflected fierily on her skin, and her hands
opened with a fluid gesture to allow twin streams of a
dark powder to fall onto the coals.

The brazier hissed, and vivid flames of blue and green
leapt up, engulfing Simorh's hands. She didn't flinch,

though by the suddenly vivid light Kyre saw her jaw
clench with momentary pain. Then, with the flames still
writhing about her fingers she began to chant.

It was a corruption of the old tongue, and the few
words he could recognize set cold claws into Kyre's
spine. Simorh's voice was pitched to the lowest register
her throat could produce, her tone guttural, the words
twining and twisting on her tongue. The chant grew more
rhythmic, more insistent; shadows danced about the
room, forming brief and strange images that made Kyre
shudder, and the air seemed to thicken and grow clammy
with a claustrophobic sense of anticipation, as though
something that lurked and waited beyond the borders of
the senses was slowly closing in. The power that
emanated from Simorh's quivering form was building,
building; still she chanted, calling on every reserve
within her—

And Gamora's eyes snapped open.

The strangled cry that broke from DiMag's throat was
stifled instantly as the brazier went out, plunging them
into darkness. For a moment that seemed to last an
eternity the silence crawled with near-unbearable tension, while Kyre's shocked mind wondered if he had
imagined what he'd thought he saw in the instant before
the brazier was extinguished. Then a new light began to
glow from the pallet where the child lay: a cold, green-
white glow, phosphorescent and sickly. It gained strength
until Gamora's body was haloed by it, and when Kyre
looked down at the pallet he felt his stomach lurch
violently.

Gamora's eyes had indeed opened. She was staring
into the room, and on her face was a smile never seen
before on the face of any child ever born. Behind her,
Simorh's expression was frozen into a look of paralyzed

horror; as DiMag started forward she held up her hands,
palms out, warning him to stay back.

The little girl began to sit up. She moved as though
controlled by invisible hands, her back rigid, arms by her
sides, and there was something repulsive about the
apparent lack of effort it took her to rise. She sat bolt
upright, and her head turned slowly, jerkily, first to one
side, then to the other. Her gaze swept the room and the
four appalled witnesses, then her mouth opened, and a
voice that made Kyre swallow back bile issued from her
throat.

Calthar's voice.

*"I believe I almost pity you, Simorh who calls herself
sorceress!"* The familiar mockery lent an uglier edge to
the words. DiMag stared at his daughter, transfixed, and
Simorh could only utter a faint, gagging sound. It was
echoed by Calthar's laughter.

*"You can't lift the enchantment, foolish child. The
little one sleeps, and only I can wake her—should I
choose. But you have angered me. You have angered my
Mothers. It would be fit punishment, I think, were I to
reach out my hand and sever the fragile cord of your
daughter's life!"*

"No!" Simorh's cry was anguished with impotent
fury, and Kyre felt his pulse throb with a rage that
matched hers. He spoke without thinking, unable to
prevent the words from spilling out.

"I should have stayed to see you dead, and consigned
you back to the putrefaction from which you came! May
the Eye help me, I should have dismembered your
corrupting body and scattered the pieces to the tide for
sea worms to devour!"

"Ah . . ." The dreadful voice issuing from
Gamora's lips took on a quality like poisoned honey. *"So*

*Haven's little dog is among you, is he? My salutations,
Sun-Cur. You did well to escape me, but you should have
realized that the Mothers take good care of their own.''*

"Damn you!" Simorh shrieked. "Release my daughter!"

Gamora's head turned, the small body twisting about
until she faced her mother. Simorh started to shake
violently, but forced herself not to look away. *"It seems
we have reached the heart of this matter,"* Calthar said
sweetly. *"You want your child restored to you. And I, in
my turn, want something from you.''*

There was a sharp silence. Then Simorh took a deep
breath, and whispered: "What . . . ?"

Calthar laughed. The low chuckle from the little girl's
throat was horrible. *"This, Simorh who calls herself
sorceress, I tell you now, and I tell you once. If you want
your child to live, then the girl Talliann must be brought
to the ruin on the shingle strand, on the night of the
Great Conjunction. There you will give her into my
keeping—and only then will I lift the bewitchment.''*

Kyre spat an involuntary protest and, forgetting in his
fury that Calthar wasn't physically present in the room,
started toward the pallet with murder in his eyes. DiMag
moved quickly to intercept him, grabbing hold of his arm
and hissing urgently in his ear, *"No!* Hear her out!"

"Prince DiMag?" Gamora's head swiveled again and
her unseeing eyes glared at the prince. *"It seems I am
in the most exalted of company. How interesting to encounter you again, after . . . what must it be? Nine
years?"*

DiMag's expression tightened, but he kept his voice
even. "Don't waste your breath mocking me. You say
that you will break the spell you have cast on my
daughter if Talliann is returned to you on Dead Night. Do

you seriously expect us to believe that if such a bargain is made, you'll keep your word?"

Gamora uttered a long, fluttering sigh, and Calthar's voice said, *"Prince, you flatter yourself! I have no interest in you, or your witch-wife, or your child, or the troublesome mongrel you keep on your leash. Your options are simple. Do as I have told you, and I will release the little girl. Fail, and as the Hag's light strikes your gates, your daughter will die and my Mothers will destroy Haven.*

"You have heard my terms, Prince DiMag, and I have no more to say to you. You have five more nights to ponder your decision. And then I will be waiting."

As Calthar spoke the last word, the cold halo around Gamora's small frame flickered and dimmed. The child's eyes rolled and, for an instant only, something resembling terrified intelligence flickered behind their blindness. Then the halo vanished, and the child fell soundlessly back onto the pallet.

"Gamora!" Simorh almost stumbled over in her frantic effort to reach the little girl's side. She grasped her shoulders, hugging her, shaking her. "Gamora!"

DiMag pulled her back, gently but implacably. "Simorh, it's no use!" He drew her against him, and buried his face in her hair. "You won't wake her—you can't fight this!"

She was quiet for a few moments, her shaking gradually subsiding. Then, her voice under an iron-hard but painfully thin shell of self-control, she said, "Light. I want light. The lamps, the curtains . . . *quickly!*"

Kyre stumbled across the room to where he could just make out the faint outline of a window. He dragged the curtain back, but it made little difference; only the faintest hint of dawn glimmered through the mist outside. But it was enough to show him a lamp bracket, and flint and tinder on a table beneath. Fumbling, he lit the lantern and a yellow glow banished the worst of the shadows. Talliann hastened to light a second lamp, and as it flared he felt the thick, claustrophobic atmosphere receding a little. They all looked at each other, no one knowing what to say. Eventually, it was Talliann who broke the silence.

"She tried to touch me . . ." Her voice was barely audible. "I felt her, like a—like a dead hand inside my mind. But she couldn't reach me."

"No . . ." Simorh said. She glanced quickly at Kyre, frowned. "You're safe from her here. As Kyre said you would be. But Gamora . . ." She bit her lip, hard.

DiMag turned toward the window. "Five nights." His tone was grim; then he shook his head and pinched the bridge of his nose tiredly between thumb and forefinger. "I must summon the council. We daren't lose another moment—I have to tell them what's happened."

He stared toward the door without waiting for anyone to reply, and Kyre caught his arm. "Prince DiMag, you don't believe that Calthar meant what she said? That she'd keep her part of any bargain?"

"Of course I don't believe it!" DiMag fired back angrily.

"The council may not agree with you."

"That's a risk I'll have to take. I can't face this alone, Kyre. None of us can." The furious light died from his eyes then and his shoulders slumped. He disengaged his arm from Kyre's grip and patted the other man's shoulder. "You'd best come to the court hall. You'll want to hear what the council has to say."

"Prince DiMag . . ."

DiMag and Kyre looked in surprise at Talliann. The black-haired girl's eyes were wide and frightened, but there was a determined set to her jaw. She met the prince's gaze and said, "I'll go back."

"No, Talliann!" Kyre was aghast.

"Yes," she argued stubbornly, and looked unhappily around the room. "I can't stay here. It isn't right; I—I'm endangering you all. And the little girl . . ."

"Talliann, you can't!" Kyre protested. "If I were to—"

DiMag held up a hand, forestalling what Kyre had been about to say. He addressed Talliann, and his voice was gentle.

"Lady, there's nothing to be gained from sending you back to the citadel. Believe me, if I thought my daughter would profit from giving you back into Calthar's hands, I'd drag you to the temple on Dead Night myself—Kyre might put your well-being first: I don't." He smiled thinly. "But Kyre's right. Calthar won't keep her word—but while we have you, she won't dare do Gamora any further harm for fear of losing her bargaining power. So you must remain with us, and we must find a way to thwart her." He glanced at Simorh for confirmation, and the sorceress nodded curtly.

"Yes. You must stay, Talliann. You're our hostage to Gamora's survival."

"It's a miserable stalemate," DiMag said, to no one in particular. "And we have so little time."

Simorh crossed the room to join him. As she stood beside him DiMag thought that she was about to reach out and touch him, link her arm with his, and though the contact would have been unfamiliar he found himself longing for the comfort it might bring. But instead she withdrew her hand, and only gave him a quick, sad smile through the tawny curtain of her hair.

"You'd best send for the councillors," she said quietly. "Take Kyre with you—Talliann can stay with me for a while. I want to ensure Gamora is watched and guarded. We'll join you as soon as we can."

DiMag nodded. "There are a few councillors who won't take kindly to being hauled from their beds before daybreak. They'd best get accustomed to it—I doubt if any of us will sleep soundly again until this is over." He turned, gazed at her for a moment, then kissed her, lightly and briefly, on the brow.

Simorh stood very still as DiMag and Kyre left the room. The kiss had been unexpected, and it both gladdened and hurt. Such a small, apparently meaningless gesture; and it had cost DiMag little. But it was a beginning.

Morning was advancing but the sun was invisible behind a dense layer of cloud when the meeting in the court hall came to its chaotic and unhappy end. As the councillors filed out with his words of dismissal still ringing in their ears, DiMag sat rigid on his great chair, listening to the sounds drifting to the hall from the palace's main courtyard. Distant, stentorian voices, the clash of metal, the concerted tattoo of a myriad boots stamping on flagstones . . . Haven's army drilled intensively under the commands of its sergeants and masters-at-arms, and DiMag wondered wearily what point there was to it all. Whatever Dead Night held in store, it wasn't the readiness or otherwise of the fighting men that would decide the outcome of the battle.

Nor, he thought bitterly, would it be the wisdom of the court council that would come to Haven's aid now. He

had expected some skepticism in the face of the story he
had told them; he had expected opposition to the
decisions he had made: what he hadn't anticipated was
the intensity of that opposition. And he realized now that
he might have made a very grave mistake.

It was, of course, Vaoran who had led the main faction
against him; though the swordsmaster had cleverly
managed to give the appearance of merely being swept
along by the prevailing tide of opinion, DiMag had seen
the triumph in his eyes when the arguments began. The
prince had told the council the full truth—he had
revealed the identities of Kyre and Talliann, had de-
scribed Simorh's attempt to break the bewitchment of
Gamora and the consequence that had followed; he had
apprised them of Calther's ultimatum. They had listened
in silence, they had conferred together while the prince
watched uneasily and Kyre sat cross-legged on the dais
beside him—and then the condemnation had started.

The council was not willing to believe that the Sun-
Hound had returned from the dead. With respect, as
Councillor Grai, whom DiMag had never trusted, unctuously prefaced his speech, if such a miracle were
possible it would be enshrined in the city's historical
manuscripts. But their most erudite historians, over
many generations, had found no trace of such a concept.

"Councillor," DiMag retorted sharply, "you are as
aware as I am that our records are flawed. The old tongue
had declined; we can't be sure of the accuracy of our
translations. Besides, we have the Sun-Hound's lost
amulet. I don't think even you can deny the reality of
that!"

"Indeed, my lord." Grai bowed in thin acknowledgment of the point. "No one here disputes that the quartz
is what it purports to be: that at least is documented. But

if it has been in the possession of the sea demons, who's to say that they might not use it for their own ends?" He glanced over his shoulder at the councillors behind him, and more than a few nodded assent. "We have no proof that this Sun-Hound is anything more than a cipher who has been corrupted to their use!"

"Or was in league with them from the beginning," someone said in a deliberately carrying aside.

DiMag turned a basalt gaze on the speaker, who stood just two paces from Vaoran. "You presume to doubt the integrity of my wife?" he demanded ferociously.

The man reddened. "No, my lord: I merely—"

Vaoran interrupted smoothly. It was the first time he had spoken directly to DiMag, and that, the prince thought, was a dangerous sign. "My colleague intended no slight to the Princess Simorh's efforts to aid our city by creating a cipher to be its champion, sir," he said. "But he fears—as many of us fear—that the princess might also have been an unwitting victim of the sea devils' duplicity."

The innuendo was clear. DiMag sat back. "Then you believe I have been duped?" There was a challenging undercurrent in his voice.

Vaoran inclined his head. "I'm not in a position to judge, my lord. But if this man is Kyre—the real Kyre— I might have anticipated some more positive evidence to back his claim."

Kyre's eyes narrowed. "I'm not in the business of performing miracles, swordsmaster. I never was, as you'd know if you read your own history."

"Nonetheless, Prince DiMag, I'm sure you must appreciate the council's reluctance to accept his story without sound proof. We have only Haven's interests at heart, and—if I may speak bluntly—we've seen enough of what the sea demons can do to take nothing on trust now."

Grai stepped forward again before DiMag could respond. "My lord prince, as your senior adviser my considered opinion is this: we accept and acknowledge that our astronomers were mistaken in their calculations, and that the Dead Night conjunction will occur five nights from now. To that end, Swordsmaster Vaoran has already issued orders to our army to intensify their efforts to make ready in what little time we have left."

Vaoran gazed modestly at the floor and smiled faintly. Though he begrudged it, DiMag had at least to give him credit for his prompt action.

"As to the other matters you have placed before us, I cannot accept the assertion, nor even the likelihood, that the Sun-Hound has truly returned to us." He licked his lips. "Indeed, under less urgent circumstances I'd urge the council to look on such an assertion as blasphemy."

DiMag sighed, but said nothing.

"And the third matter—the ultimatum delivered by the sorceress Calthar." Grai shook his head. "My lord, the choice is clear. We can't trust the sea demons, but neither can we afford to lose the smallest chance to help our little princess. On Dead Night, the girl must be returned whence she came. And her return must be part of our own strategy to best the sorceress."

Kyre jerked forward as though he meant to start to his feet, but DiMag gripped his arm, fingers digging painfully into his bicep.

"Strategy?" the prince said dangerously. "What strategy?"

Grai looked at Vaoran, who cleared his throat.

"As yet I can't be more specific, my lord. There hasn't been the time for concrete proposals to be suggested, but that can soon be rectified. If our scholars and historians join forces with our military tacticians, we can find a means by which the sorceress can be overpowered, and—''

Kyre could keep silent no longer. *"Overpowered?"* he interrupted explosively, and this time DiMag's restraining hand wasn't enough to stop him from leaping to his feet. "Are you insane?" He fought back the impulse to wade in among the councillors and smash Vaoran's complacency with his fist, and with a great effort brought his fury under control. "If you have ever come face to face with Calthar, swordsmaster, you'd know that what you're suggesting is *suicidal*!"

Vaoran smiled thinly. "We're speaking now of a full military detachment, my friend; perhaps an ambush, perhaps something more subtle. That bitch from the sea is only mortal—"

"She is not mortal!" Seething, Kyre wondered if the councillors had listened to a word of the story DiMag had recounted to them. "Not in any sense that you or I understand the word! By all the laws of nature she should have been dead half a century ago, yet she lives, and she has the appearance of youth! How long do you think your military strategies will last against the kind of power which can grant her that?"

Vaoran inclined his head and made a gesture that suggested the helplessness of a man faced with blind unreason. When he spoke, it was to DiMag.

"My lord, I fully appreciate the—ah—Sun-Hound's agitation. However, I submit that his arguments are unhappily colored by his personal concerns—and I believe that my views accord with those of the majority in this hall?"

The interrogative brought murmurs of assent; too

many, DiMag realized, to give the lie to Vaoran's
presumption. He waved to Kyre to sit down again,
shaking his head in a swift warning gesture as the other
man seemed about to speak again, and cleared his throat.

"Swordsmaster Vaoran—Councillor Grai—gentlemen. You have heard the facts of this matter from me,
and I in turn have listened to your arguments." His eyes
were as hard and cold as unpolished brass. "I was
unaware, before Councillor Grai gave us all the benefit
of his considered opinion, that the question of Kyre's
identity was at issue. I have all the evidence I need to
convince me, as does the Princess Simorh. I have also
decided that there will be no attempt to treat with
Calthar, duplicitously or otherwise. Talliann will not be
used as part of any scheme to outwit her."

"My lord!" Grai protested. "If the ultimatum is
ignored—"

"If the ultimatum is ignored, it won't make our
situation any worse. No, Grai: I won't be argued with.
Talliann is and will remain under my protection."

Vaoran glared at him. "Prince DiMag, I must add my
protest to Grai's! I would remind you—"

"No!" DiMag was rapidly losing his temper. "I
would remind you, Vaoran, that the council is my servant
and not my master! Talliann stays in Haven—and if she
is what I believe her to be, then by the Eye you'll thank
me for that decision before this is over!"

Vaoran's face was granite and the prince saw rebellion
in his eyes. DiMag's command of the situation was
teetering on the edge of a deadly precipice: his decision
had added a good deal of fuel to the fires of those who
were subtly trying to prove him unfit to rule. If Vaoran
chose this moment to challenge his leadership, he could
well have enough of the council behind him to sway a
large majority in his favor.

Vaoran said, with great care, "My lord, duty compels me to urge you to think again." The words had a clear double meaning.

"Your duty," DiMag retorted, "is to ensure that our armed forces are properly drilled and trained, and in that capacity to keep me informed of progress. I'd suggest, Vaoran, that you look to that, rather than to matters on which you are not qualified to advise your prince." He smiled, but the smile was coldly hostile. "Do I make myself clear?"

There was a long pause. Then Vaoran, face flushing with anger, said: "*Quite* clear, my lord."

"Good. Then I wish you good morning." DiMag's gaze raked the entire assembly. "All of you."

And now the great doors had closed behind the last of the councillors, leaving DiMag and Kyre alone, but for a handful of silent stewards, in the court hall.

Kyre got slowly to his feet and stood looking at the prince, who ignored him. "My lord—"

DiMag's head turned. His face was rigid with tension. "Don't call me that," he said. "Coming from you, it sounds ironic to say the least."

"It shouldn't," Kyre replied. "You are the ruler here."

"Am I?" DiMag countered bitterly. "I'm beginning to wonder." Then as Kyre was about to say something more he waved an impatient hand. "I don't want to discuss that, or anything else, at the moment. Let it be, Kyre; keep what you were going to say for another time." He stood up stiffly, then paused as the small door behind the dais opened.

Simorh entered. She looked weary but there was a resolute set to her face: seeing that the hall was all but empty, she stopped, surprised, and looked queryingly at the prince. "Is the meeting over?"

"It's over." DiMag stepped awkwardly down from the dais. "You missed all the fun, Simorh."

"What was the outcome?"

He stared resentfully at her, but the resentment was for the world at large. "Precisely what I should have anticipated," he said, and headed for the door. Simorh made as though to follow, but the anger in his face, the rebuff in his eyes, stopped her. She watched until the door had closed behind him, and the curtain had fallen back into place, then turned slowly and looked at Kyre.

"It went badly." It was a statement, not a question, and Kyre nodded.

"Very." Briefly, he told her of the councillors' views and the near confrontation that had prefaced DiMag's angry dismissal. She listened in silence, then, when he had finished, sighed.

"I expected something like this." She shivered, hugged herself, then added with a trace of defiance in her voice, "DiMag won't be persuaded to change his mind."

"There's no reason why he should."

Simorh looked up at him. "You and I might be alone in that view."

There was still a faint edge of resentment in every word she addressed to him. She mistrusted him—now that she knew what he was, she wondered whether he might have ambitions to rule in her husband's stead.

She said abruptly, "I thought better of bringing Talliann with me. She's sleeping now, in my tower. The poor child's close to exhaustion."

"And . . . Gamora?"

"Guarded, and as safe as any power I possess can make her." She looked toward him again, but didn't quite seem able to meet his eyes directly. "I haven't . . . thanked you for what you did. Without you,

Gamora would have been lost to us forever." A pause.
"I don't want you to think that I'm not aware of the debt
I owe you."

"You owe me nothing, Princess," Kyre said gently,
suddenly pitying her. "I owe you my life—or had you
forgotten that?"

She grimaced. "Perhaps I had."

"Or perhaps you wanted to?"

She frowned. "I don't understand you." But her
expression was wary.

On an impulse Kyre moved toward her and laid his
hands on her shoulders. She flinched away, then froze,
staring at him with the frown fixed on her face.

"Simorh, I tried just now to explain to DiMag, but he
didn't want to hear me out. But I must say this—I have to
make you understand."

"Understand what?" She was still reluctant to look at
him.

"That I don't present any threat to the prince, or to
you. I might have ruled here once, but that was long,
long ago; I don't have ambitions to rule again." He
smiled. "Even if I had, so much has changed in Haven
since my time that I wouldn't know where to begin."

A sharp color had come to her face. "I didn't think—"

"Yes, you did. And I don't blame you. But believe
me, Simorh, I don't want to oust DiMag from his rightful
place!"

She gave a curt, bitter laugh, shrugging his hands
away, and turned her back. "If that's true, then you must
be one of the few men in the palace who hasn't harbored
such thoughts!"

"Maybe. In which case I want to help you ensure that
none of those men fulfill their secret ambitions."

"I wish you could."

"I think I can. I, and Talliann. If only we can find the lost amulet."

She looked back at him then and there was such agonizing despair in her eyes that his heart went out to her. He said: "Simorh, I can only ask you to trust me. Even in the midst of this crisis I know there are knives poised at DiMag's back. Will you try to believe that mine isn't one of the hands holding them?"

She thought about that for a long time, then, finally nodded.

"I understand you, Kyre," she said. "And I think I believe you." Now the barrier was down and she looked fully at him, her eyes candid. "I want to believe you."

"Isn't that a beginning?"

"A beginning . . . yes." An odd smile played about her mouth. "It's a beginning."

Vaoran was gratified to find that fifteen men of the seventeen to whom he'd sent his cryptic message were ready and able to answer the summons. Uncluttered though his room was, such a number made it crowded, and the majority were forced to choose between perching on the narrow window ledge or standing.

Vaoran dispensed with the social niceties; no wine was offered, no idle small talk preceded the matter at hand. The swordsmaster spoke bluntly and to the point, and the fifteen were equally pragmatic in their responses. Their view—as he had hoped but not dared to assume—was unanimous.

"So it's decided." Grai, who had elected himself spokesman for the visitors, nodded with satisfaction. "We will make our move on the day of Dead Night itself." He blinked sidelong at Vaoran. "My only reservation concerns the advisability of leaving it so late."

"I take your point," Vaoran said, "but to act earlier might be to take an even greater risk. We need to ensure that anyone who might oppose us will be too preoccupied with the imminent conflict to cause any trouble. Our strategy—our own strategy—for facing the sea demons needn't suffer in the meantime. We may not have overt control of the army, but we have all the influence we need in practice. The vast majority of our soldiers aren't, of course, privy to court matters; they simply obey orders, and it doesn't occur to them to question where those orders originate. We need only ensure that all concerned are well drilled in precisely what they must do, and precisely when they must do it."

Grai smiled, satisfied. "Then I have no further reservations. And I congratulate you, Vaoran, on such a skilled and thorough plan."

There were murmurs of agreement on which Vaoran inclined his head in acknowledgment "Thank you, my friends. And before we go our separate ways, I'd remind you once more that our first priority must always be the safety of the Princess Simorh and the little Princess Gamora. If DiMag has his way, that poor child will never open her eyes on this world again."

A short, burly army captain cleared his throat. "The sea-demon girl won't present any problem in that regard, sir. But I'm a little concerned about the . . ." He hesitated, not sure how to refer to Kyre in Vaoran's presence, then finished, "The one who calls himself the Sun-Hound."

"Mmm." Vaoran stroked his chin. "You're right to mention it, captain. I've been thinking about that, and I suspect it might be wiser to modify our original intention. Rather than take him prisoner as we intended, I think it would be more prudent to kill him."

He looked around the room to gauge the general reaction to his remark. No one spoke for a minute or so, then Grai coughed delicately.

"If I may add my voice to Vaoran's, I agree. That one could be trouble—safer to dispatch him altogether, rather than run the risk."

Any who might have had doubts found them submerged in the majority view. Vaoran nodded, and rose to his feet.

"Very well, gentlemen. We have only to await the moment. I thank you for coming, and I wish you all the best of fortune. Let's hope that this marks a new beginning for the city we all love!"

They left, as they had arrived, in twos and threes to avoid arousing comment. Grai was among the last to go, and as Vaoran escorted him to the door the plump councilor turned and smiled.

"Prince Vaoran," he said, and looked the other man up and down. "It suits you well, my friend. And it's my belief that yours will be the best dynasty Haven has had in a very long while!"

Chapter 17

HAVEN PREPARED ITSELF FOR DEAD NIGHT, AND WITH each day that dawned Kyre's forebodings grew.

He had to acknowledge that DiMag's forces were doing all they could to meet the threat from the sea, but he knew in his heart that it wasn't enough. On the rare occasions when sheer exhaustion forced him to snatch an hour or two of sleep, images of Calthar as he had last seen her stalked his dreams—Calthar, and her monstrous, rotting predecessors, the unbroken chain of Mothers that had passed down the centuries from that first traitress and founder of the city in the sea.

Malhareq: the quintessence of spiritual corruption; a rogue scion of her race—but as well as sorcerous power she had possessed charisma, and that charisma had been enough to earn her a willing following ready to challenge the Sun-Hound's rule and elevate her in his stead. With Brigrandon's help, Kyre had pieced together much of what had taken place after the attempted uprising that led to his demise. Malhareq had failed in her ultimate ambition to rule Haven: far from ensuring her victory, the death of their lord had aroused such fury in the warriors who opposed her that she had been forced to flee with her followers. She had taken refuge in the deeps of the sea— in those days, Kyre remembered, the people of Haven had been at home in both elements—and in her new domain she had founded a dynasty that had now grown strong enough to destroy the people from which it sprang so many centuries ago.

The two races could be one again, if only the cancerous legacy of the Mothers could be defied and their sway broken. But all Haven's army, and all Simorh's sorcery, couldn't hope to prevail against the power Calthar would wield on Dead Night. If there was any hope left for the city, it lay in the discovery of the lost amulet that was twin to Kyre's own.

Sometimes, as he sat in Brigrandon's rooms among the mind-numbing heaps of manuscripts, scrolls, and documents that the scholar had unearthed from the palace archives, Kyre came close to despair. Though Brigrandon had pressed every man and woman capable of understanding the old tongue into his service, their chances of finding the manuscript that would lead them to the talisman—if, indeed, such a manuscript existed at all—were remote, and worsening with each hour that passed. Their efforts were further hampered by the fact that their ability to translate the ancient language accurately was flawed at best: Kyre himself was the only man alive who could read the oldest of the documents with any fluency. And though he had learned much of Haven's history since his death, he had found not the smallest reference to what he so desperately sought.

If only Talliann could have remembered . . .

Simorh had tried to unlock the memories frozen in Talliann's mind, but she had failed. And the black-haired

girl's inability to recall her past life brought Kyre another
and more personal pain. She had been his lover, his
consort, his wife; the moon around which his sun
revolved. But although those memories were alive and
vital in his mind, to her they meant nothing. She had lost
the past, and he couldn't touch her, couldn't reach her—
and couldn't explain to her what they had once been to
each other. If he had tried to take up the threads of their
old life, Talliann couldn't have understood his reasons,
and he would run the risk of alienating her. And when he
looked at her, and saw the blankness in her dark eyes, the
emotion he felt was worse than bereavement.

For that reason alone he had forced himself to keep his
distance from Talliann. If she wondered at his reluctance
to spend time with her, she never voiced it: Simorh had
had a room prepared for her in her own tower, and the
girl spent most of each day either there or closeted with
the sorceress. She had found an unexpected champion in
Simorh; a bond had developed between the two, and
Kyre sometimes wondered if Simorh saw in Talliann's
estrangement from him an echo of her own estrangement
from DiMag.

As for DiMag himself, the prince seemed to have
become possessed by a ravening energy that drove him
day and night. He never slept—the daylight hours saw
him roving the palace, arguing with councillors, watching the drilling of the soldiers, conferring with those few
advisers he still felt he could trust; while at night he kept
vigil with Gamora or joined the weary-eyed scholars in
Brigrandon's rooms to pore fruitlessly for hour upon hour
over the ancient documents. The desperation he felt was
eating to the core of his being, his health was deteriorating fast; but nothing would persuade him to allow
himself a moment's ease.

And with each hour that trickled by, each manuscript

that yielded nothing and was set aside, Dead Night drew
nearer: until at last the sun set in a blaze that shot
ominous, angry shadows through the rising bank of fog
on the last night before the conflict.

Kyre felt as though his legs were about to give way
under him as he climbed the stairs to his own room in the
Sunrise Tower. He had been banished from his labors by
Brigrandon when he fell asleep for the third time over the
pile of parchments before him: the scholar, himself red-
eyed with weariness, had ordered him to sleep until
morning; his place would be taken by another and the
search would continue. Kyre was too dazed to argue. He
simply nodded, and walked slowly, joints stiff, from the
room.

His own chamber hadn't been occupied since his
return from the sea citadel and was damp and bitterly
cold, but he was past caring. He shut the door behind
him, stumbled to the bed, and didn't have the strength to
do more than pull a blanket roughly over himself before
he was asleep.

As soon as he opened his eyes in the darkness, he
realized that he hadn't woken naturally. Something had
disturbed his sleep; as his eyes grew a little better
accustomed to the dim, unnatural light refracted through
the window by the fog outside, he realized that he wasn't
alone in the room.

A fearful reflex made him sit up and reach out for a
weapon that wasn't there, but before he could coherently
challenge the human-shaped shadow lurking by the door
it moved, groping toward his bed.

"Kyre . . . ?" Her voice was soft and frightened,
and recognition stunned him. He had time to speak her
name, wonderingly, before Talliann had reached him and
flung her arms around him, her body quivering. He held

her tightly, unable to speak, kissing the crown of her black hair. She was crying—he could feel the wetness of her tears on his shoulder—and at last she whispered.

"I can't sleep. Not tonight, not—knowing what tomorrow will bring." Her whole frame shuddered. "Kyre, I'm so afraid!"

He turned her face toward his and kissed her again, first her brow, then her cheek, then, very lightly and tentatively, her lips. Fresh tears welled in her eyes.

"Don't send me away, Kyre. Please don't. I don't think I could bear being alone . . ."

Kyre pulled back the blanket and she climbed into the bed beside him. There was barely room for them both, but neither cared; Talliann nestled as close as she could to Kyre and he held her, protectively as he used to do, her head cradled in the crook of his arm. Her body felt as familiar to him as his own and her touch awoke yet more memories, insignificant in that they recalled only fleeting moments of their lives, yet precious to him nonetheless.

They didn't speak again. They simply lay in the moonshot darkness, easing their fear by sharing it in silence and stillness, only thankful not to be alone. And after a while, they slept.

In the chilly gray light of dawn, the city was unnervingly silent. From her window Simorh had seen the sky turn briefly roseate with the sunrise before a blanket of cloud moved in to cut off the brilliance. She had refused to look for an omen in the weather, good or bad, feeling that she could no longer trust her instincts. But her heart felt like a solid ball of lead beneath her ribs.

Thean came in softly, bearing a covered tray which she set down on a table near the sorceress's bed.

"Bread and a herb beverage, lady, as you asked," she said.

Simorh turned her head and managed a bleak smile. "Thank you, Thean. I won't need you again for a while yet. You should try to sleep a little longer."

The girl nodded and left as quietly as she had come. Simorh stared at the tray for a few moments—bread was all she would allow herself to eat today, but she didn't even want that—then she left the window and walked down the stairs and through the anteroom to her inner sanctum, where she stood for a long time gazing at the motionless figure on the couch.

The curtains had been drawn in the room, and the only illumination came from four small lamps set at the cardinal points around the couch. Gamora lay under a light blanket with her feet together and arms folded over her breast: her face was a peaceful mask and she might have been naturally sleeping.

Or dead. Though the room's trappings were a vital precaution to protect the child, the tableau reminded Simorh of the day twelve years ago when the body of DiMag's father had lain in state to receive the last farewells of a grieving family before he went to his funeral pyre. *Omens*, she thought again, and to reassure herself she moved to the couch and touched Gamora's forehead with light fingers. Her warmth banished the worst of Simorh's fears but gave her little comfort, and she turned and left the room—to find DiMag waiting for her.

"Thean said you were awake." DiMag looked hag-ridden, then glanced toward the door of the inner room. "No change?"

"Nothing." She shook her head and blinked back tears, angry with herself for giving way to weakness at this late hour. "You should try to sleep yourself, DiMag."

He shrugged. "I would if I could. But it doesn't matter

now, does it? When tomorrow dawns I'll either be resting easy in my bed, or sleeping for eternity." He tried to smile, but the attempt at levity hadn't worked for either of them, Sighing, he turned toward the window. "Kyre at least has rested. Brigrandon ordered him to bed last night when he all but collapsed over his manuscripts." This time he did smile. "I sent a servant to check on him a little while ago. He's still asleep—and Talliann's with him."

"Talliann? She went to him?"

"So it would seem. Perhaps after all she's beginning to regain her memory without the aid of the amulet."

Simorh felt a pang of bitter envy stab through her, and quelled it. "I wish that could be true," she said, then added: "The manuscripts—I suppose there's still no clue?"

"Nothing. DiMag shook his head and scuffed at a threadbare patch in the carpet with the toe of one boot. "We must, I think, face up to the prospect of meeting our enemies without the help we'd hoped for." He blinked, then his expression hardened and his voice became brisk. "With that in mind, I've ordered the full council to meet three hours before sunset, in the court hall. There are bound to be last-minute details to clarify. I thought you'd better know, in case you want to attend." His eyes were frank. "I'd appreciate it if you did."

"Of course I'll attend." If she could do nothing more than lend her voice in support to his, Simorh thought, it would at least be something.

The prince nodded. "Then I'd best get down to the courtyard. Our foot-soldiery are about to be put through their paces one last time; for whatever little good it may do, I should give them the benefit of my moral support." He hesitated, then moved toward her and, to her surprise, took hold of her hand. "I'm sorry, Simorh," he said, and there was terrible weariness and terrible sadness in his voice. "I wish things could have been different . . ." And he raised her hand to his lips and kissed her fingers.

"Don't, DiMag!" She turned her head away in distress, and abruptly he released her.

"I know," he said. "It's too late. I'm sorry . . ." And he turned and limped out of the room.

Haven was as ready as it could ever hope to be. The army had completed its final drill; in the city itself, every able-bodied man and not a few women prepared weapons that ranged from well-honed swords and daggers to fish-gutting knives, staves, and horsewhips. DiMag had issued no order to press the citizens into service, but, knowing what was at stake, they would fight without the need for compulsion, lending their numbers to the ranks of trained soldiers.

The sun passed meridian, and the first thin trails of mist formed again in the lower-lying streets. As councillors began to file into the court hall for their final meeting, Kyre and Brigrandon sat in the scholar's room with the now nightmarishly familiar heaps of documents before them. Brigrandon had slept for a while in the predawn hours while his team worked on, and when Kyre returned he had dispatched the others to their beds; now they were alone with the manuscripts and their diminishing hopes.

Talliann, too, was sleeping. When Kyre woke he had found her gone, and when he went in search of her Falla had told him that she was with Simorh, helping the sorceress to make her preparations. When the sun set, Kyre thought, he would go to her . . .

In the court hall, the gathering was all but complete. Liveried stewards opened the double doors for DiMag and Simorh as they approached together, Simorh's hand

resting in a formal posture on DiMag's arm. She wore
her black robe rather than more customary court attire as
a deliberate reminder to the council that she was a
sorceress as well as a princess; seeing her, DiMag had
acknowledged the gesture with a small smile and his eyes
had been momentarily warm. They walked side by side
toward the great chair, watched by the silent ranks of
advisers. Together they mounted the dais, and DiMag
took his seat.

"Gentlemen," he said, "as you are all aware, this is
our last meeting before Dead Night—and there's little
point in pretending that it might not be the last meeting
that will ever be convened in the court of Haven. I thank
you for taking time from your urgent duties, and I assure
you that I won't keep you longer than necessary. I intend
simply to apprise you of the position as it now stands,
and to reiterate the strategy that will be put into operation
at sunset. I—And he stopped, frowning, as a group of
councillors moved aside suddenly and Vaoran stepped
out of the ranks to stand before the dais.

The swordsmaster looked up at the throne, and there
was a smile on his face. He laid a hand on the hilt of his
sheathed sword, and said in a cool voice that carried
easily through the hall, "I think not, my lord."

Thean and Falla tried to stop the six men who forced
their way into the tower ten minutes after Simorh had
left, but against such a strength they could do nothing.
Two of the intruders—one sporting livid parallel
scratches on his face where Thean's nails had raked him
as they struggled—pinned the girls' arms behind their
backs and held them, while another went into Simorh's
inner sanctum and the remaining three took the stairs to
the rooms above. Moments later the girls heard shouting,
scuffles, a woman's scream of protest, and the three

reappeared with Talliann struggling like a wildcat in their grasp. She was biting, kicking, flailing wildly; only when one of the men bunched his fist and hit her on the jaw did she subside.

They dragged her toward the door, and the sixth of their number emerged from the sanctum with Gamora in his arms.

A short, burly army captain entered the barracks flanked by two of his most trusted sergeants. His men, who had gathered in the mess hall, were baffled by his unexpected summons—but the captain soon allayed their puzzlement. A minor change in strategy, nothing more; and it took only minutes to clarify. The soldiers were content.

The small detachment of armed men who gathered in the palace's entrance hall had been carefully and precisely instructed in their task. The man they wanted would be with the scholar Brigrandon, and their orders were clear. The old man wasn't to be harmed beyond the demands of restraint, but his companion was another matter. Their sergeant had told them to do what must be done as quickly and as cleanly as possible, then bring the corpse back to the barracks.

The men waited until their numbers were complete, then they formed up and moved off toward the terrace.

DiMag stared white-faced at Vaoran and said, his voice shaking with rage: "I don't think I believe what I'm hearing! You dare to stand before me and speak such treachery—"

"I dare because I must, Prince DiMag!" Vaoran raised his voice to cut across the prince's fury. "You have left Haven with no other choice, for you have proved yourself unfit to rule—therefore your rule must end!"

DiMag got to his feet. "Guards!" He gestured to the uniformed men ranged in a line behind the dais. "Arrest Swordsmaster Vaoran! The charge is treason!"

The guards didn't move, only continued to stare blank-faced ahead of them. Vaoran smiled.

"The guardsmen are aware of their duty to Haven, Prince DiMag. Their loyalty is to our city before all else."

Realizing the full extent of the betrayal, DiMag snatched at the hilt of his sword. He had half drawn it from its scabbard when Vaoran spoke again.

"The guardsmen also have orders to kill anyone who makes an attempt on the life of an appointed councillor," he said, and his smile widened sardonically. "As a matter of self-denfense, such an order is quite justified." He nodded to the guards, and as one they drew their swords and held them at a threatening angle toward the throne.

DiMag felt Simorh's hand take his in a viselike clasp, but he couldn't respond. Shock made his pulse pound as though his whole body were being assaulted by hammers, and his only coherent thought was: *I should have known . . . may the Eye help me, I should have known!*

"Traitor . . ." His voice grated and he could barely get the word out. *"Traitor!"*

Grai cleared his throat and stepped forward to stand at Vaoran's side. The prince turned a searing, accusing gaze on him, but Grai ignored it. "This is not treachery, Prince DiMag, but the just and necessary decision of the properly appointed members of the court council of Haven," he said. "And as spokesman for that council, it is my duty to inform you that the decision to remove you from office has been ratified by a sufficient majority to make any question of treason irrelevant." Beside him, Vaoran glanced round at his colleagues, his eyes speculative as his gaze rested on certain individuals whose support he couldn't yet count on. That, he thought, would change in good time.

DiMag continued to stare at Grai for a few moments longer, then slowly sat down as the last vestiges of his strength suddenly drained away.

"Grai," he said desperately, "do you have any idea of what this insanity means? In three hours the sun will set, and we'll face the deadliest threat we've ever known. To choose this moment to pursue your self-seeking ambitions, when Haven is on the brink of disaster—" He shook his head helplessly. "You're mad; all of you!"

"Plans for fighting the sea demons will suffer no setback," Vaoran countered. "But not your plans, Prince DiMag—ours."

DiMag sucked in breath with a hissing sound. "You've been scheming for this moment since the first—"

"For long enough to ensure that we give our city its best chance—its only chance—of survival!" Vaoran snapped. "We've suffered under the burden of your whims and obsessions for too long, prince! You can rant, you can rage—but there's not a thing you can do to stop us!" He shook off Grai's attempt to lay a restraining hand on his arm. "We have had enough, *my lord*." He gestured to the guard behind DiMag's chair. "Disarm the prince, and detain him."

DiMag hadn't the time to do more than rise and turn before strong hands pinioned his arms and pulled him from the dais. His sword was dragged from its scabbard and he found himself surrounded by armed men. He couldn't react in any way. Shock had taken him in a rigid grip, and he felt as if he were dreaming.

Vaoran looked up at Simorh, who still stood on the dais. She seemed as stunned as DiMag, and the swordsmaster gave her a smile that was intended to be encouraging.

"Lady—may I assist you down?"

She snatched her hand away as he reached toward her. "Swordsmaster Vaoran." Her voice was pitched low. "What you have done here today, your perfidy, is—is" She grimaced, striving to control herself. "You are scum!"

Vaoran's face clouded. "Lady, it pains me to hear such condemnation from you, and I hope that when this crisis is over I can convince you of my sincerity. We have no quarrel with you—indeed, your well-being is of paramount importance to all loyal citizens, as is that of the Princess Gamora."

She looked at him with withering contempt. "You are a liar, Swordsmaster Vaoran."

"Madam, I am not." He placed one foot on the dais, chagrined by the way she immediately stepped back, then suddenly drew his sword and held it up before his face in a formal salute.

"Princess Simorh, it will now be my privilege to take the throne of Haven as its new ruler. In that capacity, I pledge to you the honor which is your right." He completed the salute, returned the sword to its scabbard, and though his smile was for her alone he was unable to resist glancing surreptitiously at DiMag. "And though I make no presumptions, madam, it's my fervent hope that you will one day consent to take up again your role of consort."

Simorh stared at him in utter disbelief, and DiMag made a violent movement to free himself from his guards which was instantly restrained. He didn't speak, and Simorh struggled to find words that would adequately express her loathing for the burly man who stood before her. She longed to raise one hand and blast Vaoran where he stood, but she had no such power: her sorcery wasn't in the order of Calthar's. But Vaoran must have seen something of that longing in her eyes, for he stepped back, and signaled to the rest of the guardsmen.

"Please escort the Princess Simorh to her tower," he said, and bowed to the sorceress. "With your permission, lady, I'll wait on you as soon as my business here is concluded. I've prepared a strategy that I hope will restore the Princess Gamora back to us and it's only right that you should know the details."

White-lipped, Simorh said curtly, "Very well. You have my permission." She was aware of DiMag's hot gaze on her, but didn't dare look at him lest she gave herself away. Intuition was telling her to make no attempt to argue with Vaoran, but instead to appear to comply with his wishes. If she could keep some measure of her freedom, she might yet find a way of working against the usurper. She only prayed that DiMag didn't believe she would betray him.

DiMag watched as she was led from the hall. His face was a mask, and if Vaoran had hoped to see distress or fear in his eyes he was disappointed. When Simorh and her escort had gone, he stepped up onto the dais and looked first at the throne and then at the man he had deposed.

"Take the ex-prince to his rooms, and see that he's well-guarded," he said. DiMag went without demur, and Vaoran turned to face the council.

"Gentlemen." He lowered himself slowly onto the great chair, settled himself on the uncomfortable seat. "To business . . ."

Brigrandon said in a tightly controlled voice: "Kyre . . ."

Kyre looked up, blinking as his eyes tried to refocus

from the crabbed script he had been reading, and when he saw Brigrandon's face his heart missed a beat painfully. He stood up. "You haven't—"

"I don't know. A lot of it's badly faded, and I can't translate some of the words. But I think you'd better come and look."

The scholar pulled the lamp on his table closer as Kyre bent to peer over his shoulder at the document. It was, Kyre saw from the first words on the page, an account of the construction of a temple to honor Haven's dead hero, and the thought that it was the same building which now stood in ruins on the shingle bar gave him a peculiar frisson.

"Here," Brigrandon said, stabbing with one dusty finger. "That sentence; something about an enshrining. What, exactly, does it say?"

Kyre's eyes followed the line he indicated. For a moment he couldn't let himself believe it . . . but it was there. *It was there!*

"Brigrandon," he said, his voice soft with awe, "this is it . . . this is what we've been searching for. *Talliann's amulet is in the old temple!*"

And at the dedication of the crypt, beneath the central flagstone was placed the talisman of our Sun-Hound's beloved consort—a symbol here which, Kyre remembered, had always been used to depict Talliann's name—*who gave herself to the embrace of death in grief at her lord's passing. This amulet will stand sentinel between Haven and her enemies, until such time as it may be reunited with its lost twin and shall bring back to us all that we have lost . . .*

"Oh, Kyre . . ." Brigrandon said in an old, old voice. "And we'd almost given up hope . . ."

"DiMag must be told—and Simorh." Kyre started toward the door, but before he reached it it was flung open from outside. On the threshold stood Nirn, Brigrandon's young servant. His face was flushed and he was breathless; he stumbled into the room and slammed the door at his back.

"Master, there's a detachment of soldiers on their way here—"

"Soldiers?" Brigrandon was nonplussed, and Nirn nodded, gulping down lungfuls of air.

"They're coming for the Sun-Hound—to arrest him. Master, the palace has been taken over, the prince deposed, and—"

"What?" Brigrandon was on his feet. *"Deposed?* Nirn, are you out of your mind?"

"No, Brigrandon; wait." Kyre waved the old man to silence and addressed the breathless servant. "Nirn, are you sure of this?"

"Yes, sir. It happened a bare twenty minutes ago; there was a meeting in the court hall, the royal guard had been corrupted, and Swordsmaster Vaoran—"

"Vaoran . . ." Suddenly disbelief changed to understanding in Brigrandon's eyes. "Of course: *Vaoran.* But I didn't think he'd be so stupid as to choose a moment like this!"

"On the contrary; he couldn't have chosen better," Kyre said grimly. "Nirn, what else do you know?"

"Very little, sir; only that it all seems to have been accomplished without trouble. There's talk of prisoners, but not many."

Prisoners . . . *Talliann!* Kyre thought in alarm. He moved toward the door. "Brigrandon, I must go!"

"No, sir!" Nirn cried. "The soldiers are coming for you—if you go out on the terrace you won't be able to avoid them!"

"The lad's right," Brigrandon said tersely. "And with Vaoran in power, you can be sure they don't mean to

carry you into the palace with a laurel crown on your
head." He looked round the room, and his gaze lit on a
window. "Can you get through that?"

Kyre eyed it. "I think so."

"Then go. Out there is a disused herb garden; it isn't
overlooked, and it's overgrown enough to offer plenty of
hiding places. I'll send the soldiers on a wild goose chase
and find out as much as I can at the same time. Stay put
until I come for you personally."

"Brigrandon, there isn't time to waste hiding! If I
could get to the old temple—"

"You'll never get out of the palace, let alone the city.
Don't argue, Kyre—if they find you here, we three won't
be able to fend them off!"

He had no choice . . . Kyre stepped up on a table
and, as Brigrandon thumped the window open with a
clenched fist, squeezed himself through. The scholar
slammed the window behind him, and as he did so, the
sound of tramping boots approached along the terrace.

"Sit down," the scholar said hastily to Nirn. "Sit
where Kyre was, spread those documents around and
pretend to be asleep. Did anyone see you coming here?"

"No, master."

"Good." Brigrandon hesitated, then snatched up a
half-full ale jug and refilled the cup by his own chair,
taking care to spill a fair amount. "They'll find us both
sleeping, and me more than a little drunk. When they
wake us, we've been here since this morning going
through the manuscripts. Kyre was here, but he left just
after noon. You don't know where he's gone; I'll offer
several confusing suggestions. Got that?"

"Yes, sir." Nirn slid into his place. When the soldiers
hammered on the door, both men had their heads
pillowed on their arms, eyes shut, and Brigrandon was
snoring gently.

* * *

"So," Simorh said carefully, "you believe that you will succeed in leading the sea demons' sorceress into a trap."

Vaoran inclined his head in acknowledgment. "It's the best chance we can give to the little princess. And believe me when I say that every man involved will fight to save her."

"Oh, yes; I believe you." She rose and went to the window; at her movement the guard by the door tensed, but Vaoran waved him back. Simorh was no threat: he'd ensured that all her sorcerous accoutrements were removed to a place where she couldn't reach them, and beyond that no other precautions were needed. Indeed, he'd made better progress with her than he'd thought possible, for the simple reason that he knew and had played on her one weakness: Gamora. He was aware of the value in presenting himself as the child's champion; and if his plan succeeded—as he believed it would—then he would earn Simorh's lifelong gratitude, and in time that could develop into far more.

"The girl will be taken to the strand at sunset, as I originally exhorted the pr—the ex-prince to do," he told her. As he spoke he watched her face to see how she would react to the change in DiMag's title; but her expression gave away nothing. "The trap will be set, and—providing only that Calthar keeps the rendezvous—there's no reason why she shouldn't take the bait."

Simorh nodded. "And the—and Kyre?"

His mouth pursed. "I'm reluctant to say it, lady, but he could be a danger to our plans and therefore to the little princess. There's no doubt in my mind that he has attempted to dupe us with his claim to be the true Sun-

Hound, and I suspect that he may even be in league with our enemies in some way." He studied her for a moment, then decided to take the risk of being frank. "I dared not take any chances, madam, and by now Kyre will be dead."

With a tremendous effort Simorh managed to maintain her expression, though inside she felt horribly sick. Dead . . . With DiMag locked and guarded in his room, Gamora taken to a "place of safety," and Talliann imprisoned and awaiting the moment when she would be taken to the strand, Kyre had been her last hope. Now, there was nothing.

She gazed out of the window. The clouds were beginning to break up, and long shafts of light lay low and mellow across the city. Two hours or less until the sun set . . .

A step sounded behind her and a hand came to rest lightly on her shoulder. She forced herself not to shudder at Vaoran's touch, but her stomach muscles tensed involuntarily.

"Don't despair, lady." The swordsmaster's voice was kind. "Haven will triumph. I'm sure of it."

She couldn't bring herself to answer him: if she had tried, she would have lost all self-control and spat in his face. The hand withdrew from her shoulder and she heard his heavy tread as he and the guard made their way out, leaving her alone with the hatred burning like a volcano inside her.

Chapter 18

BRIGRANDON PRIDED HIMSELF THAT HE KNEW THE LESSER byways of Haven's palace better than almost any man alive. But he'd never dreamed that his knowledge would be put to such an urgent and alarming use.

Walking along the terrace to the main entrance, he knew he was in full view of anyone who might be watching and so took good care to weave and stagger a few times to keep up appearances. By now, he calculated, the soldiers would have searched the Sunrise Tower and found it empty, and they'd be spreading out through the palace, looking for their quarry and cursing Brigrandon for his drunken incoherence. Kyre would be safe enough from their efforts: the old scholar doubted if the soldiers even knew of the herb garden's existence.

He turned in at the main door and loitered in the hall for a few moments, as though he'd forgotten where it was he meant to go. Two servants scurried by, but ignored him; Haven's new master had no interest in an aging sot of a scholar and, provided he didn't arouse anyone's suspicions, Brigrandon would be left alone.

The servants disappeared, and for a moment there was quiet—then a slight figure moved out of the shadows of the stairwell and beckoned. Brigrandon checked quickly over his shoulder and hurried to meet her.

"Falla—you had Nirn's message? What news?" He kept his voice to a whisper.

The dark-haired girl hugged her shawl around herself. "The princess is unguarded, Master Brigrandon; she's free to move about the palace. I told her you needed to see her urgently and she said she would meet you in your rooms. She's on her way there now."

He patted her shoulder gratefully. "*Thank* you, Falla! Is there any word of the prince?"

She shook her head. "No. The princess tried to see him, but he's too heavily guarded. All we know is that he's still alive."

"Very well. You'd best go back."

"If I can do anything more—"

"I'll send word." Brigrandon patted her shoulder again and hastened away.

As he opened the door of his room, Simorh rose from where she had been crouching before the fireplace.

"Brigrandon—" She got to her feet, and only force of habit stopped her from running forward to embrace him. "Falla gave me your message—is it true? Is Kyre still alive?"

The tutor smiled reassuringly at her. "Unless Vaoran is more concerned with gardening than I think he is, madam, yes." And as she frowned uncomprehendingly he crossed the room and thumped open the window. "Kyre!" His voice was soft but carried on the still air. "It's Brigrandon—you can come back now!"

A tangle of bushes in the overgrown herb garden rustled, and Kyre emerged. He ran to the window, keeping low, and Brigrandon helped him over the sill.

"Princess . . ." Kyre froze, surprise and relief on his face as he saw Simorh. He recovered himself, brushed dry leaves from his hair and clothing. "I'd thought—when we heard the news—"

"Oh, it's true, all right," Brigrandon told him. "Vaoran is now effectively ruler of Haven, and controls both the council and the army. The prince is a prisoner; but we know at least that he's still alive."

"Vaoran has other plans for me," Simorh interjected bitterly, her tone leaving them in no doubt of what she meant. "So far, that has enabled me to keep my freedom." She shuddered.

"What of Talliann?" Kyre asked urgently.

She met his eyes. "They've taken her, Kyre. Vaoran took good care to explain his plan to me, because he thinks his concern for Gamora will inveigle him into my favor. He means to keep the rendezvous with Calthar."

Kyre swore, then looked at Brigrandon. "What's the hour?"

Brigrandon knew what he was thinking, and glanced toward the window. "Less than an hour until sunset."

"Will the tide have cleared the strand yet?"

The scholar made a rapid mental calculation, then nodded. "By the time you can reach the temple, yes."

Simorh looked quickly from one to the other. "What is this? I don't understand."

"Princess," Kyre said, "when we heard that Vaoran's men were hunting for me, Brigrandon and I had that very moment discovered the whereabouts of Talliann's lost amulet. It's in the ruined temple, under the central flagstone of the crypt floor."

Her face was immobile with astonishment for a
moment—then hope flared in her eyes. "Oh, by the
Eye . . . Kyre, are you sure?"

"There's no possible doubt."

"Then we must retrieve it, and return it to Talliann! If
the two stones can be linked—"

"Lady, there isn't time," Brigrandon interrupted. "If
Vaoran means to take Talliann to the strand at sunset,
he'll be moving out in less than an hour, and the army
will be on his heels."

He was right. "There's only one chance," Kyre said.
"Vaoran's party must be intercepted, and stopped!"

"And where would you find enough trustworthy men
to stand against them, let alone in such a short time?"
Brigrandon demanded. "No, it wouldn't work. It—"

"Wait!" Simorh held up a hand. She was staring at
something propped in one corner of the room. The sea
warrior's spear that Kyre had snatched in the citadel—he
had left it with Brigrandon, almost forgotten its existence.

"They say you wield that like a master," Simorh said,
her look wry. "Is it true?"

"Yes . . ."

"Then take it, and you and I will go to the temple.
Now, before Vaoran and his men set out."

"Lady, we can't hope to prevail against them!"

It needn't come to that. If the amulet is in our hands
before they arrive, there'll be no need for fighting." Her
eyes were ablaze now. "There's a spell—I learned it as
part of my training, though without the two amulets it
can't be used. If I can remember it, and I believe I can,
Vaoran will present no threat to us!" She smiled at him,
vulpine. "I may not be a warrior, but I have other skills
which are as valuable. All I need is for you to guard me
while the work is done."

Kyre hesitated—then returned her smile and with it a good measure of respect. There was still a chance for them all . . .

"Lady," he said, and kissed her hand, "we may triumph over Calthar yet!"

Their leave-taking of Brigrandon was hurried but intense. Kyre and the old scholar clasped arms, neither able to voice the thought that this might be the last time they would ever meet. Then Simorh hugged Brigrandon, and kissed his cheek soundly.

"We'll return," she said, resolution and emotion making her voice harsh. "And when the Hag rises, we'll be ready to meet her!"

Brigrandon nodded, and Kyre realized the old man was biting back tears. "I'll try to get word to the prince, madam. I'll tell him what you've done . . ."

She hugged him again and whispered, "Thank you, Brigrandon—thank you for your loyalty!"

And then Kyre and Simorh were outside in the raw, crimson glare of the lowering sun.

The city was a place of ghosts. Empty streets, silent houses, the few windows not yet shuttered staring into the evening light like blood-filled eyes. Mist crept around their ankles, sometimes to their knees, intensifying the quiet. Somewhere in the distance a young child was crying . . . the people had done all they could, and now they waited.

As they hastened through the still town Kyre glanced occasionally at the woman beside him. He had begun by hating Simorh; now he had learned to respect her, pity her, and, in a strange, brotherly way, love her. She was a true champion of the city and the husband and child she sought to save, and she deserved better fortune than life

had so far dealt her. He thought of DiMag, imprisoned
and under threat of his life; Gamora, little better than
dead with Calthar's enchantment still upon her . . .
reflexively his hand went to the amulet which now hung
on its repaired chain about his neck. He had failed Haven
once, though Haven might argue it, and his failure had
brought them all to this. If any power in the world could
prevent it, he wouldn't fail again.

The wind was rising. As they emerged from the
sandstone arch it came blustering to meet them, ripping
their hair back from their faces, punching and buffeting
them, and raising whirling clouds of dry sand that stung
their skin like whiplashes. Vast shadows reached out
from the cliffs toward the sea, and the sea itself where the
sun still touched it was gory, waves beginning to tumble
and agitate as the wind strengthened.

Simorh ducked her head aside and said, raising her
voice to be heard, "This may be to our advantage! The
wind will wipe out our footprints—otherwise, we'd have
had to keep to the cliff edge and waste precious time!"

He nodded, and took her arm as she stepped out from
the arch's comparative shelter. Leaning into the gale,
they ploughed through soft sand toward the shingle bar,
both painfully aware that Vaoran's party might emerge
from the gateway and see them before they could reach
cover. The bar loomed ahead; reaching it, they paused
and looked back.

The bay was deserted. But the sun was now no more
than a sliver of furious brilliance above the headland: in
minutes it would be swallowed.

"There'll be no fog tonight!" Simorh shouted, trying
to counter the terror that was threatening to dig its claws
deep into her. "We mustn't delay—come on!"

They ran, as far as running was possible, along the

shingle bar toward the monstrous silhouette of the ruin
ahead. Once Simorh fell, swore, but was on her feet
again before Kyre could stop to help her. They hastened
on, and he tried not to look at the brooding sea to his
right or listen to its booming, angry voice. Then shingle
and shale gave way to rubble and the twisted shapes of
fallen masonry, and they came to a gasping, breathless
halt amid the towering pillars of the temple.

For a few moments they stood still, gratefully dragging air into their burning lungs. Kyre was about to
speak to the sorceress—but as he opened his mouth, a
cold wing of shadow seemed to brush by him. He looked
seaward. And the sun's last crimson glow was gone,
turning the ocean to a churning, endless gray.

He gripped Simorh's arm. *"Sunset!"*

She looked, and bit down hard on her lower lip.
"Quickly," she hissed.

They found the narrow embrasure that was all that
remained of the crypt's original entrance, and squeezed
through. The stairs beyond were pitch dark—neither of
them had thought to bring a lantern—and they felt their
way carefully, step by uneven step, down the short flight
to the chamber below. Here, phosphorescent algae and
sea lichen gave off a faint, eldritch glow, and Simorh
stepped cautiously across a litter of stones and small
rocks to the middle of the floor. Judging where she
thought the central flagstone must be she crouched down
and Kyre joined her. As they cleared away the debris that
covered the floor—weed, broken shells, a thin covering
of sand—the sorceress said: "When the temple was built
it stood on a bank fifty feet above the high tide line. Until
nine years ago, the sea had never entered this chamber."
She paused in her work and looked up. "It makes me
wonder what our fate might be this time."

"Only pray, then, that we'll be in time." Kyre brushed at a layer of sand—and abruptly stopped as his fingers encountered something that didn't yield to his attempt to move it aside. Quickly he crouched lower, peering in the gloom, and Simorh said tensely, "What is it?"

"I don't know . . . a pattern, I think, slightly raised . . ."

She all but shouldered him aside in her eagerness, putting her face close to the floor. "I think . . . oh, damn this darkness; I should have had the sense to bring a lamp!" Her fingers traced the outline Kyre had found, then she sat back on her heels. In the dimness her face was alight with excitement.

"Yes!" She clenched her fists triumphantly. "This is the one—I remember it; there's a relief of the Eye in the very center. Hurry—we must clear the debris from the slab!"

Feverishly they cleared the litter, and in less than a minute the outline of a single massive flagstone was revealed.

"How can we lift it?" Kyre asked.

The sorceress scrambled to her feet and back away from the stone. "Take your spear, and insert the blade into the crack between it and its neighbor."

He didn't argue, though the idea seemed ludicrous: the spear blade would snap long before the slab could be levered up. But a new light had crept into Simorh's eyes, and as he did as she bade him he realized that she intended to use other means.

"There—hold it there!" Her voice had taken on a harsh timbre, and she closed her eyes, drawing in a deep breath. He saw her lips move though she made no sound; then her body tensed and an aura—faint, but clearly discernible—flickered into life about her. The salty air seemed to shiver and he felt a sensation like the close, tingling awareness of an electric storm raise the hairs on his arms and shiver through his scalp. The spear in his hand bucked; momentarily the floor lurched under his feet—

And the stone slab came up. It moved as though an immensely powerful fist had punched it from below, springing upright, teetering for a moment on its end, before it crashed with a heavy thump onto its neighbor, and cracked across.

Simorh's eyes met Kyre's over the hollow space that had been exposed, and he grinned, suddenly feeling light-headed with their triumph.

"I never was a sorcerer," he said. "That was always Talliann's skill, not mine."

The light faded from Simorh's eyes. "Talliann . . ." she said; and glanced toward the stairs. "They must be on their way, if not already at the rendezvous."

The thought sobered him abruptly and he dropped to his knees beside the dank, musty hole. It wasn't deep, and at first it seemed that there was nothing there but sodden sand and the broken foundations of the temple. Then he saw the faint, metallic glimmer . . .

Centuries had neither worn the quartz pendant nor tarnished the chain from which it hung. In size and form it was the perfect twin to the one that hung about Kyre's neck, but he could just make out that the quartz of Talliann's amulet was a deep orange-red, and embedded within it was not the Eye of Day but an image of the eye of night—a silver-flecked pearl.

Kyre's fist clenched around the amulet as old memories flooded into his mind. Now that both stones were in his possession he recalled some of the properties they had had when used in harmony; the power that Talliann,

with her seeking mind and her magical skills, had been
able to wield. Suddenly, on an impulse, he held the
pendant out to Simorh.

"Wear it," he told her. "For Talliann's sake. You
stand in the place she once occupied—you can use her
power!"

Her eyes widened and she made no attempt to take the
quartz from him. "I can't, Kyre. It wouldn't be right."

"It is right! Until it can be restored to her—wear it,
Simorh. Please."

She hesitated a moment longer, then reached out to
take the jewel, looping the chain over her head so that the
quartz lay between her breasts. Kyre saw surprise
register briefly in her eyes as she sensed the stone's
power; then she reached out and took his hand.

"We can't delay any longer," she said, and there was a
warmth in her voice that he'd never heard before; the
warmth of sharing even the direst danger with a known
and trusted friend. "Whatever awaits us out there, we
must go and meet it."

Emerging first through the slit of rock that formed the
crypt exit, Kyre saw something that made him freeze and
hold out a hand to halt Simorh.

"What is it?" Her whisper echoed eerily in the
confined dark, and he put a finger to his lips, flattening
himself against the rock wall and pointing to the visible
patch of nightscape beyond the entrance.

Etched in the last dim glow from the sky, a man was
standing alert and attentive among the shattered pillars.
His back was toward them, but Kyre saw the glint of an
unsheathed sword, and recognized the uniform of a
Haven warrior.

He put his mouth to Simorh's ear. "They're waiting
for Calthar. They've set an ambush."

"Fools!"

"I can't see Vaoran . . . he must be on the shingle bar." Kyre frowned. "We've no chance of helping Talliann while we're trapped here. But that guard—"

"Wait . . ." Simorh touched his arm, gesturing toward the embrasure. He looked, and saw that the warrior had dropped to a crouch, leaning tensely forward. As they watched, the man began to inch his way awkwardly toward the cover of a broken wall. He reached it, settled, and Simorh touched Kyre's arm again.

"We daren't wait for a better opportunity—we have to be able to see what's happening!" she whispered. "Ease out, and turn to the right; there's a fallen pillar there that will shelter us well enough. And watch the rubble under your feet."

He nodded, and they moved forward. The soldier's back was still toward them; the man didn't move as they emerged from the rock slit and made for the shelter of the pillar. Deeper shadow swallowed them, and Kyre heard Simorh let out a pent breath. He turned his head to get his bearings—and his heart lurched.

"Simorh!" His urgent hiss was barely audible over the sounds of the sea and the rising wind, but she heard him, and swung round as he pointed out to sea.

Something moved among the tumbling chaos of the waves, a dark shape against the sea's uneasy phosphorescence. As they watched, the shape drew nearer—and a figure, lithe-limbed, crowned with a nimbus of wild hair, rose from the shallows. For a moment she stood motionless, her outline etched by a cold, silvery glimmer from somewhere out over the sea; then she shook a stream of water from her hair and stalked toward the shingle bar.

Simorh looked at Kyre. *"Calthar?"*

He nodded, his face grim. "Calthar." With a gesture warning her to silence, he eased himself out from the shelter of the pillar and crossed quickly to the lee of a jagged wall.

And from this vantage point he could see all he needed to see.

Vaoran stood just off the shingle bar, some twenty yards from the ruin. Behind him, two men held Talliann, who stood erect and immobile, facing the sea. The wind whipped her hair back, and her face in the night's eerie glow was a sickly white. She looked just as she had done when he first saw her on the strand, and Kyre had to fight back a compulsive urge to break from his cover and attack Vaoran and the two guards single-handed.

A hand closed on his forearm as he still struggled with himself, and he started, then looked down into Simorh's eyes.

"No, Kyre," she said, her voice hard. "Don't do it— don't think it. There's a better way." She smiled, a ghastly grimace in the dimness. "The spell I told you of: it may turn the tide in our favor, and with the amulet's help I think I can make it work. Wait, watch, and take your chance when it comes."

Calthar had emerged from the sea. She stepped onto the shingle and stood gazing at Vaoran's small party. Though the hump of the bar set her at a height above them, Vaoran, on firm sand, had the better advantage. Talliann turned her head abruptly away as the sorceress stared at her.

"A strange welcome." Calthar's husky voice carried clearly even above the moaning sea and the gusting wind. "No Prince DiMag or his little wife to greet me? No ranks of soldiery to form a guard of honor?" Her voice was mocking, and her gaze raked the ruin with undisguised contempt. "Or are your men too shy to show themselves?"

Vaoran ignored the taunt, and shouted back, "It has been decided to grant your request, Calthar. The girl Talliann, in exchange for our little Princess Gamora's release from bewitchment. A straightforward bargain."

Kyre glimpsed movement at the edge of his vision. *"Down!"* he hissed, and drove the heel of his hand between Simorh's shoulder blades, sending her sprawling as he fell almost on top of her. From the far side of the broken wall another warrior emerged, crouched low, edging round the ruin toward the sand. They held their breath; the warrior slowed, stopped, froze . . .

"A straightforward bargain," Calthar repeated, smiling in a way that Kyre recognized all too well. "So be it." She held out one hand, in imperious gesture. "I have no further interest in Haven's brat. You may release the girl. She won't try to flee."

As she spoke she was staring at Talliann again and, drawn by a compulsion she couldn't fight, Talliann raised her head and looked directly into Calthar's eyes. Vaoran stepped aside and the two guards led the girl forward. One pace, two, three—they were now walking up the gentle slope of the shingle bar, and Calthar took a lazy pace toward them. Kyre's stomach muscles tensed agonizingly; the motionless warrior a few feet from their hiding place began to move stealthily forward again.

The amulet at Simorh's breast was suddenly lit from within by a vivid glow like a tiny flame. The sorceress's hands moved convulsively, covering the quartz; but still the light shone through the lattice of her fingers, its intensity growing. Her face was lit by it, her eyes were tightly closed and her lips moved rapidly, silently, as she

mouthed the words of a conjuration. Kyre moved quickly
to shield her and the amulet from sight: as he did so
Calthar raised both arms, holding them out toward
Talliann as though to enfold her in an obscene embrace.
The two guards released their hold on the girl and pushed
her so that, involuntarily, she stumbled the last few paces
toward Calthar before falling at her feet. She lay huddled
on the shingle like a mesmerized animal, and did not
move.

Calthar stared down at the two men who had guarded
Talliann, then turned her face toward Vaoran. Her mouth
widened in a smile that was almost pitying.

"Go back to Haven, little man," she said. "Go back,
and watch over your city in the hour of its death." She
snapped her fingers, once, and Talliann, like a puppet
whose strings had abruptly jerked it to life, rose. "Your
little princess will wake, for I would have her see the
final destruction of her heritage! Her life, like all your
lives, will be short enough!" The smile became a terrible
grin. "You are a gullible fool, my friend. A very gullible
fool." And, the tatters of her robe sweeping around her,
she turned—and stopped.

Vaoran said evenly: "You speak a little too soon,
Calthar."

Haven's warriors stood between Calthar and the sea.
Each had drawn his sword, and they formed an apparently impassable barrier. For a few moments no one moved
as the sorceress gazed at the men, and Kyre almost felt
pity for Vaoran. The swordsmaster still believed that he
could best this monster. He had so much to learn . . .

"Ah, little man," Calthar said. "Such a little man.
Such a simple trap. Do you know no better than that?"

She turned—and met the point of Vaoran's sword as he
lunged at her. The blade rammed into her heart; she

stopped, rigid, and for an instant a look of surprised
irony showed on her face. Then it metamorphosed into a
sly and ugly smile. Slowly, deliberately, she gripped the
hilt of the sword protruding from her body, and with a
swift, economical movement wrenched it free.

There was no blood on the blade. No blood spilling
from what should have been a fatal wound. Calthar's
smile widened, and as Vaoran stared in dumb shock,
eyes almost bursting from their sockets, she took a single
pace toward him.

Kyre had a premonition of what was to happen.
Vaoran was transfixed, his body immobilized by the
impossibility that his mind couldn't assimilate. Calthar
tossed the sword carelessly into the air. It hung unsup-
ported, drawing the swordsmaster's hypnotized gaze—
and the sorceress clenched her fist in a swift, violent
gesture.

The sword twisted in midair, turned and hovered
quivering for a single moment, before it came sweeping
down in a murderous, arcing slash. At the last instant
before the sword struck, intelligence and appalled understanding returned to Vaoran's eyes; but it was too late.
The blade sheared through his neck, the impact not even
slowing its deadly sweep, and the swordsmaster's de-
capitated body crashed to the sand.

Calthar turned her face up to the sky, her laughter
echoing from the cliffs—

And at Kyre's side, Simorh shrieked a single word.
Kyre felt a terrific jolt hit him as a blast of raw power
ripped from the amulet at her throat and almost threw
him to the ground. An instant later the sky was torn apart
by a howling, thunderous crimson flash that lit the scene
with stunning brilliance. Calthar whirled round, the
soldiers fell back, yelling in fear—

"Now!" Simorh screamed. Kyre didn't stop to think
what he was doing; he *couldn't* stop, couldn't control the
surge of furious and desperate energy that erupted within
him. He broke from cover and leaped up the slope of the
shingle bank toward Calthar and Talliann. The sorceress
spun to face him, snarling like an animal; he swung the
spear, bringing the blade shearing toward her, saw her
jerk back as it skimmed by an inch from her skull. She
recovered her balance instantly, sprang at him as the sky
split open again—he had no time to do anything other
than snatch at Talliann's arm, pulling her out of Calthar's
reach, before the sorceress's hands clamped on the spear
haft.

Talliann fell heavily, rolling from the bank onto the
sand, but Kyre could do nothing to help her. For a
moment that seemed to freeze them in another dimension
he and Calthar were locked motionless, face to face, only
the spear a flimsy and precarious barrier between them.
In the grim light he saw Calthar smile, and the deranged
eyes of Malhareq, alive even in death, glared out from
her twisted face. Hatred gave him strength; he wrenched,
kicked out, and his heel slammed against Calthar's
breastbone, sending her spinning backward.

"Simorh!!" Kyre's frantic yell resounded over the
howl of wind, sea, and sky. He plunged down the bank,
almost losing his footing, and saw Simorh's pale figure
emerge, running, from her hiding place.

"The amulet!" He grabbed Talliann, who was trying
to climb to her feet but seeed too dazed to coordinate her
limbs, and lifted her up so Simorh reached them. The
princess was trying to pull the pendant from around her
neck, but the chain had caught in her hair: she struggled
with it, cursing—and suddenly Talliann gave a small,
moaning cry of fear, and pointed back toward the shingle
bar.

Calthar stood on the crown of the bank, framed by a ghastly, phosphorescent halo. For a moment Kyre thought that the Mothers were again manifesting their unholy, vampiric existence through her living flesh—but no; the cold glow was spreading along the bar, shimmering on the wet shingle, etching the temple ruins into stark relief. And the churning, rolling wavetops beyond the bar were shot through with silver light.

The Dead Night moon was rising.

Calthar spread her arms wide, and her wild laughter rang to the sky, challenging the wind as it rose to a yelling gale. Raw power radiated from her; as though summoned by her voice, the first furious edge of the Hag's livid silver face lifted above the sea on the distant horizon, and a single shaft of light speared across the bay to strike full on the gate of Haven. Calthar howled like a wolf, and her triumphant cry ricocheted from the cliffs.

"You are too late!"

"No!" Simorh's answering protest was a shriek of defiance. She tore the amulet free, ripping out a hank of her own hair with it, and lunged toward Talliann. The chain slipped over the dark girl's neck: Talliann gasped as the quartz touched her skin, and Krye saw the deep colors within it flare briefly into a brilliance that challenged the rising Hag—

"Kyre!" It was a wail, a cry of agony and joy and despair, as Talliann's memories smashed out of their prison and into her conscious mind. Her body jerked violently as though some titanic force had struck her full on; Kyre caught her as she reeled, and they staggered chaotically back together. Simorh was buffeted aside, stumbled—then every muscle in her body locked rigid as, beyond Calthar's wild figure, the light of the moon went out.

Far out in the bay, a black wall of water was lifting itself from the surface of the sea, blotting the Hag's deadly brilliance from view. The vast wave gathered strength, gathered speed, and Simorh's mind was hurled nine years into the past, to the hideous night when the tide had flowed twice without ebbing.

No sorcery she knew, nor any power that Kyre and Talliann might command, could combat this. Calthar was summoning the full, awesome power of the Mothers—and the huge tidal wave was racing chaotically toward Haven was their herald!

Simorh tore at Kyre's sleeve, wrenching him round with more strength than she'd believed she possessed. She sucked salt air into her lungs, and screamed to him at the top of her voice, striving to combat the howling of the elements and the distant, shattering roar of the oncoming wave.

"RUN!!"

Kyre and Talliann both looked seaward, saw Calthar now in silhouette, saw what was eclipsing the Hag's light. Horrified understanding dawned on their faces; they turned and, with Simorh beside them, raced for the sanctuary of the portal. Behind them Calthar's laughter rang madly on the back of the gale, but her mockery meant nothing—to stay on the beach and face what hurtled toward them would be insanity; their only hope of survival lay in flight.

Kyre thought suddenly of Vaoran's ambush party and the fate that would await them if they didn't reach safety, and he slowed, turning to look back. Far behind, three or four figures pelted across the sand; of the rest there was no sign.

"Kyre, don't stop!" Simorh yelled. "It's too late to help them—run for your own life!"

She was right: to delay now would be to kill them all. The warriors must take their chance. With a last, despairing look at the frantically running men, Kyre turned again and raced on.

The lights of Haven's gateway shone ahead, but they still seemed impossibly distant—and behind them, the sound of the oncoming wave was swelling toward a crescendo. The sand beneath their feet vibrated, the cliffs shouted back the wave's roar in deafening echoes. *They wouldn't reach the arch in time*—then suddenly they were on drier, looser sand, whirlwinds of it stinging their bodies and whipping them to greater effort. The green witchlights danced crazily, closer, closer; the arch opened up before them. And as they hurled themselves through the sandstone gateway, a massive, thundering concussion of sound smashed into their ears as the tidal wave exploded against the cliffs.

Chapter 19

TITANIC COLUMNS OF SPRAY REARED HUNDREDS OF FEET into the night sky, and the roaring sea funneled into the bay. Kyre was behind Talliann and Simorh, trying to shield them as they ran, flagging now, through the lower streets of the town, when what felt like a gigantic fist slammed into his back and lifted him off his feet. Water struck like a solid wall and he fell, the two women flailing beneath him; he swallowed a mouthful of sea and rolled, gagging and choking. The edge of the wave swirled around them, but its strength was expended, and as suddenly as it had come the water drained away, leaving them sprawled, drenched, on the paved road.

They staggered to their feet, clutching each other for support as water streamed from their clothes and hair. Kyre was the first to recover from the shock, and as he looked back he felt as though his stomach had turned over within him.

The arch and the wall that protected Haven from the sea were gone. The furious energy of the tidal wave had

smashed the sandstone to rubble, and though the massive
undertow had already dragged water back from the gate,
there was nothing now to save half the town from being
overwhelmed by a second onslaught. Out in the bay,
where minutes before there had been smooth sand, the
sea rolled and churned like a gigantic, boiling caldron,
its surface turned to a maelstrom of tossing silver as the
Hag, a huge hemisphere now on the horizon as she
continued to rise, glared malevolently over the scene.

And far away, carried on the shrieking wind, he heard
a sound that made him feel that his veins were filled with
ice. A wailing, howling sound, as though a thousand
voices joined together in a monstrous nightmare of a
song. *Or a battle cry.*

He had heard that dreadful howling once before, and
when he looked at Talliann and Simorh he knew that
they, too, recognized it. Coming toward them over the
sea, challenging the courage and resolve of every living
soul in Haven, it was the war song of the citadel army.

They were out on the sea, and they were mustering
their forces. At the moment when the malignant moon
cleared the horizon, the Dead Night battle would begin.
And that wailing song would be the signal for Haven's
warriors to march out from the city to meet their
nemesis.

He had to reach DiMag! Haven's only hope lay in the
power invested in the amulets; but he couldn't use them,
dared not use them, until the prince was restored to his
rightful place. The quartz gems would smash open a
gateway between the present and the long-dead past—
time and space would collide, and their collision could
hurl the world into chaos. Only through DiMag and
Simorh, the true inheritors of the throne of Haven, could
he and Talliann hope to control the forces that would be
unleashed.

He looked wildly at Talliann, saw that she shared his unspoken knowledge, and yelled above the turmoil of gale and sea and the eerie swell of the far-off voices. *"Simorh!"* He snatched at the sorceress's arm. "Get to your tower, *quickly*! Talliann will go with you—we need your strength, and we need your skill! *Go!"*

He caught Talliann in his arms, kissed her briefly, fiercely, then turned and started away at a run up the street.

"Kyre!" Simorh yelled against the gale. "Kyre, where are you going?"

"To DiMag!" And he was gone.

Talliann pulled ferociously at Simorh's wrist. "Hurry!" she cried. "There's so little time left!"

Simorh didn't understand; couldn't even begin to understand—but the frantic urgency in Talliann's voice sheared like a knife through her confusion. Her fingers tangled with the black-haired girl's, and hand in hand they raced away through the streets in Kyre's wake.

Kyre burst through the wicket gate into the palace gardens with the faraway wailing of the sea warriors ringing in his ears above the racket of the wind. He stumbled onto the path that cut through the dying shrubbery, gagging at the decayed flowers' stench—then from the direction of the palace he heard something that brought him to a flailing halt.

It came from the barracks courtyard—the sound of hundreds of tramping feet, the stentorian shouts of sergeants: and then, like a physical blow on the air, the rhythmic, relentless war chant of Haven's warriors.

They were moving out. And DiMag, who should be leading them, was still a prisoner . . . Kyre inhaled a deep lungful of the sickly-sweet air and ran on toward the

palace, taking the terrace steps four at a time and
sprinting for the main door.

Only two lamps glowed dimly in the entrance hall,
casting foreboding shadows and lending an eerie unreali-
ty to the scenes embroidered on the worn tapestries. Kyre
started for the stairs—and as he ducked into the stairwell
arch, he cannoned into Brigrandon.

"Kyre!" The old scholar's face was pale. "I feared
you must be dead—thank the Eye for your safe return!
But where's the Princess Simorh?"

"Gone to her tower, with Talliann." Kyre leaned
against the wall to catch his breath. "We found the lost
amulet, and Vaoran's dead—"

"Dead?"

"Calthar killed him. Brigrandon, there's no time to
explain—I must reach DiMag: the army's moving out
and he has to lead them!"

"He's still guarded," Brigrandon said. "I tried to see
him just now, but—"

"Damn the guards!" Fury rose in Kyre: he quelled it
with difficulty and grasped the old man's shoulders.
"Stay in the palace and do what you can, Brigrandon.
The battle's about to begin, and those who shelter here
will need all the strength and comfort you can give
them."

Brigrandon's eyes narrowed angrily. "I'm joining the
city's defenders."

"No. When this is over, Haven will need you as a live
scholar, not a dead warrior!" He set one foot on the first
stair. "May the Eye watch over you, Brigrandon!"

Brigrandon stared at the shadows of the stairwell as
the sound of Kyre's running footsteps diminished up the
steps.

* * *

There were two armed soldiers outside DiMag's door. They were little more than children, Kyre realized; clearly Vaoran hadn't been willing to spare more seasoned men at such a time of crisis. He ran toward them and they raised their swords menacingly.

Kyre stopped. "Get out of my way."

Whether or not they recognized him he didn't know; but he sensed fear underlying their uncertainty. "No one is permitted to see the ex-prince," one said, his unsteady voice belying the challenge. "Not without Prince Vaoran's express permission—"

"Swordsmaster Vaoran is dead!" Kyre snapped, and had the sour gratification of seeing their eyes widen in shock. "He was murdered by the sea sorceress not half an hour ago—and that means that Prince DiMag is still your ruler!"

These two weren't traitors, he realized: they had become embroiled in this whole ugly affair through no fault or will of their own, simply because they were soldiers constrained to obey their commander or suffer for it.

More kindly, he said, "Haven's forces are leaving the barracks now. You'd best join them, quickly."

They glanced at each other: then, hastily, their spokesman bowed to him. "Yes . . . sir." He licked his lips. "Thank you . . ."

Kyre paused only a moment to watch them go, then unlocked DiMag's door.

The prince was standing by the window. At the sound of the latch he whirled—and his face went rigid with astonishment.

"Kyre!" He stumbled forward. "They told me you were dead!"

Kyre smiled grimly. "They were premature. Vaoran took my place."

"Vaoran?" DiMag swung back toward the window.
"But the Hag has risen—the army is moving out to meet
our enemies! *Who leads them?*"

"Only their captains. And I doubt if half the men even
know what happened in the court hall."

The prince paused. "You mean . . . ?" He saw
confirmation in Kyre's eyes and didn't finish the question. Instead he limped to a cupboard, opened it, and
began to rummage hastily through its contents. Moments
later he pulled out a heavy, padded black jerkin made of
supple leather, black trousers, a wide belt, a pair of
boots.

"Tell me what happened," he said as he began to
dress.

Briefly, Kyre recounted Brigrandon's discovery of the
amulet's whereabouts, his hasty flight to the ruined
temple with Simorh, Vaoran's attempt to dupe Calthar
which had resulted in the swordsmaster's death, and the
tidal wave—invisible from DiMag's window—that had
roared in to the bay as they fled back to Haven. When he
finished, DiMag looked up, his face drawn with worry.

"Gamora," he said tensely. "What happened to her?"

"I don't know; I've had no chance yet to check. But I
think Calthar might be perverse enough to have meant
what she said. She wants to savor her triumph in any way
she can."

DiMag nodded dourly. "Yes. I can believe that of
her." He sucked air sharply between his teeth. "I can't
afford the delay of finding out. All I can do is
hope . . ." He reached into the cupboard again and,
with some difficulty, pulled out a massive scabbard from
which protruded the ornate hilt of a broadsword. It must,
Kyre thought, have been twice as heavy as the blade the
prince habitually carried.

"This belonged to my father," DiMag said with a wry

grin. "Vaoran took my own blade, but he didn't know of this one's existence." He hefted it, raising his eyebrows at its prodigious length and weight. "My father was a taller man than I am."

"Can you wield it?" Kyre asked.

He laughed bitterly. "There's strength in my arms, if not in my legs. While I can still sit a horse, I can handle this well enough to cause some havoc among our enemies' ranks." He looked up. "You'll ride with me, Kyre?"

"Yes."

DiMag cinched the belt at his waist. "Then let's be on our way."

Simorh raced breathlessly up the last stairs to her tower door, thankful to find it unguarded. Behind her came Talliann, glancing back over her shoulder to ensure they weren't being followed. They hastened into the anteroom and Simorh ran to the window, from where she had a clear view over the city. Though the chanting and tramping of the departing warriors could be heard on the wind, they weren't as yet in view. *So little time*, she thought, her mind in chaos, and turned to Talliann.

"I don't know what I must do!" Panic welled up in her; she felt so bereft, so impotent. "Talliann, help me— tell me what you need of me!"

"I need your mind, and your will," Talliann said. A great change had come over the black-haired girl; all trace of the bewildered and hapless innocent were gone with the return of her memories, revealing the formidable strength of the soul beneath. Her aura was almost tangible, and Simorh realized with a shock just how great a sorceress she had been when she had ruled at Kyre's side.

"Kyre rides out with DiMag," Talliann continued.

"When they reach the bay, my mind and his will become one, and we'll awaken the amulets and call their power into the world from our own time. But it's dangerous, Simorh—by summoning that force we break down the barriers between past and present: they can't rightly exist together, and they'll clash. We must keep control of that force if we're to prevent time from running amok, and only you and DiMag can help us. We need you to hold us to *your* time, to this night, by any means you can. And it won't be easy."

Simorh looked into her stern yet sad black eyes, and understood. Time running amok . . . the thought was awesome. But a price must be paid for calling such power out of the distant past—and it was Haven's only hope.

She said, forcing strength and conviction into her voice, "We won't fail you."

DiMag and Kyre burst out of a side alley into the main thoroughfare just as the first ranks of Haven's warriors reached the junction. They had taken a shortcut to intercept the army, urging their horses at dangerous speed through a maze of narrow lanes, and as they hauled the animals to a snorting, rearing halt, the two captains at the head of the first mounted column yelled in consternation for their men to halt. A horn sounded, echoing; there was confused shouting as horses bumped one another; a standard-bearer was almost unseated—then the captains were staring, openmouthed in astonishment, at their prince.

In the moonshot darkness DiMag looked dangerous. His black war garb made his body a shadow among shadows, and his tense, pale face, framed by the fair hair streaming in the gale, was ghastly and almost unhuman. His eyes were alight with the anger that had lurked pent

and twisted within him for nine years—but at last that
anger had an outlet to cleanse it of its taint. He stood up
in his stirrups, ignoring the pain that shot through his leg,
and smiled grimly as the ripple of shock at his unexpected appearance ran back through the ranks like a
breaking wave. He looked at the two captains. One, the
younger and stockier, had been Vaoran's right-hand man;
the other—Revannic, the prince recalled—had taken up
arms as a foot soldier under DiMag's father, and was a
militiaman above all else. The prince's gaze rested a little
longer on the older captain, then he shouted, the wind
carrying his words across the heads of the throng.

"Swordsmaster Vaoran is dead, and his attempt to
overthrow me has failed! I come to lead you to triumph
over our *real* enemy, and I bring the Sun-Hound with
me!"

From somewhere behind the horsemen, among the
lines of foot soldiers, a ragged cheer went up. Vaoran
had had many followers among the higher echelons, but
he had never been popular in the ranks. DiMag smiled
again, less grimly this time, and looked once more at the
two captains.

"Gentlemen," he said, and his voice was eerily
counterpointed by the scream of the gale and the more
distant roar of the sea, "you have a simple choice.
Accept me as your rightful leader, and Kyre as our
champion—or kill us both here and now."

From far away they could all hear the chanting of the
sea warriors, rising toward a crescendo now as they
prepared to move in on the tide. The younger captain
shifted uneasily in his saddle and made as if to speak, but
the elder held up a warning hand. The look in his eyes, as
he glanced at his fellow commander, froze any words the
other might have uttered. The stocky man hesitated—
then he cast his own gaze down and conceded with a curt
nod of acquiescence.

Captain Revannic drew his sword and in a practiced, economic gesture, saluted the prince.

"My lord," he said crisply, and there was relief in his eyes. "We hadn't thought to see you lead us tonight." He glanced at the prince's maimed leg, his meaning clear; then he smiled. "Your father Prince MeGran, would have been proud of such courage." And with no further pause he signaled to the herald who rode beside him.

A long, wailing horn blast wound the length of the street, followed by three short, staccato notes. DiMag returned both Revannic's salute and his smile, then turned his horse about and spurred it forward. Kyre swung his own mount around as the horn sounded again, imperative now; the standards of Haven rose, snapping on the mind with a sound like cracking whips—and the army surged toward the city wall.

The mass of men gathered momentum, spurred on by the racket of the elements and by the ever more urgent howling of their enemies far out on the sea. The shattered wall loomed before them, the sandstone arch and its eternal witchlights smashed and indistinguishable among the rubble: they were gaining speed—

"KYRE!"

At the same moment that Talliann's disembodied voice resounded in his head, Kyre felt the quartz around his neck pulse with a violent flash of awakened energy. He yelled aloud without realizing it as his consciousness locked with hers, and with a peripheral part of his mind saw DiMag look round in surprise as he urged his horse on. What he saw Kyre couldn't even begin to guess, but the amulet at his throat burned suddenly hot, and a cold light sparked from it that lit the prince's face and his vulpine smile as he understood.

Talliann was chanting a litany in Kyre's mind, and he joined his voice with hers. Somewhere deep in his soul he felt a lurching sensation, and his inner vision focused on a gate, a dark, titanic gate, that stood between this world and the ancient past over which they had once reigned together. He saw Talliann's face within the gate, powerful and knowledgeable as she had been then, her black eyes almost closed in trance and only the twin brilliant slivers of her pupils shining through the blackness. He felt another surge of searing heat as the fire-red glow of her amulet merged with the glacial brilliance of his, and he saw her mouth open, as he opened, to scream the final, the ultimate word of the rite that would shatter the gate and bring the ancient forces roaring through.

And as the word rang out, the Hag cleared the horizon like something from a primeval nightmare, hurling her silver-green spear across the surface of the tossing sea to strike the leading ranks of Haven's army full on. With a suddenness that sent a shock through Kyre's bones, the sea warriors' eerie chanting stopped—then DiMag's voice called above the wind's howl: *"They're coming! Haven—Haven, and our triumph!!"*

The horn shrieked a challenge, a wild, primitive incitement, and a yell of furious defiance rose from massed throats. Kyre's horse bucked under him, smelling battle and terror on the battering gale, and like a living wave the warriors of Haven streamed through the shattered city gate.

And as the wave of humanity smashed into the bay, Kyre's voice and mind and soul joined with Talliann's in a cry that rang like supernatural thunder on the night.
"NOW!"

Beyond the shining sand where the tidal wave had drawn back, the incoming sea erupted like a volcano. And riding the maelstrom, carried on the back of the silver spear of light that the grim moon flung across the ocean, came a howling host, distorted by the pounding

surf into an army of inhuman phantoms, monsters made
of spray and foam, leaping and diving shoreward and
shrieking demonically.

DiMag howled a war cry, and Kyre heard his own
voice screaming in cacophonic harmony. They were
galloping now, their mounts crazed and racing while the
warriors of Haven streamed and yelled behind them. As
they crossed the smooth acreage of sand where half of
Kyre's city and DiMag's city had been buried nine years
before, the ground beneath them rumbled and shifted, as
though something that slumbered deep under the bay had
awoken and was clawing its way toward the surface—

*In Simorh's tower, Talliann shrieked. Simorh clutched
her, tried to hold her, but the dark girl's arms flailed
with a mad, unhuman strength and she was slung aside,
against the wall. She scrambled to her feet as the room
rocked wildly, then threw herself toward Talliann,
grasped her, held her, screamed at her—*

Kyre saw the first of them explode from under the sand
as the horses thundered over their graves. They had the
hideous semblance of living statues, their flesh shrunken,
petrified, bones and muscles standing out like cords
under skin stretched taut over their frames. *But they
lived!* The dead of Haven, men, women, children, rising
through the sand that had been their tomb and joining
their howling voices to those of the charging warriors.
Their eyes were livid sparks of hellfire in sand-encrusted
skulls, their ossified limbs jerked and bent in motions
their dead brains had long forgotten. They carried
swords, staves, axes, knives, clubs—anything that
would serve as a weapon—and they hurled themselves
into the ranks of the army, the living and the dead racing
together to meet the sea.

* * *

*Talliann screamed again while Simorh struggled to pin
her arms to the floor, and out on the bay Kyre screamed
with her—*

They were galloping at breakneck speed toward the
surging surf and the creatures who rode howling toward
them. Closer, closer to the line of tide—and ahead,
where the sea crashed on the shingle bar, water boiled
suddenly into a foaming explosion and something blacker than night, blacker than the ocean depths, erupted
from the waves. It was a shell—a gigantic shell,
towering into the night, blotting out the moon—and in
the shell, riding in it like passengers in a nightmare
chariot, stood Calthar and her Mothers. The sea sorceress had performed the ultimate rite, and her appalling
predecessors had risen from death as Haven's own had
risen, decayed, grinning corpses, their mortal remains
reanimated to join with their spiritual daughter in the last
conflict. And presiding over them all, most evil of them
all, most deadly of them all, Kyre saw the rotted,
triumphant face of Malhareq, his own betrayer.

He thought he cried out, but he could never know. The
sea was roaring to meet them—then he felt a massive
shock wave strike him full on, and time and space
imploded around him as the enemy army came surging
out of the tide.

DiMag heard his own voice yelling insanely as the
leading ranks of Haven's horsemen clashed with the first
line of the sea warriors. His blade was a murderous steel-
silver blur in the chaotic darkness; alien faces sprang out
of the night and he hewed at them, felt the sword bite
home, saw blood flying like dark sea spray. His horse
reared and shrieked in warning, and he arched his body

to block the shearing glitter of a spear, disarmed its wielder with a powerful twist of his arm, hacked at a pale shoulder, and saw the wounded sea warrior go down into a melee of trampling hooves. To his left he glimpsed the fiery flicker of Kyre's hair and the flash of the spear in his hands; then suddenly he was beset by three more howling warriors coming at him from the right. The sword sheared down and the first enemy flailed back with an ugly, dying shriek, but the second lunged in behind his comrade and the prince felt blood flow over his leg as the spear gashed his horse's flank. The animal bucked crazily under him, panicking; struggling to control it he had no chance to defend himself as the third warrior attacked. For a terrible instant DiMag saw the spear blade hurtling out of the dark toward his torso and he knew in that second that he couldn't evade it—then another horseman appeared from nowhere; a massive blade, swung two-handed, cut the spear in half and, as its owner turned in shock, sliced again with a sharp, whining whistle, to sever the warrior before he could jump clear.

The horseman grinned ferally at DiMag from a blood-streaked face—and the prince recognized the hawk nose, dark beard, and lean body of his own father, MeGran, in the instant before horse and rider winked out into nothingness.

MeGran, who had been dead eleven years! Shock slammed DiMag back in his saddle as his horse wheeled and plunged once more into the battle, and suddenly his mind and his body and the raging world around him were out of control as the tides of past and present collided into a maelstrom. DiMag rode a black horse that bore a great scar along its neck where it had been cut down in the battle of nine years ago to die shrieking and kicking on the sand, and at his side fought MeGran, while a lithe young woman with short dark curls and a warrior's garb

and Gamora's face sounded the horn that rallied the
Haven army, living and dead, to fresh onslaughts. And
there were children among the carnage, children with his
own fair hair and hazel eyes who yelled and shouted and
wielded swords and spears. And Brigrandon was young
again and fighting with the rest, and on the prince's right
flank Vaoran yelled a warning and spurred his horse to
intercept a silver-faced warrior launching himself at
DiMag, and between them they slew the attacker and
three more who came behind him, and their eyes met and
they laughed together, while DiMag thought of his baby
daughter sleeping in the palace and of the wife he loved
and whose sorcery was aiding him.

And everywhere he looked was Kyre. Kyre riding
through a press of enemy warriors, his spear twisting and
turning and spinning in his hands; Kyre on foot at the
edge of the sea, his horse dead beside him, in hand-to-
hand combat with three silver-haired warriors; Kyre
leading a charge of foot soldiers, the royal standard of
Haven streaming above his head. He saw Calthar, a
sinuous and vicious-faced child; he saw sea warriors he'd
slain nine years before, he saw dead men and living men
and men not yet born, and over the deafening clamor of
the battle came again and again the frantic, insistent
winding of the horn. Out on the shingle bar the temple
was changing and changing and changing, one moment a
ruin, the next new-built and whole, the next gone
without trace. Only the moon was constant, glaring
down on the carnage with her mad eye—the moon, and
the monstrous black shell that rose above the waves
while the impossible, hideous parodies of humanity that
rode within it laughed and screamed and urged their
followers to further madness.

"I CAN'T CONTROL IT!!" The words thundered in
DiMag's head and he realized that they didn't come from

within himself, but from Kyre. Somehow their minds
had fused, and the prince felt the Sun-Hound's desperation ricochet through his bones. The warp of time was
running amok as two ages and the chaotic centuries
between came together and battled to tear each other's
fabric apart.

*"WE SHOULDN'T EXIST TOGETHER! HELP ME,
DIMAG—HELP ME, OR YOUR WORLD WILL BE
LOST!!"*

DiMag's horse reared, whinnying, and through a
forest of writhing, clashing forms he saw Kyre again. He
was at the tide's edge, mounted still, and he was trying to
fight his way through to the prince. Goaded by a violent
intuition, DiMag spurred his horse toward the tideline,
only to find the path blocked by some twenty embattled
men. He swerved, saw a gap, kicked his mount's
flanks—and he was flung backward as a sea warrior
sprang from the dark, spear whirling low and deadly to
slash the horse's legs from under it. The animal shrieked
in terrified agony and DiMag pitched out of the saddle,
hitting the wet sand with bone-cracking force and rolling
clear as the animal's body crashed down an inch from his
head. Pain shot through the prince's crippled leg as he
got to his feet, but five more Haven men were closing on
his attacker and he was able to get clear—to find himself
at the edge of the crashing, tumbling sea.

"DiMag!" This time Kyre's voice wasn't in his head:
DiMag looked wildly round and saw the Sun-Hound,
also dismounted, racing toward him. They were on the
fringe of the battle now, clear of the tumult—but as the
prince limped into the shallows to meet Kyre, a warrior
appeared seemingly from nowhere, stumbling across his
path. He was unarmed and blood ran down one shoulder:
the prince caught a glimpse of black-streaked silver hair,
and snarled, raising his sword—

"No, DiMag!" Kyre flung himself between the two men as he recognized the distinctive hair, the disfiguring facial mark. The sea warrior faced him, shoulders heaving as he fought for breath. Wounded and disarmed, he'd broken free from the melee only to find himself confronted now with almost certain death. He stared at Kyre with glazed eyes—then recognition dawned.

"Sun-Hound . . ." Akrivir coughed, and spat.

Impulsively, Kyre held out a sword he'd taken from a dead Haven warrior. "Take it, Akrivir. Save yourself, if you can!"

The young man's hand closed round the hilt, and he flashed Kyre a look of intense gratitude. "Kill her, Kyre," he said. "It's the only way to save us all!" And before the astounded DiMag could stop him he was gone, running back into the chaotic dark.

The prince grasped Kyre's arm, shouting above the din. *"What d'you think you're doing? That was—"*

"There's no time to explain!" Kyre yelled back. *"DiMag, I can't hold the power! It's running out of control—I've got to lock my mind with yours, we must fight as one!"*

The prince shook his head, utterly confused but knowing he had to trust Kyre. *"I don't know how!"*

A riderless horse careered out of the chaos straight toward them; they sprang aside and it galloped by into the surf, its hooves hurling up a fountain of spray and soaking them.

"The amulet!" Kyre shouted. *"You've got to take the amulet! It'll hold your mind to this world, this time—I can control the power through you!"*

He snatched at the chain around his neck, pulling it free and thrusting it over DiMag's head. The prince's consciousness jolted as the quartz touched his skin: for an instant he thought the entire bay was lifting, humping toward the black sky like a vast, uncoiling serpent, and he flailed out as he seemed to pitch backward, over, tumbling into limitless dark.

"Hold on to the present, DiMag!" Kyre shouted. *"Don't let go!"*

His voice was eclipsed suddenly by a shriek of unhuman delight and triumph that snatched DiMag back into the world. A wave broke against the prince's thighs; as he swayed with its onslaught his eyes snapped open and he saw a vast black silhouette looming toward him. *The giant shell—*

"Kyre!" DiMag yelled in horror as the shell disgorged a plethora of flowing, serpentine shapes. Under the moonlight they resolved into hideously animated corpses, skeletons with tatters of skin clinging to their fleshless bones, worm-eaten monsters with empty eyes and brittle, colorless hair flying like scum about their skulls—the Mothers, the dead, reanimated Mothers, spilling from their carriage and surging toward the prince. Ten of them, fifteen, twenty, impossible horrors that opened their rotted mouths and screamed mayhem above the gale. And at their head—DiMag staggered back, clapping a hand over his mouth in a desperate effort to stop himself from vomiting—at their head was a skeleton with eyes like twin coals in the crumbling skull. Oldest of them all, founder and inspiration of them all, she was—she was—

She was changing, flesh growing on the bones, sinew and muscle overlaid by shining, green-tinged skin, while a wild corona of hair whipped about a face whose eyes and smile the prince knew all too well. And as she changed it seemed that the rest of the hell-inspired horde flowed toward her and around her and into her, until she stood alone, tall and erect and evil, the tattered robe clinging obscenely to her sinuous body, her eyes glittering white slits and the gigantic spear, twice the length of that borne by any of her followers, balanced effortlessly in her hand.

The years rolled back and the battle raging around him seemed to recede into a vast distance as DiMag, lonely and suddenly cold as ice, faced Calthar for the second time in his life—and for what he knew must also be the last.

In the tower, Talliann cried out as the echo of Kyre's frantic call to DiMag resounded in her mind. The room still rocked madly like a ship in a tempest, and she and Simorh staggered back from the window as lightning-shot darkness engulfed them. In their inner vision they could see the battle and the terrible clashing and warping of time, and Talliann felt Kyre's terror as the chaos of the amulets' power roiled uncontrollably about him. She saw him reach DiMag, felt the sudden surge of his intention—

"*Simorh!*" Talliann clutched at the sorceress in the swirling blackness that churned ever more wildly as time ran crazed. "Simorh, the amulet! You must take the amulet—*you must be strong*!" Even as she called out she was pulling the chain from around her throat, and Simorh, understanding the peril, ran to help her.

Then suddenly Simorh was Talliann and Talliann was Simorh, and the fair-haired sorceress flung back her head and raised her arms heavenward as power surged through her veins. All around her she felt it vibrating, calling, holding her to the world: she drew on her strength, fists clenching as she focused all the will she could muster to the aid of DiMag and Kyre. Through the channel opened by Talliann's mind she felt other presences: names from history, faces from her own past and from an indefinable

future. Her own mother, MeGran's sister, fair and
serene, a sorceress in her own right. The dead consorts of
princes past, who had worked their own magic down the
long centuries to the aid of Haven. Gamora grown to
beauty and to power. Thean and Falla, old and skilled in
arcane ways. Her nurse, at rest these twenty years. And
Talliann, black-haired Talliann, the greatest of all Haven's sorceresses, who stood beside her and held her like
a sister and merged her mind with Simorh's as the great
wheel of power spun faster, faster, faster—

Calthar laughed. She moved toward DiMag through the
waves, and DiMag stood his ground. In her face, glaring
out through the sockets of her eyes, the awful madness of
the Mothers shone like white-hot fire, and in his mind's
eye DiMag saw again the countenances of the appalling
creatures that had merged their bones and their souls and
their power with her.

*He couldn't fight that power! Something so old, so
corrupt—he was nothing more than a mortal man; he
couldn't hope to triumph over such evil!*

She came on, slowly, like a predator savoring a
paralyzed and helpless victim. DiMag tasted bile in his
throat, and hefted his sword, though he knew, knew, that
he was lost.

Calthar smiled—and suddenly she was Calthar no
longer. Her form changed, shifted—great ropes of wine-
dark hair swung about her shoulders and cascaded down
her back, and her face was younger, her pale body clad in
a long, slit-skirted robe, belted at her narrow waist, and
over her shoulder was slung the crimson sash of a Haven
councillor—

And where DiMag had stood, Kyre's green eyes and
flame-red hair flared in the darkness as he faced the
woman who centuries upon centuries ago had betrayed

her city and her people and her prince, and by whose hand the glory that had once been Haven had been sundered.

Then suddenly there was no battle. It was as though every other living soul had flared out of existence, leaving only the dark bay, the sand and the sea, and the old, pocked moon riding the sky above. There was just the entity that was both Kyre and DiMag, a lone figure facing the creature into which Calthar and Malhareq had merged. The gale was gone; and the stillness was acute.

The woman with the wine-dark hair raised her spear as though in mocking salute, and Calthar smiled. Kyre's voice broke the silence.

"Ah, Malhareq." DiMag heard the words in his tumbling mind, and in sharing Kyre's thoughts he at last understood the truth of the legacy that the Sun-Hound had left behind. "Will you kill me, this time?"

Her voice was warm, rich. "I will, Prince. The Hag's hand is on me, and she will not fail."

"The Hag is no enemy of mine. Your people were Haven's people once: before you fled to found the city under the sea. It could be so again."

Malhareq laughed softly. "It will not be so again, Kyre. Not while my daughter Calthar lives."

"And if Calthar should die?"

"There will be others." That smile again, alluring, beautiful, deadly. "Your day is long gone, Prince."

"As is yours, sorceress."

"Ah, no. Through the Mothers, I live on." Her outline flickered, wavered; maggots moved under her translucent skin and the part of her adversary that was DiMag recoiled in revulsion. He felt Kyre's mind touch his, drawing him back: the fear faded and he knew what he must do.

She was the heart of it, the core of it, this monstrous creature who lived on still through the Mothers. Once there had been but one people—the people of Haven. And then had come this power-hungry predator . . .

Without Malhareq, there need be no war. Without her malignant influence crossing the centuries to feed still on the minds and wills of her descendants, Haven and the sea citadel could live at peace together. She was a vampire, she and her daughter-in-spirit, Calthar. Through Calthar's living flesh, dead Malhareq fed on power and lust, and her thirst would only be shaken when the last of Haven's citizens lay dead among its shattered rubble.

It must be. Time must be defied, and the sway of the power that Malhareq had handed down through the long and grim line of the Mothers must be broken in the only way possible—at its source. Malhareq must die. And he—Kyre, DiMag; he no longer knew who he was, and it hardly seemed to matter—was the only one who could slay her.

He raised a weapon that was both sword and spear, and in his mind, from a great distance, he heard Talliann and Simorh cry out as the power of the amulets swamped him. The spell that had held them in limbo shattered, and the world of the shrieking gale and the screaming, battling warriors erupted volcanically back into being as DiMag and Calthar, Kyre and Malhareq, lunged forward and met in a clashing cacophony of steel.

Chapter 20

Hands clamped on Simorh's wrists, and Talliann's voice shrieked in her ear.

"Now, Simorh! Call on the power—now!"

Simorh's mind seemed to spear upward into the night, until she gazed down from a vast height on the tumult of the battle. Men struggled like a single writhing black entity on the beach, the tide of bodies surging this way and that as the armies fought. And where white surf churned at the edge of the sea there were other men, horses milling about them, knee-deep in the water and engaged in desperate single combat. Simorh looked for DiMag, but couldn't find him; at her neck the amulet pulsed hotter, hotter—

"There!" Talliann screamed, and a stunning force turned Simorh's disembodied mind about. "On the shingle bar!"

DiMag! But his hair was red, and he wielded a spear instead of a sword as he swung and hacked at a shimmering, leaping creature who seemed to be composed of flesh and foam and light and decay all at once . . .

"Call on the stone!" Talliann cried, and in the tower room her hands gripped Simorh's shoulders and shook her with a violence that made her teeth snap together. *"Now! Call on it—that monstrosity must die!"*

Simorh's mind swept back nine years and she saw again DiMag being dragged into their bedchamber on a makeshift stretcher, his face gray with shock and pain, blood from Calthar's festering, sorcerous wound soaking his clothes, while she, struck dumb by the ravages of her own failed sorcery, could only stare and stare at him, too weak even to cry. Calthar had destroyed their lives that night . . . and with the thought came a wild uprising of hatred and vengeful fury that took hold of her like a whirlwind. Her hands clawed around the quartz and the quartz burned her as she dragged from it, from her mind, from Talliann's mind, the last vestiges of the power she needed, and found the strength to hurl it on flying black wings at the battling figures on the shingle bar before the world spun madly about her and she collapsed.

Kyre saw the spear coming down at him in the instant before a fireball of brilliant scarlet light exploded above his head. It lit Malhareq's upturned, snarling face, froze her lithe figure like a stone statue in its glare, and in that one moment he realized what Simorh and Talliann had done. He yelled a name—DiMag's, his own, he didn't know—and heard an answering scream from the amulet as his consciousness ripped free from the entity that was himself and the prince, and merged with the blazing wheel of light. Blue and red spun together, he felt Talliann in his head, in his soul, her power blending with his as Malhareq's face twisted in dawning horror—

And DiMag, his mind spinning as the link with Kyre was torn apart, saw Calthar bearing down on him. Simorh's last power bolt fired his mind with the strength of vengeance, and he swung the great sword as a woodsman might swing an ax. He saw the blade bite deep, heard Calthar's howling laughter as it embedded itself in her flesh. *She didn't bleed*—and in an instant the prince's mind went spinning back nine years. He saw her snarling face as he had seen it on that night; saw the spear glittering, felt again the agony as it slashed his leg open, baring muscle and bone and searing his flesh with its sorcerous poison.

He couldn't kill her! He had failed then; he would fail now—

And something seemed to take hold of his free arm. With an involuntary jerk his hand came up and he felt the cold quartz of Kyre's amulet beneath his fingers. *And suddenly he knew what had to be done!*

Calthar was twisting her serpentine body in an obscene, contemptuous gesture, to rid herself of the sword. DiMag snapped the amulet's chain, gripped the quartz tightly—then lunged again and drove the pendant at her heart.

Her scream was something he'd remember in his nightmares for as long as he lived. It wasn't human, nor even animal: as she doubled over, jerking in a fit, the scream rose above the gale, above the din of battle, higher and higher as rage and frustration and disbelief and terror and a hatred beyond comprehension was ripped from Calthar's throat along with her life and the hideous, unnatural life of the Mothers on whose black legacy she had fed for so long. Her hands became claws that tore at her own hair, her legs kicked, out of her control: the scream went on and on, while behind

Calthar's eyes Malhareq writhed in horror and agony, and the long line of Malhareq's unholy progeny squirmed and shriveled and shared Calthar's death as they had shared her living.

The sorceress rolled over, and for one moment stared madly at DiMag in a last blaze of impotent loathing. The prince felt pain shoot through his leg and his head together; he reeled, then the world swelled, receded, roared in his ears, and he keeled unconscious to the ground as the spark of life fled from Calthar's eyes.

The darkness in the tower room seemed to swell to a suffocating density—then with a vast, silent concussion it was gone. Simorh raised her head but couldn't focus her eyes; she'd cracked her skull on a table leg and any sudden movement made her feel sick and dizzy. But there was light . . . the faint glimmer of a single lamp, and moonlight shining in at the window . . .

Trying to remember what had happened, she crawled slowly and painfully across the floor, clutching the windowsill for support as she dragged herself upright. Her legs were weak and the sickness still roiled in her stomach: but the power, the shattering force, the madness were all gone, and the room was quiet.

Quiet . . . She shook her head, winced at the pain— and remembered.

"Talliann?" Her voice was hollow against the silence, and no one answered her. She was alone in the room. But Talliann had been with her. Together, they had called on the power of—

Something fell from her right hand, which she didn't even know she'd been clenching. A shower of tiny, glittering fragments, scattering on the floor like glass shards and winking redly up at her. Simorh gasped and dropped to a crouch, her hands scrabbling. And there, under her fingers among the broken scraps of orange-red quartz, was a single, silver-flecked pearl . . .

"Talliann . . ." The sorceress jammed a fist against her mouth, biting back a flood of emotion. Talliann was gone—and her amulet, her legacy, lay shattered on the floor at Simorh's feet.

But where could she—

The door eased open a crack, stopped, opened a fraction more, stopped again. Simorh's heart pounded and she whispered, "Who's there?"

"Mother . . . ?" The door opened wide at last and Gamora stood on the threshold, her small face drawn with fear and her eyes huge under the tousled curls. "Oh, Mother!" She flung herself across the room to Simorh, hugging her with all her strength. "I was so frightened! I woke up in a room with drawn curtains and candles, and there was no one else there, and I couldn't find anyone, and I've had such horrible *dreams*!"

Simorh dropped to her knees on the worn carpet, clutching the child to her. *She was alive, she was safe, the enchantment was broken*—"Gamora, Gamora!" She couldn't say anything more; grief and joy combined to make her incoherent. Tears streamed down her cheeks and Gamora was crying too: they stayed, hugging each other without speaking, sharing feelings that neither understood, in the silence of the dimly lit room.

It was Revannic, the captain DiMag had confronted as the army rode out, who finally found the prince sprawled among the rubble of the ruined temple, and in his carrying, parade-ground voice he shouted into the confusion of milling horses and bewildered troops whose sergeants were trying to muster them into some sem-

blance of order. Two men detached themselves from the
nearest of several small parties engaged in the grim task
of separating the wounded from the dead on both sides,
and came running to the strand.

"The Eye preserve me." One of them stared down at
DiMag in amazement. "We'd thought the prince must be
dead, sir! We've already combed most of the bay,
and—"

"Then let's be thankful you were wrong." Revannic
ran his hands over the prince's legs and along his back.
"I'm no surgeon, but I don't think he's broken any
bones. And there's no blood."

DiMag stirred. Hastily the men moved to help him as
his eyes opened dazedly, and he struggled into a sitting
position on the wet shale.

"Revannic . . . what—"

"The battle's over, my lord. Haven's safe."

"But the moon's still up . . ." He could see her
pockmarked face lurking near the cliffs, throwing grotesque black shadows over the sand and the turning tide.

"I know, and I can't claim to understand it, sir."
Revannic took off her jerkin and cast it around DiMag's
shoulders as the prince began to shiver. "My detachment
was in the thick of it when we heard this sudden noise:
like a scream, a wailing. It must have been some kind of
retreat signal, because they just turned, the sea demons I
mean, and started fighting their way back to the
shoreline." He paused, licked his lips. "When it became
obvious what they were about, I—forgive me, my lord, I
called our men off and let them flee." He frowned. "We
thought you dead and someone had to make a decision;
and we'd already lost so many . . ."

DiMag nodded. "You did right. Thank you." He
knew now what Revannic had heard, and why the enemy
warriors had withdrawn. It all made sense . . . but—

"Kyre!" he said suddenly. "The Sun-Hound—is he alive?"

Revannic's face, which had cleared at his approbation, clouded again. "He hasn't been found yet, sir, among the dead or among the survivors."

"You're *sure*?"

"Certain as I can be; though there are still several parties yet to report back to me."

He had to be here . . . DiMag tried to get up, and grimaced as his maimed leg refused to support him. Revannic steadied him until he could settle the hilt of his sword under his arm to use as a makeshift crutch, then the prince looked speculatively round at the gaunt shadows of the temple. He couldn't even remember reaching the place, and his recollection of what had happened was hazy at best. All he knew was that he and Kyre had fought side by side . . . "Search the ruin," he said grimly, praying that they wouldn't find what he feared they would. "If Kyre's alive, he must be injured. I want him found!"

The two warriors saluted and hastened away, and the prince looked at Revannic. "Are there many dead?" he asked quietly.

Revannic hunched his shoulders against the chilly, invasive breeze that had replaced the gale. "It could have been worse." He paused, staring down at the uneven ground, then said in a peculiar voice: "My lord . . ."

"What is it?" Though DiMag thought he already knew.

The captain bit his lower lip. "My lord, I—I don't know how to put it: you'll think I'm mad. But . . ." He met DiMag's gaze, but only briefly before looking away again. "At the height of the battle, sir, I thought I saw . . . Prince MeGran. Your father. And others. I couldn't be sure about them, but I thought I recognized friends who died in the last conflict: it was just that I knew your father the old prince so well . . ." His throat muscles worked as he swallowed. "*Am* I mad, my lord?"

"No," DiMag said gently. "You're not mad, Revannic. I, too, fought alongside dead friends. And Prince MeGran saved my life." He smiled bleakly, sadly. "If you knew my father well, I knew him better. I don't think either of us was mistaken."

Revannic hugged himself, and shivered. "I don't understand, sir . . ."

"Neither do I; not fully. But something happened here tonight that . . ." DiMag's voice trailed off as he realized he had been about to say *that will change the course of all our lives*, and that it would have sounded pitifully banal. Instead he shifted awkwardly round until he was facing the muttering sea.

"When the aftermath is over, there'll be changes, Revannic. And maybe then I'll be able to explain it to myself and to you."

A voice rose hoarsely from the deep shadows among the ruins, and both men looked up. One of the soldiers was signaling frantically and DiMag made what speed he could toward the man, cursing his lameness and wishing that Revannic would go on ahead. As they finally came up to where the two warriors waited, one pointed to something that lay beside a shattered pillar, and DiMag swallowed back sickness as he steeled himself to look.

It wasn't Kyre. It was the body of a woman with an ugly, bloodless gash in her stomach. She was curled, limbs locked rigid, in a crude fetal posture, and her skin shone with the faint but growing phosphorescence of decay. Her eyes were empty, and her full lips were drawn back in a snarl that was frozen forever on her face; and for a moment only DiMag saw wine-dark hair like a rich cloud around her shoulders. He blinked, startled—and the hair and the evilly beautiful face changed to the silver nimbus and the cruel countenance of Calthar.

The prince looked sidelong at Revannic just in time to catch the other man's eye. Revannic, he realized, had seen the change, the fleeting echo of Malhareq in Calthar's corpse; now, staring down at her again, DiMag saw that she was already aging and withering. It was final confirmation that the sorcery which had allowed her to live years beyond her rightful time was broken.

"So that was it . . ." Revannic spoke softly, with the reverence, DiMag thought, of a soldier's grudging respect for a hated but defeated enemy. "They must have known. And when she died, it broke their power. That was why they went back to the sea . . ."

"She was our only real enemy," DiMag said quietly.

Revannic frowned, not comprehending. "My lord?"

"Never mind . . . there'll be time enough to explain." Something glittered among the shreds of Calthar's rotting robe, and DiMag dropped to a clumsy crouch to look more closely. Glass . . . or quartz . . . tiny, brilliant blue shards, as though a jewel had shattered and fallen among the decayed fabric. And draped across the sorceress's motionless breast, a thin, silver chain.

Suddenly DiMag knew why Kyre hadn't been found, and he got to his feet, staring out to sea as the pain of sorrowing regret twisted within him.

There had been so much he wanted to say. Haven owed all it had to Kyre and Talliann; and DiMag in particular had the Sun-Hound to thank for his life. He and Talliann had brought hope where before there had been only despair; there was a chance now that the city might live again, and the prince wished with all his heart that he could have seen and spoken to the Sun-Hound one last time. Thanks were desperately inadequate; but he wished he could have expressed them nonetheless.

But it was too late now. Time had opened its black gates for him once: it wouldn't do so again. And though he was gone, Kyre had left Haven a legacy beyond price.

He turned to Revannic once more, and asked quietly, "Are there prisoners?"

"Some fifty or more wounded."

The prince nodded. "Have them taken to the city, and see to it that they're tended and treated well."

Revannic was a wise soldier, and the prince's earlier remark had given him a small insight into the nature of Calthar's influence upon her followers. There was more behind DiMag's command than was yet clear, and Revannic believed it boded well.

"As you say, my lord." He bowed; a quick, economical inclination of his head. "And . . . that?" He indicated the thing that had been been Calthar.

DiMag looked for the last time on his enemy, then turned away. "Let the sea have her," he said. "She means nothing now."

They had returned in small bands, swimming into the sea cave and somehow finding the strength to pull themselves onto the rock ledge and make their way through the maze of tunnels to a place where they could rest. Many were wounded; more still were dazed, shocked by the impossible event which had stunned them all. None spoke a word, and the forebodings of the men who had taken no part in the battle but who now watched the returning warriors from the shadows grew.

Akrivir was among the last to return. One arm was stiff where blood had caked into a scab at the shoulder joint, and there was a long, fierce gash above his hairline which was still bleeding sluggishly.

Hodek saw him emerge from the water, and hastened forward from the knot of anxious senior councillors. To Akrivir the old man looked like some scrawny and wind-tossed scavenger bird, and he felt the dully familiar hatred rising in him again. But this time, there was a difference . . .

"Where is she?" Hodek's voice was shrill with petulant frustration. "Where? Answer me!"

Akrivir stared at his father, and his face was like stone. "Where is who?"

Unease flickered in Hodek's expression; he'd never seen Akrivir behave in such a way, and it worried him. *But no matter—when she came back, she'd deal with the whelp easily enough . . .*

"Calthar!" he snapped back. "Why does she delay? And what's the meaning of—"

Akrivir interrupted him in a voice so cold that Hodek's unease flowered suddenly into real fear. He said: "Calthar is dead."

"Wh . . . wh . . ." The pale eyes before him bulged in a mixture of disbelief and helpless horror. "No . . ." Hodek croaked. "You're lying, you're—"

"Calthar is dead," Akrivir repeated, and the ghost of an icy smile cracked the stony indifference on his face as he realized the full extent of his sire's terror, and what Calthar's demise would mean to the old man in particular. "Calthar, and her Mothers. Gone, Father. *Gone*." He raised the sword Kyre had given him; the movement was calculatedly slow, and Hodek hardly seemed to notice it. Suddenly Akrivir felt as though the sea was flowing through his veins and washing away a taint so old and so deep-rooted that he'd barely been aware of its existence. He felt clean—and freer than he'd ever done in his life.

Hodek's mouth was working in ugly spasms, but he couldn't utter a word; shock had robbed him of speech, and spittle foamed on his lips, dribbling down his chin. Akrivir's fist tightened on the sword hilt.

"There'll be no more of it, Father," he said, almost kindly now that the moment had come. "You're the last of the corruption." And with a swift, economic movement he thrust the point of the sword into Hodek's heart.

He turned away, with the blank and terrified stares of his father's fellow councillors fixed on him. Akrivir looked at the bloodied sword for a few moments, then released his hold on it and let it fall to the ground.

The warriors who had struggled back through the sea with him were gathered at the tunnel mouth. He couldn't read clearly what was in their eyes, but they didn't fear him. And they had no reason to do so. One of them had taken a bad sword cut to the leg and had lost a good deal of blood; a companion had tied a crude tourniquet round his thigh, but the man urgently needed attention. Akrivir approached him, nodded to a second warrior, and between them they put their shoulders under the wounded man's arms, supporting him. Ignoring the cowering councillors, the small group turned and moved away into the tunnel.

From where they stood, they could see the dark figures moving on the bay, the quiet exodus that began back to the city as the tide turned and the sea began to cover the strand once more. In Haven's streets and squares, and in the palace whose three towers rose loftily above the town, lights began to glow, scattered at first but increasing in number like tiny, distant beacons; and Kyre's thoughts went back over the centuries to Haven as it had once been; not the sad remnants of a city on the brink of disaster, but thriving, its walls and its thoroughfares spreading cheerfully and triumphantly out over the bay. Those days couldn't be recalled. The clash of time engendered by the amulets had broken down the barriers, but briefly: now the sand lay smooth over the buried streets, the dead had returned to their graves and would not rise again. The gates of time had closed on the past, and that was as it should be.

But with the closing of the gates, there was no place now in this world for Kyre and Talliann. They had returned to the city they had once ruled and loved, and they had fulfilled the promise of the ancient legacy they had left behind. Now, their names must pass again into memory and history. At the moment when Prince DiMag had slain Calthar—and with her the soul of Malhareq—the amulets had given up the last of their power and, their work done, had shattered. As they had left the world, so, Kyre knew, a part of himself and his consort had also departed. They stood now between dimensions, gazing into DiMag and Simorh's world as though looking at a window through which they could no longer pass.

But Haven no longer needed them. Kyre had glimpsed the sea citadel captives being led or carried back toward the town, and knew that their fate would be very different from that of comrades who had gone before them. With Malhareq's black spell finally broken, there would be wise and far-seeing minds on both sides who would meet and talk and understand the follies of the past. Not blind and self-aggrandizing fools like Vaoran or Hodek; but others with enough courage to admit to their own wrongs and forgive those of others, and bring about a lasting peace. One day, perhaps, the Hag would be a friend to Haven again, and the sea dwellers would no longer fear the sun.

Talliann's small hands touched his arms and he turned to her. The pillars of the old temple cast strange and fleeting shadows over her face; but her black eyes shone serenely and he knew she had seen and understood his thoughts.

"They will prosper, Kyre," she said softly. "This is their world; and they will make it thrive again." Her gaze left his face and focused at a distance, taking in the dark strand and the shimmer of moonlight on the slowly moving sea. "There's nothing more for us here."

He stroked her face. "Does that sadden you?"

"No." She smiled up at him. "DiMag and Simorh are what Haven needs now, and I have no ambitions to take their place. I want only peace, with you. We were parted for so long—"

"Never again," he said.

"No," she agreed softly. "Never again."

"There are other places," he told her. "Not worlds as we've known them, but places where time has no meaning. Where neither the past nor the future need exist." His fingers hesitated on her brow, then he bent forward to kiss her, a light touch. "We could find peace."

"Peace after strife, and after centuries of nothing . . ." She looked at the sea again. "Yes. I would like that."

He smiled, a slow, quiet smile. "Haven no longer needs us. We can be free, Talliann."

"Free . . ." Her arms slipped through his; her skin was chilled by the night wind. There was no more to say, and no farewells to make to the city or the sea or the old temple. They looked just once toward Haven, but neither spoke. Then they turned, two figures as faint as phantoms or dreams against the towering ruin, and moved slowly toward the shimmering, endless ocean. A mote of light danced briefly on the sea's surface then flickered out; and only the restless, ever-moving surf remained to disturb the night.

Epilogue: Haven

DAWN HAD BROKEN QUIETLY THROUGH VEILS OF PALE, shimmering mist that crept in from the sea to soften harsh edges and cast a milky luminescence over the city. As the morning wore on the mist slowly cleared, and Haven basked in the mellow and faintly melancholy warmth of a perfect autumn day.

In the market squares a few traders set up their stalls, though they knew that more talking than trading would be done at their booths today. Children ran shrieking through the streets, playing games incomprehensible to their elders; now and again a woman's voice would call out from a window, admonishing them to be quiet lest they wake the exhausted menfolk who slept in the aftermath of the battle. Other people, in twos and threes, stood on the heaps of broken rubble where the city wall had been, watching the full tide surging in the bay and thinking their own thoughts.

In the palace the barracks were quiet. Most men slept, though one or two wakeful sergeants sat drinking mugs

of ale and tried not to think of the numbers of empty
pallets in their sleeping quarters. And in the lofty palace
rooms with their faded tapestries, lamps were extinguished as the sun shone through tall windows, and servants prepared the court hall for the meeting that Prince
DiMag had ordered to be convened that afternoon.

DiMag hadn't slept. He had allowed himself only the
luxury of bathing and changing his war regalia for a
loose woolen shirt and trousers, the comfort of which
contrasted sharply with the dull ache suffusing through
his bones, the stiffness of his sword arm, and the
frequent stabbing pains that assailed his maimed leg. He
had wondered, briefly, if with Calthar dead that old,
sorcerous wound might now begin to heal: ingrained
cynicism made him doubt it, but he was no longer sure
whether it mattered. Crippled or whole, to his army and
his people he had become a hero. Word had traveled like
fire in dry kindling, and the story of his slaying of
Calthar was already widely known; though Haven's
accolade discomfited DiMag, he could neither stem it nor
escape it. And, in ways he was reluctant to admit even to
himself, he was glad of his people's approbation, for it
gave him the chance he needed to put right so much that
had been wrong these past nine years. There would be no
more talk of deposing him. And though by rights the
heroic mantle should have been placed upon Kyre's
shoulders, DiMag believed that the Sun-Hound would
have understood and been glad for him.

Before he completed his preparations to attend the
court hall, the prince made one visit; and it was the most
important of all. He stood in Gamora's room, looking
down at his daughter's peaceful face as she slept with one
thumb in her mouth. Simorh stood beside him, her arm
linked with his in a posture that was neither casual nor
quite formal. Her expression was pensive and a little

wistful; though her face still reflected great strain he thought that the lines were beginning to soften, showing reawakened hints of the beauty she had possessed before the bitter times had darkened both their lives.

There need be no more bitterness . . . DiMag pressed her arm gently against his and she looked up quickly, something close to a smile flickering across her face.

He said: "We should leave her to sleep. If I know Gamora, she'll come running to find us the moment she wakes."

Simorh made as if to laugh but quelled it, suspecting that it might have turned too easily to tears. "If she comes to the court hall, they'll cheer her even more loudly than they cheer her father," she replied quietly, and smiled. "She deserves it. She's had little enough joy in her life." They moved toward the door, and she added, "But she'll miss Kyre. I wish I could have seen him and Talliann one last time before they left us. We owe them so much."

"I believe they must know it." They would have much to say to each other about Kyre and Talliann, but not yet: memories were too close, and private contemplation must come first. But it wasn't too early for some of the lessons they had learned to take form. Twelve years ago, Prince MeGran's dying wish had been that his son should rule Haven justly, strongly, and wisely: a duty that, DiMag believed, he had sorely neglected. That would change now, along with so much else. He had lost his fears and his suspicions, and in their place was hope.

In the corridor outside Gamora's room, a senior steward was waiting. He bowed as they emerged, and there was an odd expression on his face that the prince couldn't interpret.

"My lord—lady. Please forgive my intrusion, but there is an emissary in the palace, asking that his presence be made known to you."

DiMag frowned, surprised. "An emissary? From where?"

"He says his name is Akrivir, my lord, and that for want of a better title he has styled himself Protector of the Citadel. A temporary measure, he says, sir, until such time as true order can be restored." The steward paused. "He was careful to stress the word *true*, sir, as though it has some special significance."

Akrivir . . . the name was familiar, and then DiMag recalled a face in the madness of the battle, a wounded warrior to whom Kyre had given a sword. And he remembered, too, that Kyre had told him about Akrivir . . .

"Yes," he said thoughtfully. "Perhaps it has . . . Tell me, does he come alone?"

"Quite alone, my lord, and unarmed."

DiMag looked questioningly at Simorh. "It could be a beginning . . ." she said, and she couldn't disguise the eagerness in her voice. They exchanged a look of shared understanding.

DiMag turned to the steward again. "Have our welcome guest conducted to the court hall," he said, "and tell him that the princess and I will join him immediately."

The man bowed and hastened away, and DiMag held out his arm to his wife.

"Are you ready to greet the Protector of the Citadel?" he asked, and his eyes were warm.

She smiled a brilliant smile that recalled the Simorh of a decade ago, and laid her hand over his. "I am, my lord."